Praise for William Brashler's *Traders*

"As contemporary as tomorrow, William Brashler's TRAD-
ERS is a no-holds-barred look at the eat-or-be-eaten world of
the Chicago Board of Trade . . . Cook Review*

"Timely . . . A qu_____greed—
the necessary ing_____vel . . .
Brashler makes it w_____ and re-
alistic, believable di_____

— *Chicago Tribune*

"A provocative portrait of the Chicago Board of Trade . . .
Brisk narrative . . . Readers will devour this brash and trashy
overview of an intriguing occupation by a well-known crime
writer and novelist."

— *Booklist*

"Moves with the madhouse pace of the trading floor. And
Joanie is an extremely endearing commercial pirate with no
deplorable yuppie characteristics."

— *Kirkus Reviews*

"This fast-paced melodrama . . . bristles with authentic details of the frenzied trading pits. Brashler, novelist, former
Wall Street Journal reporter and former employee of a Chicago
trading firm, shows an easy familiarity with the manic-de-
pressive commodities market and the traders who make or
lose big fortunes on it."

— *Publishers Weekly*

"Brashler's well-researched novel about a woman in the market does a good job of conveying the frenzied action in the 'pit'
at the Chicago Board of Trade . . . the insider's view of the
high-stakes commodities world will have wide audience appeal."

— *Library Journal*

BLOCKBUSTER FICTION FROM PINNACLE BOOKS!

THE FINAL VOYAGE OF THE S.S.N. SKATE   (17-157, $3.95)
by Stephen Cassell
The "leper" of the U.S. Pacific Fleet, SSN 578 nuclear attack sub
SKATE, has one final mission to perform — an impossible act of
piracy that will pit the underwater deathtrap and its inexperienced
crew against the combined might of the Soviet Navy's finest!

QUEENS GATE RECKONING   (17-164, $3.95)
by Lewis Purdue
Only a wounded CIA operative and a defecting Soviet ballerina
stand in the way of a vast consortium of treason that speeds toward the hour of mankind's ultimate reckoning! From the best-
selling author of THE LINZ TESTAMENT.

FAREWELL TO RUSSIA   (17-165, $4.50)
by Richard Hugo
A KGB agent must race against time to infiltrate the confines of
U.S. nuclear technology after a terrifying accident threatens to
unleash unmitigated devastation!

THE NICODEMUS CODE   (17-133, $3.95)
by Graham N. Smith and Donna Smith
A two-thousand-year-old parchment has been unearthed, un-
leashing a terrifying conspiracy unlike any the world has previously known, one that threatens the life of the Pope himself, and
the ultimate destruction of Christianity!

*Available wherever paperbacks are sold, or order direct from the
Publisher. Send cover price plus 50¢ per copy for mailing and
handling to Pinnacle Books, Dept.17-460, 475 Park Avenue
South, New York, N.Y. 10016. Residents of New York, New Jer-
sey and Pennsylvania must include sales tax. DO NOT SEND
CASH.*

TRADERS

WILLIAM BRASHLER

PINNACLE BOOKS
WINDSOR PUBLISHING CORP.

PINNACLE BOOKS

is published by

Windsor Publishing Corp.
475 Park Avenue South
New York, NY 10016

Copyright © 1989 by William Brashler. Published by arrangement with Atheneum Publishers.

All rights reserved. No part of this book may be reproduced in any form or by any means without the prior written consent of the Publisher, excepting brief quotes used in reviews.

First Pinnacle Books printing: December, 1990

Printed in the United States of America

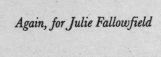

Again, for Julie Fallowfield

When Albert Einstein died, he was met at the Pearly Gates by St. Peter himself.

"We're glad to see you, Mr. Einstein," St. Peter said, "but we're not sure we have enough suitable companions for a man of your intellect. So we've decided to let you choose your own company."

Einstein agreed and proceeded to ask each new arrival his IQ. Some of the replies were astounding — 180, 195, even one individual who admitted to an IQ of 220.

Yet Einstein waved them all away.

Then one young man answered, "Seventy-eight."

At that, Einstein's face lit up and he exclaimed, "Finally, the person I've been looking for! Where did May pork bellies close?"

—Anonymous, but often told

PART ONE

Chapter One

The seedlings cracked the moist black soil of Iowa and Illinois like champions. They were strong, blight-resistant corn hybrids and soybeans with surplus written all over them, the kind of plants that make the Kremlin weep.

The boys in the pits knew this. They also knew of ambitious new government programs hell-bent on keeping harvests down and prices up. But the boys in the colored jackets and blown-dry hair, who looked like grocery clerks but who daily bartered millions of bushels of soybeans, corn, oats, and wheat, also knew the good old American farmer.

Oh, how they knew him. How he grumbled fiercely about the low price of grain and the high price to grow it. How he petitioned and picketed and muttered bitterly to television reporters as he stood in the mud of a neighbor's foreclosure sale. How, having done all that, he pulled his smudged hat over his furrowed brow, jumped inside his computerized, air-conditioned, mortgaged tractor and harvested more grain than storage silos could handle.

So that spring, beneath the fluorescent glare and the flickering tapes on the great floor of the Chicago Board of Trade, the largest commodity market in the world, the boys with the sandpaper throats and the raging hemorrhoids screamed the price of beans and corn ever downward.

They did it as part of a market that has been around for 150 years yet which remains a noisy, confusing mystery to a public that does not know a soybean from a pork belly. They did it in open, octagonal pits by shouting and flailing their hands in the air in an exercise that looks to outsiders like total madness but to them is a poetry of supply and demand. With those hearty corn and soybean seedlings in the ground, with all

9

parts of the nation's verdant agri-industry humming, it was just a matter of how much grain was too much grain, how low the price could go. To find out, the traders shouted themselves hoarse. They jumped and pumped and thrust fingers into each other's eyes.

A few days later the first heat wave hit. It was a muggy, sweltering block of stagnant air that came up from the Gulf of Mexico and hung over the Midwest. It lasted a week, drove temperatures into the 90s, and brought not a drop of rain. Farmers didn't mind because the heat dried out fields damp from spring rains; the boys in the pits, apart from adjusting the air conditioning in their Jaguars and BMW 735s, took no interest whatsoever.

Ken Korngold was one of them. His specialty, his métier, his arena was soybeans. Though he was city-born and sub-urb-reared, educated, Jewish, possessor of stubby, soft, gen-trified hands suited for little more than hefting a salad fork, Ken Korngold knew as much about soybeans, those round little nuggets of protein, as any black-dirt Iowa farmer.

Not the actual farming of the beans — Korngold himself could raise the dead easier than he could cultivate an actual plant — but he intimately knew the ingredients necessary for soybean production. He was aware of weather, field condi-tions, plantings, harvests: the raw data necessary for bringing beans to market. And when they got there they were his, to be bought and sold with those same stubby fingers, fingers work-ing on orders from a trading mind that was awesomely effi-cient, even magical, and which, over the course of nearly two decades of bean trading, had made him a fortune.

With such seasoned expertise, Korngold, the bean trader, hardly flinched at a freak punch of spring heat in the Mid-west. Korngold, the frail, vulnerable, sweating Midwest com-muter, was another story.

That searing Monday afternoon he found himself mired in expressway traffic in his cocoa-brown Mercedes 450 SL, a sculpted, finely tuned piece of German engineering except for the fact that its air conditioning was *kaput*. The dead AC was partly Korngold's fault for failing to leave the car with the dealer, and partly the dealer's fault for not reminding him. It was only May, and it wasn't supposed to get this hot in May.

So Korngold, who was thirty-eight—an elder among his fellow floor traders—sweltered and cursed for the two hours it took him to go forty-three miles from LaSalle Street in downtown Chicago to White Oak Lane and his split-level, thirteen-room home in Highland Park. This kind of heat and humidity was no good for him. It overworked his sweat glands and parched his skin. It drooped the already drooping skin beneath his tired eyes into the pouches of an old man. He stroked the soft skin of his chin and wondered when it, too, would sag.

Apart from his tired eyes and his thinning hair, however, Korngold looked to the world to be a fit man. He stepped lively. No trace of a belly slipped between the buttons of his shirt. He did not smoke, had a mouth full of cavity-free, ivory teeth, and a laugh that cut through partitions. Yet he himself knew what lay beneath the laughter. He knew that the years of trading and spitting in the pits had brought him a duodenal ulcer, a nagging lower-back disk, a chronic raw throat, hypertension, varicose veins, and occasionally—usually around the holidays—roaring hemorrhoids.

All of those hurts screamed approaching morbidity until he lowered himself into the waters of his home's undulating indoor pool. He cradled a tumbler of Absolut on the rocks. Steam rose from his forehead. It subsided only after he dialed the Mercedes dealer and told him to deliver a new 450 SL, same color, same everything, that afternoon. He never wanted to see the heap currently in his driveway again.

Korngold's presence at home this early in the evening drew his daughter, Rachel, from her bedroom sanctuary. She was fifteen, with straight black hair, straightened white teeth, and many imported sweaters. Even without the elegant trappings of her wardrobe, Rachel Korngold was beautiful, one of the rare, lucky teenagers breezing her way through puberty without a hint of a blemish.

Rachel's most amazing quality, however, was not her good looks but the fact that she considered her father, normally an ogre in the eyes of teenagers, to be a great guy. That her opinion of him was not shared by her mother only served to galvanize her sentiments. To Rachel Korngold her father was a big puppy dog, cute, rich, and misunderstood. She loved to cuddle up to him while he watched television. Occasionally she reached inside his shirt and tugged his graying chest hair. Regularly she assured him that everything was all right.

Rachel Korngold also knew exactly what her father did to make his considerable income. She read the commodity tables in the financial pages as if they were summaries of soap operas. She relished trips to the futures markets to watch the action in the pits even though she was well aware of what six hours of jumping and screaming did to a person. She monitored her father's aches, how they flared and subsided with the fates of his financial positions, something Rachel, with the help of her personal computer, figured to the penny. The figures told her when his fleshy eyes would lift or droop, when he'd made a killing or gotten gored.

To Rachel Korngold knowing all of this was fun, even exciting. And, she came to realize, it gave her a lopsided edge over her mother, who did not know a soybean from a Bonwit's credit card.

Rachel's response to her father's discontent that steamy afternoon was remarkable even for her.

"One man's heat wave is another man's fortune, Daddy," she said.

"Kahlil Gibran?" he said.

"El Niño."

"Huh?"

"And it's going to get a lot worse," she said.

"Okay. Let's have it," he said.

Rachel skipped off to her room and returned with a school notebook. On the kitchen table she spread out a sheaf of colored maps and handwritten reports.

"It's all here," she said.

Korngold, wearing a monogrammed terrycloth robe, leaned over the papers. They were Rachel's physical science report, a three-week research project on something called *"El Niño."*

"It's Spanish for 'the infant,' " she said.

It referred to a freak pattern of weather in South America,

12

she went on, that precipitated severe changes on climate all over the world. It happened every ten or twenty years for reasons scientists still were not sure of and often emerged around Christmastime. Hence the name *"El Niño."*

"It's all in the trade winds," Rachel said. "They usually sweep from the east like this. But during *El Niño* they move way over here. That raises the temperature of ocean currents and then you get storms. Big ones.

"See. This is the Humboldt current off Peru. It's usually cold, but *El Niño* warms it up."

"I know," said Korngold, not taking his eyes from the maps.

To be sure, he did know, but had forgotten. Some years before, similar conditions had warmed the Humboldt current and all but wiped out the anchovy harvest. Korngold didn't know the specifics at the time, or anything at all about *El Niño*. He didn't even know then that anchovies were a major component of fish meal used in poultry and cattle feed. He was too busy trading soybeans with his Uncle Levi's firm, trying to learn the commodities game and earn his keep. But he was to become anchovy-literate in a hurry, for the vanished critter took soybeans from $4.50 to $12.50 a bushel, and Korngold scalped profits every bit of the way. It was his first six-figure year.

Others followed. A few years later he bought his seat on the exchange outright—for $150,000 in cash—and became a power hitter in the pits. With the blessings of his uncle, he formed his own trading firm.

"It's the worst in forty-five years," Rachel went on.

"So it is," Korngold said, studying his daughter's colored pencil drawings. The sweeping black arrows designating winds and currents across the North and South Pacific oceans looked like a World War II map of marauding Axis powers.

Korngold was not reminded of anchovies, however, for they had long since ceased to be a major ingredient in cattle feed. In fact, soybean meal had taken their place. What snared Korngold's attention was the severity of *El Niño* as documented by Rachel's rough sketches. Its aberrant winds and currents had caused killer droughts in Africa as well as ruinous winter storms as far north as California. At the same time it brought the mildest winter ever to the Midwest—62 F. in Chicago on Christmas day.

"Are you thinking what I think you are?" Rachel said, as her fingernail traced the coast of Brazil.

"This heat is *El Niño* on the backside," he said.

"You got it."

There were hosts of variables, she had written, but *El Niño* could spill over into summer. And the effects would be clear: a season of torrid heat and no rain. For long moments Ken Korngold pondered images of baked soil and stunted plants.

Rachel put her arm around him. "Now, can we negotiate a price for this information?" she cooed.

In the days that followed, Korngold quietly researched *El Niño*. Like all the boys in the pits, he had access to mountains of data, research, and opinion ranging from computerized deductions to almanacs and astrology. Much of it was ignored, especially when it concerned the weather. Traders reacted to rumors, speculations, and events of all stripes. They leaped within seconds on news of a freeze or a freak flood. But they didn't predict. They played the numbers and let the market take care of itself. Korngold usually did the same, caring not if the market went up or down or for what reason as long as he was a fraction of a beat ahead of it.

But *El Niño* was too good to be true, he decided, a powerful force with the potential of bringing turmoil into the market. He also knew that if he failed to move, if he waited for another dry spell, it would be too late. He wondered how many traders might know, how many were long in anticipation. The bean market was known to erupt on much, much less. Korngold watched and listened more closely than ever before in his trading career, trying to sense the slightest adumbration of *El Niño*. But nothing, no stirring of any sort, came back to him. The prices of corn and soybeans continued their seasonal slides.

Then one afternoon he jumped in. Near the end of a somnolent trading session he bought 1,000 bean and 1,000 corn contracts. Each contract was for delivery of 5,000 bushels, 10 million bushels of grain in all, in September. It cost him $3 million, approximately 5 percent of the grain's market value of $60 million. Such margin was typical of trading in commodities: a proportionally small amount of cash to control a great quantity of product, and key to its volatile potential for profit or loss.

For Korngold, the position was hefty and bullish, and other traders took notice. Yet in an arena where giants like General Mills or Ralston Purina regularly bought millions of bushels of grain to be used for dog food and breakfast cereal, where individual brokers bought and sold similar quantities for customers all over the globe, where floor traders who did not intend to take delivery of even one kernel of grain regularly took on million-dollar positions, Ken Korngold's buy was exceptional, but not extraordinary.

That night he told his daughter.

"I went long in the grains today. A hundred lot in corn and beans," he said, unsure as he spoke why he understated the positions.

Rachel's deep brown eyes widened.

"My first official buy," she said, and she hugged him with her head on his chest.

Her exuberance didn't help him sleep well that night. He'd gambled three mil on the stinking weather. It was a gutsy move that could hurt him badly if the price went against him, if *El Niño* faded and corn and bean plants thrived as they usually had in the past and record harvests depressed the price. He lay in bed and stared at the ceiling, seeing the grain boards' palpitating, menacing digits.

At 5:00 A.M., an hour earlier than usual, he left for work. He eased his new Mercedes out of his paved drive and past the broad, tile-roofed homes of his neighbors. Well-heeled all, they nevertheless had little comprehension of what he did for a living, of the degree of leverage it took to control at this very moment 10 million bushels of September grain. He wished he were a pediatrician like Fred Cahan on the corner.

He parked his car across the street from the Board of Trade in an exclusive underground lot crammed with Mercedes', Rollses, and twelve-cylinder Jaguars, most with vanity plates such as "GNYMAES," "CBOT 1," "BEANPIT," and other related ciphers. A half dozen black attendants incessantly buffed the autos with chamois. Traders not-so-jokingly called the garage the "credit" lot because of the fortunes parked here. Insiders could look at a car and tell you how its owner made it—the soybean market of '73, the bond market of '80, and so on. The "debit" lots were a few blocks away, and though dotted with Mercedes' and BMWs, were the domain of traders still looking for the ring.

Two agonizing weeks passed. Trading in soybeans was directionless, sideways. Korngold's positions eroded by more than $300,000. Then another heat wave hit the Midwest. This one was hotter and drier than the last. It was interrupted by rumbling, lightning-laced thunderstorms that lasted a half hour and left barely a trace of rain before another surge of hot Gulf air settled in. Korngold luxuriated in it, leaving his auto's air conditioning off and letting the sweat stream down his face.

What followed was the summer of *El Niño,* weeks of the hottest, driest weather the Midwest had known since the dust storms of the Depression. Unirrigated soybean fields became parched and blistered wastelands. Seedlings that had been puffy and moist in spring withered into brittle stalks. Crop forecasts shrunk, then plummeted. *El Niño* became a buzz word of newspaper and magazine articles, complete with illustrations and colorful maps of winds and currents that looked as if they had been lifted from Rachel Korngold's science project.

The pits went wild. Anything that grew was affected: wheat, oats, feeder cattle, live beef cattle, live hogs, pork bellies, but especially corn, soybeans, soybean meal, and soybean oil. The boys traded furiously, reaching the limit set for a day's trading range sometimes only minutes after the opening gong. Television camera crews sick of shooting packed city beaches or the insides of commercial ice houses came down and trained their equipment on the frenzied trading floors.

In the middle of it all was Korngold. His positions turned into a rout of profits, a whirlwind that danced and howled amidst the pandemonium of flailing hands and ravaged throats. He sold his first block of 100 contracts for double what they had cost him weeks earlier. The rest of his trades

16

followed accordingly. By the heat of mid-summer he had gradually liquidated most of his positions. His $3 million had increased to $20 million.

Even by Board of Trade standards it was a nifty bit of trading, enough to put Korngold among the legends of the pits: Bill and Ed O'Connor, the quiet Irish bean-trading brothers who played the bull market of the seventies for $25 million; Eugene Cashman, the former Chicago cop who rode the '73 bean market for an estimated $50 million; or Richard Dennis, the mild-mannered Treasury bond trader who built a $50 million fortune in the late 1970s when interest rates went crazy. Korngold's coup could not match these strikes, but his was not bad.

It was also enough to persuade him to take the rest of the summer off, maybe the rest of the year. He needed a vacation. He would visit West Palm Beach and his mother, take care of a nagging problem involving her finances, and play some golf.

He also thought it might be time to take Rachel on a real vacation, to Paris or London, the French Riviera. Then he considered how raptly she followed the market, how she rushed home from school to get the final closings on Channel 26, how she met him at the door every night knowing to the penny what shape he was in. She deserved a special place. Just him and her.

He knew the spot. He would take her to Hong Kong, that fortress of capitalism, and its fabulous gold markets. The Chinese were some of the best traders in the world. Or so he had been told.

At the suggestion, Rachel squealed and jumped and gave Korngold her characteristic overhug.

Then she stepped back and smiled slyly.

"*Anything* to get out of this heat," she said.

Chapter Two

When she was a little girl Joanie's favorite story in the whole world was how she got her golden curly hair.

The angels were making cotton candy one day, her mother, whose hair was brown and straight, used to say, big swirls of it out of fluffy white clouds and sugar, when one of the angels dropped a handful of the marvelous stuff. It fell out of heaven, through the clouds, past bluebirds who swooped close to see if they might make nests with it, down, down toward earth where — just as an angel was about to reach out and catch it — it landed on the pink head of a pudgy baby called Jo-Jo lying naked on a blanket in the grass.

When she was a little older, Joanie was told that she got her blond hair from her mother, who claimed that her hair had been white and wispy before it turned brown.

When she was old enough, Joanie was told about Trader's.

It was in Pensacola and famous because of the fly-boys from the Naval Air Base who hung out there. Especially the Blue Angels, the Navy's hotshot PR fliers, the guys with a couple years of missions in Korea or Nam and several hundred carrier landings who had exchanged flak-dodging for cloudbursts and peel-away formations in front of festival crowds.

Full-color photos of the Angels standing rigid in their blue-and-gold dress uniforms before a sleek blue F-15 fighter jet covered Trader's walls like icons.

Joanie's mother met her father there. Oh no, she said, he wasn't a Blue Angel. You could not find his face in any of the photos on the walls. He was just a sailor, she went on, a mechanic who kept the planes flying in and out of the base. She left it at that.

As a matter of fact, her mother really had very little more to add, because Chief Petty Officer Harold Yff—rhymes with "if," she always added—had come in and out of her life just about that fast. Not two ships passing in the night, she used to sigh. More like a Navy jet on a refueling stop.

He was a tall, shy Dutch kid from Holland, Michigan, just about the most gorgeous boy Joanie's mother had ever seen. He had a blond brush cut and a blond moustache and skin so smooth and baby-soft she could kiss it all night long. One night she did just that, whispering into his pink ears that of all the guys she met at Trader's he was the one she would be naughty with.

He was so excited he made little squealy sounds and got the hiccups. His arms and legs flailed about, like a mammoth, fuzzy, crazed blond octopus ensnaring her whole. She gasped and tried to slow him down, but he was so aroused, just a dervish of energy and sweaty sex.

"What do they *feed* you in Holland, Michigan, makes you so frisky?" she said.

When she told him she was pregnant he cried. He raised his arms to his temples and sobbed and said his dad and mom would be ashamed. She cried, too, but not so hard. She had pinned the tail on the mule. And he was so cute.

Then Harold Yff took off, not without a trace, but with a rambling, tear-smeared letter in which he spoke of sin and the lusts of the flesh. He also promised to pay for his "transgression," as he repeatedly referred to it, starting with the enclosed $40 in cash and continuing with as much per month as he could afford until the child was eighteen years old. When she read it she wept, quite hard this time, with cramping sobs that nearly made her black out.

The miracle of it all was that he sent the money. Every month for years, the amount steadily increasing, in cash at first, then money orders, finally crisp, insured checks drawn from an account in a Michigan bank. There was never a letter or a note inside—though later on the contents included religious tracts from an organization called the World Home Bible League—just the money.

19

From the beginning she took every penny of it. She wiped her tears and had the baby, a little girl named Joan Olivia, and committed herself to keeping it. She gave the baby its father's name and said to anyone who asked that he was away at sea.

At first the baby was her cross, then her jewel, then her best friend. When little Joanie asked questions about her daddy she was told about sailors and big ships that never came in. She said it, however, without bitterness or rancor. Whenever they went to the beach Joanie looked out on the horizon and tried to find her father's boat.

Many years later, a few months after her eighteenth birthday (he'd guessed wrong, of course), the mysterious monthly checks stopped coming in the mail. By that time Joanie and her mother were living in a two-bedroom house trailer on the outskirts of West Palm Beach. Joanie had a high school graduation tassel swinging from her Honda's rearview mirror and was a month away from starting college.

To celebrate she and a couple of friends decided to spend a week's holiday in Pensacola. Joanie's mother said nothing, but the mere mention of the panhandle city sent her thoughts hurtling.

Joanie fought with the idea for two days before she looked up the place called Trader's. She was surprised and not a little scared when she found it. It was the same place, a joint, a dark, seedy saloon in the middle of downtown run by an old swabbie who loved Navy fliers. Joanie and her girlfriends didn't dare go inside until Trader himself came out and ushered them in. He sat them down in dentists' chairs lining one side of the bar and told them to feel at home. Then he set them up with bottles of beer.

Joanie swiveled her chair and looked around. The saloon was a junkyard of naval memorabilia. Dusty souvenirs, wacky hats, and model planes hung in a jumble from the ceiling. Every open space was cluttered with artifacts, authentic or otherwise, and junk from jet cockpits and seagoing vessels. The walls were papered with those color photographs of the Blue Angels and their jets, dozens of teams going back several years, all of them handsome, square-jawed boys with sandy

20

hair and grimacing smiles.

Sitting around, at the bar and amidst the clutter of chairs and tables, were a few locals and a handful of sailors. So, too, were the girls, waitresses and barmaids, but it was immediately obvious to Joanie that these girls were not innocents with high school class rings hanging from necklaces. They were dancing girls, floozies in skimpy outfits who sipped watered-down drinks and let the sailors nuzzle their boobs.

Every so often one of them put Mick Jagger on a cheap stereo and danced on the tables, grinding and gyrating, pulling away her top and bottom so the sailors could see the merchandise. Then they sat down and rubbed thighs and whispered boozy promises into crimson ears.

The girls ignored Joanie and her friends, but Joanie could not take her eyes off them.

Finally she got up the courage to ask. She beckoned to Trader and asked not about the girls but if he knew any of the boys in the photographs.

"Knew 'em all, young lady," he said. "Remember every one."

"How about officers who weren't fliers? Mechanics," she said.

"Call 'em 'Baby Hueys.' They're up over there," he said, grinning a toothless smile and pointing to a far corner. "Go take a look."

She got up and wandered over, carrying a bottle of beer in her hand, ignoring the dozens of pairs of eyes that followed her. In the corner were rows of yellowed photos. But unlike the glossy, professional composites of the Blue Angels, these were homemade, candidly struck eight-by-ten snapshots. There was not a face among them. The favored pose of the Baby Hueys was a group moon shot, dozens of white backsides bared for posterity.

Joanie was startled, then transfixed, her eyes panning the wall of fannies. A thin smile broke over her face, then faded and dissolved. She felt herself growing enormously sad. She stood and stared, thinking of the stories she had been told as a child, of her mother as a young girl in this stale, smoky place, and tears leaked down her face.

* * *

Several days later Joanie returned to West Palm Beach and her trailer home. Her mother was waiting, sitting in her La-Z-Boy doing her needlepoint. She did cross-stitch and embroidery on meticulous, demanding patterns copied from eighteenth-century designs. They were masterpieces, tapestries of thread and concentration. They took her months to complete, sitting for hours in good light in her chair. When she was not doing them she worked the keyboard of a word processor in a downtown law office. Before that she had been a beautician in one of West Palm Beach's many hair salons, creating wonders in blue rinse. She had great hands.

She looked up and smiled at Joanie, her lips counting, fingers a blur. She let Joanie fix herself a cup of instant coffee and sit down before she spoke.

"So now what do you think?"

She kept her eyes fast on the needlework.

Joanie looked at her across the room. They talked best like this, the needlework preventing their eyes from meeting, or avoiding, each other.

"That guy Trader," Joanie began. "He's incredible. Marcy gave him a ten-dollar bill and—"

"He took it and didn't give her change," her mother said.

"Right! And kept serving us."

"And when you were ready to leave he gave you, what, six, seven dollars back?"

"Eight," Joanie replied.

Her mother smiled, keeping her eyes on her work.

"A guy told us he decides how much change you get by how much he likes you," Joanie said, sipping her coffee.

"Never wears a matched pair of socks," she continued. "Wore this Yankees baseball cap. An article on the wall says he owns half of downtown Pensacola."

Her mother leaned over to study the thread color chart. She studied her design, then her fingers took off again.

"To answer your first question," she said, "the place hasn't changed a bit."

Joanie stared at her.

"And my second?" she said.

22

"It wasn't because I needed the money, which I did. Or because I was running away from my folks, which I was."

She stopped.

"Kidnapped into white slavery?" Joanie said.

Her mother wrinkled her nose. "Trader never paid us any attention. All he cared about was his boys."

"So why, Mother? I mean, that *place*. One of those babes danced to 'Light My Fire' with candles stuck to her boobs. It was really gross."

Her mother remained silent, her eyes never lifting from her needlework.

"I liked it," she finally said. "All the attention I got. Those guys snuggling up close with their warm noses. They'd offer me their paychecks. They'd say I was the best thing since home."

"And you believed it?"

"Every word."

"Until you got pregnant. Raped and abandoned."

"Maybe."

"Maybe? C'mon, Mom, the creep never even made an honest woman out of you."

At that her mother looked up, the needlework dropping in her lap.

"Now tell me what in hell is an honest woman?"

"You know what I mean."

"That creep, as you call him, was responsible for that gorgeous face of yours and that smooth skin. Long legs, blond hair, the works. You did okay."

"You defend him! It's amazing."

"No, I don't defend him. Can't and never would. But don't *you* complain about the deal," her mother said.

"I never got a father. I've heard they can be okay."

"That's my fault."

"So why didn't you go after him? If you wanted him in the first place, why'd you let him run out?"

Her mother looked up, her hands suddenly motionless.

"I was free, white, and over eighteen. Thought I could get away with anything. Even working at Trader's.

"Then this sailor started coming in. All the girls had their eye on him but I — *me* — I thought I could get him. He'd fall for me. I took the chance."

"You mean those chicks think sailors will start up with them?" Joanie said.

"You think we were working there for the money?"

Joanie shrugged.

"So I paid my nickel and took the dance. I timed it right and got pregnant with his baby and offered to follow him anywhere. And zip — he took off. Like they all did. The only difference was that he paid the bill."

"You could have forced him to marry you."

"I thought about it. Especially when I saw all that Christian guilt flowing through his veins. But I didn't do it. I finally convinced myself I didn't want him that way."

"God," Joanie said. "Pregnant, alone — you had to be desperate."

Her mother's eyebrows lifted.

"One day I'll tell you about how I packed a suitcase and bundled you up and took a bus to Michigan. Or maybe I'll show you a bunch of letters I wrote but never sent. Or the times on Christmas Eve or my birthday — or *your* birthday — that I called long distance and hung up after that voice answered," she said.

Joanie stared at her mother, and she saw those curled, black-and-white photographs of her mother at the beach, at a picnic, on Easter Sunday, always squinting in the glaring sunlight and holding the baby, the blond, bubble-cheeked baby, not like a burden but a prize.

"You were a good baby, that helped," her mother said.

"That's something," Joanie said.

"Look, Jo, I took a chance. Miss Fancy Pants. Nobody could tell me what to do. And I got slapped down. Best lesson I ever had."

"That sounds like mother-daughter talk," Joanie said.

"You started it," she said.

Then she smiled. "If you ever work at Trader's, I'll kill you."

Joanie laughed, then she exhaled and slouched back on the sofa, thinking.

"You never got married . . ." she said, and left the thought hanging.

"I was scared to. I wasn't ever going to pin my hopes on one man again," she said.

Then her attention went back to her embroidery. Joanie watched her, turning her words over in her mind. Finally, she got up to put her cup in the sink.

Returning, Joanie ran her hands through her hair, that very same blond, angelic hair.

"I don't know for sure," she said, "but I think he had a cute ass."

Her mother laughed.

"It was adorable."

The one promise Joanie's mother made her keep was to enroll in beauty school and get its diploma. It was but a few months and a few hundred dollars out of her life, but it would always be a cushion, her mother insisted, something to bring in hard cash when the dreams went soft.

To Joanie it was ridiculous, but she did it anyway and did it easily, having inherited her mother's manual finesse. In no time she could do hair. Then she went after her own degree. She enrolled in a newly created business course at West Palm Beach Junior College. The curriculum was specially designed for part-time students and those who wanted to go on to four-year business majors. Joanie was a part-timer, taking three classes a semester while she worked and built up her assets. To do that she got a job at The New Wave, a loud, multilevel, unisex beauty salon. She was one of twenty-nine stylists on duty, and while the place drove her nuts, the money was good and the hours flexible.

For the next two years she studied the theory and practice of American business and worked five, sometimes six, days a week at The New Wave, an example of American free enterprise at its purest. She took home $500 a week, paid each Friday morning in cash, which she immediately banked in an interest-bearing checking account. When the balance went above $1,000 she sent $500 to her money market fund.

By the spring of her second year she had $3,107 in money

25

market funds with interest reinvested, and one of her professors suggested she invest in a high-rated utility stock for an even better yield. She looked into it, into electric utility companies that heretofore had been as interesting to her as real estate in Kuwait, and made her choice. More importantly, she found that she liked doing it, that researching a company and making an investment in it was a lark.

In the meantime she still drove her Honda Civic, an '83 and getting older, but paid for. Several credit cards fattened her wallet and she used them rather than paying cash, knowing very well that paying off all balances in full at the end of the month saved her any finance charges. Her credit line became so solid that her bank charge card beseeched her to borrow cash, making it as effortless for her as writing out a check. But Joanie read the fine print, took one look at the 19 percent interest rate, and declined. Her investment class was studying hard assets. She considered buying an Oriental rug.

Again, she liked it. She liked having her own money and being master of it. It was something no sailor could take away from her.

At the beginning of her second year at West Palm, a professor asked her where she was going to complete her business degree.

"You will, won't you?" he said. "You're far too bright not to go on."

She beamed. More than just getting good grades, she was good at this, at the study of business, at money in all its green goodness.

Any one of the major Florida colleges offered business and economic programs, yet the more she considered her move, the wider afield she looked, as far as Harvard, Wharton, Chicago, Stanford. She rolled those famous names across her tongue, schools and places so far outside of her sphere of existence as to be locales of fairy tales, east, west, and north, beyond Atlanta and the Carolinas, as far up as Chicago.

It was that place that stuck in her mind, a germ reinforced by one of her professors who cited the work of Nobel Prize-winners Milton Friedman and George Stigler of the University of Chicago as if it were gospel. He used Friedman's public

26

television series to augment his lectures. But the University of Chicago, Joanie soon discovered, even if she were somehow able to get accepted into its School of Economics, was sorely expensive. Way beyond her means.

Yet Chicago, that place best left to the Eskimos, as Randy Newman sang on Joanie's tapes, offered something else. She learned of it in chapter 8 of her investment text, a world that stirred the book's prose into new adjectives and rare anecdotes. It was called commodities, the buying and selling of grains, staples, and currencies in what the textbook described as "curious, dangerous, fascinating, lightning-like" futures markets.

Joanie's professor, the same one whose expression grew beatific at the mention of Milton Friedman, lifted his eyes heavenward when he introduced the chapter.

"Commodities make Wall Street look like a retirement village," he said.

Most of the class's tanned Florida undergrads laughed when he said it. Joanie perked her ears and let her mind race as the professor went on. The material was dynamite.

Still, Joanie would have relegated the whole phenomenon of commodities trading to but an intriguing interlude in her business studies were it not for the day she met the trader, one very different from the old sailor in Pensacola.

Chapter Three

Korngold drove down Bexley Avenue in West Palm Beach. He was alone, having flown into town for a few days to take care of business. Then he was off to Pinehurst, North Carolina, to play some golf. It was the kind of match he loved, a foursome including a club pro, usually one who occasionally made the cut on the tour but whose main talent lay in taking money from hackers like Korngold who loved to bet and press on every hole.

But first, Korngold was driving to West Palm's First Federal Savings Bank. It was time to put a leash on his mother. He had come to instruct bank officials not to allow Birdie Korngold to withdraw a penny more than $1,000 at any one time, and that he was to be notified immediately if she tried. As much as he loved her and wanted his mother to enjoy her postharvest days, Korngold was afraid Birdie was going *meshugge* on him.

Why else would a penny-wise Jewish mother from the old neighborhood air mail a $5,000 cashier's check to the Reverend Jack Benny Evers of Ascension City, Tennessee, for a seat on his Space Shuttle to Jesus?

Why else would the widow of Sidney Korngold, the penurious operator of three Chicago currency exchanges, throw $3,500 to Brother Peter Pettinga of Ada, Michigan, for one of the spikes used to nail Jesus to the tree?

Why else would she regularly donate drips of $200 and drabs of $350 totaling who knows how much to toupee'd faith healers and speakers-of-tongues?

So contemplated Ken Korngold as he cursed Florida's geriatric traffic, the dozens of retirees on their way to the bank to withdraw their children's money. He had bought Birdie the condominium ostensibly as an investment, taking maximum

28

write-offs for depreciation, maintenance, and expenses, renting it to her at the lowest figure allowable by the IRS. The rent payments came, of course, from a generous monthly stipend, a figure he felt would allow her to live out her years in Florida in upper-middle-class luxury were it not for the bloodletting of her account by TV's Jesus Boys.

That is what put him in downtown West Palm Beach that day, and that is what totally left his mind when he saw the girl in the fedora.

His Mercedes (leased to his mother, Illinois license "BOYCHK") had been stranded in the middle of the crosswalk by a left-turn artist who decided that a yellow light was too late to make the turn. So the car forced pedestrians to walk scowling and muttering around its front fender. Among them was the girl, who was dressed in a snug but not outrageous pair of jeans, a loose-fitting shortsleeve blouse with something written in blood-red Japanese script across the back, a pair of running shoes, and that hat. From the hat trailed a single, blond braid.

She was tilting a bottle of diet soda to her lips as she passed and Korngold would have done little more than admire her outlines had she not stopped in front of the car, tapped a nail on the chrome, and mouthed, "I'm walking here."

"Ratso Rizzo!" Korngold yelled, his voice trapped by the Mercedes's soundproof windows.

It was only his favorite character from one of his favorite movies. He pounded the steering wheel. This chick could not possibly know about Ratso. Or could she? And he laughed and craned his neck to follow her as she walked, doing so long into the next series of traffic signals, and suddenly he was jarred by the honking horns of senior citizens behind him.

He looked ahead, then behind him, then across the street to see where she had gone. By then she was a half block east down Bexley. Korngold no longer wanted to turn left, and tried to slip ahead through the intersection. The honkers went berserk, and Korngold opened his window and thrust his arm out in the Chicago Salute, a frigging motion known to travelers throughout the world.

No appointment with any banker would keep him from cutting across two lanes of traffic and illegally parking the SEL in order to follow her. Korngold could do things like this nowadays, even get away with them. She had gone, he thought, into what looked like a beauty salon.

He followed, walking into The New Wave, a cluttered menagerie of mirrors, clippers, scissors, curlers, drip cages, the piss odor of perm solution, and pounding rock music. Standing everywhere were beauticians, glittering, garish young girls standing behind a wet head in a chair. Atop their own skulls were hauls of red, auburn, and raven hair, poofed, primped, curled, teased, and cellophaned. Some wore sparkled T-shirts and jeans, Bon Jour, Sasson, Sergio Valente; others wore minis, ankle socks, and suffocating leather pants.

None of them, as far as Korngold could see, was the girl on Bexley.

"Do you have an appointment?" the phone girl said, looking at him sideways as she cradled a receiver on her shoulder, put another caller on hold, and scribbled on a docket. She had magenta fingernails as long as shrimp forks.

Korngold laughed.

"Why not?" he said.

"With who?"

He laughed again, nervously, to his surprise, and half in awe of this place. Behind him sat six appointments: two fifteen-year-old girls, a two-hundred-pound mechanic, an old lady in a wig, a guy in a corduroy suit, a three-year-old kid reading *Playboy*.

"So who?" she repeated, the phone now out of her neck.

"Uh, a girl with a hat, blond maybe, white, uh, shirt?"

"You gotta name? We got twenty-nine stylists here."

"They all wear hats and shirts with, uh, red banzai writing on it?"

"So what's your name?"

"Me? Leo."

She picked up a microphone.

"Joanie"—her voice cutting into the thump of the stereo—"you have Leo."

She nodded at Korngold over her shoulder. "Up the steps and right."

30

He waded into the shop, walking between chairs, around carts of curlers, in and out of the blasts of a dozen whining hair dryers, past a row of bored stylists sitting in canvas chairs who smoked and picked at their nails. One looked up at him and broke a trace of a smile. He had the feeling he was intruding. He felt eighty years old. He didn't need a haircut and these girls knew it.

"Hi, Leo. How ya doin'?"

It was her. She was all smiles, minus the fedora, with great white teeth that kind of bit into her lower lip, one foot on the pedal of the chair. He sat down as if he knew what he was doing.

"I can't do a thing with it," he said, gesturing to his salt-and-pepper, naturally curly hair, looking at her in the mirror as she moved behind him.

Joanie ran her fingers through his hair, pulling lightly at a few wisps. It was thinning, she noted, but she did not say as much. With little effort she could clear a circular bare spot at the crown of his head. She was certain he was aware of it, and that whoever cut his hair less than two weeks earlier had made certain to cover it.

"This is nice work," she said.

"Mr. Marcel — best there is," he said.

"Does good hands, too," she said, touching his manicured forefinger.

"That's Miss Alexis," he said.

"So what do you want me to do?" she said, jiggling a comb on her fingers.

"Oh, shampoo, comb out, blow dry. Maybe hover around and whisper at it a little while."

She laughed. He guessed she did not recognize him from the intersection.

Her eyes narrowed, and she tried to read him. What she scanned was a guy in his late thirties who was run-down but had the money to hide the damage. Except for his eyes. They were quick, even flashing, but lined with sagging skin that made him look like a politician, or one of those old English actors who introduces dramas on public TV. He could have something done to those pouches, she knew. If you have the dough, you can have something done to anything.

"Ah, c'mon. If you got the time, I got the fee," he said.

She clipped a towel around his neck and released the back of the chair, dropping his head down to the lavatory.

"Name's Ken," he said.

"Leo Ken? Sounds Oriental," she said.

She shot a spray of water onto his scalp.

"Put some heat in it, what say?" he said.

Joanie sniffed.

As she worked, Korngold started to jabber. He tried for a rise, for some kind of reaction, working like he did when one bad trade put him in a hole and he had to scalp and scratch his way through twenty-five small trades to get even. He used all his good lines, wit, double entendre, a trace of the risqué here and there.

Little of it seemed to score. At his definition of Polish foreplay, she smiled. At his story of the elephant trunk and the hard rolls, she chortled. When he poked his thumb out of his fly and showed her how a one-armed blind man counted his change, she gave in and laughed out loud.

"Let me guess," she said. "Stockbroker. Wall Street. High-tech issues."

"No cigar," he said. "Commodities. Board of Trade. Beans."

"The *pits,*" she said, suddenly brightening.

She stepped in front of him. "A floor trader?"

It was his turn to look startled.

"Whattaya know from a floor trader?" he said.

"I've read all about it," she said, then stopped short.

"I'm taking business classes at West Palm J.C.," she went on. "We covered a section on futures trading in my finance course."

He interrupted, "I bet the whole class bought an imaginary portfolio."

"That's right! We did it for a month. Unlimited trades. The biggest winner gets a pizza. I'm still up six cents in December oats."

"Sell them and short Deece beans," he said.

"Why? — oh, this is great," she said. "You *are* a trader."

She kept it up for several minutes, maneuvering around

him, going through the motions of combing and recombing his hair while she asked him about trading and the pits. Her questions were intelligent. She was animated, and utterly beautiful.

"You really *do* it. You take that risk every day," she said. "We only did it on paper. . . ."

He never took his eyes off her, having long since confirmed that everything he had seen on the street was bona fide. She was one of those rare people who looked better up close, whose flash and gloss enhanced instead of covered. She could not be more than twenty-two.

"I tell you what," he said. "I gotta shoot some golf in North Carolina tomorrow. Why don't you fly up there with me and I'll explain things in detail."

She laughed and tossed her head to one side.

"I bet you would," she said.

"You can caddy."

"Nuts. I'd play."

"That's negotiable. Pick you up tomorrow morning at seven. You on?"

"You're serious."

"Of course."

"You come in here for a haircut and offer me a plane ride. How do I know you're not some Ted Bundy creep?"

"Who's Ted Bundy?"

"Cute guy who got his kicks killing women. Several."

"Get outta here. I'm a nice Jewish boy from Chicago."

"Richard Speck."

"Him I know and he wasn't Jewish. What is it, you got a library on mass murderers?"

"If you only knew how many guys come in here and offer girls plane rides, penthouse suites, overnights to Nassau. Takes only one weirdo."

"That's the chance you take. No guts, no glory."

"I've heard that," she said.

Just then the intercom announced her next appointment.

"So tonight? Dinner at a public place. You can frisk me before you get in the car."

"Love to, but I got a class."

"Class? I'll teach you more in an hour than you learn all year."

"Okay, come to class with me. Show and tell," she said.

"Hold it. I couldn't handle that," he said.

She frowned.

He looked in the mirror and patted his already overpampered locks, then started out of the chair.

"If you change your mind, mine is the Lear jet in the small-craft hangar. Seven-thirty takeoff."

"Tempting," she said. "Give me a rain check and a business card."

From a gold clip he withdrew a card and a $50 bill. He wrapped the bill around the card and reached out to tuck it in her waist.

She intercepted his hand in midair and plucked the package from his fingers.

"Thank you, Mr. . . . Korngold. Korngold Commodities. Kenneth I. Korngold, President," she read. "I am genuinely impressed. I mean that."

"But not enough to fly," he said, swiveling around off the chair.

She shrugged and smiled.

He shrugged and smiled, having given it his best, and turned to leave.

"Hey," she said suddenly.

He turned back to her.

"Are there women in your business?" she said.

He grinned, then dropped his voice an octave.

"Are there *women,*" he said, then gave her one more head-to-toe scan.

She lifted her eyes slightly, then watched as he wound his way out of the salon.

"Did that guy come on or did that guy come on?" said Tina, stopping work on her customer in the next chair. "I heard every word."

"A private jet, a condo in North Carolina, and a million or so net worth. Interested?" Joanie said.

"I'd be out the *door* right *now,*" said Tina.

Joanie absently palmed the bill and rubbed her fingers

34

along the embossed letters of Korngold's business card.

In class that night, and for the remainder of the semester, she used the card as a bookmark.

At dawn the next morning she was wide awake, and she lay in bed with her thoughts running. He was out there waiting. The clock said she had time, if only she had the courage. Finally she decided: it was ridiculous to lie awake in bed, at least she would get up and get dressed. As she did, her resolve grew, and soon she found herself hurrying.

Because of the trailer's close quarters her mother would probably hear her, but Joanie knew she would not stir. Minutes later Joanie softly shut the trailer door and drove off toward the airport.

The morning's shimmering sunlight shone in her face and she put on dark glasses. Private planes were parked on the south end of the airfield, and she followed a single-lane road toward it. As she neared the gate her foot began to flutter against the accelerator, and suddenly she pulled the car off the road. Her heart was beating in her throat, and she opened the door and got out.

An unoccupied parking lot shack stood about fifty yards away, and she walked to it. From there she could see the airfield.

And there he was. Alone, readying the sleek silver jet. Every so often he stopped and looked up, sometimes in her direction, seemingly right at the spot where she stood, as if he expected her to appear. She wanted to step out and shout or wave, to ask him if he was the kind of man she could pin her hopes on.

But she only stood and watched, trembling, her mouth dry.

At 7:30, just as he had said, Korngold tripped the engines and maneuvered the jet toward takeoff. Joanie watched, frozen, her hands clenched and her breath rapid, as the gleaming, whining machine taxied, caught a glint of sunlight, and effortlessly rose into the yellow sky.

It flew off like a blue angel. And just before it disappeared, its jet stream spelled her name.

35

She was certain of it.

By next May it was time to go. She finished her exams, tied up her affairs in West Palm Beach — including a long-standing, warm, occasionally torrid but doomed relationship with a medical student named Wilson — and made inquiries about life and school in Chicago. The in-city campus of the University of Illinois, she had learned, offered an accredited business degree. And they were eager to have her, offering housing, financial aid, even part-time employment. They made it sound too easy.

She knew she was serious when she gave The New Wave two weeks' notice. Near the end of her last week, as she worked late one night, she sensed something odd going on around her. Too many stylists were hanging around after their last appointment instead of running for the door. Just before ten, when only a few customers remained, including one last-minute trim that had, for some reason, been sent over to her, the lights flickered and the stereo system went off.

Joanie looked up, then around, and realized what was going on. Her hands dropped to her side and she groaned. Suddenly the stereo offered an awful Johnny Mathis song about going far, far away. From the front of the salon a half dozen stylists wearing party hats and hefting a cake with hissing sparklers stumbled toward her. Everybody cheered.

"Oh, come *on!*" she wailed, then sunk into her now vacant chair and started laughing. She spotted her mother, who came through the crowd, and gave her a hug. Both of them had all they could do to keep from crying.

Besides the cake, which read "Go for It, Joanie" in green icing, they popped a half dozen bottles of champagne, then urged Joanie to open the stack of farewell gifts. The first was a Chicago Cubs cap. The second was a toy tommy gun. The third was a purse-size can of Mace.

"That city has an image problem," she declared.

"Worse than that," someone shouted, and pointed to the other packages. Inside were several pairs of leg warmers, long underwear, a pillow with a filler that magically warmed when you sat on it, earmuffs in the shape of small animals, mittens, a ski mask, cough drops, cold medicine, and a can of Sterno.

"I'm going to Chicago, not the North Pole," Joanie protested, and withered under the cries that there was no difference.

The last gift was a game of Pit, an old favorite in which players screamed trades at each other in an effort to complete their hands. Joanie howled and raised the game in the air for all to see. She had played the game as a kid.

She read out loud from the label. " 'At the sound of the bell, everyone tries to corner the market on hay, barley, corn, rye, flax, oats, or wheat—just like a trader in a real grain exchange.' "

"That's you!" someone shouted.

"Aaaiiiyyeee!" she squealed, and thrust her hands in the air.

The party carried on for more than an hour. Someone broke open the Pit game and four girls began playing, screaming out the crops and laughing hysterically. Stylists Joanie hardly knew came over and wished her the best.

"I can see New York or Hollywood," said one. "But I *never* heard of going up to those markets."

Joanie laughed, then shrugged.

"It's the new Hollywood," she said.

A few days later, after the laughter and the cake and the farewells, Joanie silently packed the Honda. Her mother helped, saying little but the most mundane comments about this blouse or that pair of shoes.

Most of the talking, the preparation, the anticipation, had been done. Joanie was determined not to look like one of those dopey kids in the airline ads on TV. Then she saw the earmuffs, the ones shaped like puppie snouts, and she thought of how she had never seen snow except on television. A blizzard was out of the question. Did they occur often in Chicago? Daily?

She put on the muffs and turned to her mother, and suddenly she felt like the dopey kids in the airline commercials. They hugged and cried and Joanie tried to make out what her mother was saying.

"You got guts, Jo," her mother said.

"Yours," Joanie said, hugging and loving this woman more than ever.

"I'm not scared," Joanie added. Then she stepped back to look at her mother. "Am I?"

Soon she was on the road. With her was $2,000 withdrawn from her money market fund and changed into traveler's checks, her "A" list wardrobe, her portable cassette recorder and a dozen tapes she couldn't survive without, her hair paraphernalia — she was sure she could get a job cutting hair in any city on earth — a small library of her business textbooks, and a guidebook of Chicago. The rest of her possessions could stay in the trailer until she got settled.

She had a Chicago address (two, counting that precious business card from LaSalle Street) where she could live until she got her affairs in order. It was an apartment on West Polk Street near campus. With the help of a wonderful lady named Deena in the Student Affairs Office at the university, Joanie had secured a summer sublet. After three days of lonesome, uneventful travel, she found the campus and Deena's office.

"Look at *you*," gushed Deena, a gorgeous, shoelace-thin black woman. "You're just like you sound on the phone."

Everything to do with the apartment was ready and waiting, she went on.

"I did this personally for Professor Miller. He went to England. Oh, he's my honey. Good thing he went 'fore he got a look at *you*."

She laughed and patted Joanie's cheek, then gave her the keys.

"Things are fine around here. You'll like it. 'Course you got to watch yourself no matter what. Nighttime there's thugs. Don't talk to them joggers. They wear those outfits and they look okay. But underneath, girl, they don't wear no shorts, you hear?"

Joanie howled.

"Got problems get back to Deena, you know? I come from Georgia myself. Us southern girls got to stick together."

Joanie leaned over and gave her a kiss, and Deena's eyes

38

lifted into slight surprise and genuine affection.

Only minutes later Joanie walked up the stone steps of an eighty-year-old, renovated, Victorian graystone. It was a tall, imposing building, rock-solid, much like the others on the quiet city street only blocks away from the campus. She unlocked the oak front door and stepped inside. The glossy wood floors were partially covered with Persian rugs. The furniture—leather wingback chairs and a matching sofa—was carefully—almost too carefully—arranged. The walls were white and lined with chrome-framed architectural drawings. The windowsills held bulbous, fearsome-looking cactuses, each with watering instructions printed on a small card beneath the pot.

Joanie silently inspected the flat, her soft shoes creaking lightly over the floorboards. It was different from anything she had ever seen in Florida, and absolutely perfect. The rest of the day she moved in, feeling all the time like an intruder. That night she hardly slept, feeling alone but terribly excited, hearing all the building's strange bumps and groans, an occasional siren on the streets, and a seemingly incessant hum that she was certain came from the heart of this big, strange city.

The next day she went after a job. Before she could go to school she had to support herself. Michigan Avenue. Go to the Magnificent Mile, she had been told. She auditioned at Paul B., a tony second-floor salon, before Paul B. himself in his spiked hair and pantaloons. He liked her work—"As long as you ain't a one-cut ticket, honey"—and loved her Florida accent. She could start as soon as she wanted to.

Before she did, however, Joanie found her way to the Board of Trade.

The building was spectacular, granite, marble, the art deco lobby echoing the swarm of people pushing and weaving their way through it. The place was everything she had hoped it to be. So were its inhabitants, men and women, most of them no older than she was, in colored jackets, who hustled around her as if they were in a chase.

She asked directions, then rode an elevator packed with those jacketed workers, to the fifth floor. There she followed the signs to the visitors' gallery. She was startled when she opened the door and heard the noise, a pitched din of shouts, like a crowd at a ball game.

Joanie walked quickly over to the floor-to-ceiling windows and looked down onto a massive, three-story trading floor. It was a scene even beyond her expectations. Below was a crush of bodies, the same men and women in colored coats who had rushed by her in the lobby, now rushing in all directions beneath the flickering glow of the electronic price boards on the walls all around.

It was truly a human hive, with workers in the aisles and onto the tiered phone banks which surrounded the floor, all madly fulfilling their specific jobs. Their efforts were concentrated, of course, on the half dozen octagonal pits — yes, the *pits,* Joanie whispered — where more men and women in colored jackets shouted and waved their arms in what looked like panic.

With overhead speakers providing a live sound track of the clamor, Joanie stared at the frenzied action, at the bodies, at traders literally climbing on each other's backs.

She stood and marveled for several minutes. Then a slight smile broke on her lips. She was here, in the place that she had read and dreamed about for so long. She felt honored, almost weak.

Below her, only a few hundred yards away, Ken Korngold stood on the top step of the soybean pit checking his totals. There was a lull in trading, and he was nudged in the ribs by a fellow local. The trader nodded up at the glass of the visitors' gallery.

"Catch that," he said.

Korngold looked up and saw the figure, the blond hair, the bronzed legs crossed at the ankle. She was looking out over the trading floor, studying the price boards. She was dressed differently, a knee-length skirt, a waist-length blazer. She seemed intensely interested, her expression incredulous. She had a marvelous Florida tan.

"Couldn't be," Korngold said.

Chapter Four

Korngold was not in when she had visited his office that afternoon. She left him a mauve-colored Paul B. appointment card with her name penciled in at the top.

A week later, however, a Mr. Leo Ken called and scheduled for 2:45.

Joanie recognized him instantly. She smiled.

"How was Pinehurst?" she said.

As if it were yesterday.

But it was not, and she knew it. The months that had passed in between, the resolve that it took to pack up and leave her mother and Florida, to come up to this city, *Chicago*, and live on her own—all that had changed things. Changed her. Joanie felt it the moment she set foot in the Loop and she felt it with each new day, every time she stepped off the bus and moved with the crowds on Michigan Avenue, saw her reflection in shop windows, kept pace with the hustle and grab of this big, new, northern place.

Korngold laughed out loud and sat in the chair, eyeing her in the mirror as he had in Florida. In the cold light of Chicago, he decided, she looked different, gorgeous, to be sure, but different.

Joanie leaned into him as she worked, occasionally but not altogether accidentally grazing his arm with a breast. She cut his hair as if it were mink.

"The thing is *margin*," Joanie said. "You put ten cents down as margin—deposit—say on a coat or a car, and you control that thing for a certain amount of time."

"Go on," Korngold said.

"Then you either come up with the balance on what you bought and take it home with you, or you sell your deposit to

41

someone else because the value of what you've held has gone up. So the deposit is worth, say, twenty cents."

Since the day she had met Korngold, she had prepared this pitch. She had pored over her materials on commodities trading, mastering the fundamentals and imagining the reality, the incredible risk of the business. Great risk and great money, she pondered, absolutely amazing money. Gains that made her investments, her carefully weighed investments, seem piddling.

"The idea is a hundred years old," she went on. "Wheat farmers came to market with their fall harvest and there would be so much crop around they couldn't sell it. The price dropped like a brick. Some of them dumped it into the lake rather than take a loss. So they decided to set up a market where they could sell some of their crop now for delivery in the future. Buy wheat in October and deliver it in January. Then the price would remain fairly stable and the market more orderly."

"You could be a teacher," he said.

As she shaped and styled Korngold's hair, she inhaled the musky scent of his cologne and caught glimpses of the matted hair on his chest. It was all amazingly familiar to her. He wore a thread-thin gold necklace, a piece of glitter less noticeable than the thick, gold Rolex watch on his left wrist. She liked the watch second only to his Gucci loafers, which were so soft they didn't even seem like leather.

"Stop me if I'm boring you," she said.

"I never learned any of this stuff," he said.

"At first it was done just with crops — corn, soybeans, wheat," she said. "Commodities. They put tables on the floor with the varieties of wheat so the traders could touch it. The people involved were big grain houses and food processors. But to have a market you had to have some action besides just producers and buyers. You had to have some traders who just wanted to buy and sell the futures contracts for the money, not the crop, to give the market liquidity. They're the speculators who just trade to see if they can buy and sell a contract for more than they originally paid for it."

"Sounds good to me," he said.

"They're buying and selling something they don't own, and never will."

"Absolutely."

"That's you," she concluded.

"That's me," he replied.

"And that is one impressive lesson, Miss Yff," he added, pronouncing it "Yife."

"If," she said, and stepped back with a mirror to show him the back of his scalp.

"As in 'What if?' " he said.

"No . . ." she said, then paused. "As in 'If he hollers, let him go.' "

"I see," he said.

"So what am I doing cutting hair?" she said.

"There's the question," he said.

From that day back in West Palm Beach Joanie knew it would happen if she gave him an opening. Looking up Ken Korngold on his home turf was an opening. He asked her out to dinner that very night, and she stuttered, hemmed, and agreed.

He told her to meet him at a place called Kelly Mendelly's on Clark Street, and she found it without much difficulty. Chicago was big and crowded, but directions made sense. Arriving a half hour early, she sat on a stool near the front of the bar, a dark but apparently popular place with single men and women, many of them looking the age of Ken Korngold. With her bare, coppery legs crossed and one foot jiggling an open-toed high-heel, she attracted attention and tried to ignore it. She played idly with a drink stir. In the quick sip she took of her white wine, her glossed lower lip met the thin rim of the glass and ever so slightly quivered.

This was more than just a weekend fling with a sharp guy who owned a jet. She was taking her chances now, pressing the issue. She told herself she knew what to expect; she shuddered and admitted that she had no idea of what to expect.

When Korngold arrived, he stopped and took her in. He smiled, she noticed, with teeth that were amazingly white. He

43

grasped her hand and kissed her lightly on cheek, inhaling a trace of Charlie. She was gorgeous, almost too gorgeous, eyes shaded steel-gray. She had loosely curled and layered her hair, letting it fall about the shoulders of a conservative blue silk blouse. A flint-gray suede skirt slit just above the knee.

The outfit was a problem, he noted. Here was a starlet dressed like a stockbroker, and he hated stockbrokers. He decided she had worked very hard on this look, maybe too hard. But that was okay, because beneath that proper suede was a southern girl, right here in Chicago, blond, so beach-sweet he could taste her.

He put one leg onto a stool and waved over a Scotch and rocks.

"Want a hot tip on the market, doll?" he said, and laughed.

He put a hand on her arm, and she liked that.

"Sure, mister," she said.

He leaned close and whispered into her ear.

"Buy low, sell high."

Her eyes widened.

"Really?"

He clinked his glass gently to hers. Hers trembled.

She watched as he took a long drink. She liked his tan, even though it deepened the lines around his eyes, lines that told her he was older but which made it difficult to tell just how much. He wore the same gold chain tightly around his neck and a rust-colored leather sport coat, contrasting with a monogrammed blue shirt, cream-colored slacks, no socks, and those lovely leather loafers. They were clothes you could press to your cheek, clothes that fairly dripped price.

"A lot of sharks in here," he said.

"I've noticed," she said.

"That's what you get. You look terrific," he said.

"Thanks," she said.

"And relax," he said, smiling and lightly covering her hand with his. "Come straight from work?"

"You kidding?" she said.

"From what I could see every girl in that joint looks like a million bucks every minute of the day."

"Some of them, sure, but others . . ."

44

"Everything's in *place,* know what I mean?" he said.

"They're stylists," she said. She had had this conversation before. "How you look is your life."

"I smoke a cigar, but once in a while I take it outta my mouth."

"Thank you, Groucho."

He perked. "You're not supposed to know about Groucho."

"They're vain, but that goes with the job," Joanie went on. "They spend ten hours a day looking in a mirror and pushing their fingers through other people's hair. And they always see something wrong. There's always a strand they're bored with."

"That's *great,*" he said. "Always a strand you're bored with. I gotta remember that."

She smiled weakly.

"You say 'they.' "

"Yeah. Hair is their life. Not mine."

He lifted his glass, and his other hand once again touched her arm. He was still a toucher, this time his fingers lingering.

"Okay. Now that we got that out of the way. Let's let the alcohol kill some brain cells," he said.

Just then two men walked in and he turned to them. They were loud and smiley, dressed as he was. They eyed her without reserve and he introduced them by their first names. They were traders.

"This is a club," she said, after the two went off to the bar.

"A lot of guys come in here. It's a no-hassle joint. Like that showerhead up there."

He pointed in a corner over the bar.

"It's just up there. Doesn't work."

She looked at it.

"And the jukebox. Lot of sixties stuff. This is the kind of place where you can feel at home in a tie or a flannel shirt."

He rattled the ice in his glass and set it down. He faced her and grabbed her wrists. Their knees touched.

"You know what I wanna do?" he said, his eyes widening.

"I think so," she said quickly.

He laughed loudly and crunched an ice cube.

"Wrongo. But close. I wanna dance. What say?" he said.

With that he hopped off his stool and gave the bartender a

creased twenty. He didn't wait for change.

He put his arm around her shoulder and guided her toward the door. "I loves a girl what can *boo*-gie."

"I'm a maniac," she said, and slipped off her stool.

She was okay now, she decided, the jitters gone.

His car was a silver Porsche, polished, parked illegally. She slid into a soft, calfskin bucket seat that smelled as if the calf had been killed yesterday. A second after her door was shut he pulled a U-turn across Clark Street and headed south.

"Don't break the law for me," she said.

"Po-lice just wink at me," he said.

She turned toward him, her knees slightly apart and millimeters away from his hand as it lay on the gearshift. She reached over and pushed in the cassette tape.

"The Righteous Brothers," he said.

"Huh?"

"I got *Little Richard's Greatest Hits,* if that'll do ya."

She grimaced. "Where we gonna dance, Harlem?"

He laughed, then swerved around a bus on the right.

"Joanie If—whatever kind of name that is—you're a funny shit."

She smiled. She was trying her best.

"It's Dutch," she said.

In no time they were angling down North State Parkway, past the cardinal's digs, then down a few blocks past the former Playboy mansion, squeezing by cabs and Lincoln Continentals, yielding to matrons walking twin Pekinese. Korngold double-parked in front of the Ambassador East Hotel, left the engine idling, and nodded at the doorman.

"Evening, Mr. Korngold," the doorman said. "And to you, miss."

He held Joanie's door as she stepped out.

She paused, and waited as Korngold stepped around and took her arm. She felt as if she had stepped into a television commercial, complete with chiffon gown, a full orchestra, and gentle breezes.

Inside the hotel they crossed the lobby to a small cabaret. Its bar was crowded with men in sport coats and women with long legs and short dresses, draped on stools, sipping on white wine spritzers. A five-piece electric band covered their small talk with sheer volume and passable imitations of what was on the charts. A dance floor the size of Joanie's bedroom was choked with bodies.

Holding Joanie's hand, Korngold squeezed through the maze to a semiuninhabited cove near the end of the bar. He caught the eye of the bartender, mouthed something, and in what seemed like seconds he was handed a pair of drinks.

Joanie smiled, impressed at how casually he managed such treatment. She sipped, feeling the band's beat, then dipped her shoulder to it, tucked her lower lip beneath her upper teeth, closed her eyes. She was feeling good, the night even better so far than she had hoped, and she would ride it as long as it held.

He watched her, thought no woman was sexier than when she started to slither, especially this one here and now. He nodded toward the floor.

"Thought you'd never ask," she said.

They didn't dance as much as they moved with the group, a mash of bodies lost in the sound and light, an undulating, sensual sway. She loved to dance with her eyes closed, with herself, letting her whole being float with the music, the glide of rhythm and beat. But she saw that Korngold had his eyes trained on her, as if to follow her every move, so she met his stare. She pursed her lips.

Korngold, who couldn't dance a lick, was sold. He could not take his eyes off her, her mouth, her skin, the trace of perspiration forming on her forehead. Dancing could do that to you, could meld your senses as well as your hips and crotch, could transmit something raw and electric and reckless. Her. Right now.

Then the band went into a golden hit of Smokey Robinson and the Miracles. Korngold got crazy, lip-syncing lyrics he thought he remembered. She laughed and let him flail away, not sure of just how young he thought he was or how old he wanted her to be. A little later he stood back and let her go with one of her favorites, a dance number from a rock movie starring a hunk she once had a mindless crush on.

They danced until the band stopped, then wound their way

47

back to the bar. Their drinks had been replaced with fresh ones, and Joanie gulped hers as if it were lemonade. She shook herself with the cool rush of the alcohol, and winked at him. She was having a great time. His neck glistened with perspiration. He smiled back at her, approving of how cool and cocky she was, reveling in the infatuation, the undiluted lust he felt for her.

"Let's skip this joint," he said.

On the way through the lobby she swayed on his arm.

They waited for the carhop to fetch the Porsche. It hurtled around the corner and braked abruptly before them. Korngold scowled.

"Such service," she said.

"I got a few points in the bar—it's not part of the hotel. So . . ."

She swung into the front seat. He joined her, slammed the front door, and in a single motion put the car into gear.

"What else do you own?" she asked.

"Thought you'd never ask," he said.

Korngold's in-town place was a condominium in Harbor Point, a sleek, black-skinned high rise on the east side of the Drive that seemed to grow out of the lake itself. They were there in minutes, scooting into the dimly lit garage underneath.

Korngold got out and came around to her door. When he opened it she did not move to get out.

"This is a little weird for me," she began, peering up at him.

"Why?" he said. His voice echoed.

"Well," she began, "I don't know if I should go up . . . I mean . . ." she stammered, "what do you expect?"

"Not to worry," he said.

She turned slowly in the seat.

"This isn't a three-day weekend," he said. "Just a look at the lake from forty-two floors up. If you don't want, I can take you home."

He looked off.

She sighed. They always took it that way.

"Great view?" she said.

He smiled and she took his hand.

48

They went up the forty-two stories, so high, she noticed immediately, that the world became quiet, the street below a ribbon of soundless motion. The interior of the apartment was white, the shag carpeting, the high-gloss walls and ceiling, broken by color from chrome-framed geometric prints and a bold LeRoy Neiman original of a soccer match. The furniture was glass and chrome, with cushions of kid leather that looked as if they had been lifted out of Korngold's Porsche. In the corners were huge, green, living plants with polished leaves that shone in the glare of recessed lights.

The apartment was spotless and uncluttered. Magazines were arranged alphabetically on the coffee table. Table lamps were turned on by wall switches. It reminded Joanie of the $400-a-night suite one of her girlfriend's father had rented in a Miami Beach hotel.

As Korngold promised, the view of the lake was dramatic, lit tonight by a wide platter of a moon. The black water shimmered, dotted by the red and green lights of a few boats anchored just offshore and the rhythmical flashing signals of a municipal pumping station out near the breakwater. Beyond them lay the vast dark lake and the unblemished horizon.

"So what do you think of Chicago so far?" Korngold said.

Joanie stood and stared.

"I'm awed," she said. "I haven't been here a week and I've got a great apartment, a job, and now look at this view."

Korngold went across the living room to a wall of built-in cabinets and shelves.

"People think they come to Chicago and they're going to be met by a guy with a machine gun," he said. "That won't happen for at least a week or so."

He stood before a giant-screen television and a video cassette recorder. Next to it was a stereo, a compact disc player, and eight shelves of components, discs, and records and a remote control console the size of a lap-top computer.

She turned and surveyed the equipment, shaking her head.

"Wants for nothing," she said.

"Not right now," he said.

"Live here alone?"

"Here, yes."

"And away from here?"

"There's the house in Highland Park. That's a suburb. And a few other getaway shacks in out-of-the-way places."

"Just for you?"

"There's a wife, if that's what you're asking. And a daughter, Rachel, who's fifteen."

He left it at that. He stood beside her, close now, enough to hear her breathe. Slowly, like a bead of perspiration, he ran the tip of a single finger down the side of her face, tracing the contours of her cheek, then her lips. She leaned toward him ever so slightly, faltering. His hand slipped behind her neck and he drew her to him. She met his kiss, the salt of his lips, tasted, lingered for a moment. Oh, she wanted to, how she wanted to. Then she pulled away and stepped around him.

"Tell me all about this equipment. It's fantastic," she blurted, her head spinning.

He stood where he was.

"Forget the equipment," he said.

"I'd love a glass of ice water," she said.

She turned up the volume on a compact disc of light jazz. She longed to see what was on his face, to see if he was frustrated or angry or both, but she did not dare look. She snapped her fingers, a motion to hide the fact that she was shaking, now almost scared out of her wits.

After what seemed like long moments he came over next to her.

"Who's Ramsey Lewis?" she said.

"Chicago guy. Damn good," he said.

He was silent. She did not move. He spoke.

"What in the hell'd you come here for?" he said.

She turned and faced him.

"From the day I met you—" she began, then exhaled loudly, her voice wavering. She started over again.

"I'm going to go to school. I really want to learn about the markets, you know, maybe even—"

"So do something about it," he said. "Make your bid."

Her lip began to tremble.

"Shit," she said softly. "I'm sorry. I knew or I thought I knew what—"

50

He sniffed impatiently, cutting her off. He rubbed his hands over his face, stopping to massage his forehead.

"You don't know the first thing, Joanie *Yife*," he muttered.

He turned and went to the kitchen. She could hear him open the refrigerator and take out a tray of ice cubes, fumble with it, then suddenly he whacked it against the countertop and she jumped. The cubes skittered about the floor. He appeared with a glass of ice water.

"Here. Enjoy the scenery."

He sat down in the middle of the sofa, looking off, then began snapping his fingers to the music and slapping his palm against his thigh. She was afraid to say anything.

"I do a lot of things," he finally said, looking at her with a blank stare. "I rob, plunder, murder, commit savage acts. All in the name of trading. Well, most of the time in the name of trading. But no matter what anyone says, I don't rape little girls."

She looked at him. His expression was unflinching, totally honest.

"I'm not a little girl," she said.

He chuckled.

"Too late," he said. "Trading's over."

"Excuse me?" she said.

He made a telephone call and told her she would be driven home. She nodded, forgetting that her car was parked on the North Side near the bar where they had met. As they waited he told her about her new neighborhood. Years ago it had been the city's Little Italy, called the Patch, he said. Taylor Street, its most famous thoroughfare, spawned some of the city's most notorious gangsters. The campus, which he simply referred to as "Circle," had pretty much decimated the old neighborhood, though there were still some hangouts and some fine old Italian stores and restaurants. What was there now was actually a pretty fair neighborhood, he granted, though you still had to be careful. Just to the south was Maxwell Street, the famous street bazaar, where Korngold said some of his relatives got their start.

Joanie heard very little of it, thinking only that she had ruined everything. She had pressed too hard and too fast, and when the rush came she could not handle it — did not handle it. She should have waited, should have done her homework, should have — Her mind crowded with should haves.

The phone interrupted her thoughts. The car was here.

She turned to him.

"Thanks," she began, looking at him for some clue as to just what to say. He gave no sign whatsoever, standing as if he were waiting for the mailman. Then he smiled.

"You're a hell of a dancer," he said.

"I'm sorry that I —"

"No," he said. "Rule number one in the big city: don't be sorry."

She smiled and he opened the door.

"Good night," she said.

He nodded.

The car was a black limousine with tinted windows. She sat alone in the enormous backseat. It was dark and quiet. She felt like a little girl being punished.

The driver went directly to her flat and held the car door for her without a word. She hurried up the steps, unlocked the door, fumbled for a light and knocked against a hanging plant. She swung her hand at it, missing. Again missing. When the light came on, her cheeks were already wet with tears.

Just over a week later, in mid-morning, as Joanie worked the fashionable tresses of a Near North Side cocktail waitress and would-be television model, she got a phone call.

It was his voice.

"I've got an open spot for a clerk if you want it," Korngold said.

Joanie gasped. "You're not *serious*."

"Serious, yes. Crazy, too, maybe," he replied.

"When?"

"Now."

"My *God*. I'm in the middle of a cut."

"Want the job or not?"

"What time is it? I'll be there in forty-five minutes."

He laughed.

"Don't panic. Give that fruitcake you work for notice and see if you can stop by this afternoon."

He waited for a reply and heard what sounded like a squeal muffled through a hand placed over the receiver.

"Very unprofessional," he said. "But I like the sentiment."

"Thanks," she gushed. "And 'bye."

Korngold normally would not have taken the time to give a new employee directions to the washroom, much less show him around the trading floor. Only potential clients — and big ones at that — got the tour guide routine. Even blood relatives were pushed off on a clerk.

But this new hire was different. Korngold's firm was known for having the best-looking women on the floor, and the new blonde sustained the reputation.

When Korngold's fellow bean traders caught sight of the two of them, they began to throw bets on every possibility, the length of her employment being the most tasteful. Korngold pretended to ignore them, the hand signals, the gestures, the whistles and wolf calls.

"As far as you're concerned, the only traders on the face of this earth are Korngold traders," he said, taking Joanie by the elbow. "If you got an order and a trader from another company drops dead right in front of you, step over him and get to our man."

It was mid-afternoon and they bumped shoulders with the scurrying hordes even though activity was light. The trading floor was brightly lit, as usual, crowded, whirling, and Joanie, who had a temporary floor pass, was stunned. She felt assaulted, as if she were onstage, in a noisy ticker tape parade, lost in a huge train station. For she had made it; she was on the floor. She could not believe it.

"How many Korngold traders are there?" Joanie said, trying to ask an intelligent question.

"We've got fourteen right now, but the way things are going

we could have twice that many by year end."

"Is that a lot?" she asked, looking up and around as if she were a tourist in downtown Tokyo.

"There's only so many seats available. Fourteen hundred and one, to be exact. That's set by the Board of Trade. You can buy a seat for the going rate—that's about three hundred and fifty thousand right now—or you can rent one. A lot of partial trading badges will let you in certain pits. The Board issues them to bring in more traders, especially in the newer options and indexes," he said, not sure if she heard or understood what he was saying.

"Do you have to qualify or something?" Joanie asked.

"Just with bucks. You want to trade, you rent a seat and put up capital with a clearinghouse. That backs your trades. Then you get in the pit and go to it. Not much different than driving a taxi except you have to know English. I got in a cab the other day and this towel head thinks the Wrigley Building is where the Cubs play. I didn't ask him what he thought went on in the Hancock."

Joanie kept staring, then she laughed, his words registering.

"A little late on that," he said.

"Sorry," she said.

She paused and asked, "With enough money anyone can trade?"

"You got it. It's the last frontier of capitalism."

"Not even a test to qualify?"

"When the gong sounds, then you take the stiffest test of your life. Called trade or die."

Joanie noticed the clock, then absently slipped her hands inside the trading coat Korngold had given her. It was beige with a maroon *K* and a small white-and-black emblem of a soccer ball on the breast pocket.

"That's the glory of this place," Korngold added, moving through the aisle. "You got the scratch and you're in. No papers, no pedigree. No M.B.A. from the U. of C. We got traders who used to be cops on the beat. College grads, high school dropouts, priests, lawyers, beer salesmen, and brain surgeons.

"C'mon, I've got to see Tommy on the desk before the opening."

They moved through the crowd, into the already hazy corridor leading to the financial side of the floor. Korngold kept chattering as they walked. They hopped up the steps onto the bridge between the Treasury bond and Treasury note pits.

"Take a good look at the faces down there. In six months about four out of every five guys you see will be gone. The twenty K or whatever they put up to get in will be wiped out."

"Then what do they do?" Joanie said.

"Go back to selling shoes or get a loan and get back in. Most never come back. They get picked clean. It's a fact of life that eighty percent of the money is made by twenty percent of the traders."

"And you're one of the twenty percent," Joanie said.

"So far," he said.

He turned and nodded at Tommy Haggarty, one of his assistants.

"That's my *shtick* for now. Tommy here'll show you the ropes," he said.

"That's not all I'll show her," Tommy said.

Korngold ignored the remark and said something to Tommy which made no sense to Joanie. Then he turned to her.

"You all set? You wanna work here?" he said.

She looked into his face, at a countenance altogether different from the one she'd encountered a few nights before in his condominium, a look very firm and professional yet remarkably warm, almost like that of a kindly father.

She smiled broadly.

"Why are you so nice to me?" she said.

He looked sideways at her.

"Trading's begun," he said, and he hustled off to the bean pit.

55

Chapter Five

He was young, red-faced, just out of high school, with thin auburn hair parted down the middle and feathered back over his ears: the look of thousands of kids from Chicago's neighborhoods. Only today he was wearing a shirt and tie, the thick knot off-center and shoved beneath the collar.

His name was Brian Boyer. He was wearing a tie and seeking out a strange address because he was in desperate need of a job—and the scratch that went along with it. Hanging out was expensive, as was keeping fumes in the gas tank, and staying current with the chicks.

(Who was he kidding? Chicks was chick, *uno*, Rhonda, to be specific, his girlfriend/squeeze/ol' lady, who'd been around since the ninth grade and was no knockout but was about the only girl he really felt loose with, in fact, felt real good with, and who, as the years went by, let him get to know her better than he ever dreamed, if you can dig it, and who wanted to get married someday in a white dress with a forty-foot veil trailing behind her in a church with all her friends and folks and a priest and her little nephew Josh who has leg braces from some birth defect as ring-bearer which would be a big thrill for him in front of the family and all.)

All that: Rhonda, his life, took money. Scratch.

"Try working," his father said. "Get a job."

Then his father added that because a graduation tassel was swinging from the rearview mirror, Brian's allowance was a memory. Free room and board was enough, and even that would have a price tag before long. So get a paycheck.

Yeah, sure, Brian said under his breath.

Saying aloud, "How 'bout midnights at a beer store? Sell

booze and rubbers and *Hustler* magazines and get held up by gangbangers?"

"Sounds good to me," the old man said.

But Pop finally came through. "I got a friend at the Board of Trade. He'll put ya to work on the floor if you can handle it."

"You serious?" Brian said.

"If you can handle it. Ain't easy down there," his father said.

"Aaaaaayyyy," Brian twanged, his eyes half-closed, his thumbs wagging. "Mr. High Finance. You're lookin' at him."

And he grinned like the job was something he'd maneuvered himself.

So on that fateful day he put on a pair of corduroys, a clean shirt, the tie, and aimed his '82 Camaro north and east through the streets of Beverly, his southwest side Chicago neighborhood of green grass and bungalows and Irishmen. He headed toward the Dan Ryan Expressway, which went downtown, not to the beach or the North Side, Wells Street and Second City, where he once went to impress a girl, not Rhonda, only to blow twenty bucks and get nothing like he expected in return. No, he was headed downtown to the South Loop.

The address on West Jackson Boulevard was but a skyscraper among the skyscrapers, a building with no parking to be had anywhere. He circled the block four times, between the support beams of the el tracks along Wells and Van Buren, almost getting sideswiped by a taxi. In frustration he wedged the Camaro into an illegal space next to a loading dock in an alley. To hell with five bucks on a parking lot. Get a ticket and toss it. If they tow the heap, then they can have it. He kept saying this to himself, shoring up his guts to put himself on the altar and ask for a job.

He hit the revolving door and the elevator, found the office on the twenty-first floor, knocked, got no answer, and walked in. It looked pretty usual — desks, a sofa, magazines — except for a pile of shoes lined up outside a closet. Among them was a pair of cowboy boots must have run $200.

"Help ya?" came a voice, and he saw some chick in blue jeans sitting in a corner chewing on a Big Mac.

"Looking for Mr. Korngold."

57

"They're all on the floor," she said, chewing, trying to turn a page of a paperback.

Just above her head was a television set, the screen dotted with clusters of green numbers. He noticed other sets nearby, all with the same rows of numbers. The girl paid no attention to the sets, or him.

Real friendly, he thought, but said, "When will he be back?" He sounded like a mope, looked like one.

"Who knows? Comes up once in a while during the day. You can catch him when the market closes," she said.

She was kind of good-looking, but with the frizzy hair he hated, no makeup to speak of, and a pair of jeans he wouldn't wear to take out kitty litter.

"When's that?" he said.

"After two," she said.

It wasn't even one o'clock yet.

"Can I wait?" he said.

"Why not?" she said.

He sat down and put his hands on his knees. The morning's *Sun-Times* lay on the floor, so he picked it up and started paging through it. He didn't come here to read the newspaper. He had chapped lips. He began to pick at the skin and noticed his fingers were already smudged with ink from the paper. He hated that. It was enough to keep him from reading the papers except for the ball scores or to look up a show. He wondered if he had black smudge on his lip but didn't dare rub it. It was hot in this place. The girl picked the lettuce off the Mac, which was stupid. Why buy the thing if you don't like what's inside?

"Go over and watch," she said.

What is it, my deodorant? he thought.

"Thanks," he said.

He had no idea what she was talking about. But he walked out and got back on the elevator. In the lobby he saw a black guy behind a desk doing nothing. For whatever reason buildings like this had guys all over the place sitting on stools and telling you which elevator to get on. Like that was some difficult thing.

"Hey, where's the market?" he said.

The black guy looked at him and smiled. "Look all around you, my man," he said.

All of 'em think they're Richard Pryor, he thought.

"Fifth floor. You ain't got much time," he said.

"I'm fast," Brian said.

"You better be," he said, and laughed with white false teeth, not Pryor, but Scatman Crothers.

He rode the escalator with a couple of guys in colored jackets who got off on the fourth floor. On five he found his way to the visitors' gallery and walked in and over to the windows. He looked down and shook his head.

"Look at those crazy bastards," he said.

"Can you run, kid?" said the guy with curly hair and the weird eyes.

"Yeah, y'know," Brian replied.

What kind of question is that? he said to himself.

"Let's see."

"Huh?"

"Yeah. Let's see you go full out to the desk, grab that Sox mug, and put it on that desk over there," the guy said.

"You serious?"

"Not really, but do it anyway."

Brian looked at him, standing there with his hands on his hips, his jacket open and tie loose. The guy wasn't shitting him. So he took off, three strides across the office, grabbed the mug, pivoted, then lost his balance, slipped, and kicked the steel desk with his left foot, but righted himself and hustled over to the other desk.

"You're hired," the guy said, laughing.

His badge said "KIK." Kenneth I. Korngold. Mr. Korngold to Brian, a guy who looked older than everybody else. Bags under his eyes made him look like he hadn't slept since Christmas.

"Get a form from Mary Beth for your floor pass. She'll tell you where to go. Be here at seven A.M. tomorrow. If you're not, I don't want to know about it and you're out of a job."

"Seven sharp," said Brian.

59

"You got it," said Korngold. "And give me my Sox mug back."

A stupid grin broke over Brian's face. He handed the mug to Korngold but stood still for a moment, transfixed. He was still smiling.

"You do that, don't you?" he finally said.

"What?" said Korngold.

Brian shot his fingers in the air, mimicking what he'd just seen from the fifth floor observatory.

"That I do," Korngold said, and went off to his private office.

"God *damn,*" Brian said.

"C'mon, kids. Right now we take care of business," Tommy said.

He walked quickly, his sneakers squeaking on the gleaming tile floor, his beige jacket flapping. It was seven-thirty in the morning, and Joanie and Brian Boyer, Korngold's two new hires, trailed behind him.

Joanie had been up since five. She was scrubbed and radiant, wearing a white pantsuit, her hair pulled back into a braid. She was as nervous as she could be. That subsided somewhat with the paperwork, the forms to be filled out for floor credentials.

As she walked, she eyed Brian, and she wondered how many minutes had passed since he had graduated from high school. He wore his tie like a neck brace. As for Tommy Haggarty, their guide and apparent mentor, he was not much older than Brian, but acted as if he were his father. He snapped his fingers as he walked, made popping noises with his mouth.

Suddenly he elbowed an approaching clerk in a blue jacket.

"Aayyy Tommy," the clerk said, offering a palm.

Tommy thrust his out, then pulled it back, made a pistol out of his thumb and finger and pulled the trigger.

"Yer mother swims out to meet troop ships, Donnelly," he yelled.

"Bite the big one," came the reply.

Tommy snorted.

"Bite the big one," he muttered.

They turned into an office. Brian and Joanie handed a secretary their Board of Trade registration forms, then went into an adjoining room, had their pictures taken, and emerged with still-warm plastic badges on which their faces stared blankly out of the left-hand corner.

"Hang on to that," said Tommy. "It'll get you on the floor and entitles you to one free blow job from the security guard. 'Course, he's eighty-two. But he's got false teeth . . ."

Tommy hung a quick glance at Joanie when he said it.

Joanie shook her head. Brian sort of laughed.

Minutes later they were heading toward the escalators.

"Don't worry about a thing, kids. Ask any stupid question you want," Tommy said.

"Yeah?" Brian said.

Tommy said, "If I don't know the answer, it ain't worth knowin'."

"Uh, okay, here goes: Those guys in the pit, like Mr. Korngold . . ."

"Right—"

". . . like what in hell are they doin'?"

Tommy rubbed his hands on his face and exhaled. "Oh, boy," he said.

"Okay. Good question," Tommy went on. "One word: megabucks. You can make more money in the pits than anywhere, okay? Wall Street, Vegas, you name it."

"Yeah, but how? I don't see no money," Brian said.

"So stick with me," said Tommy, eyeing Joanie to see if she was digging him. "Listen to every word I say, and·in no time you'll see plenty of money.

"That is," he added with one eye shut, "if you know what to look for."

Joanie loved it, aware of how hard Tommy was working to entertain her.

They turned down a long hall, past the research library and a huge, attended cloakroom.

"Like right there," said Tommy. He pointed to a rack of shoes that ran down one side of the hallway. "Street shoes.

Most guys change their shoes first thing, okay? Take off the boots and the Guccis in favor of somethin' fast and loose. You gotta move in the pits.

"They don't mind what it looks like, usually a lucky pair they been wearin' for months and looks like shit. That along with the trading coats — and a lot of them wear the same one for weeks if it's goin' good — and a loose shirt. Just lookin' at some of 'em you wouldn't think they were worth a rat's turd.

"It's Board rules that you got to wear a tie, okay? Over to the Merc you got to have five buttons on the shirt, which rules out your Izods and Ralph Laurens. Had to do it 'cuz those clowns over there'd wear dago shirts if they could. And no blue jeans. This is big business, no fuckin' 'American Bandstand.'

"Still, half these guys look like bums, you know what I mean? Guys with red faces and shaving cuts. There's this bond trader who don't pinch his blackheads."

"Oh, please . . ." groaned Joanie.

"Yeah. They just sit there on his nose lookin' at you like rotten spuds, okay? Yeah. And on paper that guy's worth a couple mil. Zits and all.

"Heatseeker, man. Fuckin' heatseeker."

"Huh?" said Brian.

"Listen up, Boyer. This is a good one for ya. There's this missile, see, that the Air Force uses. Called a 'Heatseeker' because that's what guides it. They shoot it at other jets, especially if they belong to that jagoff Khaddafi, and the damn thing usually runs right up the exhaust tank. I mean right up their ass. Kaboom!

"Yer good traders here, man, they are fuckin' *heatseekers.* Got it?"

"Yeah," Brian said.

"Stop rubbin' yer ass then," Haggarty said.

Joanie turned her head to hide her laughter.

Haggarty's words trailed behind him as he stepped onto the escalator. The moving stairs full of men and women in colored jackets like themselves.

"Tommy!" came a shout from the down escalator.

Tommy made his finger pistol again.

"Your sister, too," the voice shouted.

They got off with the crowd at the fourth floor and walked through the foyer. Once again the place was a crush of bodies, like a commuter terminal, with people charging in all directions but mostly toward the entrance to the trading floors.

"There's two floors here, agricultural and financial. You work both depending on who needs you. This way first."

Tommy went to his right. Brian stayed on his shoulder. Joanie walked a step behind, though Tommy occasionally slowed in an effort to get next to her. Mostly Tommy kept nodding and shooting his finger at other clerks and runners, particularly the females, as if he was president of the place.

They passed through a narrow, smoky hallway, a tunnel, really, banked on one side by cushions and chrome chairs where traders and others sat and smoked, and on the other side by sixteen bright-red telephones. The telephones were free, and several people crouched over them, demonstratively talking prices and strategies, or whispering, their eyes turned downward, oblivious to the traffic coming and going.

Then the tunnel opened dramatically to the light and sound of the trading floor itself. Brian was jolted at the sight of it. It was what he had seen yesterday, but now he was in it, a gymnasium of motion and shouts.

"Hold on to your noogies, kids," said Tommy. "We in the ball park now."

Brian had to admit, it *was* like a ball park, like the day he first walked into Comiskey Park, seeing how big it was, how bright and alive, with real ballplayers in uniforms white like choir robes. He gazed upward at the massive price boards, the electronic fields ablaze with green and yellow digits, like the Sox scoreboard during a night game, the schedule boards at O'Hare, only these were bigger, numbers everywhere. He stared at stationary electronic ticker tapes, television monitors, even the red digital clocks on each wall. His pause caused another runner to bump into him, jostling him and bringing him to his senses, and he quickly caught sight of Tommy.

"This is it," Tommy said. "The Big Leagues. Broadway. Hollywood. Vegas. You catch my drift?"

They followed Tommy into the rows of phone banks on the edge of the floor.

"This is where all the clearing firms do their floor business," said Tommy. "You got more phones here than at the race-track."

The area was a mass of desks and cubicles, stools and walls of telephones, separated by narrow aisles, through which clerks and runners moved like ants. At the Korngold desk a guy and two girls wearing beige Korngold coats stood and huddled over telephones and stacks of order blanks. The guy had a phone in each ear.

"Hey, Mary Beth. You were great last night," said Tommy.

"In your *dreams,*" the girl replied.

"And this is Lisa. And Rick. He's only got one ball but he's okay."

"Haggarty's arrived. The Roach Motel failed again," Rick said in a monotone.

"Roach? Who's got a roach?" Tommy said, then spread his arms out in front of him. "This is the Korngold Command Post, commodity traders and stud service to the world."

Lisa, a stunning, brown-haired girl with freckles and a pencil in her hair, looked at Joanie and lifted her eyes.

"Don't ever stray too far from here. We got a good sight line on the bond pit. It's where the action is on this side," said Tommy.

He hopped down the aisle steps toward the pits, the bond pit, which was filled with hundreds of traders, the smaller Treasury note pit to the right, and the Ginnie Mae pit next to it. The pits were connected by a bridge crowded with milling traders and clerks. Just beyond the bridge was a raised platform from which exchange officials monitored the trading and fed price fluctuations into computers and onto boards overhead.

Joanie and Brian once again followed, not sure of what to do, staying behind Tommy on the bridge where they could get a clear view of the entire bond pit. Joanie once again caught herself, aware suddenly of where she was, not behind the glass of a visitors' gallery but on the floor, virtually in the pit, wearing a jacket, able to reach out and touch the players.

Just then the bell rang, 8:00 A.M., the start of trading. Like sprinters out of the blocks, the traders leaped into action, jabbing pencil-clenching hands in the air like bayonets and shouting prices. Joanie and Brian were startled at the onslaught. The entire pit seemed to sway, with traders pushing and screaming, in clusters of two or three or ten or twenty, sometimes all together, as if they were a huge animal trying to fight itself.

"Holy shit," Brian shouted, his words lost in the swell.

Tommy laughed.

They stood and watched, without trying to talk over the noise, for several minutes, when Tommy motioned for Brian and Joanie to come with him. They retraced their steps, off the bridge, back through the smoky hallway, then over to the east floor.

"This is the ag side—agriculture. Soybeans, oats, corn, wheat, yummy shit like that," Tommy said.

"Where's pork bellies?" Brian asked.

"The Merc. Six blocks away and who cares," Tommy shot back. "There's Korngold traders in most every pit," he went on. "That's the bean pit. Kenny's home park. He's somewhere on the left side just about ready to make them beans jump. Our ag desk is over there."

Tommy pointed to the south wall.

The agriculture floor was only slightly different from the financial side, seemingly brighter, with blocks of quotation boards overhead. The actual floor was covered with a black, nubby rubber tile that seemed to thump beneath the feet of runners.

"It's no different. Just different stuff being traded. Lot more runners here," Tommy said.

He nodded toward the desks and phone banks along the wall, the aisles inclined even more severely than on the financial side so that they were more like chutes propelling runners and clerks toward the pits.

"Lot more brokers here, too. They're the guys with creased order blanks. They execute orders for customers, mostly. When they give a fill they drop it and the runner picks it up and brings it back to the desk."

It was uncanny, as Brian and Joanie saw it close up. The floor was awash with litter, debris, paper of every shape and kind, newspapers, bulletins, and torn trading slips. Yet whenever a trader dropped a filled order slip a clerk scooped it up almost before it landed, as if he had a scent for it, and carried it off.

"How do they trade? Where's the auctioneer?" Brian interjected.

"Ain't none. They trade with each other. Any trader can trade with anyone else. That's why they scream. To get somebody's attention. You show your price with your hands and scream it with your lungs."

"How do they keep it straight?"

"Ain't easy. You make a trade with me and we confirm it, mark it down on our cards. At the end of the day we tally up and that trade should jibe. They make mistakes, but generally the traders know each other and what they traded. If they make a mistake, then they got to settle it between themselves."

"Seems like a mess," said Brian.

"At first, yeah. But you get a hang of it pretty quick."

"Who sets the price?"

At that Joanie interjected, "The market itself. There's always a supply and demand for any good or service."

"Very good," said Tommy. " 'Course Brian here'd know that if he'd gone to school."

"I went to Rita, Haggarty. Same one as you," Brian snapped.

Joanie looked at him, surprised.

Tommy didn't respond, his attention seemingly caught by a flurry of action in the far side of the pit.

"Didn't you used to be called the Tip?" Brian asked.

"Nobody calls me that," Tommy said. "Especially you."

He slapped hands with a clerk running by.

"Kiss my what?" he yelled.

"See, the price is free to go up and down depending on the traders," Tommy went on. "You want to buy, make a bid. You want to sell, make an offer. Make a trade and yell 'Sold.' See that yellow row of numbers. That's the tick, the last price offered. It goes up or down depending how the market's going."

"So where are the beans?" said Brian.

"In beanbags, for all I know. Don't worry about it. Just concentrate on the pit. The traders. Bid and offer. And that tick, man. That's all that counts," said Tommy.

"See that black guy there. That's Big Train Trout. He used to be one of ours."

"Looks like the guy—" said Brian.

"It's him, that's why."

"Yer shittin' me? For the Cubs?" said Boyer.

"In person. 'Cept he's making more money now than he ever made hittin' a baseball. Damn good trader.

"But forget him. Your job is to keep our boys happy. Bring in the orders, bring back the fills and move your ass because if you waste time you cost people money.

"Help them keep their shit straight. Do anything they ask you. Any fuckin' thing at all, save for a blow job, and maybe that, too. Got it?" Tommy said, this time looking almost directly in Joanie's direction.

"Got it," Brian said.

Tommy looked at him and chuckled. "Sure ya do."

He turned to Joanie.

"Now this is all gonna seem like Greek to you but don't worry," he said. "With me around you can't go wrong. I can turn my back to the pits and still tell what's goin' on."

"Greek?" Joanie said. "No Greek."

"My *God*," Tommy howled. "That was *my* line."

He slapped his forehead.

"Come, come," he went on, pulling Joanie toward the pits. "As I said to bone-on back there, there's no auctioneer. Everybody trades with everybody else. Called zero sum."

"I know," Joanie said. "You win, you lose, or you scratch— that means an even trade. For every winner there's a loser. For every Rolls-Royce there are twenty guys whose kids won't go to college."

Tommy looked sideways at her.

"C'*mon*, you been here before."

She laughed.

"Tell me some of the strategies," she said.

"Sure thing. Play it all ways. Most guys are lead month scalpers—they play the tick on today's price because that's the one that moves. Up or down, don't matter, so long as it moves

67

and they can scalp it either way. The big guys take positions and sit on them for a while. Gotta have big bucks and balls — excuse the French — of some alloy to do that. Some guys are spreaders, some guys trade back months — there's all kinds of ways to do it."

"Complicated," she said.

"Don't worry. The longer you hang around, the more it makes sense. Then one day you'll want in."

Joanie nodded, still looking all around her, at the scores of unsettled, anxious grain traders in the pits before her, seeing their faces and their nervous twitches. She glanced at the clock, wondering when trading here would open.

She looked back at Tommy. "With your obvious expertise, Tommy, why aren't you trading?"

Tommy turned and said, "One day, my lovely lady. One day."

Then he smiled broadly, too broadly.

Chapter Six

They served cake and ice cream. The cake was devil's food and yellow, in sheets shaped in the form of octagons, covered with blue-and-white icing that tasted like shaving cream. The ice cream was vanilla, small bricks wrapped in paper, and tasted like Kaopectate.

It was served on paper plates with plastic forks from card tables in the low lights of the carpeted fourth floor foyer outside the trading floors. The occasion was the Chicago Board of Trade's 135th birthday — "CBT: Long 140" was the logo — and this was a little party for the floor mice. (The formal dinner and appropriate ceremony, lavishly catered — champagne, hearts of palm, baby rack of lamb — and served on the trading floor itself, had taken place the evening before, by invitation only, and a scant few of the jacketed floor personnel received an invitation.) Today's impromptu fest was CBT largess, and while the gesture meant well, it didn't improve the food.

Nevertheless, hundreds of traders, runners, and clerks in bright colored coats with overstuffed pockets elbowed each other for a helping. Even after the word on its quality got out. They pushed and jockeyed anyway, then ate the cake in huge, sloppy gulps and slurped at the runny ice cream. They did it because it was there, and they knew no other way.

"First class party," said the bean trader with the walrus moustache and the badge reading "RAZ" to a corn broker with a tight salt-and-pepper beard and a badge reading "CLL."

"Best fill I've had all day," said CLL.

"Cripes," said RAZ.

They stood among several clumps of celebrators, oblivious

to the constant rush about them of fellow traders, brokers, clerks, and runners going to and from the escalators and elevators, on and off the floor. It was mid-morning and the pits were alive, minus those who'd come out for the cake. Their clipped chatter and clouds of cigarette smoke could not mute the din of trading inside. The PA system paged incessantly.

RAZ searched his pockets for a cigarette, about to add to the thick haze that hovered over the milling crowd. He was no older than twenty-eight, yet his brown, blown-dry hair was thinning dangerously. On his wrist was a fat, gleaming, gold Rolex watch.

He put a Marlboro between his teeth and tripped a green disposable lighter. It didn't light, not to repeated thumb flicks or RAZ's muttered curses. He flipped the lighter into the trash alongside his half-eaten cake and plucked the cigarette from the mouth of MM, who snapped her head around and was about to protest when she saw it was RAZ, the same RAZ from whom she'd snatched a lovely trade only minutes earlier and who, she knew, had been taking a beating for a solid week now. RAZ sucked a light from the butt, handed it back to MM, and headed toward the floor.

"What's his problem?" said a young girl with a clerk's badge, a hank of punk purple hair on her neck, and two earrings in each ear.

"He's sucking wind in there," said MM.

"No excuse," the clerk said.

"Yes it is," said MM.

It went on for an hour, the crowd changing but seldom thinning, the dry cake and warm ice cream as served by round black ladies in yellow uniforms seemingly inexhaustible. Traders, brokers, clerks, runners, exchange officials, big hitters and small, scalpers and spreaders, winners and losers, distinguishable only by the colors of their coats and the identity of their badges, stood together like neighbors. Then, one by one, they turned and headed back onto the floor and into the pits: the financial side to the west, the agricultural side to the east.

And they were neighbors no more.

*   *   *

In those opening hours of trading, Korngold, his yellow badge reading "KIK," shut out the world and honed in on the frenzied activity at which he had become supremely talented. He was Rod Carew hitting to the opposite field, Tom Watson holing a chip shot, Boris Spassky contemplating a move.

By mid-morning a lull set in, a time of waiting and chafing in the pit as the price held steady. A single bean contract in the Board of Trade represented 5,000 bushels of soybeans. Trading was done in increments of 1/4 cent — the tick — each worth $12.50. If the price of beans went up four ticks — 1 cent — the value of a contract increased by $50. The tick right now, however, was flat, advancing two or three, then retreating. As the action slowed, traders grew listless. They could make money if the price went up or down, but not if it stayed put.

"If things don't get movin'," moaned JPL, "I'm never gonna make my payments on my IROC."

"Fuckin' A," came a reply, PPT, a row behind him. "You can't pay cash, you shouldn't buy the damn thing."

With the boredom came the nerves, and traders began taking odds on the White Sox, the possibility of a war with Yemen, a particular trader's bust measurement. Others told jokes about Polish homosexuals with incurable diseases. The pit thinned, now occupied by only two-thirds of the normal population.

Korngold held his positions, did some light trading, and awaited the day's move into the market by some of the bigger brokers. This was not the summer of *El Niño:* there were few surprises and sluggish action. Korngold was bearish but flexible. He would take what he could get, which, after his past coup, was paltry. Other traders looked at him and wondered why he was still trading. When they asked him he laughed. "What else would I *do?*" he protested. A commonly held axiom of futures trading said that once you had been in the pit, once you had inhaled its heady breath, you were unfit for any other kind of employment. Right now Korngold was short 80 contracts.

He was nudged by Bob Penneman, ROP, known as the Rope because standing straight he looked like a piece of limp clothesline, and also because he was a crafty, deadly trader who'd hogtie you with quick trades before you knew it.

"I say to hell with the General Mills," the Rope barked, loud enough for other traders to hear.

"Whattaya, Benedict Arnold?" groused Korngold.

"Arnold *Stang*," cracked a trader a step below.

"Who's that?" asked another.

"What a chunk a *chaw*-colate," came the reply.

"Prehistoric," muttered someone else.

The remarks followed like pistol shots, the traders keeping their eyes trained on the pit and the tick, fidgeting, fanning and slapping their price cards against their palms like blackjacks.

"Hear, hear," the Rope repeated. "I say my life is too important to be controlled by some damn broker for Cheerios."

A number of the bigger brokers nearby sneered. One offered an obscene but nonnegotiable gesture.

Korngold bit. "So, Roper, whattaya gonna do to prove it?"

Penneman grabbed his crotch with his left hand and stuck a finger in his throat.

Korngold motioned at his cards.

Penneman showed him his position: long 100 contracts.

"Put up the floozy, and I'll take on history," he said.

The Rope was referring to one of the favorite tales of the pits. Pork belly traders were once said to have kept ladies of dubious honor upstairs for times when trading was slack but their private parts were not. Legend held that a trader left the pit carrying a hefty position, merged with a lady of the bellies, and returned to the floor to discover that a frantic rally had improved his position by $100,000. His dalliance was thereafter referred to as "the $100,000 head."

"I want quality," Penneman said.

"I want a witness," said Korngold.

By now several traders had leaned in on their conversation.

"Tommy, your gofer," said Rope.

"No way. He'd cut a deal before you even got your pants down."

"So who?"

"New kid. Name's Brian. Hired him last week."

With that he skimmed a $100 bill off a wad in his pocket and held it in front of the Rope.

Penneman snapped the bill, slipped his cards into his pocket and backed out of the pit. The traders cheered. They watched as Penneman went over and found Brian Boyer. He nodded at Korngold and the others, broke a massive grin over his face and frigged his cupped hand in front of his face. Once again a howl rose from the pit. Then the Rope went off with Brian in tow.

It wasn't uncommon for traders to come and go from the pit, especially if they were spreaders or big hitting position traders. That kind of trading involved sitting out slight swings in the market. But Penneman was a scalper, rarely a position trader. He had gotten where he was by covering his ass, by playing each move of the tick and shaving a buck here and there. He lived to play any price gyration, especially those perpetrated by the big brokers with massive buy or sell orders. For him, taking on a 100-lot position was like laying his neck on a chopping block.

Immediately the word flew through the pit, and in minutes the heaviest action was betting on how the Rope would fare.

When the Rope reached the exit corridor, he stopped at one of the red phones, dialed, said a few brief words, then hung up and walked toward the elevators. Brian followed him like an obedient pet.

On the thirteenth floor, the Rope walked past his firm's main entrance and used a key to enter a door leading directly into his private office. He ushered Brian in and motioned to a chair next to the desk. Locking the door leading into the firm's outer offices, he went into a closet where he took off his shoes and trousers, then slipped off his boxer shorts. He shook out his penis. Then he put his trousers and shoes back on again.

"Cola?" he said, and threw Brian a can of Pepsi.

Brian pried open the top and it sprayed his arm.

The Rope mixed himself a soda and grapefruit juice on ice, and sprawled out on his soft leather sofa.

"You like spectator sports?" he said to Brian.

"Huh?" Brian said.

"Smart kid. You'll go far."

73

Only minutes later came the knock on his outer door.

The Rope looked over at Brian and unzipped his fly.

"It's open," he said, mimicking a guffaw.

The door opened and a young, dark-haired woman came in. She was short and solid, wearing a gray business suit that camouflaged her figure, a pastel blue blouse with a petite ribbon tie. In her hand was a thin, red-leather briefcase with gold initials beneath the handle. She looked very much like the lawyer who had settled Penneman's father's estate, except for her hair, which was shaggy and tinted a deep plum color. Lawyers didn't have hair like that. The briefcase was empty.

The girl looked over at Brian.

"Twosies cost double," she said.

"Hey, I like that," the Rope said. "Twosies cost double. Not to worry. He's just gonna watch."

The girl scowled.

"What *next*," she muttered.

The Rope grinned, then raised the creased C-note between two fingers.

"That's for starters. Now, Brian, my boy, this little kitchen magician'll give you an idea of what she's gonna do to my Johnson and you can take a hike."

He nodded at the girl.

She shook her head and exhaled, as if such antics went with the territory, which they usually did.

The girl took off her jacket, revealing that her blouse was badly in need of a press. The blouse revealed the outline of a plum-colored brassiere that matched her hair. Penneman admired color coordination. What he admired more was how the girl reached into her mouth and removed a partial upper bridge.

"Good Lord," he sighed.

She knelt between his legs.

Penneman snapped his fingers at Brian and pointed to the door. Brian, who had watched the proceedings to this point in stonecold, uncomprehending awe, hustled across the carpet and out of the office.

The Rope closed his eyes and smiled.

"Succubus, succubus," he murmured.

Several remarkably short minutes later, after he had regained his breathing and his pulse rate, the Rope heard the commotion down the hall. He gave the girl another C-note, dismissed her, retrieved his shorts and trousers, and went into the main office.

He glanced at the monitor.

"Beans?" he said.

"The whole farm," said his accountant. "Up twelve and counting. What the hell *you* doin' up here?"

"Leaving," the Rope said.

Moments later he leaped to the top step of the pit and snaked his way to his spot. He was met with a chorus of hoots and catcalls from traders, who, even with the sudden market flurry, acclaimed his coup. Korngold threw him a grudging nod. The price of beans had *risen* twelve ticks — 3 cents — in the Rope's absence and showed no signs of weakness. Korngold was madly covering his short position. The Rope immediately sold and took his profit. In seconds he unloaded his 100 contracts for a clean $15,000 profit.

"That's the longest you've ever been in your *life*," Korngold growled.

"That's what she said," Penneman cackled as he ripped a handful of blank cards into shreds and tossed them into the air.

Almost from the first Joanie realized why she was called a runner. She spent much of her day moving between the Korngold desk, the pits, and the office upstairs. There were times, however, when she was able to stop, when she had nothing to do but watch and wait. It was like that: wild scrambling for some runners and assistants while others sat and waited on benches near the desks, on the steps of vacant pits, on the bridges, in the chairs in the tunnel. Some of them lounged and stared, some read the *Wall Street Journal* or the *Sun-Times*, some plowed through fat paperbacks. Then, at a nod or some seemingly inaudible signal, they were up again, running — not literally, for due to past accidents and injuries there was a strict rule against any pace quicker than a swift walk — flash-

75

ing hand signals from the pit to the desk, answering phones. They were the worker bees in a hive that occasionally rested but never slept.

Joanie waited on the needs of Rick, the desk sergeant and phone man on the financial side who worked closely with the firm's bond traders. She kept her ears open, tried not to screw up, asked a lot of directions, and generally survived her first week on the job. At 2 P.M. that Thursday the final gong sounded in the bond pit, and she followed Rick and the others off the floor and back to the office. Like all of them, her ears rang and her feet hurt. Her neck was sore and she had a headache. But she felt wonderful. Her pulse raced, the tips of her fingers tingled.

The same was true for everyone else, she noticed, even Brian, who seemed to be coming out of his teenaged funk. Tommy, of course, was wired, up all day. Being Korngold's assistant kept him moving, jabbering, his jaws chomping gum. On the elevator Tommy told three bad jokes and tried to goose Lisa when she bent over to retrieve some trading cards. As soon as they got inside the office he popped open a can of beer and chugged it.

At 2:15 the traders began coming in. They moved like beaten soldiers, shirts open, ties hanging loose, their faces haggard. To Joanie they looked not just exhausted, but pounded, like men who had been doing windsprints, their faces flushed, their hair damp with perspiration. One of them turned on a hard rock tape cassette and it thumped throughout the office. A silent color television beamed the afternoon efforts of the Cubs, though no one seemed to pay attention. They sat down heavily onto the office sofas, occasionally turning to check monitors blipping prices from markets still open.

They flipped stacks of cards, the concrete evidence of hundreds of trades made during the day, to Joanie and the other clerks, who stacked them in three-inch-high piles and began to sort and date-stamp them. From there the cards went to the key puncher, who attempted to make sense of the scrawled numbers and initials — ticks made and lost — and enter them into computers for the day's tally.

Give or take a tick here and there, the traders already knew the totals. Their expressions told all, even through the exhaustion, another six hours of screaming and jostling, the aching leg muscles and roiled guts. The losers sat and stared, occasionally muttering to nobody in particular, smoking. The winners chattered, talking too loud, as if they were still in the pit, still up and galloping.

What Joanie and the others did not know was the degree. For among the dozen or so Korngold traders were big hitters, smalltimers, scared novices, garrulous veterans, and several somewhere in between. The clerks would learn who was who in due time.

The traders took off their jackets, the sleeves distressed with lead pencil marks, the backs marked with graffiti scribbled by other traders during the pit's dull periods. Some traders took off their shoes, wearing white wool socks, and padded over to the refrigerator for beer, soft drinks, or fruit juices. A few dug into sacks of hamburgers and fries from the lobby's Beef King, their first meal of the day. They milled about, trying, win or lose, to gear down.

For the first time all day the male traders became aware of Mary Beth's slacks, the white ones with the distinct panty lines. She was now no longer a runner, an asexual clerk who had to be there when they needed her. She was now a chick, with a nice ass, olive skin, tits that looked up at you, and all those other possibilities. It was as if the traders' libidos, on ice for six hours, had suddenly thawed. And Mary Beth smiled, used to it, to these strange men who grunted and farted and told the grossest jokes, and shook her butt.

Joanie wondered when it would be her turn.

But generally they were too tired to get into it. They talked, instead, of the day's trades, and particularly of the Rope's salacious, altogether nifty off-the-floor slam dunk.

Then the Rope himself walked in, stopping in mock surprise at the attention, gagging sounds and palm slaps.

"Who me?" he mouthed silently, and clutched his throat.

The entire office erupted in laughter, and the Rope disappeared into Korngold's office.

"Jagoff," Tommy said. "Hey, Boyer. I hear you saw it all."

"I guess so," Brian said, grinning like all the others but unsure of what was so funny.

"Brian, you simple shit, you witnessed trading *history,*" said Tommy.

"Yeah," said Brian, nodding his head up and down. "Uh huh."

Once the cards were safely in the domain of the key puncher and the firm's accountant, Joanie's day was over. She sat and sipped a can of Pepsi, then watched the Cubs blow a six-run lead in the eighth inning. Tommy moved about the office, jabbering nonstop.

Most of the traders did not stay long, not even for Tommy's chatter, and the office soon became dominated by the incessant stereo and the clatter of the computers. Joanie could leave at any time now. There were no time clocks, no whistles. Tommy, however, appeared as if he was going to stay all night.

Then Korngold appeared.

"You like soccer?" he said.

Joanie looked at Brian, then back at Korngold, then realized Korngold meant the both of them.

"The Clouts in town?" Tommy said.

Korngold ignored him.

"Call your mother, Boyer, and tell her you'll be a little late tonight," he said.

Then he turned to Joanie. "You free?"

She nodded, still unaware of what was going on.

Tommy's mouth dropped open.

"Ten minutes and we're gone," interjected Korngold.

Tommy grabbed a *Sun-Times* and whipped through the sports pages.

"He owns half the fuckin' franchise, ya know," he said to Brian. "Holy, shit! They're playin' in *Atlanta.*"

He tossed the paper on a desk and shook his head. He looked over at Joanie, then made sure Korngold was out of earshot.

"Kenny's time to impress the kiddies," he said coldly.

"Give it a rest," snapped Lisa as she sat at her terminal.

Fifteen minutes later Joanie and Brian walked with

Korngold to the parking garage across the street. Waiting there for them was a slim, attractive, and very young girl with long, shiny black hair. She was dressed in designer jeans, a baggy, brilliantly colored Zuzu shirt, and glittering gold chains.

"Hi, kid," Korngold said, and gave her a kiss.

"Rachel, meet Brian and Joanie, my new people," he said. "This is my daughter."

Rachel ignored Brian, but threw Joanie a look that could have put ice on the length of LaSalle Street. Minutes later they were inside Korngold's Mercedes heading onto the Stevenson Expressway toward Midway Airport. Rachel sat in the front next to her father. Korngold immediately got on his cellular phone. Instead of his office, however, he was calling the front office of the Chicago Clout. He listened as an associate there filled him in as to who among his team's kickers were healthy and what the prospects were against the Atlanta team.

"Were you good today?" Rachel asked when he put down the phone.

"Had to be just to keep my babe in style," he said, patting her hand. "Look at you—you're gorgeous."

She beamed and struck a pose, then laughed.

Sliding in and out of the late-afternoon traffic, they made it to the small southwest side airport in twenty minutes. Korngold parked in a lot reserved for the owners and operators of light planes, and ushered his young guests into his four-seater Lear Executive jet. It was exactly as Joanie had remembered it. In minutes they were in the air.

So this is it, Joanie thought to herself as she scanned the sleek insides of the plane. She was unaware that her face glowed with a sweet, benign smile. Brian Boyer held a comparable expression. He simply could not believe this was happening to him, and as the jet shot up into the sky he looked down and thought he saw his house, his father watering the tomatoes.

In the Atlanta stadium they sat in a deluxe skybox and ordered from a menu of steaks, prime rib, and prawns. Korngold, however, after a cocktail and some chatter with officials from the Atlanta club, one of whom, Joanie thought, looked like Ted Turner, left for the locker room.

Joanie looked over at Rachel, who had not spoken to her since they had been introduced.

"Do you go to a lot of the games?" Joanie ventured.

"Enough," Rachel said, her eyes locked on the playing field.

That left Brian, who interrupted his destruction of a New York strip steak with a garbled cheer at a Chicago goal.

"Look at Daddy down there," Rachel exclaimed. "You'd think he was playing, he gets so excited."

Joanie leaned forward to look and saw that Korngold was actually on the field and pacing behind the bench, exhorting the Clout and, now that the game was in progress, berating the officials.

"You'd think he was in the bean pit," Joanie said.

"Yes! Yes!" Rachel cried, and clapped her hands.

Joanie watched her, how the girl squealed when her father's team scored and groaned whenever it was scored upon. Other patrons of the sedate Atlanta skybox frowned on such emotion, yet Rachel did not care a whit.

At halftime Joanie made another try at conversation.

"Are you in high school?" she said.

Rachel nodded, then she turned in her seat and faced Joanie.

"Where'd he find you?" she said.

Joanie was momentarily startled, then composed herself and saw in that instant how naturally pretty Rachel Korngold was, and how hard she was working at it. No more than sixteen years old, yet she looked a half dozen years older.

"I'm from Florida. West Palm Beach. I applied for the job," Joanie said, slightly massaging the facts.

"I bet you did," Rachel said, and turned back to the window.

Joanie decided not to pursue things, not sure of what she might get into, or of what she had gotten into.

After an hour of what the fans seemed to think was exciting play, the Chicago Clout squeezed out a 3-2 win. Korngold rejoined them, a cold bottle of beer in his hand and a flushed but triumphant look on his face. He gave Rachel a hug and winked at Joanie.

"You were *great* tonight," Rachel said.

"Limit up," said Korngold.

On the plane ride back home Brian suddenly came alive and wanted to know everything about the game, the rules, the strategies, and every member of the Clout. Rachel fielded most of his questions, throwing out hyphenated names of players from Germany, Poland, and Brazil as if they were her schoolmates. She knew soccer the way she knew commodities, and she fairly glowed beneath her father's bemused smile. Occasionally she glanced back at Joanie, pleased that Joanie was quite unable to add to the conversation.

Joanie did not mind. The chatter about goalies and half-backs was foreign to her. She was content to listen quietly, and she wondered what Ken Korngold was all about. In the week she had worked for him she had seen him take any number of faces and poses. Now this one: the proud, generous father sitting at the controls of this magnificent and costly piece of machinery, humming as his spunky, satin-haired young daughter and a green kid from the neighborhoods jabbered about his latest toy.

"How'd you *get* all this?" Brian finally blurted.

Korngold laughed. "The fruits of the pits, my good man."

"But how'd you get started?"

"Like you."

"Yer kiddin'?"

"No, I'm not. Except I ran for my uncles. The Korngold family has been in the business for a long time."

"My old man's in heating and air conditioning," Brian said.

"Not a bad business."

"Jeez . . ."

"That's what I once thought about the pits. I quit one year and tried to sell real estate."

"What happened?"

"I wasn't any better at that than I was at wheat futures. My Uncle Levi took me back and told me to screw my head on right."

"That was it?"

"Nope. Beans were it. The market came alive in the seventies and so did I."

"That's no joke," Brian said.

"What's your father do, Joanie?" Korngold asked.

Joanie perked.

"Uh, I don't know, I mean . . . banking, I guess," she said.

"You're not sure?"

"I never knew my father," she said.

"That's too bad," Korngold said, suddenly aware that Rachel was staring at him.

"Have a good time?" he said to her, and put his hand on her knee.

A short time later Joanie felt her stomach sink. The plane dropped down and approached the vast expanse of light and haze that was Chicago. Seconds later Korngold guided the jet between the airport's blue and amber runway lights.

"Incredible," Joanie said, exhaling loudly.

"God," Brian said. "This was the most exciting day of my life."

"Thank you, ladies and gentlemen. And thank you for flying Air Korngold," Korngold said, smiling.

At that, Rachel yawned.

"Oh, Daddy," she said. "You *love* it, don't ya."

Five hours later Joanie scraped her bone-tired self out of bed and into work. Korngold did not show up; at least, he was not to be found in the soybean pit. She looked, wanting to thank him for the night before.

Long after the close that afternoon she heard noise coming from his office. Korngold was there. He was wearing yellow-striped knee socks, a pair of black shorts, and a yellow Chicago Clouts jersey. He was standing at the far end of his office in front of a large net that hung from eye hooks bolted into the ceiling.

"C'mon, Bruno!" he growled.

From the other side of the room came a loud thud and a black-and-white soccer ball shot toward the net. Korngold dove for it and tipped it against the bookshelf, where it knocked over a stereo speaker. He landed heavily on the carpet.

"Jawohl! boss," shouted a shaggy-headed kid from the cor-

ner where the ball had come from.

"Hey, Slick," Korngold shouted, catching sight of Joanie. "Meet Bruno Bollfrass. One of my guys," he said, breathing heavily and rubbing his thigh. "Scored two last night, remember?"

Joanie did, and she held out her hand. Bruno wiped the hair out of his eyes and quickly came over. He was barefoot, wearing a pair of designer blue jeans and a see-through net T-shirt.

"Watch this, Joanie. Bruno, do your warm-up."

Bollfrass laughed and fetched the ball. He spun it with his toe so that it rolled backward and up his foot. Then he lightly kicked it in the air at about the level of his chin. Alternating feet, he kept the ball airborne as if it were on a tether, kicking it no higher than his head, all the while grinning and looking at Joanie and Korngold.

"Feets do your stuff!" shouted Korngold.

Then he backed up toward the net.

"Now! you son of a bitch!" he yelled.

Bruno suddenly swept his foot back and nailed the ball on a line toward the net. It was past Korngold before he even left his feet, which he did anyway, landing once again with a thump on the floor.

"Fuckin' showoff," he muttered, and Bruno laughed.

"Okay, Joanie, you try," he said, rolling the ball to her. "Bruno, get us some suds, will ya."

Joanie looked at him, the ball at her feet.

"C'mon!" he shouted.

She wound up and kicked it with the toe of her sneaker. It sailed up and wide of the net and smacked against the window. She winced.

"No, side of your foot," he said, and came over to demonstrate the technique. He took two cold cans of beer from Bruno Bollfrass and handed one to Joanie. Bruno stood there, his eyes hard on Joanie.

"Okay, ace, take a walk. I got a lesson to give," Korngold said to him.

Bruno frowned, but picked up his shoes.

"Auf Wiedersehen," he said, and trotted out.

Joanie waved at him and turned to see Korngold back in front of the net.

"Let it fly," he shouted.

She kicked and he caught it. He rolled it slowly back to her and she kicked it again. He left his feet to catch this one, though he didn't have to. She kicked again and again, and he lunged after each one.

"You're gettin' it," he said, and again rolled the ball back to her.

"Enough!" she finally gasped.

"Great game, ain't it?" he said. "I have my guys come up here and work me all the time. I mean, how many sports are there where the owner can actually go at it with his players, huh?"

He was sweating, taking long draughts of his beer.

Joanie had nearly finished hers. She was exhausted.

"I really came to say thanks for last night. It was really a nice time," she said.

"So show me by having a bite. I got a double order of tempura coming up from Ichiban any minute now. I insist," he said.

She started to decline but thought otherwise. Not after the night before. Not after what he had done for her. She looked at Korngold, the same suave devil who had come on to her like a truck in Florida, who had come on even stronger in his penthouse, who had managed no favor from her but a reluctant kiss and yet had reciprocated with overwhelming generosity. Now standing there in shorts and funny socks and offering her yet another invitation.

"What's tempra?" she said.

"Tempura. Japanese jive. Vegetables and shit deep-fried. You'll like it."

She stepped out to go to the bathroom and saw that the office was deserted. Returning, Joanie accepted another beer. The food came soon after, and Korngold spread it on his desktop. He had ordered a half-dozen entrees and several sauces, some of them gooey and sweet, others tart and spicy. He literally lunged at the food, taking big hunks of vegetables in his fingers, dipping them in the sauces, and dropping them into his mouth. Joanie followed his lead. The food was wonderful, and sauce dripped down her chin. She worked on her third can of beer.

"Your turn," he said, nodding at the goal.

She stood upright, chewing on a piece of cauliflower, when Korngold kicked the ball at her. She squealed and turned her back and the ball smacked her in the buttocks.

"Good save!" he said.

She threw the ball back at him, licked her fingers, and crouched down for another try.

"Hold it," she said, and quickly kicked off her shoes.

Thut! went his foot against the ball and it whizzed by her into the net. He snickered. She frowned. He dribbled the ball to his right, then kicked it left. Joanie dove and pinned the ball to the carpet.

"Piece of cake," she purred, and rolled the ball back to him.

This time Korngold did not hesitate, and he smacked the ball past her into the net.

They kept at it, both of them lunging and diving and grunting in success and exasperation. Joanie had not worked this hard since she played volleyball on the beach back home. Huffing for breath, she pulled her blouse out of her slacks and fanned it against her chest. She took several swigs of beer. Korngold held his in one hand as he kicked shot after shot at her.

Then he paused, looked at her as she crouched in an expectant wiggle in front of the net, and began his approach. Instead of waiting, Joanie decided to rush him and kick it away before he could take a shot. She kicked out her leg and caught his foot as he pushed the ball and the two of them tumbled heavily to the floor.

"Got it!" she screamed, and she scrambled over him and punched the ball out of reach, landing on his chest.

She lay on him with her whole weight and gasped for breath. She flopped her head against his collarbone, her golden hair, now out of all control, splashing in his face. His arms reached around her, embracing her. She looked up at him, sweat running down her face, and pressed her mouth against his, kissing him, biting his lips, grinding her damp,

85

exhausted body against his in a sheer physical rush.

They rolled on the carpet, entwined legs and arms, caressed, fingertips and open palms. Their breathing came in gasps, in a release of heated, fierce bursts, as if they were struggling for every drop, every smell, every taste. Joanie rolled on her side, then straddled him once again, now lost in herself, feeling every part of him and wanting more.

She stood up on her knees and shed her blouse, then her brassiere. The air buffeted her damp, downy skin, and she wavered deliciously over him. He reached up and touched her breasts, now brazen, open to him, inviting. She melted, came apart, had to have him, her first man since she had left home, her first man in such a long time. She lead him, guided him, fit into the spaces and the recesses, melded with him as if it were inevitable, as if she had known it would happen.

Or he knew. She did not want to ask.

PART TWO

Chapter One

Tommy could have tapped anyone. His buddies would have lined up for the job. His clients would have volunteered. From the very moment he conceived the foray, however, Tommy knew exactly whom he wanted. That was because had he the choice of occupying the shoes of anyone on the face of God's green earth, Tommy would have chosen those of Rick Jaskula.

Rick was a sweetheart, a lean slab of a kid, a heartbreaker, the casual possessor of Polish, blond good looks, dimples, and cool — all the qualities kids his age would kill for. Girls approached him on the street. They slipped their phone numbers beneath the windshield wipers of his car. They pinched his butt at dances. They giggled about running their tongues over his big white teeth. He had lettered in three sports, and carried himself with a jock's swagger. He had even gotten decent-enough grades to snare a basketball scholarship to a small school in Iowa. He could carry on a conversation.

Yet what Tommy saw in Rick Jaskula was largely unseen by the rest of the world. He discovered it one day in a biology class during his junior year. The teacher was Mr. Braker, a short, beady-eyed mad scientist of a guy who resented anyone who didn't enjoy biology as much as he did. His room was a zoo full of tropical fish, plants, and several menacing critters including a bat, tarantula, and a boa constrictor that Braker lovingly fed a white mouse once a week.

Mr. Braker's pride and joy, however, was a coal-gray, slithering moray eel that he often lifted from the aquarium and stroked like a puppy.

To pass Mr. Braker's course, you had to perform several experiments, many of which involved small animals, particularly mice and frogs. There was a not-too-hidden suspicion among his students that Mr. Braker loved harmless little animals best when they were being maimed and eaten by bigger ones, and his class-wide experiments seemed to bear that out.

That day Mr. Braker was demonstrating the resilient aspects of the heart, both human and animal, and to do it he brought in dozens of live leopard frogs. Each student was to kill a frog, then quickly dissect it, remove its heart, and place it in a saline solution. Depending on the makeup of the solution, the frog's heart would continue beating for minutes, even hours, thumping away in a petri dish like a slimy Mexican jumping bean.

The frogs were handed out to every student. Nobody got a pass. You had to quickly kill the frog, either by whacking its skull on the tabletop or pithing its brain with an awl. Everybody but the most ghoulish began to squeal and complain. Several girls wouldn't even touch the frogs, which meant the critters were jumping all over.

Mr. Braker was adamant: you killed a frog and plucked out its heart or you failed the day. No matter, several kids couldn't do it, and they trembled and chafed over the animals. Patty Malloy started to cry. She held the frog in her cupped palms and bawled, the tears coursing down her cheeks and dripping onto her blouse.

Most of the class was too engrossed in their own killings to pay much attention. For several minutes and beneath the drama of several successful dissections, Patty continued to weep. Finally she was the only one who had not assassinated her frog. Mr. Braker stared at her, motioned for her to have at it, then he closed in. With the entire class watching, he snatched the frog from Patty Malloy's grasp, set it on the table before her, then put a pick in her right hand, lifted it above the amphibian's head, and plunged it into its brain. Patty screamed and fainted. The frog's eyes bulged as it spasmed and struggled, though its skull was stuck fast to the table.

"Oh, dammit," Mr. Braker said, looking down at Patty Malloy. Then he stalked out of the room to fetch the school nurse.

Patty Malloy's loss of consciousness was brief, and she sat up on the floor and began to sob. Nobody touched her frog.

Then someone growled, "That asshole."

It was Rick Jaskula. Without another word he pulled away from the crowd around Patty Malloy's station and went over to

Mr. Braker's menagerie. With a wide net he scooped the precious eel from the aquarium. He held the net aloft and carried it dripping across the classroom to Mr. Braker's desk. With a splat he overturned the net, and the eel wildly churned and flopped about the desktop. Then Rick Jaskula raised up his hand just as Mr. Braker had done a few moments earlier and plunged an ice pick into the eye of the eel, pinning it to the desk. It flailed and squirmed around the pick, looking, in its dying throes, like a glistening, wet streamer on a Maypole.

The class gasped, stood motionless and gaped at the dying creature, then broke out in applause. In the days that followed, nobody ever snitched. And Tommy Haggarty had found his partner.

He never told Jaskula that that was why he approached him on this deal. It was hard enough just selling Rick on the whole thing. Jaskula was a kid with a future, the kind of person who never did anything without first figuring how it fit with the total scheme of his life. He wasn't game for sprees, binges, or risks. He had never done a totally reckless thing. It'd fit, Tommy thought, if Rick were still a virgin.

Knowing all that, Tommy confronted Jaskula one night when Rick was home from college during spring break. Tommy had two pieces of leverage: the sheer challenge to Jaskula's guts, and the fact that the one thing that Rick was more in love with than himself was money. He dearly wanted to get rich, and his father being one of the many laid-off-and-never-to-be-rehired steelworkers on the far South Side meant that he'd have to make it on his own. Tommy volunteered to pay for air fare and all expenses, plus $2,000 cash, half on takeoff, half when they got back.

Rick sat on the proposition for a week before he agreed. Their cover was a white-water canoe trip to Canada, complete with brochures and bogus reservations that Tommy had arranged through another runner on the floor. What they did instead that summer day was to board a TWA flight to Miami and Bogotá, Colombia.

When they got there they checked into a $9-a-day hotel room in the middle of the city. Tommy had memorized the name of the place, as he had memorized every detail of the operation. It would take three days to consummate. In the meantime he wanted to see the sights.

"C'mon, Rick boy, put on a Hawaiian shirt, Bermuda shorts, a Japanese camera and play *turista*," Tommy said.

Rick would have none of it. He stayed near their hotel, usually inside the dank, depressing room, and looked worried.

"Three days, Haggarty. If you don't score in three days I'm outta here," he said.

"Relax," said Tommy, and went off on his own.

The next day he returned to the room with a package inside his backpack.

"A fill," he said.

Then he danced on the bed.

"It's like it's candy. The guy said there's laboratories all over, in the jungles and stuff. Runways and planes and all. He said you go down the Yarí River which we passed when we come in and you can spot the lookouts. Carry fuckin' machine guns. You fart at 'em and they'll zip you like that. And the government just winks. Guy says the Commie party here are the biggest suppliers. The Reds, can you beat that?"

"Why'd he tell you all that?" Rick said.

"Cuz who cares? My buy was probably lunch money for these guys."

He talked and fondled the package, turning it over and over like a pillow.

"Let's do it," said Rick.

"Fuckin' Gary Gilmore," said Tommy.

For the next three hours they coated their throats with honey, and swallowed 186 balloons. They had intended on packing 200, but Rick gagged at 80, and could only manage 4 more. Tommy did all 100, then two more for the hell of it.

"In Co-lahm-bia," Tommy said, raising a red balloon to his lips, "we pack only de ripest balloons." And he gulped it down with a wide grin.

The balloons cost them less than a penny a piece. Tommy bought them from a peasant in the open-air market, but they were made in Hong Kong, the kind their mothers had strung on the ceiling for Kodak Instamatic birthday parties when they were kids. The balloons were blue, yellow, red, and green.

They filled each balloon with five grams of processed, pure-grade Bolivian cocaine, tied it securely with dental floss, and swallowed it. A pound and a half in all, a total cost of 10,000 American dollars. In America, however, it would be worth thirty times that: $300,000.

If they made it.

If the balloons held, if the ties stayed secure and the skins resisted stomach acids, if the balloons worked their way into their digestive systems, shuffled through the intestines, and lodged in the bowels to be moved with laxatives at the proper time in the proper place: shitting a fortune.

Tommy grinned and gulped one last time, his Adam's apple bobbing. "I feel like Meatloaf," he said and held his stomach.

Rick didn't bite. Tommy had talked him into this thing, but laughing at his jokes wasn't part of the deal. He reached for his nylon backpack, his caramel-tan arms snaking through the straps, then picked up a heavy roll of handmade Colombian serapes. They were their cover: goods two American kids would buy cheap in South America and sell for a profit back home. Rick was nineteen years old with green eyes and a head of blond Harpo Marx curls that made the South Americans stare.

They hopped a *público*, the groaning, belching municipal bus, 10 peso fare — 1 1/2 cents — this one with the windshield held together with furnace tape, for the dusty ride to the *aeropuetro*. They clutched their charter-fare tickets for the flight back to Miami, two kids from Chicago coming home from an adventure.

Or so they intended the world to believe. According to Tommy's plan they would be in Miami in four hours, get through customs — they'd gladly show the agents their underwear and their cheap souvenirs — in another hour, and arrive by taxi at a nearby hotel room ten minutes later. Then they'd flip a coin to see who would run out for the Ex-Lax.

When the jet lifted off, Tommy gave Rick the thumbs up. Rick again didn't respond. They'd vowed to make no jokes or smug comments about their cargo. For Tommy that would be difficult: Tommy the Tip, the runner, the man to see for drugs, booze, concert tickets, pirated computer programs, video games, or rubbers. Part of the deal was putting up with his bullshit, an endless stream, even now, when they both felt as if they'd just eaten a gallon of cold oatmeal.

Tommy put on the earphones and tuned in REO Speedwagon. He tried to lose himself in the sounds.

"You remember in chemistry when Mulroy computed the chemical worth of the human body," he said, lifting the earphones from his head. "Three hundred and twelve bucks or something like that, if you were butchered and put in bottles. Not counting the fillings in your teeth. Except for Loomis who'd get three bills just for his lard alone."

He looked at Rick and saw he had his eyes closed.

"Three hundred and twelve bucks, my *ass*," Tommy said to himself, and smiled a dreamy, druggy smile that lay on his face like a limp balloon.

Rick suddenly sat up straight and began a game of solitaire on his tray. He snapped the cards and played extremely well.

The flight seemed long and ragged, the belly of the DC-10 buffeted by a Caribbean storm. The pilot never switched off the seatbelt lights. Rick groaned. Tommy tried to sleep. They refused the snack of peanuts and pretzels and the dinner of beef brisket, Tommy waving it away as if it were tainted — even though the stewardess, whose name was Andrea, was a fox. They sipped soda water and looked ill. Andrea smiled.

Shortly before landing, Rick tapped Tommy on the leg.

"I love the sky blue sky," Rick said, and giggled.

"Don't we all?" Tommy replied, and grinned, then paused. He looked at Rick and saw his head bob, as if he was about to drift off to sleep. Except he was smiling like a loon.

"Lucy in the sky-yi-yi-yi-yi . . ." Rick sang.

"Goddamm it," Tommy said, then turned to look directly into Rick's face. His brown skin was now pale, even pasty. A line of perspiration trailed down his temple. He was biting the insides of his cheeks as if they were bubble gum.

"Hell, you gotta cool it," Tommy hissed, and prayed that it wasn't what he feared: that the balloons in Rick's body were leaking.

Just then Rick exhaled, coughed, and pitched forward with his arms cradling his stomach. At the same time the wheels of the DC-10 thumped onto the runway, bounced, the fuselage groaning, and the sudden thrust of the reverse throttle threw the passengers forward in their seats. Several in the front section, a charter group from Wisconsin, applauded. Rick rolled his head and gagged.

The plane slowed, turned, and began to taxi into the terminal of Miami International. Two stewardesses walked quickly toward the front of the section while another reminded passengers to stay in their seats until the plane had stopped moving. Tommy heard none of it. Rick was bent forward, his head in his hands, his breathing coming in short, quick gasps.

"We're almost in, Rick," Tommy said, leaning close to get a look at him. When he did, he realized that through Rick's muffled breathing he was crying. The tears leaked over his fingers.

Tommy sat up and jerked around in his seat, searching for a stewardess. This could be a blessing in disguise, dammit, he thought. He motioned at Andrea, the stewardess.

"My buddy here is real sick," he said.

Andrea instinctively smiled, then her eyes widened in concern when she saw Rick.

"Has he used the air bag?" she said, leaning in between the seats.

"No. But he's gotta get off this crate in a hurry," Tommy said.

Andrea grimaced, a strand of blond hair fell across her forehead and she looked up the aisle for help.

"Can you lift him out?" she said.

Tommy unbuckled his belt and Rick's, and reached around to pull him up.

"Get your ass off of the seat," he said under his breath.

He pulled on Rick's shoulders and Rick responded, turning to him and falling drunkenly into his arms. His eyes turned upward and he swooned. His lips moved but he said nothing; a viscous foam streamed down his chin.

"I'll call in for a stretcher," the stewardess said.

"Fuck no!" Tommy yelled. "No stretcher. He needs some air. I seen him do this before."

At that he pulled Rick into the aisle, jerking him upright and supporting him with an arm around his ribs. The two of them stumbled down the aisle, the other passengers standing and staring, the stewardesses clustering to give aid.

By this time the plane had pulled in at the gate and the doors were opening. Tommy and Rick reached the front exit and were met by an airline employee with a wheelchair. Tommy angrily waved it away.

"C'mon, ya fuck," he hissed into Rick's ear. "Just make it through. *C'mon.*"

"Put him in the chair, sir. It's airline rules," the man with the wheelchair said. He pushed the chair alongside the stumbling pair as they made their way through the corridor toward customs.

"Look at him, he's walkin'," Tommy yelled. "He's feelin' better."

As he said it Rick's feet went limp, and Tommy realized he was dragging him, carrying his whole weight. He turned a corner and the baggage trays and inspection counters of the customs area came into view.

"Almost home," Tommy grunted.

As he said it Rick's head fell back, his mouth open. Blood trickled out his nose.

A massive black woman in a customs uniform saw them and hurried over. She pulled Rick from Tommy and laid him on the floor, setting on her knees and pressing two fingers to his neck. The foamy stream of saliva trailed out the side of Rick's mouth and down his jaw. Others gathered around, forming a tight circle and leaning over to see.

"Get the van!" the black woman bellowed over her shoulder, not taking her eyes from Rick, who was now totally limp.

Tommy looked around, saw the faces, then watched as the woman put her ear near to Rick's bloody nostrils. Then he saw Rick's eyes. They were wide open, the pupils frozen.

They told Tommy that the worst had happened, the only possible disaster in the "no risk" risk that he and Rick had taken on when they'd swallowed the balloons: one had ruptured and released its contents into Rick's system, taking him with it.

"He okay?" Tommy said.

The woman, her green cap pinned to a stiff black burst of straightened hair, looked up at him with her dark eyes and purple skin, and scowled.

"He's *dead,*" she said, spitting the words into Tommy's dumbstruck face.

He did not remember what happened next, only that some time later he too began to feel a little light-headed. He had been taken into a small, airless bathroom. He was given an ample quantity of a remarkable laxative called Prompt. It was true to its label, just as Tommy, in his newfound misery, feared it would be. For the next hour he groaned and grunted and delivered all 102 balloons safely into a colander positioned under the toilet seat by an agent of the Drug Enforcement Administration, an operative soon to be dubbed by his associates as a member of the DEA's "Squat Team."

That same agent, a man who looked to be not much older than Tommy, later sat across a table from him and noticeably lifted his eyebrows when Tommy told him that he worked as a runner in the commodities markets in Chicago. The man paused for a moment, then left the room for what seemed like an endless period of time.

When he returned he said, "Thomas, we're going to make a little deal with you . . ."

Chapter Two

The days and weeks ran by, and Joanie with them. She learned the job, the traders, the orders and fills, that she was a vital link between the desk and the pits. She was a gofer, be it for orders, trading cards, coffee or cigarettes, and that status brought a paycheck of $200 a week, less than half of the total she had been making in the hair salon. But she was swept up by the energy, the furious action of commodity trading. That made up for the meager salary, she told her mother over the phone during one of their regular Sunday morning calls.

"How's school?" her mother asked.

"Uh, it hasn't happened yet," Joanie said.

From the moment Korngold hired her, Joanie had all but dropped her intention of enrolling despite almost daily mailings and reminders sent to her by the university.

"Oh," said her mother.

"I really *like* this," she said.

"Met any sailors yet?" her mother asked.

"All over the place," Joanie said.

"Watch out for the tall, quiet blonds," came the reply.

"I know," Joanie said, and her mind began to drift.

"I think I've made a mistake," she suddenly added.

"How?"

Joanie immediately reconsidered.

"I'm not sure . . ." she said softly, being perfectly honest.

Along with Brian Boyer and three others, she ran for all Korngold traders, and, in keeping with the pecking order of the floor, did the bidding of clerks and trader's assistants such as Tommy Haggarty. She went to and from both trading floors, beating a path between the Korngold desks and the pits, delivering and returning orders, checking card totals and prices.

She learned quickly, not just her job, but the whole process of the market. She began to comprehend its order within the chaos. What had been only an image in a textbook back in school was now her reality: an order to buy soybeans from one of the firm's clients—a computer salesman in Tampa, a small manufacturer in Portland—came in on the phone, was delivered by her hands into those of a trader in the pits, was executed, then confirmed. It happened hundreds of times in her day, every trading day.

On some days she did not run at all. Instead, she stood on the top level of the bond pit and faced the Korngold desk. Called flashing, her job was to signal the current price to the phone clerk, and she stood with a hand in front of her face, the fingers signifying the tick as it moved up or down, as quickly as she heard it from the traders themselves. The instantaneous price fix was vital, the flashing relay precious seconds faster than that which is registered on the boards.

This job was exciting and boring, a manual exercise that, once learned, easily became tedious even within the pandemonium of the pits. On the steps of the pits she jostled other clerks, bumping rumps and trading jibes, putting up with belching and farting as if the pit were a men's room, resignedly taking the less-than-classy remarks from pimply just-out-of-high-school runners all around her. She and the other women who endured such treatment often remarked that were they to take just one of them up on his ribald suggestions, he would faint dead out.

Although there were hundreds of women like herself working as clerks, runners, and assistants, the fact is that they had only been allowed on the trading floor since 1966. For nearly a century, commodity trading floors were men's clubs. It took the Board of Trade until 1981 to install women's bathrooms on the floor level itself. Still, by the 1980's, while several hundred exchange memberships were owned by women, there were only a few dozen women actually trading in the pits. And they, Joanie soon realized, were only grudgingly accepted. Well-worn male biases, the raunchiest of raunchy humor, and a palpable macho aura hung in the air like cigar smoke over a poker table.

For the time being, however, Joanie ignored the guff, preferring instead to get a fix on the business of trading, where the money was, how the numbers on the boards and on the lips and fingers of traders translated into cash. One day, she knew, she would lock into what it was all about, the market, the dynamics of trading, the whole crazy, seductive game.

But a deadly serious game, she realized. Once the gong sounded, traders became different people: intense, strained, giddy, desperate. Their moods swung like scythes. They had ferocious tempers, and usually vented them on runners or assistants no matter who was at fault. They had raucous, almost juvenile bursts of laughter, and humor that spared no one. Yet when they were not ranting or giggling, they were afraid. More than anything, Joanie saw traders gripped with a pervasive, numbing, sweat-soaked fear that made them tremble and whimper and, on many occasions, break down and sob. She saw it time after time.

As for Korngold, he continued to be a ferocious presence in the pit, a big hitter, a trader capable of swaying the entire arena. He stood at the core of the pit's major locals and brokers, the traders who bought and sold hundreds of contracts for customers. Small traders positioned around the base of the pit watched him, trying to key off his trades, ride his moves or just feed off his scraps.

When trading was on, the tick was moving, a trader—even a veteran like Korngold—held his ego, his passion, his livelihood in his bare hands. And nothing else mattered. When Joanie came in contact with him on the floor he seldom even acknowledged her. He did not smile, nod, or remark.

Still, he depended on her to be his second set of eyes, ears, and arms. She was his portable calculator, collating his trades, keeping track of his numbers, his longs and shorts. And she loved it, sliding through the welter of bodies, literally skipping up and down steps, grabbing orders, rushing back to the desk and attacking the phones, cradling two receivers at a time. Her work was constant motion, exciting, harried, keenly mental, just a hair's width away from insanity.

She was good at it. Once, at the close of a particularly good trading session, he paused outside the pit and drew her aside.

"Thanks a lot," he said. "You did a hell of a job today."

His voice was nearly hoarse, yet it was the softest thing Joanie had ever heard in her life. He meant it, and Joanie felt so good she nearly cried. Standing there, Ken Korngold, smiling and making her feel priceless, was the nicest man on earth, a man she would do anything for. She said so to herself as he walked off.

But for days and weeks on end that was the only gesture he made toward her, and it puzzled Joanie. She knew he had not forgotten what had happened that night in his office, and that he had not taken it for granted — no, about that she could not be sure. Yet he did not pursue matters, did not ask her out, invite her to stay after, or show any interest in her outside of business.

She was not used to that. When men took an interest in her, they usually pressed. Korngold showed only occasional regard, a touch, a lingering nudge on the sleeve, a hand on her back, a slight massage of a shoulder. He would smile slightly, catching her glance at odd moments, and she smiled back. She could not help but feel uneasy, not threatened or vulnerable or abused, but as if she were in suspension or reserve, like a wine or a weapon, to be enjoyed at the appropriate moment. She was new at this, and she knew that he was not.

Not long after the trip to Atlanta, Rachel Korngold began coming downtown. She usually arrived at mid-afternoon, slipped on a Korngold jacket, and went down to the floor to watch the closing minutes of trading. Afterward she glided around the office, joking with her father, huddling over his shoulders as he sat at his desk, playing with his hair, massaging his back.

Whenever she crossed paths with Joanie, Rachel fleetingly acknowledged her, then quickly turned to something or someone else.

Joanie did not take offense, not after she observed Rachel's darting, furtive glances toward her in Korngold's presence. The girl had learned early and well how to throw daggers. As Joanie went about her work she could feel them lodge between her shoulder blades.

Apart from what she felt personally for Korngold, Joanie watched his every professional move, what he did and how. More than anything she wanted to perceive what kind of person one had to be to do battle in the pits as he did. In no time she began to know the pressure, the fury, the instincts, the risk. She commiserated with him, rooted for him, soared with his wins and plummeted with his losses.

Outwardly, however, she sought to mimic Korngold's ability to win and to lose with the same icy temperament. She strove to remain unfazed at single trades that gained or lost him $25,000 — twice the money she made in a year — a trading sum that months earlier she would not have fathomed. Likewise, Korngold's trading patterns swung up and down several hundred thousand dollars in short periods of time. He was routinely "up a mil" or "down a mil" — one million dollars. For traders of his magnitude, that figure was only a temporary hill or valley. When Joanie explained this to her mother, she did so matter-of-factly. Her mother gasped over the phone, and said that she simply did not believe it.

Indeed, no outsider could tell from just looking at Korngold as he walked around the Board of Trade with his frayed trading jacket and lucky but stained tie that he amassed such sums. And Joanie marveled at that fact. Within the course of a day, it was impossible to discern from the look on his face if he was up or down, losing a bundle or pocketing it. At the end of trading he took off his shoes and holed up in his office, holding court with traders and employees, traders from other firms, and clients who came in and out. He sipped from a tumbler of Russian vodka on ice. He played tapes — the same ones over and over — of the Righteous Brothers, Aretha Franklin, Little Richard, Gladys Knight. When Joanie passed by, he just smiled benignly, and patted her butt.

Then one morning as she hustled from the trading floor up to the office on an errand for a wheat trader, she came upon Korngold as he was interviewing a would-be trader. Korngold paid no attention to her. She rummaged through a box of trading cards, and watched and listened.

"How much you think you can lose in a day? One day?" Korngold said, pacing in front of the sofa and the trader.

He was wearing a well-tailored gray business suit and tie, looked about twenty-five.

"I don't know . . ." he began. "Maybe three, five thousand if

102

you stay —"

"I'll tell you something," Korngold interrupted, stepping in front of him. "See that chair over there? That old wooden chair? That's the crying chair. It's an old piece of shit. Stained with a lot of things unmentionable, but especially tears. *Tears.* I mean big ones that just ran down guys' faces and dripped onto their legs so you'd think they were peeing their pants.

"I took that chair with me from my uncle's firm. Guys sit in that chair when they tap out. When they go in the tank not for three K or thirty K, to answer my own question, but for *three hundred and fifty thousand.* And *more.* A hell of a lot more. Guys puke out like that. Not in a year or two. I've seen it happen in a *day.*

"They fuckin' cry because they know if they lose and lose big, if they go crazy, right? then I got no choice. You remember that, Eddie. You come back up here because I'm the guy who has to clear your losses. But then you sit down, and digest the fact that I'm gonna take your house. Your fuckin' house and all the furniture, see. I will, Eddie, so help me. And you have to sit here and think about how you're going to go home and tell the missus that you ain't got a place to live in any more. And how you may have to work as a *pisher* shoe clerk for the rest of your life just to pay me back.

"That's what this chair is for. Take a good look at it before you go down there."

Then Korngold walked out of his office. The trader, whose name was Ed McAllister, sat there with his hands on his knees, saying nothing, but staring at the battered wooden chair. Joanie looked at him, and at the chair, and forgot what she had been doing.

"Joanie!" Korngold called.

She went into his office. He was standing inside the door, and he kicked it shut when she entered.

"Where were we?" he said.

And suddenly she had her breath sucked from her.

It was a Friday afternoon after the pits had closed. The stereo in the Korngold outer office throbbed; the television was tuned to a Three Stooges movie in which the boys happened to be fixing faulty plumbing in the basement while a social gathering of ladies in evening gowns and tuxedoed gentlemen sporting a pince-nez or two was going on upstairs. It was the perfect accompaniment to the routine of totaling up for the week. Joanie, Brian, Mary Beth, Tommy Haggarty, and the others sipped soft drinks and beer, jabbered, stopped occasionally to watch Curly get rapped in the chops.

By this time most of the floor traders had taken off. They were bound by no schedules or time clocks, only the positions they held in the pits. So they came and went as they pleased, trading from start to finish, trading an hour and quitting, trading a day and sitting out the rest of the week. Theirs was a job that made them responsible only to themselves, a kind of perpetual childhood surrounded with dollars.

Just as Curly jerked his pipe wrench and unleashed a torrent of water in Moe's face, the week's money supply figures came in.

"Holy shit!" yelled a bond trader named Marty Valukas. "Nobody called that."

He and a few others gathered around a monitor flashing the current price of bonds on the cash market from New York. That market was still open, offering bonds to buyers and sellers all over the nation. Though the floor traders dealt in bond futures, they kept close watch on the current prices. The futures market would respond accordingly when it opened Monday morning.

"Look at it go," cried Valukas.

Even Tommy Haggarty put down his beer to watch.

"Christ, Monday will be a fuckin' riot," he said.

Brian Boyer leaned in. He watched for several minutes, not even sure which digits on the screen to follow.

"What's goin' on now?" he finally asked.

Tommy stepped back.

"Cash market took off. That means bombs away at opening Monday," he said.

Brian nodded. Tommy tried to explain the phenomenon, talking about money supply and its effects on interest rates and bond prices. He spoke quickly, as if the information was common knowledge. Then he turned to the other television set and howled when Larry stuck his head up through the sod of the front lawn.

"Why don't you get in, Haggarty?" Marty Valukas said to him.

"You float me?"

"Fuckin' A!"

"How 'bout you, Boyer?" Valukas said.

"Whattaya mean?" Brian said.

"Buy a contract. Get in, ride the opening and get out. Make yourself a quick buck."

"How?"

"God damn. How long you been workin' here? You give me scratch for a onesie and I'll give you a fill. *Comprende?*"

Brian took a drink from his beer. He pinched his face together as if he'd just had an attack of piles.

"Two bills. I'll do you a favor," Valukas said.

"Two hunnert? How much do I make?"

"Come *onnnnnn*, Boyer. Depends on the tick. I'll keep you in as long as it runs. Take it or leave it."

"When do you gotta know?"

"Anytime before the bell Monday."

Brian stood and gawked at him, a confused, helpless look on his glistening mug. Moe tightened a pipe wrench on Larry's nose. Brian looked at Lisa, at Joanie, then at Tommy Haggarty. He stood there looking at everybody, and they all looked back at him.

"One of *the* best Stooges of all time," crowed Tommy.

Brian's drive home was pure agony. There was no question about what he was going to do, only how. How was he going to scrape up two hundred bucks for Marty Valukas? And he had to. It was a sure thing. Marty was one of the best scalpers in the office, the kind of trader, Tommy said, who would trade his ass off just to make a few ticks.

Yet beyond his uncashed paycheck of $142 and a few bucks in cash in his wallet, Brian had not a dime. He'd spent his first few paychecks paying off debts and spreading cash among his buddies and Rhonda. His car needed a brake job and the ol' man said he was going to start charging room and board.

He decided his folks were out, even a loan against a savings bond they said he'd get once he turned twenty-one or got married, whichever came first. He knew his grandpa had money in his basement — pure silver quarters stacked in three-foot-long pipes. Grandpa had showed them to him when he was small. But he had no idea of how much was down there, or of any way he could get to it. He decided not to go to his buddies because they were assholes.

Only one person remained, and he had a date with her that night.

He waited until after the movie, which cost him eight bucks, when he and Rhonda were sitting in the front seat of his car and Rhonda began talking about the wedding, her favorite subject. The money was in her wedding fund, eight months of carefully protected paychecks.

"Do you love me?" he asked.

"Do you *really* love me?" he asked again.

When she got the cash from the drive-in teller the next morning she began to cry.

"By Monday those'll be tears of joy, Rhonda. You'll see," Brian said.

She kept crying.

"Trust me," he said.

He stuffed the money in the pocket of his trading jacket and slept fitfully all Sunday night. Monday morning he showed up for work at six.

"*Whee*-ler *dea*-ler," Marty Valukas whistled as he took the cash and tucked it in his shirt pocket. "Now let's go play the ponies."

When the bell sounded, the bond pit exploded as everybody had predicted. Though Brian was running in the grain pits, they did not open until 9:30, so he stood with the crowd of clerks and traders on the edge of the pit and watched. He had never been so nervous in his life. His heart pounded; his breath came in quick bursts. He immediately found Marty Valukas, MAV, standing smack in the middle of the teeming mass of traders on the north edge of the pit. Valukas was simply one of the fray, his hands outstretched, his eyes bugged, his mouth an oval scream. Brian watched the tick with his mouth open, as if he were trading. In minutes he had all he could do to keep from shouting out, for the tick shot upward. Ten ticks in but a few minutes, holding, then rocketing upward again.

"Hope Marty got you in," Tommy said as he elbowed by.

Brian glared at him. Was there even a chance that he couldn't? Was that possible? And what could he do? In fifteen minutes the flurry was over, the price having risen a full point—thirty-two ticks—and held. Brian was frantic. He strained to see Marty Valukas, and when he did he saw that Valukas was laughing, now seemingly oblivious to the board and the tick, his hands at his sides. Trading had settled to only an occasional burst.

Just then Valukas saw Brian and waved him in the pit. Brian jumped off the bridge and sprinted around the outside, then he elbowed his way inside to Valukas's spot. Marty handed him a card. It held three trades.

"Not bad," Valukas said, and looked away.

Brian studied it.

"How'd you do?" Tommy said, leaning over his shoulder.

Brian stared at the card, not sure of what he was reading.

"A point and a half. Son of a bitch, Boyer."

"So how much?" Brian said.

"About fourteen hunnert."

"Yer kiddin' me!"

"It's right there, shitbrain. I told ya Marty could trade."

Brian was stunned, bumped from behind as he walked drunkenly sideways. Suddenly he had to go to the bathroom.

As he stumbled toward the men's room, he stared at the piece of paper he held with two hands in front of him.

"My God," he said almost in a whisper.

"Oh, my God," he said a little louder.

Then the words dribbled out of his mouth, slowly at first, then faster, and louder.

"Hot-diggety-diggety-diggety-Jesus-H.-Holy-Christ-Oh-me-oh- my-help-me-Rhonda-Rhonda-Rhonda-God-*dammmm-mmmmm*-I-am- fuckin'-*rich!!!!!*"

Chapter Three

At dawn the clock was a scold, a jolt, a knife in her ribs. She hated it, never got used to it, never ignored it. There was no choice. When trading was hectic some traders actually tipped her to arrive in the pit at 6:00 A.M. and hold their spots. A trader's physical position in a pit could be crucial. Until the Board of Trade imposed stiff fines, fistfights often broke out over a specific square foot of trading space.

Still, Joanie was by no means the first one in the building. Some stayed all night. Others came in the early hours of the morning. All had their reasons — to check the closings of foreign markets, to collate reports or data, or simply because they could not stay away. For all the glamour and action associated with the commodities business, she marveled, its practitioners worked their asses off.

On her own time before trading began Joanie did her own homework. She checked figures, averages, forecasts, and research services. She analyzed the trading patterns of Korngold and a few of the firm's best traders, checking their track records against the charts. She studied as if she were cramming for a mid-term in school, then she filed the material away in an office drawer.

One morning she turned to find Mary Beth at her elbow.

"Almond croissant?" Mary Beth said, holding out a sticky but delicious-looking pastry.

"Love it," said Joanie.

They stood together, munching and licking their fingers.

"Why do you do all that?" Mary Beth asked, motioning toward the drawer where Joanie had stuffed her research.

"Uh, well, I just want to really know it," Joanie said.

"You wanna trade, don't ya?" Mary Beth said, pushing a frizzy bang of permed hair from her eye.

"Doesn't everybody?"

"You kiddin'? The guys, maybe. But not us. You see 'em — half the chicks on the floor are sharks. Here just to get a guy and get their hooks on his account. Why da ya think they dress that way — you see 'em," Mary Beth said.

"Sure I do, but it's part of the place —"

"Right. Like they just *love* commodities," Mary Beth said. She reached for a can of grapefruit juice.

"They're after the bucks. They see what it does to these guys, how half of em are jerks, but they don't care. Not if it can get their ass in a Vette."

Joanie pushed the last of the croissant into her mouth and eyed Mary Beth. She was no more than twenty, with thick, coal-black eye-liner, exploded hair, noisy purple plastic jewelry, yellow hightop sneakers, and as much insight on traders and trading as anyone.

"Imagine what you thought of me," Joanie said.

"Oh, *God*, that's for sure. I don't mean —" Mary Beth gulped, then clutched Joanie's sleeve and laughed. Joanie laughed with her.

"I thought I'd die when I heard you were going along with Korno and his precious little daughter. The little *bitch*."

"Not the friendliest date," Joanie said.

"Cuz she *knows*. They come after Korno in packs. He hit on you yet?" Mary Beth said, hardly pausing for an answer.

Joanie smiled.

"Korno," she said. She had never heard him called that.

"What about his wife?" she said.

"Who — Marvelous Myrna?" Mary Beth exclaimed, then she put her hand over her mouth and looked around her. Joanie giggled.

"What a *number*. But it's too expensive to get a divorce nowadays. And Korno knows how to cut his losses. Myrna'd make Johnny Carson's ex-wife look like a penny pincher."

"God, Mary Beth, you're a gold mine," Joanie said.

"It's about time you hung out a little bit," Mary Beth said. "Us girls are starting to wonder about you."

"Yeah, well, it's been kind of boring for me so far."

"We can change that," said Mary Beth.

Just then a trader yelled at Mary Beth. She lifted her eyes and sauntered off.

Several traders and other Korngold employees had trickled into the office. Most had their own schedules, some of them staying only minutes before heading down to the floor, others milling about sipping coffee and chewing warm Danish from Lou Mitchell's, a landmark restaurant down the street. Some lounged about and talked of golf games, others eyed the boards and worried about prices. Most absently rubbed their legs, readying them for the hours of standing in the pits, massaging premature varicose veins.

Joanie well appreciated the maladies even though she didn't, as yet, suffer from them. Trading was physical, even violent, and the body paid the price. Ulcers, sore knees, veins, chronically raw throats, hemorrhoids, all the hidden tariffs paid for being on their feet all day.

At 7:30 A.M. she put on her beige coat with its maroon "KORNGOLD" lettering and the soccerball patch, and her laminated badge. The upper pocket was full of pencils, the side pockets bulged with the reserve trading cards for the traders she principally ran for, and what research data she thought they might need for the day.

Then she headed for the elevators once again. Just ahead of her, wearing the same color jacket but one that was obviously just pressed, was a new face. He was a thin, angular guy named Steve Stamford, a gold trader who had just signed on with the firm. Joanie eyed him for a moment, noticing his hair as she still noticed everybody's hair, how short it was, not styled or layered or even combed with any particular conviction. He looked like a clerk in a hardware store, not like other traders, who had hairstyles like tennis pros.

He was in his mid-thirties, older than most new traders. He had come over to Korngold from Hutton. She had heard he was pretty good, a steady, disciplined scalper. She had also heard he had a temper, something positive, she thought, if it gave some color to his pale, midwestern looks.

At the elevators he turned to her.

"I'm Steve Stamford," he said.

Joanie shook his hand and looked at his badge.

110

"SDS. I've read about you," she said.

"You have?" he said.

She nodded.

"Not really. I had a high school history teacher who said American history began in the sixties. How about this: Mark Rudd?"

"Mark Rudd," he said.

"Right. And the Port Something-or-other Declaration?"

"Very good. The Port Huron Statement, founding papers of the student movement," he said, a look of mild amusement covering his face.

The elevator opened and they got on together.

"High school, huh?" he said.

"Sorry," she said.

As the car descended, they were silent. More traders stepped on at various stops, like miners going down into the earth, until the car was stuffed. Joanie looked up and eyed the thin blue vein on Steve Stamford's temple. It was coursing.

At four they walked with the crowd into the foyer. Just before parting, Stamford squeezed her arm.

"Go get 'em," he said, and smiled.

Joanie stopped, momentarily surprised at the gesture, rubbing the spot where he had touched her, and watched him disappear into the melee.

A few nights later Joanie took up Mary Beth on one of her invitations. Mary Beth called it "beat-on-the-bod." It was her term for working out. For weeks Joanie had been a slave to her routine: twelve hours a day of jostling and running at work, a bus ride back to her apartment, a take-out dinner eaten in front of the television, some puttering and reading — too often, she realized, market-related reading — some attention to her hair or her nails, then a collapse into bed before the clock struck 10:00 A.M. The glamour of it all, she sighed.

Yet tonight Mary Beth prevailed. Just about everyone on the trading floor was a member of a health club — traders insisted that the physical toll exacted by the pits could only be replenished by something equally physical — and at the close of the markets they flocked to racquet ball and tennis courts, basketball games, aerobics classes, or simply the quiet of a steam or sauna. Purge the poisons, slow down the pulse, clear the skull. Mary Beth was no exception.

"The workout? Forget it," she said. "I go to this joint to see guys. See'em in shorts, count the bulges. Then there ain't no surprises later."

"Works both ways," replied Joanie.

"No shit," said Mary Beth.

Joanie herself had never worked out, never taken aerobics, played tennis, pressed Nautilus weights, or jogged any farther than from the parking lot to the drugstore in a rainstorm. She had inhabited the beach like everybody in Florida, maintained a year-round tan, but she had always taken it all for granted. In Chicago, where beach weather was a summertime, three-month event, the indoors health club scene was an obsession. Mary Beth's invite was a chance to take it in, free of charge. Swim, take a steam, or just sip wine coolers in the lounge.

The high rollers, Joanie was told, did all this at the East Bank Club, the EBC, a posh and notorious club situated on the banks of the Chicago River just behind the Merchandise Mart. Six thousand members strong, a months-long waiting list, and exorbitant fees. The rest of the world, including the soldiers of the trading floor, sought out less-elegant, less-expensive facilities in the dozens of clubs scattered throughout the rest of the city.

Mary Beth's club was in Lincoln Park, a fashionable North Side neighborhood and playground for many of the floor's single employees, those who had just moved away from their parents.

To get there Joanie got on an elevated train at a station a block east of the Board of Trade. She rode the train around the Loop — beneath the skywalk connecting the Board of Trade and the gleaming new quarters of the Chicago Board Options Exchange — leaning with the old train as it screeched into turns only inches away from hazy second-floor windows. As the train passed over the sleepy Chicago River, Joanie spotted the East Bank Club. A few blocks north, in yet another grim contrast in Chicago real estate, stood Cabrini-Green, a fearsome, high-rise, public housing project with street gangs and sniper fire. Just north of Cabrini began Lincoln Park and the gray back porches of $200,000 graystones.

She got off at Fullerton and walked west, past DePaul University, and finally to the LakeShore Centre, a one-time factory turned all-purpose athletic club. It was an East Bank Club for clerks, runners, and neophyte traders. Its parking lots were outdoors and uncovered, exposing newly acquired BMWs to the elements.

Joanie easily found Mary Beth and the two of them headed for the locker room. Mary Beth was Joanie's size and had volunteered to let Joanie wear one of her exercise outfits. That meant a black-and-pink-striped backless leotard cut to the hipbones, black tights, and lavender leg warmers. Joanie supplied her own, well-worn, trading-floor Etonics.

"You're *it*, babe," Mary Beth said, looking Joanie over.

"Nice and low key," Joanie said, pinning her hair into a chignon.

Mary Beth added that she might not be very sociable tonight because she was going to make a lunge at one of four guys in her aerobics class.

"Make friends," Mary Beth said, and winked.

Joanie did not mind. She followed Mary Beth to a class already in progress. She filed into the back row next to a pregnant woman in a gray sweatshirt and black tights. To the incessant vamp of the disco music pounding from five-foot-high speakers on each wall, Joanie bounced and twisted. The class leader, a woman with a beak nose, small breasts, no waist, and muscled legs, shouted out the routines. The floor shook, the walls vibrated. Joanie closed her eyes and kicked, exhaling through a tight circle of her lips. It was hard work, and she hated it. She decided right then and there that she did not need this, that she was in good enough shape until a mirror told her otherwise.

Yet she stayed with it, trying to lose herself in the routines, breathing hard, straining muscles, working up a sweat. When it was over she staggered out of the room and looked for a reward. Mary Beth was hard at work on two guys at once. For a few minutes Joanie idly watched a tennis match, then tried to figure out what she should do. It would be a shame to put on these duds just to grunt and sweat next to a pregnant woman.

Then she saw a sign for the Nautilus room, something she had never visited before. Once inside she decided it was the mirrored walls, tall, endless mirrors very much like those of a beauty salon, that had drawn her here. You could not avoid looking at yourself. Even after all these months she was used to that. She looked about, surveyed, then turned to the clutter of chrome-plated machines, the kind Hollywood stars effortlessly hefted on television as they tried to shame you into buying a club membership.

She sat down in a contraption that looked like a cross between a rowboat and a physician's examination table. She gripped two handles and started pulling and pushing. She had no idea what she was doing, and soon found it was hard to do. In a single movement her arms were spread and her legs split. She did not know whether to feel challenged or exploited.

Instead she looked in the mirrors and caught the profile of a well-built blond guy working out just behind her. His eyes met hers. In no time he was on the machine next to her. She continued to struggle, now with purpose.

Finally the blond guy, who was wearing blue satin shorts and no top and whose pectoral muscles were dotted with droplets of sweat, stopped and stared at her. She turned and stared back. He had a mole on his cheek very much like Robert Redford's, and she decided that the guy probably knew it.

"You always work out that hard?" he said.

It was not an original line, but he delivered it well. Extremely well, she thought, and she fixated on his right nipple, which seemed to have an involuntary twitch. She knew women who could fall in love with just that little nub alone.

"I play harder," she said.

"That I'd like to see," he said.

"I bet you would," she said.

It was a bum's rush no different from the traders and the clerks, the Tommy Haggartys of the world. But this came from someone outside the pits. She wavered. She had not played since Korngold, and the memory lingered.

"You drive?" she said, surprising herself.

"A silver Targa. West lot. Half hour," he said.

In half an hour she emerged from the club, her hair wet and ready, wearing Mary Beth's peach-colored velour jumpsuit. The hunk was leaning against the car, wearing a loose football jersey and a pair of white canvas pants, looking perfectly beautiful and

114

appropriately thick.

She approached her new friend. He went nothing less than 210 pounds, smelling blatantly of musk, totally sure of himself. She paused in front of him, feeling his smirk, wondering if it might not be too late to stop this foolishness. He was an appealing commodity, but did she really want to take delivery? She reached for the door of the Porsche. He reached out and pulled her to him so that her hip met his crotch. He was not wearing any underwear. They never did.

Just then a jogger ran by and the hunk momentarily paused. The jogger waved and Joanie looked at him. His face—she knew him—and then she laughed. It was Steve Stamford—SDS.

"Hey!" he exhaled, running in place. He was wearing baggy sweat pants and a Cubs T-shirt. His ribs showed through the shirt.

"Steve," she said, stepping quickly, almost too quickly, over to him. "On your way inside?" she asked.

"No," he exhaled. "Cheaper out here."

"Come on, a big gold trader like you?" she said.

He coughed and let his hands go limp by his sides as he bounced. He caught sight of the Bluto by the car.

"Miles to go before I sleep," he said.

"I'll join you," she said, and began jogging in place.

He laughed, then began running backward, wondering if she was serious.

She stayed with him, clutching a plastic bag with her clothes and her purse under her arm, raising a most bewildered look on Steve's face. She turned and waved at the hunk and his Porsche.

"Wait a minute—" Steve said, not sure of what he had interrupted, or if he wanted to. The guy by the car was big enough to squash him.

But Joanie kept going and he turned and caught up with her, out of the lot and down a side street. Moments later, with a squealing of tires and a whining roar, the Porsche hurtled by them.

"Stop," Joanie gasped.

"What was that about?" Steve said.

"A real short story," she said as they stood beneath a streetlight.

"As dramatic as it looked?" he said.

"It never is," she said, then gasped. "Do we have to run any-more?"

He laughed and shook his long legs. Joanie held her sides.

"You always do this?" she said.

"Since high school," he said. "I take it you don't run?"

"Torture," she said, and began walking with him.

A few blocks later they were in front of his loft apartment, in a building that only a few years before had been used to manufac-ture compasses and slide rules but now featured four stories of light and space and two and one-half baths per loft.

"I'd ask you up for a drink but I don't have a Porsche," he said.

"A beer will do," she said.

"One night, maybe," he said. "But this is one boy who's gotta be in the pits tomorrow with both eyes open."

Joanie curled her lower lip.

"A glass of water?" she asked.

He laughed.

"Sure. I'm being a jerk," he said.

Inside he got Joanie the beer she originally suggested.

"Two minutes and I'm back smelling a whole lot better," he said, and disappeared.

Joanie looked around. The loft was authentic urban-mod-ern — an expanse of bare brick walls, green plants, varnished oak floors, and the latest in security devices. The only interior walls were those of the bathroom and closet areas, which had been placed in the middle of the apartment in order to separate the liv-ing room and galley kitchen in front from the huge open bed-room in back.

The apartment was noticeably clean and ordered, Joanie noted, but not sterile. The walls were lined with oak shelves of hardback books, and hung with huge, chrome-framed prints of Ben Shahn and *Spy*'s courtroom caricatures. The furniture was a mixture of antique oak chairs and tables, a white pine hutch, a beige, overstuffed, corduroy sofa, a hall tree with polished brass hooks covered by an assortment of baseball hats.

Joanie could hear the shower, then a rattle of drawers before Stamford emerged dripping and dressed in a gray warm-up suit.

"I love your place," she said.

"Tenement gentrification," he said.

"Huh?"

"Building used to be an empty factory nobody wanted. A few sharpies bought it for bird feed, called it a loft, and sold the apartments for a ransom," he said.

"You bought," she said, wishing she had not.

He shrugged. "That I did."

He lifted a glass of club soda and a wedge of lime.

"To real estate values," he said.

She drank from her beer and wandered over to the dining room table and its clutter of papers.

"Mind if I eat?" he said.

"Don't chew with your mouth open," she said.

He put a couple of red snapper fillets under the broiler, sliced a huge tomato, and poured himself more soda.

"Want some? Fresh from Burhop's."

"Sure," she said.

A few minutes later he handed her a plate and they sat down across from each other at the table.

"What would you be doing if I weren't here?" she asked.

"Having two helpings," he said.

She smiled and ate. It tasted wonderful.

He motioned at the work on the table, the contents of his briefcase.

"A lot of second-guessing," he said.

Before him lay a printout of his gold trades for the day, his charts, a pocket calculator, and assorted research bulletins and market materials.

"Great," she said, nibbling at her tomato.

"Not when you see my trades," he said.

"No, I mean the whole thing — you doing it like this. It's really impressive."

"You're not serious," he said.

"Oh, sure. I've started charting myself — mostly beans and Korngold's trades. Just for myself. 'Cept I don't know how to crunch it. I'd love to see how you do it."

Then she stopped short.

"I'm sorry," she said. "You've got a lot of work to do and I'm in the way."

Steve looked at her, wiping his mouth with his napkin.

"You track Korngold? Your own charts?" he said.

"Sure. This is my dream. This is what I'm going to do some-day."

"Amazing," Steve said. "Simply amazing. A girl like you finding this interesting. It's a new age."

"Yup," she echoed.

"Of course, you know how most of the guys feel about women traders," Steve said.

"Like a case of herpes," she said.

He nodded and pushed aside his plate.

"You've got work here," she said quickly.

She got up to leave.

"So do it with me," he said. "Tell me where I go wrong."

"Good luck," she said. "But I'll watch."

She pulled her chair next to him. He cleared the dishes, arranged the homework in front of them, and once again sat down. In a moment he became aware of her presence, the natural scent of her skin and her hair, the blond hair on her brown arms, her thin fingers and clear, polished nails. God, she was pretty, he thought.

He began to review his trades, explaining each one out loud, analyzing and retrading it, getting a clear fix on what he would have done, could have done, should have done, and did. It had been a decent day, not mind-boggling, but on the plus side. He had made a few hundred bucks. But—that big word—he could have done better.

Then he went to his charts. They were graphs of price, volume, short interest, and several other ingredients of the day-by-day path of the bond market. He had an orderly, methodical mind, keen on detail and minute fluctuation. He paid close attention to the numbers and what they told him, of resistance, peaks, and intensity.

Joanie listened closely, questioning only occasionally, impressed and a little intimidated by the amount of study Stamford apparently put into his trading. She had only seen the floor side of it, the action in the pits which often seemed to be guided only by emotion and guts, not carefully researched strategies.

When she said as much he replied, "Yeah, I get all this analysis together and then I get in the pit and trade on the basis of which

118

side of my butt itches."

He flipped his pencil onto the table and looked up at Joanie. It was after nine.

"Some fun, eh?" he said.

"No — I mean, yes. This is terrific."

"Not really. Just anal retentive."

She looked sideways at him.

"I'm a paper shuffler. A drone. It's the best I can do until I learn how to trade."

He pushed his chair back. She took the cue and got up to leave.

In the few minutes remaining to his night he'd read — a biography of Teddy Roosevelt — before going to bed at 9:30. Seven and one-half hours later he would begin the hard business of another trading day.

"I'm glad I shamed you into letting me watch," Joanie said.

He looked into her green eyes, the young, smooth, fearless face of a kid. He brushed a knuckle over her velour sleeve.

"I'm glad I rescued you tonight," he said. "You can do a lot better, you know."

She smiled slightly. She knew.

Chapter Four

That night Brian had the money — $1,407.25. Subtracting Valukas's $100 commission — the trade cost Valukas only a few bucks but he charged Brian $50 for the risk then suggested he throw in a $50 gratuity for future consideration — and Rhonda's $200, his total profit came to over $1,100. In cash, eleven Ben Frankies, lying against his palm like velvet.

"Put it in your pocket before it bites ya," said Valukas.

"Already has," said Tommy.

Brian folded the bills over his index finger like guys did it. Most of them were delivery boys — booze or cakes — or gas station attendants at the end of a shift. Except that their wads were fins and sawbucks, not fat Franklins. And Benny was a hell of a guy.

From the pay phone inside the Sign of the Trader he called Rhonda at work. She was a catalogue order clerk at Montgomery Ward, so if she was on a customer it could be days before she picked up.

"Brian?" she said. She'd been on break.

"Yeah, it's me, Ronnie," he said. He spoke slowly, his voice just barely audible. Rhonda would buy it.

"I gotta see ya tonight."

"We have a date anyway, silly goose," she said.

"Oh yeah? Well, don't stand me up."

There was a moment of silence.

"Huh?"

"You up to somethin' funny?"

"You hear me laughin'?"

"O-o-o-h, n-o-o-o-o, Brian," she groaned. "It's the money, ain't it. God, if my mother finds out —"

"Forget about your mother! And don't make me sit in the kitchen lookin' at yer grandma's combat boots while you're upstairs."

"She feeds you cookies and you eat like a piggy."

"So, Okay, Ronnie. We're on."

"Good-bye, Brian."

When he drove up she was sitting on the front porch steps next to her father. He was aiming the hose on the grass, smoking a Marlboro, a can of Old Style sweating at his side. Brian let the Pontiac idle, which was so rough the whole chassis shook, and got out just enough to lift his head over the car's roof.

"What say, Mr. Rooney," he yelled.

Rhonda's father lifted the hose in his direction and rolled the cigarette between his teeth. He worked for a company that made doorjambs.

Rhonda walk-skipped to the car, reached inside to open the door, and slid over to his side. A half block down the street she leaned up and kissed him on the cheek.

"It's the money, isn't it?" she said. "But it's okay, Brian. You don't have to feel, like, pressure to give it back."

He looked at her as if to take complete offense.

"It's okay, Brian. It really is."

He stopped at the end of her street, squealed a hard right onto Cicero Avenue and down-shifted, causing her to lurch forward.

"You're right," he said, staring straight ahead, his jaw hard. "It *is* the money."

Then he pulled off into an abandoned Clark Super 100 station, put the shift in neutral, and reached into his shirt pocket.

"Here's your two bills," he said, holding them between two fingers.

She took them, her eyes wide.

"And here's *fi-i-ive* more!" he sang.

He held another bound wad in front of her nose.

"Brian!!!!!" she screamed, and hugged him.

It was just about better, he thought then and there, than anything on "The Price Is Right."

"Tell me all *about* it," she said, kissing the cash.

"Ain't much to tell. Money supply came in way low last Friday. Monday's opening was a sure thing. We went long at the bell and rode the pop for a few ticks. Took our profit plus some change and got out."

"Brian, that is so mega," Rhonda exclaimed, reaching up to

121

kiss him. "I could *die* on this."

He kissed her back and slid his right hand inside her blouse and directly onto her boob. He squeezed it like a sponge.

"God, money's such a turn-on," she moaned, thrusting her breast into his hand.

They groped for a few minutes more before Brian pulled back into traffic.

"Now we go someplace special and celebrate," he said.

He drove north on Cicero, a four-lane thoroughfare that cut through the heart of Chicago's southwest side neighborhoods. On the left was Midway Airport, and then a tired strip of small motels and cocktail lounges. Most had been built after World War II to accommodate traffic at what was then Chicago's main air terminal. They went to seed when O'Hare took all but a smattering of daily flights. At Forty-fourth he turned onto the Adlai Stevenson Expressway toward downtown.

"This is just too much, Brian. In hundreds yet," Rhonda said. She unfolded the bills and laid them on top of each other.

"A C-note down there is rabbit shit," he said. "Guys use 'em for tips."

"How did you do it?"

"I told ya."

"I'm supposed to *understand* all that shit?"

"Hey, I do," he said.

She fingered the bills, smoothing each corner.

"Mr. Big Business," she mumbled, gazing at the money. Then she lifted her head. "Could you do it again?" she said softly.

"No guarantees," he said, driving with his wrist on the wheel and his hand hanging loosely. "But, then, that *is* the name of the game."

They drove in the center lane, the rumble of the Pontiac at sixty miles per hour almost too much to talk over.

Then Rhonda turned to him, swinging her knees onto the seat and into his thighs.

"Okay. Here goes," she said "What say I take the two hundred I loaned you —" she counted the bills out on her lap — "one puppy, two puppies, and then I take one hundred more, like that, for a blanket to keep those puppies warm. And put them all back beddy-bye in my savings account. *God,* that'll look so funny in the book: out on Friday and back in on Tuesday. Then I give four hundred right *back* to you, Mr. Lucky Strike, to make us a whole bundle more."

She kissed the roll and stuck it in his shirt pocket.

He flicked his finger across his nose and set a pose.

"Smart broad," he said.

She hugged him and closed her eyes.

The Stevenson Expressway took them past salvage yards, sprawling truck terminals, and the Campbell Soup factory. Then Brian followed the cloverleaf ramp onto the Dan Ryan as it passed to the west of the Loop, through Hubbard Cave and onto the Kennedy. By this time rush-hour traffic had thinned into the merging, relentless flow of cars and trucks that coursed through the expressway system every hour of the day and night.

Brian got off at Western Avenue and went straight north. The used car lots began at Belmont, dozens of them promising, in Spanish and English, an instant ride with instant credit: Walk-in. Drive-out. At Foster the secondhand lots gave way to block after block of new car dealerships, foreign and domestic, trucks, jeeps, vans, campers, and a snowblower thrown in at no extra cost if you buy before the end of the month. The avenue was a bazaar of flashing lights, neon signs, and hand-painted exhortations on showroom windows promising deals too good to be true, prices never again this low, rebates, sellathons, balloons for the kids, autographed photos of the Chicago Bears.

"Where are we *goin'*?" Rhonda said.

"This place is somethin' special," Brian said. "Trust me."

The restaurant was called Sally's Stage, and from the outside it looked like little more than a converted storefront. They were met by a girl wearing a derby hat, a red-and-white-striped jacket and short-shorts, black tights, and roller skates. She skated them to a table in an open room with a raised stage at one end and ringed by an oval track. She glided off onto the track and was re-placed by a waitress in the same outfit who gave them a menu in the shape of a beer stein. The water glasses were jelly jars. People at other tables were eating fried chicken and cheeseburgers from wicker baskets. The sound system belted out "Camptown Races" on a honky-tonk piano and a screen on the stage showed a silent Keystone Kops movie.

Rhonda beamed, craning her neck to look all around the place. Her shoulder-length light brown hair was parted in the middle and perfectly feathered back off her forehead and cheeks. By her wedding day she wanted it to be long enough so she could wear it up with sprigs of baby's breath.

Brian badly wanted a beer, but they'd card him if he ordered one and he didn't need that. They took a pitcher of cola instead. After the waitress plunked it down on the table she scampered off. The house lights went down, the movie screen went blank, and the stage lit up and came alive with a huge pipe organ pumping out "Toot Toot Tootsie Goodbye." A chorus line of waiters and waitresses sang a raucous welcome to Sally's Stage, then scrambled offstage and into the kitchen to pick up their orders.

More acts followed: a juggling trombone player, a magician who swallowed dozens of Ping-Pong balls, a dog who howled along with its singing master. Then the organ belted out some more ancient hits and the crowd sang along thanks to lyrics flashed on the movie screen. Rhonda sang her heart out, opening her mouth wide and applauding wildly after each number. Brian kept a lazy grin plastered across his face and mumbled a few lyrics.

The best was yet to come, or so Brian had been told. Not only did the waitress bring his bacon double cheeseburger and onion rings but the organ player gave way to the West Rogers Park Nursing Home and Convalescent Center Jug and Kazoo Band. They called themselves the Doo-das, three codgers in white shirts and bow ties, and two toothless crones in bathrobes, all of them wearing green high-top tennis shoes. They strummed, hooted, and stomped their way through a medley of awful songs that put the crowd on the floor. Brian laughed so hard he choked.

On the way home Rhonda burrowed into his neck and put her hand inside his belt. Her nails tickled the hair around his navel. He hated it when she did that because his hard-on got so enraged it threatened to put out the dome light.

"I'm gonna be rich I wanna be rich with you," she cooed, and pushed her hand in even further.

He smiled and drove. He had to get all the way back to the southwest side before his purple-headed monster would find relief.

Chapter Five

Each morning Steve Stamford rode the Ravenswood elevated train, the same one Joanie had taken to the health club, to work. He got off at the Wells and Jackson stop and hopped down the seventy-five-year-old iron stairs to the Board of Trade Building and its side entrance. The route was convenient and calculated, a way for Steve to avoid LaSalle Street.

He could tell himself otherwise, that LaSalle Street was just another strip of Loop concrete. But he knew that the street named after the French explorer who was murdered by his own men was a sanctuary of capitalism, that vaunted economic system in which murder was one of the lesser crimes.

Chicago's LaSalle Street was home to multinational banks with billions in assets, institutions housed in buildings of impregnable granite with doors that gleamed with polished brass, floors of Italian marble, lobbies paneled in oak and burled mahogany, sixty-foot hand-knotted rugs from Persia, Tiffany fixtures, crystal chandeliers.

Above that, on certain upper floors, were private quarters complete with sumptuous dining clubs that catered to bankers' tastes with fresh fillet of sole, Wisconsin rack of lamb, Ugandan coffees, and dry French wines.

Steve Stamford knew all this because on many occasions he had been inside these banks (though not their dining rooms) to do business. It was not his personal business, not layered deals and complicated transactions, but business that involved little guys with problems. Not so many years earlier he had been a lawyer for the people. He had pled for extensions on auto loans and installment charges, fought foreclosures and evictions. He argued with petulant loan officers who represented hidden trusts, those invisible abominations set up to insulate creditors from debtors, landlords from tenants, the moneyed from the

125

penniless. He usually lost, or, at the very best, gained some time.

As the son of the late Samuel Stamford, of Noblesville, Indiana, a slight, pale, thoroughly decent man who spent most of his life lawyering to farmers and small-town merchants, Steve's mission seemed altogether appropriate. Though his father barely made enough money to varnish the shingle outside his office, Steve idolized him. The practice of the law was a calling, a solemn duty, his father said, not a means of gaining wealth. Many of his father's clients never paid him — although Steve did not learn that until his father's death — yet they were never deprived of his services. He was a town saint. People in Noblesville used to say that the only thing Gregory Peck in *To Kill a Mockingbird* had on Sam Stamford was a little height.

His father's example, and his death of a heart attack at age fifty-seven, motivated Steve to pursue a law degree at Indiana University. He passed with high honors, and, in his only break with tradition, decided not to practice in Noblesville. Chicago was five hours north by car, and a different world as far as the law was concerned. He got a job in the public defender's office. Samuel Stamford's response would have been one of characteristic calm, and unabashed pride.

After a few years in the PD's office, Steve joined a storefront legal clinic, an arm of a feisty neighborhood organization born of the protest movement of the 1960s. The neighborhood was a tired, run-down area just south of Wrigley Field, populated largely by scared Hispanics and brash, idealistic white kids like himself. They were young, loud, broke (as long as they did not tap their trust funds), full of philosophies and political rancor born of Vietnam, the murder of Black Panther leader Fred Hampton, and the chaos of the 1968 Democratic National Convention. They displayed portraits of Che Guevara and Abbie Hoffman side-by-side. They fought City Hall, and LaSalle Street, and their emissary was the lanky beanpole of a kid from Indiana named Stamford. He was a petitioner, a crier from the wilderness of people with weak voices, an outsider looking for a break, a pass, and, if all else failed, maybe even a smidgen of justice.

On those forays downtown and into the jaws of the oppressor, Steve often walked the length of LaSalle Street, starting at the first businessman's bank on Wacker Drive and ending with the giant Federal Reserve Bank at Jackson Boulevard. Along the way he tried to make eye contact with the men in the gray flannel suits (his was corduroy with elbow patches), just to see if he could detect any life in them. He never did.

At LaSalle and Jackson he paused, giving but a glance to the Board of Trade Building. It, too, was gray like the granite of the banks, but gray limestone, a softer shade, perhaps, or just a more deceptive one. Forty-four stories up was a conical tower, and atop that, a statue of Ceres, the daughter of Saturn and the goddess of wheat. This was the commodity market, originally created, Steve knew, for the good of farmers and the management of their crops. He chuckled at the pretense, for now the noble Chicago Board of Trade was the domain of speculators and gamblers, the same ones exposed years ago in the fiction of Frank Norris, commodity traders devoted not to sodbusters or breadmakers but to the good of their pocketbooks.

That it took place under the aegis of Ceres was an appropriate touch, Steve thought, for an institution now based more on myth than reality. But in those days he seldom gave the Board of Trade more notice than that. He made his way back to Wells Street and the elevated train for the ride back to his impoverished neighborhood.

That was years ago, in another life. Nowadays he rode the same train but headed for a different destination, a different state of mind, a whole different philosophy. His briefcase was filled not with pleadings and petitions but with market data. He was now one of them, one of the rats in the nest of capitalism, and the best he could do was sidle into a secondary entrance lest the normally impassive gaze of Ceres turn into a smirk.

At her first chance the next day Joanie lingered by the gold pit. She did not immediately spot Steve among the traders. When she did she laughed to herself. He was a good head taller than most of them. He looked like a dandelion above the grass, his face stern, pinched, concentrating on the numbers.

He was a quiet, measured trader, dealing in one-or two-lots at a time, refusing to be drawn into bidding panics, yet unafraid to

127

bellow his trades when the time appeared right. To Joanie he was the personification of the calculations and graphs she had seen on his table the night before. He did not fidget or grimace, bite his nails or banter. He did not laugh or jostle or scribble doodles on the shoulders of other traders. That also meant, she knew all too well, that he probably did not fart or belch or tell lewd jokes about hermaphroditic nuns. Remarkable indeed, she thought.

His lips moved slightly as he studied his cards, always studying, Joanie observed. He did not seem to be in agony like so many of the others, nor did he seem to be enjoying himself. In the few minutes she watched him, and later at intervals throughout the day, Steve never once noticed her. She kind of wished he had. She had felt his touch on her sleeve last night, felt it right through to the bone.

For the rest of the day Joanie was consumed by her own work, the constant needs of the traders she assisted. It wasn't until an hour after the end of trading that afternoon that she saw him in the office. He was sipping a can of grapefruit juice and reading the sports page.

"How'd I do?" she said, standing next to him.

"Huh? Oh, hi," he said.

"I make any money for you today?"

He sighed.

"This is not the face of a winner," he said.

"Bad?"

"A wash. One for them, one for me."

"McGinniss calls that slow death," she said.

"Comforting," he said.

He raised the can of juice to his lips. She exhaled, realizing that was not what he wanted to hear.

"You think I should take up jogging?" she said.

He scanned her up and down.

"You don't smoke. Weight's perfect. You're under thirty. No family history of high blood pressure or heart disease — I'd say it's jog or die," he said.

"And when I'm thirty-five will I exist on broiled fish and tomatoes?"

"What a life," he said.

"You gonna run tonight?"

"Always do."

"Can I watch?"

"Lord," he said. "Am I being propositioned?"

"You can say no, but don't," she said, bending down on one knee and thumping his arm with her fist.

"Watch? You don't want to share the misery?"

"I'll hand you oranges and cups of water like they do in the marathons," she said.

They settled on the time and place, nodding and trading easy lines.

Their banter went unnoticed by others in the office, except for Tommy Haggarty. He bit the inside of his lip and wondered what the beanpole gold trader had going for him.

Chapter Six

At noon that day the pits were quiet — Korngold was away for the week — and Tommy talked Brian into a game of liar's poker. When times were slack in the pits everybody turned to some other form of gambling, usually idle but costly wagers on golf games, ball scores, and horse races. Traders at the Board of Trade once wagered more than $100,000 on whether or not one of their members, a former professional football quarterback, could stand at home plate in Comiskey Park and throw a ball into the left field bleachers in five tries. (He could not, but did so on the seventh try.) Liar's poker was Tommy's favorite. He played it with dollar bills, using bills' serial numbers as poker hands. Unused trading cards were nickel chips.

"Raise you ten and show 'em," said Tommy.

Brian studied his bills and, working up his version of a poker face, grimaced.

Just then Mary Beth tapped Tommy on the shoulder.

"Phone call at the desk," she said.

Tommy shot her a look of pain.

"Play the hand, Boyer," he snapped.

Brian suddenly grinned and displayed five M's — a rare and unbeatable flush.

"Christ almighty," Tommy said, flipped his chips at him and went to get the phone.

"Yeh," he barked into the receiver.

"This is Mr. Clark," the caller said.

Tommy momentarily gagged. His hand began to shake and he looked hurriedly around him to see if anyone was watching or listening. He frantically tried to remember what he had been told to say.

"Sure, uh, no problem," he replied, then, remembering, added, "That can be done."

The caller gave him a two-digit number. Tommy fumbled for a pencil, even though his pocket was jammed with them, and jotted it on a trading card. He hung up. Then he sprinted down the aisle and up into the bond pit. He was shaking, breathing in gasps, yet in the midst of traders who shook and gasped as a matter of routine, only Tommy was aware of his own misery.

At 3:45 that afternoon, after Tommy had attended to his totals, he left the building. A stiff wind off the lake buffeted his clothing. It was a cool, brilliant August day, the kind Chicago never gets credit for, but as he walked he began to sweat. He walked east on Jackson Boulevard to State Street, then north to the Palmer House Hotel. In the arcade below the lobby, he glanced at the number on his card. On an elevator he pressed the same number.

When he reached the floor he went to the stairs and walked down one flight. Were he not so damn nervous this would be fun, he thought. He kept telling himself that. The exit door on that floor, normally locked to anyone inside the stairwell, was wedged open by a matchbook. Tommy picked it up and walked into the hallway, letting the door close behind him. He went around the corner to the door at the very end of the hallway. He made a single knock. It was exactly four o'clock.

The door was opened by a short, brown-haired man in a lima-bean green sport coat and a paisley tie. The guy looked to be no older than Tommy. He nodded Tommy inside, an antiseptic room with two made beds. Sitting at a marble-topped table beneath a swag lamp was another man, also young, with a thick moustache that appeared to be waxed at the ends, a dark blue velour sweater, jeans with creases down the center of the legs, and cowboy boots. He reminded Tommy of Rollie Fingers.

"No problems?" said the sport coat, motioning him to a chair at the table. He didn't remind Tommy of anyone.

Tommy sat down.

"I'm Ben. This is Reed," said the sport coat.

Reed reached across the table for a thin micro-cassette recorder and placed it between himself and Tommy. He stared up at Tommy with heavy-lidded, uninterested eyes.

The sport coat pulled a padded chair away from the dresser and swung it in front of him. He straddled the seat, and leaned forward against the chair's back. The whole scene, Tommy thought, was just like something on television, with him the only one who did not know his lines.

"Now," said the sport coat. "Just like you were told down in Miami. We get together every so often for little talks. You talk. We listen. Gossip, rumor, all kinds of goodies."

"Like what?" Tommy said.

"You tell us."

"Okay . . ." he started. "There's some shit down there."

"No shit," said the sport coat.

"Hell, whattaya want!" Tommy said, looking first at the guy in the velour whose eyes had not moved from him, then to the sport coat.

"We already got your ass, Tommy," said the sport coat. "You want it back you tell us who does what, where, and how much. Don't leave anything out."

"Candy?" Tommy said.

"Good place to start."

"Guys do it in the john. Before trading. They do it on the top of the tissue paper holder. Cut lines with their badges. They blow with bills or Bic pens. Hollowed out. Some guys put it in those nasal inhalers and do it right out on the floor. A couple guys are so coked up all the time they call 'em Sneezy and Dopey."

"Who's Sneezy?"

"Some guy. Wheat trader."

"What's his name?"

"I dunno."

"Who's Dopey?"

"Another wheat trader. No, T-bills — I don't know him neither."

"Who passes?"

"Who doesn't? Guys drop bindles like chewing gum."

"A bindle?" asked the sport coat.

"Cellophane. Them envelopes you get from stamp collector stores. Holds about a gram."

"Who passes?"

"Who doesn't?"

The velour suddenly slapped the tabletop.

"One fuckin' rule right off the bat, asshole," the velour said

132

with a voice somewhere in the range of Bobby of the Oak Ridge Boys. "Don't answer a question with a question."

"Who passes?" the sport coat said.

"Runners, clerks — whoever's around."

"On the trading floors?"

"Sure. But all over. I seen traders cut commissions for a bindle. I seen them try to get some big accounts by layin' heavy shit in on the deal. Especially guys in from the coasts. Throw in a limo and a broad and that'll just about do it."

"All snow?" said the sport coat.

"Snow?"

"Cocaine."

"Yeah. Mostly."

"Crack?"

"Some."

"What else?"

"Weed, if you wanna count that. Lot of ludes. You fly, you land. I heard some guys cut coke with smack. You get too wired if you do straight coke so they cut it."

"Heroin?"

"Yeah."

"You've seen guys doing heroin?"

"No. I *heard* lot of 'em do."

"You *heard*."

"Yeah."

"No, Tommy. No 'I *heards.'* "

The sport coat got up from the chair and went over by the TV. He absently flicked the knob.

Without looking at Tommy, he said, "Give me five names."

"Huh?"

"Five guys. Users, suppliers, big buyers. Five in all."

"Jesus Christ —"

"No, Tommy. Not him."

"Ah, fuck. Names of who?"

"You heard me, Tommy." The sport coat returned to the chair.

"Let's not bullshit around. We already *know* what's down there. Give us *names*. We're your friends, Tommy. Otherwise your ass is back in Miami looking at possession, maybe accessory to murder — which in Florida is enough to *fry*. Them rednecks

133

love to see smoke come out of guys' ears. So give us some *names.*"

"Bojira. Keogh. Panagakis. Lefferts. Lipinski," Tommy said.

The sport coat smiled.

"You been practicing," he said.

He reached inside his jacket and took out a business card.

"Here's a number for you. Memorize it, then burn the card. Use the number when you have to. You get in trouble with any-body—the cops, guys on the trading floor, you call. You got something to tell us, you call and we'll meet."

He got up and went toward the door.

"We're your real friends, Tommy. Don't forget that. Keep your ears open. Stay loose."

Tommy looked at him, then at the velour who was picking his teeth with a fingernail.

"That's all? We done?"

"You ever been wired, Tommy?" the sport coat said.

"Aw shit," Tommy groaned.

So what had he done? Tommy wound his way down State Street, not walking but ambling, not seeing the gray stones of the mall or the people who jostled him. He saw only that room in the Miami airport and the vague images of the DEA agents. That had been months ago, so long that he had even begun to forget the whole episode, something not easy in light of the fact that he not only attended Rick's funeral but also had to endure two hours of Rick's old man pacing in front of him and shouting, demand-ing an explanation. The only real explanation, Tommy said, was that Rick was dead and he was not. He tried to talk Rick out of buying coke but could not. He had no idea Rick swallowed it. It was the story he had been told to tell. He clung to it until Rick's old man gave up. The Feds in Miami backed him up. Which was convenient.

Until today. That phone call. Their hooks were planted and deep, a stab he could almost feel as he walked.

He had no idea of what he would do, how he would go about his job on the floor, whom he would tell (if anyone). He wondered what the two assholes back in the hotel room would do when the five names he had given them came back blank. Five guys on his chess team in high school. He wondered how long it would take them to find him if he up and skipped, just took what money he had and got on a plane.

He stopped at a vendor and bought a hot pretzel. He pulled it apart, shoving pieces of the warm dough into his mouth, still walking. He turned and went across to the west side of the street, cutting in front of the Monroe Street CTA stairway. Sitting on the railing were two black guys, one with a Walkman plugged in his ears, the other with lazy eyes and a Pirates baseball cap. As he approached, the one in the Pirates hat opened a palm to reveal a joint.

"Reef?" he mumbled.

"Go to hell," Tommy said, and passed by.

He kept walking and thinking when it suddenly struck him. He could nail those two spades. If they were selling a joint, they no doubt have much more, much heavier stuff. And they had hit on him, Tom Haggarty, not just a guy on the street, but somebody with contacts. The Feds. DEA. Hell, for all practical purposes he was an agent himself. Undercover. Two eagle eyes waiting to nail the world.

He rolled that around a little. He tossed the pretzel paper onto the curb. Or he was a snitch? A two-bit stool? What the newspapers called an informant?

At the corner of Jackson he looked at his watch. He had a racquet ball game at six, and that was more than an hour away, so he decided to walk back to the Board of Trade and see who was still around. He headed into the Sign of the Trader, the in-house saloon on the first floor, gave a glance at the bar itself and at the crowd at the tables. There were people he knew, but first he went for the bathroom.

The urinals were open, but he did not like urinals. It was something that went way back to the eighth grade and that he did not like to talk about. He went for a stall.

Putting his hand out he pushed the door. It slammed into the back side of a guy who was standing inside. The impact jolted Tommy's arm up to his shoulder.

"Dammit!" the guy yelled and wheeled around to face Tommy.

He was a trader, a thick-necked, dark-skinned guy, Greek maybe, whom Tommy had seen in the bean pit, though he was

135

not sure. What he was sure of was what he saw in the few seconds it took him to react — the guy's moustache looking like he had just eaten a powdered donut.

Tommy put his palms up in front of his chest and backed away. "Sorry. Sorry," he said.

The guy stood and scowled.

"Asswipe," he hissed.

Regardless of his aching bladder, Tommy hustled outside. But as soon as the low light of the bar hit him, he reconsidered.

Who's he callin' asswipe? he thought. I could nail the fucker. *Ought* to.

He strode over to the bar and ordered a beer. Damn straight, he thought, and drank half the stein even though it made him have to piss even worse. Then he sat down on a stool and turned toward the washroom. He would look the guy right in his lights.

Make your move, chump.

Chapter Seven

On Wednesday of that week Brian spotted Marty Valukas hunched over a screen.

"Where's it at?" Brian said.

"Two seventy-two and a puddle of piss," said Marty.

"Huh!" exclaimed Brian. "Deece bonds at two seventy-two!"

"Cripes," snorted Valukas.

"S and P's," said Ira Roth, not looking up from his ledgers.

"Get me in bonds, Marty," Brian said.

Valukas looked up sideways from his crouch.

"Why? The market's flat."

"So?"

"So where's the play?"

"A repo maybe."

"Listen to you, Mister Bond Expert."

He stood up with his hands on hips and faced Brian.

"You even know what a system repo is, Boyer?"

"Sure. I mean, it happens all the time. Just get me in again, okay?"

Valukas shook his head.

"So okay. You want in, I'll get you in."

He turned back to the screen and exhaled loudly, then pounded the desk with his fist.

"I'm *dyin'* with these things," he moaned.

At the end of the day Valukas tossed a card at Brian.

"You're in at seventy-three ten."

Brian nodded, looking at the card. Then he hustled over to a screen, quickly looking for the closing bond price. It was 73-8.

He slapped the card against his thigh.

"Marty!" he yelled. "What the hell—"

Valukas wasn't around, and the others ignored him. Haggarty came up and took the card out of Brian's hands.

"You're down a couple a ticks. So big deal."

137

"So what if it opens lower?"

"Put in a stop."

"Where?"

"Come on, Boyer. You go long, you go short. You get in, you get out. What is this—kindergarten?"

Brian stood there, his mouth open.

He went home that night worrying about the price of bonds. All night he worried about the price of bonds. The next morning he caught up with Marty Valukas and told him to sell the contract.

"If I can," Marty said.

"Whattya mean?"

"Hey, Boyer. I'm doin' you a favor. I gotta trade my own account. I'll get you out when I can."

Marty turned and headed for the door, then turned back to face Brian.

"If you can't handle it, Boyer, what the fuck you get in for?" he said.

At mid-morning on the next day Valukas sold Brian's contract at 73-5. A loss of five ticks. Just over $160.

"I was lucky to get that," Marty said. "I need the cash plus my costs by tomorrow morning."

"What—I pay commission when I lose?" Brian said.

At that Marty, Mary Beth, Joanie, and three traders turned and glared at him as if he had just knifed a puppy.

At the end of the day Brian pulled Tommy Haggarty off to the side.

"You get me some stuff, Tommy," he said.

"Like what? Box seats, rubbers?"

"You know, some lines."

"Never touch the stuff, my man. Don't know anybody who does. Destroys brain cells and mucous membranes," Tommy said, impatiently slapping a deck of trading cards against the back of his hand.

"C'mon, Tommy."

"Hey, get a load a you, Boyer. Come in here on the Archer Avenue bus, didn't know your ass from the front door, and now you're hitting me for candy."

"You're a real asshole, Tommy."

"Try my best."

In his retreat Brian bumped into Joanie, who had witnessed his little repartee with Tommy, and knocked her can of grapefruit juice to the carpet. He dropped to his knees to retrieve it. Joanie took it from him with two fingers, then she dropped it into the waste can.

She smiled weakly, her version of a scold. Brian retreated without a word. She followed him.

"Walk me to the john," she said, nodding toward the office door.

Brian followed. For him, Joanie had always been a dream. They had started with the firm together, but that was all. Joanie was a natural. She managed Korngold's cards so well that people said she could trade for him if she had to. Joanie with her long, blond hair, her smile, the way she carried herself that was somehow very different from the other girls, that slight, yet sweet scent that accompanied her.

"You're asking for trouble, Brian," Joanie said once they were out of the office. "Those guys are sucking you in. For starters, don't buy what Tommy's selling. Just don't get into it."

"Aw, shit . . ." Brian began.

"You know what I'm saying," Joanie went on.

"And for closers, you shouldn't be trading. No *way* should you be trading. It's not a fair game, I don't care how much you scored on your first try."

She turned and walked backward down the long corridor, facing him with her arms crossed.

"You know the game. It's *hard* to make it. I don't care what trader you take, he loses most of the time. I know, I add up the numbers," she said.

He listened, looking at her, then looking away.

"But everything's cool with them, right? Big dealers. Talk your ear off about the big numbers. But ask them about taking gas. Ask them about all the times they get wiped."

She stopped and leaned against the wall just next to the door to the women's room. Her stern, unwavering stare made him self-conscious.

"You know what I'm talking about, Brian. You're a nice kid but you're gonna get clobbered. We've both seen guys break down and cry. You know, how they come out of the john with puke on their shirts. The guys on the floor begging their buddies to lend them cash."

Joanie paused as a pair of traders approached, then passed, one of them looking back at her.

"This is my stop," she said, nodding toward the unmarked door.

Brian smiled feebly at her, wanting to say something. He looked at the smooth skin at her collar, the few stray strands of blond hair along her temples. He wanted to touch them.

"Just stop it, okay? Just do your work and learn and take your paycheck home. You'll be a lot better off than most of those clowns," she said.

She reached out and hooked a finger in his shirt pocket and tugged. Then she turned, unlocked the restroom door, and disappeared.

Brian stood there wanting to follow her, feeling somewhat relieved, very sheepish, and totally in love.

It took only until the following week for Joanie's admonition to wear off. Bent on recovering his loss, infected with the bug of trading, Brian took on another bond contract. He did it on the basis of a hunch of his own. He had begun to take note of scheduled federal repurchase moves—repos—the large-scale buying and selling of Treasury bonds by the government in order to manage their accounts. Each repo, Brian saw, brought a whirlwind of activity into the pit, usually fluctuating prices by several ticks up or down.

On the morning of just such a scheduled repo he had Marty get him in. He named his price, writing out a limit order and a stop, and told Valukas to get him out at any profit he could manage.

"Aren't we getting sophisticated," said Marty upon viewing the order.

"When the shoeshine boy gets in, it's time to get out," said Dave Beston, a Ginnie Mae trader standing nearby.

Valukas sniffed, then turned to Brian.

"Just have your cash ready," he said, "win *or* lose."

At the approximate time of the fed repo, Brian joined the crowd on the bridge between the bond and the T-bill pits. He was already perspiring. Suddenly a roar emerged from the far left of the bond pit, the domain of the biggest locals and brokers. They began dealing huge lots, spurred by the fed, then goosed by their own trades. The rest of the pit followed on their heels, and the tick moved.

Brian's heart raced as he watched the board and the pit simultaneously. He was long, praying the price would shoot up once again. It did just the opposite, falling like a ball off a table, the tick skipping downward — ten, twelve, eighteen — then holding, then falling once again.

Brian's mouth dropped open and he began to gasp, witnessing a horror worse than anything he had imagined, feeling in that devastating moment that he wanted to scream, to wrench his head from its socket, then, as the reality of the price drop sunk in, to vomit.

After a half hour, but what seemed to Brian like an eternity, the action subsided and the price held. At the close of trading it was far below its opening level. Brian walked away from the bond pit, his head spinning, trying to calculate his loss. He was sweating heavily now, and breathing in gasps, as if he had just sprinted two blocks in a downpour.

At the first chance he could he sought out Marty Valukas. He found him standing at the elevator, smoking and staring at his shoes. He looked as if he'd just been in a fight. When Brian approached he said nothing, and Brian followed him onto the car.

"We all got killed," Marty said, his voice barely audible. "We were all long and we got whipsawed."

"I had a stop—" Brian began.

"Fuck your stop. Tick went right through it. I couldn't get you out."

"What?!!!?" Brian exclaimed. "You mean I'm still in?"

"Yeah. I'll get you out at the opening," Marty said.

"I'm still in? I'm still holding?"

"I told ya I'd get you out at the opening."

"But it could open lower. It could keep goin' down!"

"I'll get you out, dammit!"

The car stopped and Valukas stepped out, looking through his cards and his fills, leaving Brian without a word.

Brian tried to swallow but could not, then his teeth began to ache.

* * *

At the end of the day Brian finished up as quickly as he could, wanting to leave the place yet not sure if he wanted to go home. He could think of nothing but the bond contract. Eighteen lost ticks put him down an additional $552 and all but wiped out half of his cash. His and Rhonda's. And there was no guarantee he would not lose more. He was bleeding, that word so many traders used, just out and out bleeding.

He also had to urinate, so Brian walked over to the men's room. Already standing at one of the urinals was Tommy Haggarty.

"Don't mind me, I'm just jaggin' off," Tommy said.

Brian exhaled with relief as he washed down the china. He stared straight ahead.

Tommy fumbled with his briefs.

"No matter how you shake and dance, those last two drops always hit the pants, eh, Boyer?"

"Yeah, I guess."

"Don't guess. We're talking *urine* here, Boyer," Tommy shouted.

Brian continued to look ahead. Tommy washed his hands.

"You still got some cash from the bond trick last week?" he said.

"Yeah, I guess."

"What's to guess? You got it or you don't."

"I lost some on a trade."

"All of it?"

"No way. Just some."

"So terrific. Whattaya gonna do with the rest?"

"Bank it."

"*Bank* it? The fuckin' savings and *loin*, Boyer?"

"Yeah."

"That's no place for it."

"Whatta you suggest?"

Brian stepped back, spilling two drops on his pants.

"Hell, you made it in the pit, so put it back in the pit. Sure, you're gonna suck it up once in a while. But you can't wimp out. Maybe skim a little for a good time, but keep it in there. Hit Marty again."

"Not after —."

"C'mon, Boyer. Get with the program. You don't see guys who make it sit with their thumbs up their ass. They goose it. Take on an attitude, you know what I mean? They play a little, blow off something orbital, get their rocks off, and go right back at it."

Tommy flipped a wad of paper towel around his back and toward the wastebasket. It missed. Brian walked over and placed his used towel in the receptacle.

As they left the bathroom, a door down the corridor slammed. Tommy turned in time to see a couple walk toward the elevator.

"Great, great," he said hurriedly. "If I'm right we're in for a blocker," he said.

"What?" Brian said.

"C'mon, raisin balls, I wanna show you somethin'. Won't take a few minutes and yer gonna love it."

Brian followed Tommy to the elevator.

"Remember that time you watched the Rope get his ashes raked?"

"How could I forget?"

"This is a little play on that tune. Called a blocker."

Once off the elevator Tommy headed for the west exit.

"I think that's his garage," he said.

They stood and waited outside the door. Tommy watched the exit of a parking lot across the street.

"There. That two-seater Benz," he said.

A silver Mercedes pulled out of the garage and headed toward Van Buren, then turned right.

"Follow me," Tommy said, and he went north to Jackson.

They waited for a few moments.

"Here he comes," Tommy said.

The Mercedes passed them, moving slowly in the right lane. The man Tommy had seen in the hallway was in the front seat.

"That's Sarsany. Big corn guy. Look at the smile on his face." Tommy laughed.

"So what?" Brian said, watching the Mercedes proceed down Jackson, then turn south.

"So he ain't alone in that cockpit, dumb ass. I figure two times round the block and he'll pop," Tommy said.

They turned and looked south toward Van Buren, and a few moments later the Mercedes passed by. Moments after that it appeared on Jackson, passed in front of them, then turned right.

"See her? Huh, Boyer? Just bobbin' away. Guy did a blocker

once and hit the accelerator when he shot and damn near drove through the building."

"No shit," Brian said, a lazy grin now on his face.

"The moral being: don't mix coming with going," Tommy said and punched Brian's arm.

"There he is," he said.

About a block from them the Mercedes pulled to the curb. "Two times. Was I right or was I right?" Tommy exclaimed. "She's good."

At that a female head appeared above the dashboard. Then the passenger door opened and a girl in blue jeans and heels got out. The driver waved and the car drove off, this time with squealing tires, heading south.

"Great, huh?" Tommy said. "After a hard day in the pits traders like to do a blocker. Release a little pressure before going home to the old lady in the burbs."

"Who's the girl?" Brian said.

"Who knows?" Tommy said, and headed back inside the building.

In the elevator Tommy tapped and drummed and mouthed the words to some unidentifiable hit. Brian looked at the floor, his mind still out on Jackson Boulevard and, at least for the moment, off of his bond contract.

Just as the elevator neared their stop, he looked up at Tommy.

"God, gettin' that kind of action," Brian said.

"The American dream, Brian baby," Tommy said.

A few minutes later, as Brian took off his Korngold jacket and prepared to leave, Tommy nabbed him again.

"Hey, stick around. Couple guys and me are gonna party and you can come along," said Tommy.

"I'm s'posed to go out with my girl," Brian said.

"Ah, blow her off," said Tommy.

"I dunno . . ."

"Look, Brian. These guys get ass. You know what I mean? You and I could live on the spillover."

"Yeah, sure. I get carded everywhere I go," Brian said.

Tommy tossed him a cold can of Stroh's.

"Who says we're goin' anywhere?" said Tommy.

Brian fondled the unopened can, rolled the cool, sweating aluminum against his cheek, all the while contemplating what he would say to Rhonda when he called. He had to call. He always did.

Suddenly Tommy plucked the can from Brian's fist and stuck it a half inch from his nose. He popped the top and ice-cold fumes shot up Brian's nostrils.

"Toss it back, Boyer. Get a head start on this crowd. You'll need it," Tommy said.

Brian took a long draught, and some of the beer spilled onto his chin and down the front of his shirt.

Just then the office door flew open and banged against the wall.

"Ladies and gentlemen, start your engines!!" came a shout from the hall, followed by muffled giggles.

"Otis!" Tommy yelled. "Get your diseased mind in here!"

A clerk with a head of curls and a thick moustache sauntered in. On the curls was a blue Cubs hat with two cans of beer in pouches mounted on either side, each with plastic tubing that ran from the cans into Otis's mouth.

"And that's *all* that's diseased," he yelled.

"Better be, wise guy," said a chunky, frizzed brunette behind him.

She swatted his shoulder and Otis mock-stumbled across the room. Three more young women in molded jeans, high heels, and frilly blouses followed. They were all secretaries, vintage southwest side, not more than twenty-two years old each, with plenty of hips, make-up, jangling jewelry, and chewing gum.

"Brews all around," said Tommy, as he bent into the refrigerator and started tossing cans of Stroh's over his shoulder.

Otis and the women lunged for them like garters at a wedding, bumping and shoving each other.

"Here, babe, warm this up for me," Otis said, taking his unopened, ice-cold can and pressing it between the breasts of a well-developed blonde. He rolled it back and forth, and the blonde squealed and shimmied.

"Ya love it, ya love it, ya crazy wench!" Otis yelled.

Then he stepped back and motioned toward Haggarty.

"Tommy, this is Marcy, Jody, Erin, and Robin. Or Robin, Marcy, Erin, and Jody. Or Flopsy, Mopsy, and Cotton-tail— beats the shit out of me," Otis said.

"We got Lucy coming—and does she *come*—"

145

"How do *you* know?" said Marcy, the frizzy one.

"And Lester and Freddy and maybe, *God*, I-hope-I-hope, lovely Bridget Boom-Boom!" he went on.

Tommy shouted, "Come on in! The music's loud, the booze is free, and so am I!"

Brian stood behind him, absently sipping his beer and staring at the women. They were the foxes, the movers, the brassy, loud, untouchable girls only a couple grades ahead of him in school yet completely out of his world. They strutted around in packs and gave him as much notice as a street sign. They were not Rhonda, oh my, Brian thought, they were not Rhonda.

Suddenly one of them turned to him.

"Who's the ba-by?" cooed Jody, the blonde whose blouse now had a choice wet spot at the cleavage.

"Who? Oh, Boyer here?" said Tommy, and he pulled Brian next to him then flopped his arm around Brian's shoulders.

"He's young, he's clean, and he's only had sex with his mother at a very young age," Tommy went on.

"Come to mamma," Jody said.

She stretched her arms out in front of her and approached Brian, smiled at him, then put her hands on his cheeks and kissed him deeply, parting her lips and plunging her tongue into his mouth.

"E-e-e-e-e-o-o-o-o-o-w-w-w!" howled Tommy.

"Party hard!" yelped Otis.

They stepped around Jody and Brian as they clinched. Brian was a couple inches shorter than Jody so he kissed upward, his arms now wrapped around her as hers were around him, caressing the fabric of her blouse and feeling the outline of her brassiere. She smelt like smoke and felt like heaven.

Suddenly she stepped back and gave his cheek a not-too-gentle pat.

"You kiss good," she said. "Sloppy, but good."

Then she tousled her hair and joined the others.

Brian stood there, and took a deep breath. He had a fearsome erection.

Behind him, to the whomping sounds of the stereo and a cadence of exploding pop-tops, Tommy cleared off desks. He moved perishable data and machines against the wall. He did it as if he

146

had done it before.

"Stay out of the old man's office," he shouted to nobody and everybody. "Don't drink his booze. Don't touch his stash. Don't stain his sofa."

"Ooooooh," squealed Robin. "I love it when you talk stains."

In the next half hour they were joined by four more guys and three women. Among them was the previously acclaimed Bridget, a tall, weed-thin, frosted blonde with the long, sculpted legs of a dancer, a nonexistent waist, and breasts that were cones jutting to points beneath a loose, off-the-shoulder designer jersey. A cigarette the size of a lance jutted from her fingers. She inhaled it with a pout.

When Brian saw her he lost his breath. If she were a clerk or a runner, he was certain he had never seen her on the floor, or, he was also certain, he had never seen her looking like this. And here she was just a few feet away from him, listening to the same sounds at the same party, oblivious to his existence, sure, but hell, weirder things had happened.

By now it was after seven, the office was hazy with smoke and drowned in music and babble, and Tommy casually went over and locked the door. Then he wedged a chair beneath the handle.

"Don't want the Polack cleaning crew crashing the proceedings," he said.

With that he cranked the stereo full blast, sounds of Wham and Iggy Pop. With one eye closed he bump-danced with Marcy in the center of the office, each of them cradling a beer and a cigarette. Someone lit a joint, then another, and things were on. This was not the only party in progress in the building, not the loudest, or the rankest, but it was close.

Brian leaned against a desk and started on his second beer. Except for Tommy he knew nobody, but he did not mind just standing and watching. He accepted a joint when it was passed to him. He inhaled and held, his eyes narrowing on the image of Bridget. She was standing like a goddess against the window, absently flicking the ashes of her cigarette onto the carpet. Had she requested an ashtray, Brian would have volunteered his palm, his navel, his mouth.

It struck Brian just then that he had not called Rhonda. He had not broken their date. She would be furious. She would be worried. She would cry. And yet he could not call her now, not here with all this racket, the music and shouts, lest she discover what he was doing. He began to perspire. He thought of his bond contract, the tick, the fact that he was down five and a half bills and counting. More money than he made in two weeks lost in a few minutes. Could he get out? Could he get it back? God, what was he doing here?

He shook himself and realized that he had fixed a glassy-eyed stare on Bridget as she stood alone, seemingly preoccupied, smoking, waiting. The other women danced and swayed to the music, giggling, spilling beer, pursing their lips in mock scowls and leers. Brian's beer was warm.

Just then someone thumped loudly on the door.

"Not to worry," Tommy yelled, as he hustled over.

He knocked three times, got two thumps in return, and opened the door to Terry Breggan, a currency trader at the Merc, whose arms were loaded with four large boxes of pizza.

"Buffet!" Tommy yelled, ushered Breggan inside, then he secured the door once again.

The pizza drew everyone, even Bridget, the stone statue, and in moments they were stuffing wedges into their mouths. Bridget held a piece in each hand, biting from one, then the other. An orange line of grease slipped down her forearm.

"God, look at that woman eat," said Tommy.

Bridget flashed her long white teeth at him and snapped off another hunk of sausage and pepperoni.

"I'd like to eat that woman," growled Otis.

"Such a mouth on ya," said Marcy.

"Such a tongue on me," Otis replied.

He sidled over to Tommy.

"Is she a piece or is she a piece?" he said.

"Stanley-fuckin'-Cup," Tommy said.

"She likes the pizza—" Otis went on.

"Then she'll love my Irish beef," Tommy said.

"—but she's outta here without lines," Otis said.

"I got 'em. I got 'em," Tommy said.

At that Marcy flipped a hunk of pepperoni and hit Erin square in the chin.

"You pig!" Erin yelped, and heaved a piece of green pepper at her.

Tommy loved it, realizing that the girls were getting primed. He was convinced when Marcy popped a button on Robin's blouse and stuffed a glob of cheese down her cleavage.

Robin shrieked, bent forward, and Terry Breggan immediately jumped in front of her and plunged his nose into her bosom.

"I'll get it, I'll get it," he yelled, and licked and nuzzled the billowing confines of Robin's brassiere.

He pushed her until she backed into a desk, lost her balance and flopped on her back. Breggan went down on top of her, growling and gobbling to the cheers of the others. Suddenly the front clasp of Robin's brassiere unhooked and snapped apart, revealing spongy, ample breasts and walnut-colored nipples.

She screamed and grabbed Breggan's head, trying to push him away. Otis ran over and began slapping the desk with his palm as if he were a wrestling referee. Then he poured the remainder of his beer on Robin's chest, and Breggan lapped it like a dog. Robin's eyes bugged at the cold splash of beer and she pounded on Breggan's shoulders.

Tommy went over to the coat closet.

"Candy break," he announced, and nodded toward a small outer office.

The others looked over to him and, led by Bridget in her long heels, scurried after.

Like a laboratory technician, Tommy carefully tamped the lines in two rows of four on a round portable mirror that Mary Beth kept in her desk. His stuff was good. Top dollar, white and snowy, crystals of bliss.

Bridget could not wait to lean down, her own bill—a crisp fifty rolled as tightly as a reed—poised. Tommy gawked at the front of her shirt, now open as she crouched and revealing the caramel skin of her chest, a sheer bra, breasts sculpted and erect.

She sniffed twice, then stood and shuddered, her eyes closed. She had gotten what she had come for. She would stay. The party had finally begun.

"I'd fuckin' kill for a chance at her," Tommy hissed.

"Enough coke and all you'll have to do is ask," said Otis.

The others gathered around. Tommy tamped the powdery crystals from a brown vial that once held his mother's asthma prescription. One after another, with care and remarkable order given their beery conditions, the crowd partook of the cocaine.

Bridget leaned in for another draw, snorted quickly, then stood up and once again shook herself. Then she cocked her tousled head and looked dreamily at Tommy, the giver of that which was good, and pulled his head to hers. She kissed him as if she were devouring yet another wedge of pizza, opening and closing her mouth on his, biting his lower lip until it hurt.

With his right hand Tommy cupped her butt and pressed her crotch into his, and she fiercely complied. She was a snow slave, coming to her master, a little now, more later.

"Ham shots! Ham shots!" Otis shouted.

The women yelled and ran out of the office in mock terror. The others followed, leaving the mirror clean, and Tommy and Bridget in their grinding embrace.

Only Brian, whose head was light but whose eyes still focused, stood transfixed at the sight of Bridget straddling Tommy's thigh, riding it slowly up and down as if she were melded to it.

"Ham shots! Ham shots!" Otis chanted from the outer office.

The group pushed and taunted each other. Some of the women tugged at their neighbors' belts. Finally Erin, with her reddish-auburn hair and square shoulders, her mouth set in a grin that accentuated a slight lip scar, strode out front and kicked off her heels. The others cheered, then began to rhythmically clap.

After the shoes came the belt, then the zip of her fly. More cheers and hoots, and she bent slightly to peel the tight jeans from her buttocks. She nearly stumbled in tugging them off one leg, then the other, then whirled and flashed a pair of crimson, cotton, Calvin Klein panties. With both hands behind her head, pushing up her gorgeous hair, she did an abbreviated bump and grind en route to the copying machine.

With a single motion she whisked her panties down to her knees and hopped on top of the glass. She sat and wiggled as Otis punched the button. The bulb flashed white against the alabaster skin of her shanks. The crowd cheered as the bulb went off again and again, copies for everybody, before Robin jumped down and covered up.

They grabbed for the photocopies. Robin's cheeks, like two blobs of putty on glass, reproduced beautifully.

150

Otis rubbed the paper against his face.

"God, your ass smells like toner fluid," he said.

Meanwhile, in the comparative quiet of Ken Korngold's office, Bridget was sprawled out on the sofa, her arms outstretched and her eyes closed. Tommy Haggarty's face was buried in her naked and copious crotch, and he laved and drank to her pitched moans.

The others continued to drink and party, the ham photos completed, but the machine, having been set on infinity and long since depleted of paper, continued to flash and churn on its own.

In one corner Robin arm-wrestled with all comers, male or female, rewarding any guy who bested her with a deep, suffocating kiss. A few of the others danced serenely and sloppily in the center of the office, none of them particular about his partner.

Just then Jody, the tall, bountiful blonde, grabbed Brian, who was sitting Indian-style atop a desk and smiling dopily.

"Where were we, fuzzy face?" she said, and sloppily ambushed his mouth with hers. As she did she cupped his crotch and once again brought his member to attention. She had huge hands and it felt as if she was going to squeeze his balls into Milk Duds. Brian groaned, loving it, and sucked on her lips and her tongue and her sweet-sour saliva.

He was gone now. The real world with all of its traps and losses and nagging responsibilities was far, far away.

Lost in his groping nirvana, he did not notice two women, Lucy and Marcy, as they kneeled like two sprinters in the blocks. Both of them were barefoot, shucked of their jeans, the orbs of their panty-clad butts sticking in the air.

Robin whacked a filing cabinet with a clipboard and Lucy and Marcy sprinted toward the now-opened office door and disappeared into the hallway, their feet thumping on the carpeting. The others cheered; the relays were on.

Suddenly Jody withdrew from Brian.

"Get by the windows," she shouted.

Brian's hands fell to his sides. He wanted more of what he'd tasted. He was puzzled by what the girl was doing now.

"That guy doin' hall relays who went through the window? 'Member? *God*, he went down thirty stories. 'Member?" she said.

Brian didn't remember, and had little time to do so before Marcy and Lucy came barreling back through the office. Jody lunged at them and caught them around the chest before they slammed into the desks.

They hugged and laughed and puffed.

"I told ya I'd whip your butt!" gasped Lucy.

She looked around her for a beer and palm slaps and realized that besides Brian Boyer, there were no men in the room.

The door to Korngold's office was open, and the women, leaving Brian by himself, went over to it.

Brian sat on the carpet, his legs askew, feeling dopey, a little off-balance. He had no idea of what time it was or where he belonged. The party was still going on, but without him, if, in fact, he had ever really been a part of it. He felt bloated and sore, the inside of his mouth rancid from beer and smoke. He was a loser, still holding a contract he couldn't afford, for Chrissakes, his pockets were empty. He looked over at the crowd outside Korngold's office door. He had no idea who they were, and he doubted that he ever would.

Inside the office, huddled around and on the sofa, stood Breggan, Otis, and the other guys, all of them with their pants down to their ankles and their organs in their hands. Bridget, just barely visible to the spectators at the doorway, was now totally nude and reclining spread-eagle in their midst. She writhed and groaned, running her hands about her breasts and stomach and her glistening pubic hair. Tommy, who was also naked, crouched between her legs, alternately tonguing her, then pulling back and sprinkling a few grains of coke from a small envelope onto the gelatinous folds of her crotch.

The others watched and pulled on their peckers and fondled Bridget's breasts. With each tamp of coke Bridget swung her head from side to side. Then suddenly she emitted a choked, high-pitched cry, and thrust her fingers into her vagina. She masturbated furiously, her fingers a blur against the pink flesh. She gasped and screamed, lifting herself off the sofa, her body convulsed, and the men around her pounded themselves, ejaculating onto the writhing, sweaty inferno before them.

"*God*, that's gross," hissed Erin.

"*Good* for the skin," whispered Robin.

Chapter Eight

Joanie had looked for Korngold all day Monday. She did not find him until late in the afternoon.

He was sitting behind his desk, his hands cradling a tumbler of vodka, his attention on the television and another Cubs game.

"Drink?" he said to Joanie, raising his glass.

"Just this," she said, lifting her can of diet cola.

"No buzz in that," he said.

Joanie shrugged.

He lifted his stocking feet onto the desk. He had not gone into the pits, yet he was dressed in his trading clothes, a striped dress shirt so frayed it had to be charmed to avoid the rag pile. A fat, soiled, purple tie that also held some mystical power lay open around his neck.

"There's something going on in the office, Ken. Something you should know about," Joanie began.

"Oh, my."

"It's those guys and Brian. They're trading for him. He's getting in way over his head."

"How much?"

"Just one-lots. Bonds, mostly, but he —"

"Big deal. They're screwin' around. Pitching pennies."

"He can't handle it. He's too young."

"Kid loses a paycheck or two and he'll grow up in a hurry."

"You should stop them."

He looked up at the TV.

"Bullshit, Harry! It was low and outside," he yelled.

Joanie glared at him, until he finally looked at her.

"Don't play mother, Joanie. You don't look the part."

He sipped his drink and looked back at the television.

"I'm serious, Ken. Somebody's going to get hurt bad."

"With a onesie?"

"Yes. To somebody like Brian—"

"Hey! Shut up! Count's three-and-two on my man Leon. Swing! Fuck!!! Ya overpaid little *pisher!*"

Joanie put her hands on her hips.

"Don't worry about it, Joanie. Just don't worry about it. The kid sucks some wind and gets cleaned out. Every little shit in this place should be so lucky," he said.

She turned and walked out.

More than an hour later, with only a handful of people still in the office, she heard him call her name.

When she went into his office the TV was off and the stereo was jumping with the Temptations. Korngold was sitting on the carpet in front of the sofa, the glass full once again. He looked up at her and smiled lazily.

"So look at you," Korngold said. "Joanie Yff. The Camptown lady hairdresser. Doo-da, doo-da. Worried about her fellow-man."

He patted the carpet.

"C'mon down. Talk to me."

She leaned against the end of the sofa.

"I'll stay up here. You're dangerous on the floor."

He laughed loudly, then belched.

"Who'd a thunk it?" he said. "You're damn good, you know that. Best little worker bee I've ever had. Gorgeous broad like you, belong somewhere with staples in your belly button. Maybe selling perfume on TV."

He clumsily bounced his heels on the floor.

"But no," he went on. "Joanie's right down here wearing the Korngold jacket and doin' the hokey-pokey. Like you were some Jew kid from Highland Park born with a calculator in your head."

Joanie exhaled. Then she lifted her can of cola.

"Cheers," she said, not wanting to reengage him in his present state.

"Aaaah, c'mon, let's fight," he said, a sloppy grin washing over his face.

"Why?" she said. "Because I think it's shitty that those guys—"

"Forget about that," he said.

He started tapping rhythms on his thighs.

154

"I'm gonna total up," she said.

"Stick around. I'm just in my cups a little."

He fell sideways, landing on his elbows like a little kid trying to get comfortable in front of a TV, cradling his chin in his hands.

"You know my girl, Rachel — God love her — she don't like you at all. Puts out her cat claws every time your name comes up."

"I know," said Joanie.

"That's a point in your favor. Little scamp feels threatened. Ain't that something?"

"I guess so."

"Ain't that somethin . . . ?"

"She's crazy about you. She really is," Joanie said.

"I *know* that," he said, then tilted his head and looked cockeyed at her. "What in hell did I do right?"

Joanie lifted her eyes and shrugged.

"It's nice," Korngold said, his voice trailing off. "Nice."

He stared blankly up at her.

She shifted her weight, tired, wanting to go home. She tried to block out her gut reaction to this, to Korngold the drunk, the lout. He was her boss, the reason she was even in this business, and she would never forget that. He was a master trader, a powerhouse on the floor, a wealthy man, and yet he was this: a pudgy slob sitting on his butt on the floor of his office lobbing snide remarks at her. That instant she felt as she had in his condominium that first night.

"You wanna trade?" he said.

"Huh?"

"Yeah. Beans, maybe? On the floor. You know what I mean."

"Oh, come on, Ken. That takes capital. . . . I couldn't —"

"I'll back you. Don't put out a dime. Just feel your way in. Make a little, lose a little. Get a handle on it."

"You're kidding."

"Why not? That's what you want, isn't it?"

She was stunned. He said it without blinking, as if he had just suggested she run out and buy a newspaper.

"Everybody wants something. Even little Rachel wants something. She's like her mother. Now there's a lulu. You ever meet Myrna? No, you never met her. But don't worry about it," he said.

Joanie stood up and ran her hand through her hair.

"Wanna sit on my lap?" he said, and laughed again. He drained his glass of vodka and lost an ice cube down the front of his shirt.

"It's too quick. Too impossible," she said.

"What is?" he said.

"Me trading so soon," she answered. "It's just too incredible."

"Of course it is," he said, rolling the glass across the carpet. "Don't worry about it."

She sighed and realized he was fogged in. She went for the door.

"Goal!" he shouted.

The next afternoon, as the clerks closed out the day, the few traders still in the office huddled around Jimmy Bilandic, a squarejawed Croatian who had been with Korngold only a few weeks. Bilandic was hacking on a computer, filling the screen with twenty- and thirty-day moving averages, bar graphs, and volatility charts. The office hammered with rock music, the television was tuned to a "Leave It to Beaver" rerun. Soda and fruit juices had been replaced by beer.

Bilandic's specialty was currencies. They were traded on the IMM, the International Monetary Market, which was part of the Mercantile Exchange, the Board of Trade's feisty competitor. Originally started as a butter and egg market, the Merc had burst into the forefront of commodity trading in the 1970s via the IMM and the public's growing obsession with gold, silver, and currencies — called the "ultimate commodities."

A spunkier, flashier floor than the Board of Trade, the Merc had increased its action and volume even further in the 1980s by trading the Standard and Poor's Index of 500 stocks, the S&P 500. That, in turn, moved the Chicago Board Options Exchange to create similar trading on the Standard and Poor's Index of 100 stocks, the S&P 100, and the wildly volatile and successful industry of stock market index trading was born.

In 1986 the Merc opened its new building at Wacker and Monroe, a glittering glass and chrome high rise and a perfect testimony to its meteoric and intrepid presence in the futures industry. The slick, daring building was an appropriate home for Merc traders who, by and large, were younger than many of those at the CBT (with the exception of the Treasury bond pit) and had a reputation, deserved or otherwise, of being even less sane than Board of Trade traders.

The business, however, was the same. The pits and the players confronted the same perilous risks and played with the same leverage. Traders, brokers, and their clients speculated in the hot commodity of the day, from Eurodollars to pork bellies, wherever the action was.

Jimmy Bilandic was talking deutsche marks. He brimmed with data which showed that the German buck was ready to break out. His words were those of a tout, an insider, a sharpy who was cocksure of his information and his instincts.

"There it is, boys and girls. A sure-fuckin'-thing," he said.

"Sure things make my roids throb," said Lorn Vogel, a pork belly trader.

"So you want a maybe instead?"

"I hate bettin' against the dollar," said Marty Valukas.

"Whattaya, Nathan Hale?" said Bilandic.

"Look, assholes," he went on, turning in his chair. "I got raw data and a bitchin' track record. Throw in some timing, and I'm J. P. Morgan."

They went back and forth until Bilandic lost interest in being an evangelist.

Brian pulled Tommy aside. "Bilandic's good, ain't he?"

"Good? Put him in Texas and his dick could find oil."

"You gettin' in, Tommy?"

"Between you and me, Boyer, if I had any guts I'd mortgage the ol' man's house on him."

"Don't bullshit me, Tommy."

"I'm not, you little jerk. Jimmy's on a roll. He's up a half mil and change. Spreadin' the currencies like whores. If you don't get in it's your problem."

Brian scowled and turned away, more unsettled than ever. Up a half million. God, what would it be like to be up a half million dollars? You always heard that, like it was Monopoly money. It was just a matter of hooking on with a guy when he was hot, just grabbing his shirttail and hanging on. But which guy? And when? And how long?

All Brian really knew right now was the pain of his last two losses. Even though Valukas had gotten him out of his position with no more harm done, holding the losing bond contract overnight had been excruciating. In all, he had lost more than $700 in his last two flings, over half of the cash he had made in his first try.

On the way home he decided to wait. He had to recover his losses, yet he could not afford to get burned again. He could not bear the thought of *losing* every penny of that $1,100 pot. (Traders seldom said "lose," he knew. They preferred to say "give back," as if the money they had made on a trade was just a loan and they would give it back sooner or later. Brian could not think of it that way. He had the money, the gain, in his hand. He could not and would not accept the notion that it was not his to keep.)

So he would wait. No decision was a decision, he told himself. He had heard someone say that and he liked it. He would wait a week and watch Jimmy Bilandic's deutsche marks. Wait and watch, jump in if they broke, sigh relief if they fell.

At the start of the next week his eye fixed on the mark board — all commodity prices were posted no matter where they were traded — and he watched the price as nervously as if he had invested. For three days the price traded sideways, showing no trend one way or another, staying in line with the rest of the European currencies as they sold against the dollar. A blip here or there was usually due to some bit of news — speculation about the trade deficit, inflation figures, money supply — was temporary, and generally did not sustain itself in the face of the overall market. What counted was the American dollar, how strong or how weak it was in the eyes of the rest of the world.

Then on Thursday the D-mark opened strong, got stronger, and exploded. At first Brian thought it was a misposting, but not for long. Volume was staggering, the pit itself was in pandemonium. Not being on the Merc floor itself, Brian could not find out why and had to rely on whatever rumors he picked up. One said the German Bundesbank had come in and bought huge sums of D-marks to support its price; another said that the Germans had wiggled out of disastrous South American loan commitments.

The D-mark closed the day limit up, the maximum amount of gain allowed by the Exchange in any single trading day. What it

158

meant in dollars and cents, from the opening price to the limit-up close, was a profit of $1,250 per contract.

Bilandic's numbers were right. He was greeted with high-five palm slaps when he came into the office after the close. Tommy grinned at him as if he, too, had made a bundle.

That night, as Brian sat in the back of the crowded Archer Avenue bus, as he mulled over and over the percentage gain of the D-mark for that day alone, he felt as much pain as he had losing fifteen ticks in Treasury bonds.

By the time he got home, however, he had turned his mopery into a plan. He figured several strategies for taking the money he still had—almost $400—and getting into the D-mark play. He would put on a spread—buying one contract and hedging it against another some months further out. He wasn't sure of the math involved, but guys did it and said it was safer than just putting everything into a single long or short position. It was either that, he decided, or he would get a line on what Bilandic was doing and follow his lead. Or maybe he would get some guts and give his whole roll to Bilandic and let him goose it.

Whatever his strategy, he needed more capital. And there was only one place to get that. No problem. In Rhonda's eyes right now he was golden, a genius. She did not know of his losses. She would not understand, Brian reasoned, so he had not told her. She would give him the cash he needed as easily as she was giving him other things nowadays, her eyes dreamily focused on that fine day next summer.

He ate supper at home that night, something he did infrequently because of the late hours he kept at the Board of Trade. His mother made city chicken—breaded chunks of veal skewered on a stick—and boiled potatoes. His father harvested a half dozen tomatoes from the backyard, cut them up in thin slices and fanned them out on a platter like playing cards. Then he laid a dozen slices on his own plate, slathered them with great gobs of mayonnaise, and shoveled the mess home with hunks of sweet butter on dark rye bread.

It was a meal that had been served in the Boyer home hundreds of times but which showed nary a sign of fatigue. Brian's mother, Rose, hovered around the table like a traffic cop, never sitting, directing food and removing platters. His old man chewed and slurped and occasionally pointed at something—salt, apple sauce—and snapped his fingers. Brian ate what his mother put on his plate, and occasionally snarled at his sister, Mary Rose, who pushed aside whatever her mother put on her plate.

That night it was Brian who started the conversation, a rarity at the Boyer table apart from his grunts to pass this or that. His topic was deutsche marks, and the remarkable run-up they had had that day. Mary Rose, who was fourteen and in love with her fingernails, looked at him as if he was speaking in tongues.

Brian went on for ten minutes of unqualified exuberance over currencies, throwing in a few technical terms like "upside resistance" and "thirty-day moving average."

"That's interesting, Brian. You *understand* all that," his mother said.

"It ain't *interesting,* Mother, it's *real.* There's a market there where they make more money in a day than most people make in a lifetime. It's like—"

His father looked at him and frowned.

"—yeah. Hey, Dad, you ever thought of getting into the market? I can get you a discount on commissions—next to nothing like you'd pay a broker," Brian said.

Mr. Boyer drank the rest of his milk.

"It's bad enough I got to listen to you," he said. "Make us all millionaires overnight."

"So what's wrong with that?" Brian said.

"I wanna Fiero turbo," said Mary Rose.

"Die," said Brian.

His mother finally sat down on the edge of a chair and began to chew on a cold piece of chicken, her first bite of the meal.

"You could make some real money, Dad," Brian went on.

"Been workin' down there three months," his father grumbled, smacking his lips and wiping his fingers on his pants. "All of a sudden you're a big wheeler-dealer."

"No, I ain't. It's just—I mean, you get to know the markets. Like you see how the big dollars are made."

"People lose big, too," Mr. Boyer said.

"Sure, that's the risk. No pain, no gain. No guts, no glory."

"That from Prince?" said Mary Rose.

"But if you play it right, man, the upside is outta sight," Brian went on. "Megabucks. You should see some of the guys down there."

His father continued to eat, pointing to his empty coffee cup and waiting as Rose scurried to fill it. He added half-and-half, then stirred it with the spoon clanging against the inside of the cup as if he were at a wedding reception.

"Trouble is," he began, sitting back and pushing his plate away from his belly, "and I ain't saying you shouldn't be working there seein' as it got you off the streets — but the trouble is that it's Funnyland. Goofy, you know? It ain't the real world. Listen to what's coming outta yer mouth, Brian. You don't even talk about money so's you can understand it. You say 'ticks' and 'down risk' or some such baloney. You don't say dollars and cents."

He brought his coffee cup to his lips and sipped noisily.

"None of those birds down there know the value of a dollar. You go down some rathole of a basement on Stony Island, pull out the oil burner and ductwork been there sixty years, then chop holes for new ducts and the whole git-go, all the time worryin' if some niggers ain't runnin' away with your truck and every tool you own. Do that first. Then come back and tell me what makin' a buck is all about."

Brian gritted his teeth. Since he had been twelve he had heard the rip-out-an-oil-burner lecture a hundred times.

"You make some sweat dollars and you won't be so eager to piss 'em away on Nazi money," his father added.

"For God's sake, Dad, I made over a thousand bucks in a half day! A grand. That's a shitload of oil burners."

"Brian!" his mother exclaimed.

"Moolah!" yelled Mary Rose.

"Oh, you *didn't* do that—" his mother said, her mouth wide open.

"You bet I did, Mother. Played a bond contract and it hit."

His father looked at him suspiciously.

"We oughtta be seein' some room and board, Mother," he said.

Then he got up and went into the den to see if the Sox were on.

"How much?" Mary Rose asked, her eyes wider than her plate.

"You heard me," Brian said.

His mother began to stack the dishes, still picking at her own food with her fingers.

"What you gonna get?" said Mary Rose.

"What? Like I'm gonna blow it on blue jeans and tapes? No way, José, you build an account. Put on new positions."

His mother shook her head, glanced off toward the living room, then looked back at Brian, her expression long.

"You shouldn't a told your father how much you made. You know how much that bothers him," his mother said.

Brian stared at her.

"What — he'd be happier if I was some burnout on the corner?"

"Stop that."

"So tell me."

"He's a very proud man. You can't rub his nose in things."

Brian slapped his forehead.

"Jesus Christ," he said.

He grabbed a stick eaten clean of city chicken and began to pick his teeth.

"You know, Mother, I ain't loadin' freight or workin' bump shops like half the guys around here. But I would be if it weren't for the floor, ya know? You can make money with your head instead of your back, like the nuns used to say at Rita. And I'm doin' it — I wasn't kiddin' about that money I made. It's incredible down there.

"I gotta chance to go somewhere and do somethin' nobody would a given me a prayer to do — especially Dad — and now I gotta apologize for it."

Rose looked at him and smiled, her lower lip quivering slightly. She patted the backs of his hands.

"Just listen to my big boy," she said.

Brian put the request to Rhonda later that night at Wendy's. She hadn't eaten since she'd gotten home from work and told him to wait until she finished her cheese-and-broccoli baked potato.

"How much do you need?" she said.

"Five bills."

She smiled.

"My bank branch opens at eight. I'll get it on the way to work

162

tomorrow morning," she said.

Brian was momentarily startled, but managed to convert the response into a confident smile.

"You're star quality, Rhonda," he said.

"Lover," she said, and beneath the table she wrapped her calf around his.

She could not stop thinking about Korngold's offer to back her—even if he had reneged on it. Joanie's first impulse was to search out Steve. She felt like a kid running home with a good report card.

That night, over a late-night full slab of ribs at Twin Anchors, a legendary Old Town tap, she started in.

"When do you think I should start trading?" she said.

He winced and dropped a bone into his plate.

"As if the thought never entered your mind," she said.

"The thought—of course. The reality. . . ?" he said.

"I've got what it takes, I think," she went on.

"Yeah? What does it take?"

"Oh, come on. I know the pit."

"Only the sublime side. You come and go. You take home a paycheck if your man wins or loses," he said.

"But I could *do* it," Joanie said.

She leaned on both elbows, gnawing on a bone, her fingers brown with sauce.

"I know the trades of half those bozos better than they do themselves," she continued.

He exhaled loudly.

"That has nothing to do with trading," he said.

"It doesn't?"

"Technically, yes. But a trader's assistant does not a trader make, or something like that."

"Give me a break. Not the old you-ain't-done-it-until-you-done-it routine."

"Not at all. I fully agree that you could probably function quite well in the pit."

"So when do you think I should trade?"

"Never."

163

"Why?!"

He reached over for some of her French fries.

"Okay. You're damn good. You read the market like a map. You know the *feel* of it. You could grab Korngold's cards in a minute and run with them. Knowing that, I should be the first to urge you to take the big move. But I'm not going to. I know you. And I like you. I'd hate to see you change."

"Come on. I'm twenty-one years old. Change is what it's all about," Joanie said.

She reached across the table and nabbed three ribs still intact on his plate.

"Besides," she went on, "Korngold offered to back me today."

"Oh, he did, did he?" Steve said.

"Out of pocket. Said I wouldn't have to put up a thing. Just say the word."

"Congratulations. I guess," he said.

"Right. I know what you're thinking: anybody but Korngold and it would mean something."

"No, that's not it. Kenny's a hitter. If he backs you, you're in, you know that. Lot of guys would rape and pillage to have that offer."

She looked directly at him.

"He can be such a prick sometimes," she said.

Steve unwrapped a wet napkin and went to work on his fingers.

"Goes with his territory. Those guys are in a different cosmos," he said, looking off across the nearly empty restaurant.

As they left the restaurant he put his arm around her and they walked slowly through the narrow, quaint streets of Old Town. One of the first of the reborn neighborhoods on the North Side and the heart of the sixties hippie scene, Old Town was now filled with ivy-covered row houses and Chicago cottages. The night was warm and muggy, a last push of summer before September and autumn set in.

"All right, try this. The path to becoming a trader is a twist on Faust," Steve began. "You don't completely sell your soul to the devil, but he says, 'Hey, you wanna trade? Then you gotta become an asshole for the next five years. Chuck all your best instincts down the toilet. Walk over your grandmother. Step on baby turtles, kick winos, put slugs in the Salvation Army buckets. Then do a lotta coke, wear a six-pound Rolex and a solid gold miniature of your trading badge around your neck, buy a BMW with a cellular phone and scream down Lake Shore Drive with the receiver cradled in your neck.' "

He looked down at her.

"That's what he says."

Joanie pulled away from him and met his glance.

"Shit, Steve," she said. "That's exactly what I was planning to do."

"It could happen," he said.

"Vote of confidence," she said.

Chapter Nine

That morning Brian left the house an hour earlier than usual, made his bus and train connections, and was in the office just after six. He was early, though by no means first. Several Korngold traders came in at 4:00 A.M. to catch the closings of overseas markets. Brian was there not to prepare for the day's running, but rather to gear himself up for a run on D-marks. In his pocket was $1,000 cash, ten bills, burning as it had never burned before.

An hour later he caught Jimmy Bilandic and asked him to get him a five-lot, a position that committed Brian to five futures contracts controlling the fate of 625,000 deutsche marks, the equivalent of more than $200,000. Bilandic whistled through his teeth when Brian showed him the $1,000, then he laughed and waved it off.

"Give it to me when I get you a fill," he said, adding the order to scores of others he would control that day, to be bought and sold at his discretion.

Brian pocketed his money with a broad smile.

The currency markets opened at 9:30. At that very moment Brian began to sweat.

The D-mark pit began trading with the same frenzy with which it closed. The gust of activity was based mostly on anticipation, not of events in Germany, though they counted some, but of the American dollar. The dollar's strength or weakness pegged the worth of all the currencies in the world. After months of remarkable strength, the buck seemed to be leveling off, and that meant a possible end to daily lows in the other currencies.

Just as in earlier rallies, the deutsche mark was one of the first to respond. The Swiss franc and British pound would follow, due to the fact that they, like the German mark, were part of the European Monetary System and their paths were usually similar. The strong opening suggested that the rally was not about to weaken. The action was furious, the pit a frenzy of buying. Jimmy Bilandic bought aggressively, whirling and leaping, taking on the market in a shower of energy and spit.

Bilandic was a former Golden Gloves bantamweight from Blue Island, a tough, working-class southern suburb of Chicago, and he came to the pits with his jab and uppercut intact. He had been around the floor since he was a teenager, boasting that he made his first trade when he was eighteen by simply jumping in the pit and making a bid. Now he was twenty-four, with thick brown hair parted down the middle of his skull and plastered back over his ears. Just above his collarbone he wore a gold chain with a pointed gold tooth on it. His ancestors came from a small town in Croatia known, he claimed, for cannibalistic mules.

Within an hour of the opening the D-mark threatened to challenge its up limit for the day. Volume was enormous, the trading frantic. By mid-morning Jimmy Bilandic had nearly lost his voice, yet he remained in the center of the storm, trading wildly, remaining long and going longer, holding bigger positions than he had ever taken on before.

Then, just after noon, the market collapsed. The same anticipation, the rumors, the pent-up bullish urges that fueled the rally suddenly evaporated. The U.S. government put out several reports that restated its belief in the strength of the dollar at the same time that the pit was swept by a rumor that the German Bundesbank was unloading D-marks and taking profits. Through it all, the D-mark fell like a stone.

Over at the Board of Trade, Brian stopped in the middle of a run and stood dead still, watching the plummeting D-mark board in stunned disbelief. He began to breathe in gasps, his heart beating in his throat. After several long moments during which the price of the mark continued to flicker downward, Brian ran to the Korngold desk.

"Look at the mark!" he shouted at Tommy Haggarty.

Tommy nonchalantly looked up.

"You in?" he asked Brian.

"Damn right! Ain't you?"

Tommy snickered.

"Better hope Bilandic got you out," he said.

"Call his desk," Brian said.

"Get outta here. He's in the pit."

For the rest of the trading, until 1:20, when the D-mark pit closed, Brian was frantic, like a mother whose baby had just been plucked from her arms, yet he was unable to do anything. Five minutes after the close of trading, he was on the phone to the Korngold floor desk at the Mercantile Exchange. With all the noise from markets still in session he could barely hear the clerk who answered. The clerk said Bilandic wasn't around and hung up.

Brian looked in panic at the receiver in his hand. Then he ran to find Mary Beth.

"You gotta cover for me! I'm sick!" he shouted, and thrust his cards and orders into her hands. Then he sprinted off the floor to the escalators. In seconds he was out the door and running down Jackson Boulevard toward the Merc. It was an eight-block sprint. Brian jostled other pedestrians as he ran, slithered through traffic against the lights, and burst through the building's front doors. He did not have credentials to get on the trading floor, so he took the elevator to the visitors' observatory. He had to see what Bilandic was doing.

From behind the glass he frantically scanned the faces of the traders remaining in the D-mark pit, not finding Jimmy's. He had one more resort, a firm that provided office space in the building for Korngold traders. In minutes he was there.

"Where's Bilandic?" he shouted to a girl sitting on a desk.

She shrugged her shoulders. Brian pounded his fists together, and the girl's eyes widened. Another Korngold trader Brian had never seen before appeared.

"Who you want?" he said.

"Jimmy Bilandic."

"He took off."

"Whattaya mean?"

"He left the pit. Didn't even close himself out."

"Where is he?" Brian said, his voice cracking.

"I heard Vegas. Somebody said he walked off the floor, right out the front door, flagged a cab, and went to O'Hare. It's either that or he's at his office on his hands and knees."

"Oh, *shit*," Brian moaned. "What do I do? I gotta find him."

The trader shook his head and sighed, looking at the girl.

"Guys do that," the trader said to her. "They take a hit and go West and shoot craps all night. Don't even check into a hotel. Then they come back the next morning, change their shirt, and get right back into the pit."

He looked back at Brian. "You want him I'd try there first thing."

Brian stood and stared at him, hearing every word and not wanting to believe any one of them. His shoulders sank. Now he was sick.

For the rest of the afternoon he moved about without feeling, vaguely conscious of his co-workers, carrying out his duties. When trading ended he tossed aside his unused order slips and sat heavily down on the steps of the bond pit.

Tommy came over.

"Heard Bilandic pulled an O'Hare spread—buy Vegas, sell Chicago," he said. "Didn't even close out."

Brian did not respond, did not blink.

He left the office after eight that night. The streets were dark. It seemed as if he waited a good hour for a bus. At home he did not have anything to eat. He went to his bedroom and lay on his bed fully clothed, staring at the ceiling. At some time in the night he fell asleep. His mother woke him the next morning and could not pry a word out of him.

On the floor Marty Valukas pulled him aside.

"Bilandic's back. You want out?" Valukas said.

"What—he's back in?"

"Trying to stop the bleeding."

"Where am I—I mean, how bad is it?"

"First degree murder. He got us in at the top, or close. Get out now—what with a onesie—and you'll live."

Brian grimaced.

"I got more."

"How many?"

169

"Five-lot."

"Fuck, Boyer! That's way over your head! Jesus—I'll try to get your ass out."

"Okay," Brian said softly, and Valukas went off.

After the close of trading there were no palm slaps awaiting Jimmy Bilandic. He filed quietly into the Korngold office, recorded his trades, and left. Valukas brought Brian the receipt.

"Pretty bad. Eighty ticks," he said.

Brian began to figure. Each commodity traded in different units, and a tick held a different value in each. In D-marks a tick was worth $12.50.

"That's total?" Brian asked.

"Per lot."

Brian gasped and fell back against the wall.

"On a five lot that's . . . that's . . . that's—"

"Five K," said Valukas.

"Oh, my *God*," Brian cried. "What do I do?"

"Hell—that's pissant," said Tommy Haggarty, who was standing nearby. "Bilandic was holding a couple hunnerd in his own account. And he ain't got it. Korngold's gonna use him like a dildo to get it back."

Brian did not hear him. He began to shake, and crossed his arms tightly around himself. His eyes flooded with tears.

That night was Rhonda's bowling league. Her team, a clique of girls from work who called themselves the Splits, was tied for last place. But they did not mind. Beneath the windshield wiper of his car where it was parked in front of the house Brian saw a note. It was on pink stationery with a drawing of two pigs at the top and the caption, "I pledge thee my trough."

On it Rhonda had written:

"I'll roll a X for you, lover. R. XXXOOO."

The O's were made in the shape of hearts.

Brian stuffed the paper in his pocket and went into the house. Again he did not eat supper, but went to his room and sat on his bed. He put on his stereo headphones and tucked in a cassette of Pink Floyd's *The Wall*, his all-time favorite tape. It ran and reran, the sound glazing his eyes and shutting out the

170

world.

Just after ten o'clock he left the house and drove his Grand Prix down to the White Castle. He sat in the front seat and ate nine sliders and a Coke. Then he drove around. The Pontiac's gas gauge registered not a fume of gas, but he went on, stopping in an alley near his house. He cut the engine and sat there. He saw a neighbor and his motorcycle, the rear end of someone leaning under the hood of a Trans Am in an open garage.

Brian sat for long minutes, hearing and seeing very little in the cool, late-summer night — lost in the desolate wave that washed over his dreams.

That night it was Steve's turn.

"I apologize. I was wrong. I lay awake all last night thinking about it. I'm a selfish, self-centered jerk and I want to change my mind. You should trade. You should trade as soon as you feel ready to trade. Grab Korngold's offer, set up your system, get a badge and get in. Period," he said.

Then he clutched each side of her head and kissed her on the lips.

"Oooooh!" she said.

"And there's more where that came from," he said. "Come on."

They stopped at a fishery for a pair of fresh swordfish steaks and went back to his place for a session at the round table.

"So I don't know," Joanie began. "Should I start small — maybe the MidAm, or what?"

"Give me a break. The MidAm — that's Little League. You could jump in the bond pit tomorrow and feel no pain," Steve said.

She rubbed her hands together nervously.

"It's so insane! I just got here yesterday. God, I remember the first day, the very moment I walked on to the floor . . . and now, trading myself? Impossible."

"Only to you. And only when you think about it too hard. Look at the pits. The average trader is in his mid-twenties. I'm thirty-five and an old fart. You just get in and do it. I'm not telling you anything you don't know."

She smiled weakly.

"What about Dr. Faust and the Rolex watch and walking over my grandmother?" she said.

"Scratch that," he said.

She leaned over and kissed him lightly, yet let her lips lingered close to his.

"It's like sex when you're sixteen," she said, her voice just above a whisper. "You know you *want* to do it. You're sure you *can* do it. But you haven't got the faintest idea if you *should* do it."

"I don't remember," he said.

She kissed him again. This time harder, reaching her hands around his neck, stroking his hair.

"I want to do it," she said.

"Trade?" he said.

"That, too," she said, pulling him to her.

"Whoa!" he said, trying to keep his balance.

"No, not this time," she said.

She turned in her chair and wrapped her legs around his, then leaned forward so that her forehead touched his.

"Here you are, Steven Stamford, telling me I shouldn't trade then telling me I should trade. You tell me you're a shit and I'm terrific and how good I'd be in the pit. You just lay it on and I love you for it and then I wonder what's going on with us? Huh? Huh?"

"So what's going on?" he said, now smiling with her.

She tugged on his hair.

"Look at you, Mr. Hector Protector. Just about the cutest, nicest person I've met in my whole life," she said.

She kissed him again, this time caught up in it, in her own words, in the emotion of having made a decision about a dream.

"I want you to do something for me," she said. "If you think I'd be such a great trader, then okay, I will be, I promise. But first of all I want some *stuff* out of you. Some *feeling*. Something that isn't an apology, like something you thought about all last

172

night and then prepared like some kind of brief in law school. Something just for me. From your gut—no—from your heart. How 'bout that?"

He was momentarily captive, his attention locked onto her determined, resolute, gorgeous face and her wide, luminous, shining eyes.

She said, "I want you to love me. To slide up and slither around and bang those bony hips. Make me go *ooh, ooh.*"

He did not object, did not philosophize or quip or foul things up by jabbering. He just hugged her.

They kissed, pecking, him biting her lower lip, then tugging and pressing and inhaling one another.

He had had his own dreams lately, and this was one of them: this young, beautiful, electric girl one day being full of him.

He kept his mouth shut and felt his crotch tighten, his whole being desiring nothing more than what was in his grasp. He took her hand and led her off.

Brian started his car and backed out of the alley. He went south a few blocks to Rhonda's house, cutting his engine just down the street. He got out and walked. The block was bright from the yellow-pink glare of the streetlight, yet deserted. The light in Rhonda's bedroom was on. Her car was parked in a graveled space alongside the driveway. It was locked but Brian had a key. Soundlessly he let himself in and sat in the front seat.

This was her: her smell, the candy-sweet perfume, her pie-eyed dolls and fuzzy elephants stuck to the dash and hanging from the mirror, a plastic magnet on the dashboard saying, "Thank God I'm Irish." In the coin tray between the seats was the kazoo she had kept from their trip to the goofy restaurant on the North Side.

He sat there with his hands on the steering wheel for a few more minutes then took the envelope out of his shirt. Inside was a note telling Rhonda that she was terrific but that he was not, that everything he touched turned to shit. With it was the

173

$1,000 in cash.

He left as quietly as he had come, going back to his car. He passed the house and went toward home. A block away from his place the Pontiac sputtered and died, coasting like a wounded moose over to the curb. Brian got out and did not look back. He walked to his house, up the drive and inside the side door of the garage, where the family Mercury was parked. He closed the door behind him. The garage was pitch-dark. He fumbled for the car door and got in, sitting back, closing his eyes and feeling utterly exhausted. The car smelled like furnace filters.

He flicked on the radio dial but it would not play without the key in the ignition. He cursed, then opened the door and from the slight light of the dome bulb found it in a metallic keybox stuck magnetically to the inside of the front bumper. It was the first place anyone interested in the heap would look.

He got back in the front seat and dark silence. The radio was tuned to an all-talk station and two stiffs were complaining about coho salmon fishing in Lake Michigan. He shut it off and laid his head back on the seat. He stared at the car's ceiling, seeing nothing but the green lights of the price boards at the Board of Trade. The din of trading filled his head as if he were on the steps of a pit. Prices were dropping, the D-mark a disaster. When Korngold found out he would keep him on just long enough to pay back his debt. Then he would fire him and he would be out. It had happened to other guys.

A line of sweat formed on his neck in the stale air of the car's interior, yet Brian began to shiver. He reached up and turned on the ignition. The motor raced as if the accelerator were stuck and he tapped the pedal and it slowed. Still shivering, he turned on the heater, then the radio. Finally a station with some sounds, a wailing, whining guitar with some guy on a harmonica. Brian smiled, his head feeling suddenly light, clear of flickering green digits and bids and offers and Rhonda and the smell of furnace filters.

Chapter Ten

It was Brian Boyer's mother who called the office. Mary Beth answered. She strained to hear the voice on the other end. Then her face lost its color.

The news swept through the office, then passed quickly among Korngold employees on the floor. All except Joanie, who was madly trying to attend to a dozen different traders in a dozen different directions.

"Hey!" she said angrily when Tommy Haggarty got in her way.

"You heard?" he said.

"What now, Tommy?"

"Whole office is up for grabs. Boyer zapped himself last night."

"Brian what?" she said.

"Asshole went and sucked wind for five K on D-marks. Bilandic got him in. Lost his ass and he couldn't take it."

"What happened to him?"

"Gassed himself in a garage. Used his old man's car."

"He died?"

"You got it."

"I don't believe it," Joanie cried, suddenly seeing Brian's face in her mind, envisioning what he had done.

"Korngold is gonna raise hell. It'll be my ass, you just wait," Tommy went on. "I got Boyer in to start with. You know, usual shit of guys tradin' in the office. And he won big. Took home a K his first trade—"

"C'mon, Tommy, Brian's dead?" Joanie said.

"Yeah! His ol' lady called. Stupid shit. He goes and becomes a fuckin' monster. Gets in with Jimmy Bilandic on the Merc and gets pounded. Bilandic went to *Vegas*. Didn't even close himself out. And you-know-who is gonna take

175

the enema for it all."

Joanie slumped and held her head. Tommy angrily pounded his hands together.

"Forget about yourself for one second, okay, Tommy?" Joanie said looking up at him. "My God, how could it happen . . . ?"

"Handwriting's on the wall," he said.

"Little Brian Boyer," Joanie said, her throat constricting, her thoughts filling with images of Brian on his — and her — first day in the office, his fresh babyface.

"Little *me*," Tommy said.

"Dammit, Tommy. Why don't *you* find yourself a garage," she said, and tried to walk around him.

"Nice," Tommy said, letting her pass.

Joanie hurried over to the desk on the financial floor.

"Is it true about Brian?" she said to Lisa.

Lisa, who had a phone receiver against each ear, nodded.

"Where's Ken?"

"Nobody knows," came the reply.

It was late afternoon when Korngold learned of it, and then only because Ira Roth was finally able to reach him on his car phone. Korngold blinked and wondered if he had heard right. Boyer? The runner? The Irish kid who never said anything? As he drove on he remembered the trip with Brian to Atlanta, how the kid had sat wide-eyed in the cockpit, asking all the questions.

The first person Korngold spotted when he came in was Mary Beth, and he motioned her into his office.

"What in the hell happened?" he said.

In a quiet, fragile voice, Mary Beth recounted the late afternoon scenes in the office, how Brian lingered around the edges like a little boy on tiptoes trying to see over the crowd, how he hung that gimpy smile on his face when they picked on him, how he grew more and more in awe of the traders and wished one day to be one of them, one of the boys. As she spoke her voice wavered, then she began to cry.

Korngold was still, facing Mary Beth's grief, unsure of what to say.

"But it wasn't their fault, Ken," she quickly said.

"Why not?"

"You can't blame Marty and them. You really can't. It's a big game that they all play. Me, too. Brian just didn't know," she said, looking off at the carpet.

"Haggarty?" he asked.

"Shit. You know Tommy . . ."

At the close of trading that afternoon the clerks shuffled back into the office, none of them saying much. In this business, suicide was for traders or brokers, the high fliers who tapped out for millions and could not face the fall. The runners, clerks, and trader's assistants were the kids, the worker bees, the carefree apprentices who supposedly were spared the psychotic highs and lows of trading.

Korngold traders, on the other hand, came in and out of the office, their expressions reflecting only the day's fortunes or failures in the pit. They exchanged the usual market talk, drank soft drinks and juices, and lounged on the furniture. None of them mentioned Brian, many did not even know his last name.

Finally Joanie couldn't take it anymore.

"Shouldn't we *do* something?" she said out loud.

Everyone stopped what they were doing and looked at her.

She waited. She looked at Tommy, at a pair of T-bill traders on the sofa, at Ira Roth.

"He was one of us. He . . . he . . . I mean, doesn't anyone here feel responsible?"

"For what?" said Marty Valukas. He was standing near the refrigerator. "I lost a hell of a lot more than Boyer and I didn't put my head in the oven."

177

"But you're a *trader*, Marty," said Mary Beth.

"So was he. Anybody who takes on a five-lot ain't a virgin," Marty replied.

"So what now? Do we just step over the body and keep on with the bids and offers?" said Joanie.

Nobody responded. Ira Roth began tapping the keys on his computer console. Others turned back to their work.

"And where's the boss, I'd like to know?" Joanie said.

"He's here," Mary Beth said. "He knows."

"He does?" Joanie said.

She headed off toward Korngold's office. Korngold was sitting behind his desk. The office was quiet, the computer screens blank. He was reading a research report.

"What about Brian?" Joanie said.

"What about him?" he said, looking up from his paper.

"You knew what he was doing. I told you —" she said.

"Get a grip, Joanie," he said.

He sat back, tossing the report on the desk, and cupped his palms behind his head.

"There's no way in hell I can keep these guys out of shit. Fuckin' kids gamble on everything, the Cubs, poker with dollar bills, for God's sakes."

"What Brian was doing wasn't liar's poker," she said.

"I don't know what he was up to. For all I know he killed himself over a broad, not because of his losses," he said.

Joanie exhaled, feeling more exasperated than ever.

"It's pathetic, if you ask me. People always say, 'Hey, you can get a heart attack in the pits and the traders will just step over you and keep on trading.' Well, it's true. Just look at Korngold Commodities right now."

"Miss Bleeding Heart," he said.

He sat up, kicking the desk as he did.

"I'm as sorry for the kid as you are," he went on. "I talked to his mother. I'll do what I can for the family. But that's it. The little jerk was trading D-marks. He wins he gets shit-faced drunk. He loses he kills himself."

Joanie looked off, searching for something to say. Suddenly she was startled by someone standing in the doorway behind her. It was Rachel Korngold. She was staring at Joanie, her expression, her dark eyes, fixed in a look that Joanie had seen before. Only now Joanie was too upset to acknowledge it or Rachel herself.

She strode quickly toward the doorway. Rachel stepped sideways to let her by. But Joanie stopped, glanced at the girl, then turned back to Korngold.

"It stinks, if you ask me. Brian was *eighteen* years old," she said, and she hurried out.

She went past the others in the outer office, all of whom had heard her, and went to the restroom down the hall. When she reached the door she began to cry. She held onto the lavatory and shook, the sobs convulsing her entire body, her tears falling onto the backs of her hands.

"This place is on tilt," said Tommy Haggarty.

An hour later Jimmy Bilandic came in and went directly into Korngold's office. Korngold tossed a printout of Bilandic's D-mark losses to the edge of the desk.

"Cover these and find another firm," he said.

Bilandic scowled.

"Fine," he said, and walked out.

Marty Valukas was next.

Korngold said, "Anybody trading fills out an application. And it has my signature on it before a fuckin' one-lot trades. You got that, Marty?"

Valukas nodded.

Finally, Korngold found Tommy. Tommy gave him the cocked pistol and the finger snaps, then followed him into his office and turned to search the liquor cabinet for a bottle of club soda.

"So this guy is cutting his lawn and the blade of the mower flies off and cuts his dick clean off," Tommy began, shoving the words out past a wad of gum the size of a golf ball in his mouth.

"You got two weeks to find another job," Korngold said.

179

Tommy turned and stared, his hands on his hips.

"Son of a *bitch*," he said. "I didn't have a fuckin' thing to do with that little asshole."

"Keep telling yourself that."

"Aw, *c'mon*, Ken. Don't tell me you're gonna pile the guilt on the first guy on the list."

"You're not the first guy, Tommy. But close enough."

"Look: I didn't *tell* him to get in. I didn't *lean* on him. I didn't *push* him. I didn't do *nothin'*."

"Two weeks. Now get outta here."

"Aw, fuck—"

He whirled and walked for the door, then kicked it with the heel of his shoe. His fists clenched, he turned back to Korngold.

"Did I *call* it or did I *call* it?" he shouted.

They had a date later that night but Joanie could not wait that long. Steve had left the office at noon, and knew nothing of what had gone on later. Joanie left the Board of Trade and took the train up to his place, got no answer when she rang, and sat on the concrete step outside the door. It was still light out, but she hardly noticed the brilliant, diagonal rays of sun. Her head was still back in the office.

Steve finally appeared on the long end of a four-mile run. He was winded and dank.

As he changed and showered, Joanie raced through the afternoon's confrontations.

Steve listened and said nothing, not having to.

"Korngold was such a *prick* about it. And I told him where to stuff it," she said.

"Not really," Steve said.

She stopped short, looking up at him.

"You should have quit."

"Quit?" Joanie said.

"Yeah. Life and death is as good a reason as I know of."

180

"Very funny."

"It's not a joke."

"What about *you?* You're just as involved."

"By association, yes."

"Quit? I couldn't *quit*. Korngold is the reason I'm here! If it weren't for him I'd be cutting hair in Florida—"

"And Brian Boyer would still be alive."

"Oh, come on. . . . I mean, is that what you would have done back in the glorious sixties?" she said.

"In a minute," he said.

He paused before turning to the mirror.

"Got any guts?" he said.

"That's not fair," Joanie said.

Why am I doing this? Why am I jeopardizing everything? What will Mom say? Does she have to know? Steve says I can get another job in a minute, but what if I can't? What if Korngold has some kind of blackball? What if they just laugh in my face, say, hey, Joanie baby, you'll never work on the floor again? Could I go back to cutting hair? I couldn't. Could I? It would be different between Steve and me. He's interested because I'm down there. I know what it means to trade. He knows that I know. But what if I don't know anymore? What if he loses interest? Says he doesn't go out with hairdressers? How long will my savings hold out? What would I sell first? My utilities are hurting thanks to that plant shutdown. What if I lost all my money? What if I lost everything?

The refrain was endless, tripping through her mind most of the night after the day she told Korngold, who shrugged his shoulders and said, "Stupid cunt," that she was quitting.

Early on the following Saturday morning, she went down to the Korngold offices to clear out her things.

When she cracked the door she heard the tapping of a

181

computer keyboard. Mary Beth, Lisa, maybe Ira Roth, the ever-present accountant. Yet inside Joanie saw no one. The noise came from Korngold's office. She stepped near the door to get a peek. There, staring into the computer's screen, was a head of glistening dark hair. It belonged to Rachel Korngold, the princess herself.

Rachel turned and saw her.

"Hello," Joanie said softly.

Rachel frowned.

"Oh," she said, but just barely, and she turned back to the computer. Next to her were stacks of her father's trading cards.

Joanie watched for a moment, oddly curious.

"Doing his log?" she said.

"Always have. It was my idea in the first place," Rachel said.

"You're kidding."

"I'm not," Rachel said, rapping the keys.

She was entering the details of Korngold's daily trading into a program that translated it into flow charts and bar graphs. Every trend and every quirk in his trading was recorded, and easily assessed.

"That's really good work. He uses it all the time," Joanie said.

"He does?" Rachel said, her eyes lifting.

"Oh yeah. I thought he pulled it from some service, or something. But *you* do it?"

"I got the program from school. There's a kid there who pirates software and he and I messed with it. His dad trades S and P's," she said, still facing the screen.

"Amazing."

"And Daddy uses it a lot?"

"Always," Joanie said. "I figured he paid a fortune for it."

"Nope. It's me. Miss Cheap Data Entry," Rachel said.

Her face fairly glowed as she said it. She punched up different graphs and charts as she spoke, all of them done in multicolor. Then she turned in her chair.

"Done. Daddy's clear. Ira said everybody else is okay, too," she said.

She was obviously pleased with herself, and pleased with Joanie's compliments.

"That's great," Joanie said.

She began to move away.

Then she stopped.

"Your father here?" she asked.

"On Saturday? You kidding? I take the train down," Rachel said.

Joanie shook her head.

"You love it, too, huh?" she said.

"Of course," Rachel said.

But too quickly. She sighed.

"A lot of my friends do it. Like a family thing. Daddy used to bring me down when I was five years old and have me stack his cards."

"That explains it," Joanie said.

"What?"

"Why everybody is related to somebody down here. Like you said, it's one big family business."

"It's just easy that way," Rachel said.

Joanie smiled.

"You're lucky. I never knew the markets existed until college. You—geez—for you it's natural. Like a kid learning baseball."

Rachel nodded, looking to Joanie at that moment neither lucky nor natural.

"Does your mother get involved?" Joanie said.

"Get serious. Mrs. American Express Platinum Card?"

Joanie laughed. Rachel did not.

"Your dad's lucky," Joanie said quickly.

"You don't know my mother," said Rachel.

"No, I mean you."

"Oh . . ." Rachel said.

"You really like him."

"Sure. Why not?"

"I'm the wrong one to ask. I never had a father."

Rachel looked up at her. "Oh, yeah, I remember."

Joanie smiled very slightly, seeing features in Rachel's face, the sleek contour of her cheeks, a trait she did not draw from her father.

"But you have a mother," Rachel said.

"Oh, that I do," Joanie said. "A champ."

Rachel looked at the computer screen once again.

"How come you're here today?" she said.

"Moving out," Joanie said.

"Why?" Rachel said, turning in her chair and clutching Joanie's wrist. "You quit? Over what happened?"

Joanie nodded silently.

"That's *incredible*. I mean, God, Daddy must have been *zapped*," she said.

"He didn't take it real well," Joanie said.

"He doesn't take *anything* real well. I can't believe it. I wouldn't have the balls—"

Joanie shook her head. "I was scared stiff," she said.

"No, I didn't mean that. It's just that—God, *quitting*. Like on principle."

"Yeah, you could say that," Joanie said.

"You got another job?"

"No."

"Wow."

"Monday morning I start looking."

"No sweat. You'll get hired as soon as you walk in the door."

Joanie smiled. "You're a sweet kid, Rachel."

It was Rachel's turn to smile.

"God. *Quitting*. That is so neat," she said.

Joanie went over to the closet to get her things. It did not take long. She glanced at the clock and made a phone call. She was supposed to meet Steve at noon. She tilted her head to the side and her hair fell over the receiver.

"Checking in," she said.

"Forget about the beach," Steve said. "It's eighty degrees

184

and the wind's blowing out. That means fun at the old ball park."

"Where?" Joanie asked.

"Where? Why in God's green ball yard—Wrigley Field."

"The Cubbies."

"The Cubs, please. Bleachers. I've got the ducats and plenty of beer money."

"Mr. Fun," she said.

"Joanie, you're not a Chicagoan 'til you've been there. So put on some shorts and a tank top. Get on the el and I'll meet you at Addison and Sheffield in a half hour."

"Such an offer," she said.

"Damn right, Cub fans," he said, and hung up.

She put down the phone and turned to see Rachel standing in the doorway. Joanie paused, taking in the slender, beautiful, solitary girl on a summertime Saturday morning.

"You like the Cubs?" Joanie said.

"My friends go sometimes."

"Come on along," Joanie said.

"Oh, no—"

"Yeah. It'll be a good time. Get some sun. You can tell me which team is the Cubs."

"But it's your *date*."

"So what? Steve can sit in the middle and everybody'll think he's a big stud or something."

Rachel laughed. "You serious? It'd be a gas."

"Come on," Joanie said, and nodded toward the door.

Rachel skipped after her, leaving her father's computer quietly humming, its screen alive with figures, the flashing cursor awaiting command.

In minutes Joanie and Rachel were on an elevated train heading north. At each stop they were joined by blue-capped fans on their way to the park. This was Cubs mania, Joanie realized, a fact of life in Chicago every bit as well known as State Street. Traders were infected with it. Several were season ticket holders, which meant that when the team was home they fled the pits after lunch in order to

185

make the first inning. Those that did not go put down bets on the game, and kept runners hopping back to the office to check on the score.

Joanic, though not a baseball fan, was mildly fascinated by it all, especially the recent fuss over Wrigley Field and its newly installed lights. Until today she had never seen the team or been inside its park. At the Addison Street stop she and Rachel followed the wave of fans onto the sidewalk.

The field was located in the middle of a typical Chicago neighborhood, with two-flats and stoops and one-way side streets. Impromptu souvenir stands cluttered street corners; kids and old ladies waved cars into cramped parking places in alleys and vacant lots. People streamed everywhere, police directed traffic, corner bars had smoky grills out front loaded with hotdogs and bratwurst, clusters of beer-drinking fans clogged the sidewalks.

On the designated corner, wearing his jogging shorts, a T-shirt with "Bud Man, Bud Fan" on front, and a ridiculous blue-and-white Cubs painter's hat, was Steve. He waved and cut across the street toward them.

"You made good time," he said, then eyed Rachel.

"Brought along a friend," Joanie said. "Rachel, you know Steve Stamford, one of your dad's men."

"Hi," Rachel said meekly, looking as if she wanted to get back on the train and go back to the office.

"Hey, what a surprise," Steve said, then he turned and scanned the sidewalk. "So what do we do about a ticket?"

"I know a guy," Rachel said.

"Huh? Who?" said Steve.

"Daddy always uses him," she said.

She led them around the corner to a souvenir stand near the fire station. Joanie and Steve hung back while Rachel approached a young guy with a chrome coin changer on his belt and blue kerchief on his forehead. Moments later she returned with a ticket and smile.

"That was easy," Joanie said.

"He used to run for us," said Rachel. "Now he does this."

"Figures," said Steve.

He put his arm around them both and pushed them down the sidewalk. Joanie loved him for it.

"I got a buddy saving us some seats. They're numbered but nobody gives a shit. First come, first serve, so you gotta know a bird dog. Especially with the Mets here. Hey, good to see you at the ball game, kids," he said, and squeezed their lovely shoulders.

"Slow down, big guy," Joanie said.

In no time they were in the bleachers. It was a baked area of benches packed with beer-swilling fans, most of them young and nearly naked.

"Great, huh?" Steve proclaimed as they wedged into their spots. "Today, Joanie, you're a Bleacher Bum. Full rights to heckle the enemy, get a suntan, and dive for a home run or two."

"I need a scorecard," Joanie said.

"You're sitting next to one. Whattaya wanna know?" he said.

Joanie laughed, looking around at the beach of humanity, guys without shirts, girls in cut-off jeans and halter tops, all of them wearing Cubs visors, painter's hats, blue team caps or beanies, and working on Old Style beer in paper cups. Above them to the rear was the broad, olive-green, ancient scoreboard bedecked with metal numbers for the line scores. Inside the sweltering metal compartment were three men who watched the game and read a teletype machine in order to post the scores, a routine that had been followed since the scoreboard was built fifty years before.

In the top row of the bleachers a couple of kids were collecting empty cups and wedging them in the cyclone fence to spell out "Cubs." A sweating black guy stood up and led a cheer, punctuating it with death-rattling shrieks.

"He ought to trade beans with that voice," Joanie said.

"That's Ronnie. Long-time Bleacher Bum. It's a club, as you can see. They even wrote a play about the Bums a few years ago," Steve said.

187

"And right over there," he went on, pointing at the front row, "was where Bill Veeck sat every day."

"Who was he?" Joanie said.

"A hero," Steve said.

At that the crowd rose for the National Anthem, and then the game began. Joanie looked around and felt the buzz of the fans, the heat of the sun. She glanced at Rachel. She was sipping a soft drink, occasionally tilting her head skyward, but mostly taking in the carnival all around her. Joanie wondered if, indeed, Rachel had ever been here before, had ever come in with a gaggle of friends and spent the afternoon being silly in the bleachers.

"Anybody ever hit a home run out here?" Joanie asked.

"Constantly," Steve said. "But nobody's ever hit the scoreboard."

"Wrongo!" shouted a woman in front of them. She turned to them to expound. "Sammy Snead hit it with a five iron in 1951. Roberto Clemente hit the steps right below it."

"Okay, okay," Steve said.

Joanie was stunned. "You got to pass a test to sit out here?"

"We're talking hard-core fans," Steve said.

For the rest of the afternoon they baked in the sun, screamed with the Bleacher Bums, washed down pints of beer, perspired more than they thought possible, and made regular trips to the restroom.

The game was a good one, with the Cubs and Mets trading runs, many brought in by rocket shots into the bleachers. With each one the fans jumped to their feet, and those near the ball lunged at it in a phalanx of hands and arms madly grasping for the hissing white blur. It was a wild, collapsing crush of sweaty humanity, reminding Joanie of the soybean pit in the midst of a spiraling rally.

If the home run had been hit by the Cubs, the ball was kept. By the Mets, and it was tossed back onto the field to a burst of cheers and applause.

"I thought the ball was a souvenir?" Joanie said.

188

"No self-respecting Cub fan would keep such a thing," he said.

In the ninth they stood up with the throng as the Cub relief pitcher humiliated the final Mets hitter, then whistled at the victory. They filed out, tired, drained, a little burnt around the edges. The vacated bleachers were a sea of debris.

"Let's do the Sheffield stagger," Steve said. "We walk back toward my place stopping at each corner tap for a draught."

Joanie's eyes rolled upward, then she looked at Rachel.

"I'm outta here. You guys have been super," Rachel said.

She turned and gave Joanie a hug.

"How will you get home?" Joanie said.

"No sweat. I flag a cab to the Lawrence station and catch the train. For a suburban brat, I can get around," she said. She made a victory fist.

"Hey, thanks for comin' along, brat," Joanie said, and hugged her.

"Brat," Rachel replied, and stuck out her tongue. Then she dashed into the street after an empty cab.

"Well, well, well," Steve said, draping his arm around Joanie. "Interesting little social arrangement."

"I don't know about that," Joanie said.

They made two blocks and two stops before Joanie began to stagger. The beer was cold and delicious, but it went from her throat directly to her brain. Steve mercifully hailed a cab.

"I would kill defenseless women and children for a cold shower," she said as they stepped inside his apartment.

"Spare them and use the first door on the right."

The cold water was a godsend. She was sunburned, a little drunk, yet, with the rush of the cool water and the caress of the soap bar against her body, she began to feel a little frisky.

She emerged from the bathroom wrapped in a towel, her hair wet, her nose the color of a radish.

"My turn," he said, and brushed by her.

She fixed herself a tumbler of ice water and returned to the door of the bathroom. She waited. He took long showers.

When he opened the door she was standing there.

"That was a great time," she said.

"Even with the boss's daughter along," he said.

"Former boss," Joanie said.

"Current daughter."

"She's a good kid. She can be saved," Joanie said.

"From what?"

"No," Joanie said, "from *whom*."

"Looks like dangerous territory to me," he said.

He shook his head, then flicked water from his hair in her direction.

"You can't beat fun at the old ball park," he said.

She loosened her towel, and it fell to the floor.

"Wanna bet?" she said.

By the time she got back to her apartment it was close to midnight. It had been a golden day, culminating in a careless evening sitting in an outdoors restaurant sipping champagne. Now Joanie was exhausted.

The phone was ringing as she unlocked her door.

She answered it.

"I don't know what you're doing or what you're trying to prove, but you're not doing it with my daughter," the voice said.

She began to respond, but was interrupted.

"This is not a conversation. Just a statement of fact. Stay away from Rachel."

Then Korngold hung up.

PART THREE

Chapter One

Rachel Korngold had been right: it was not a matter of whether Joanie would find another job but which company she would go with. Other firms were unaware of her falling out with Korngold, and did not seem interested in the flap. Floor personnel routinely jumped from firm to firm. Most were eager to take on experienced assistants, especially when they looked like Joanie Yff.

It was Steve's idea that she seek out a small company, one with active partners and a paternal eye over its traders. It was heartfelt advice, for only a day after Joanie quit, Steve himself left Korngold to go with Cunningham, a partnership made up of a handful of traders Steve knew from the bond pit. It was a quiet, bloodless parting that seemed to come as no surprise or insult to Korngold himself. As for Joanie, Steve knew of a spot with Trout Trading, a fledgling house made up of two soybean traders. The company's name came from Ballard Trout, a tall, intense black man whose baritone voice thundered through the pits like a ghost of Paul Robeson.

Yet it was not Trout's voice nor his trading prowess—though he was a tough, aggressive trader—that put the members of the floor in awe of him. It was his former career. In his not too distant past, Ballard Trout could hit a baseball as well as any man alive.

"What are people gonna think when they see the likes of you workin' for the likes of me?" Trout said when Joanie applied to him. Then he roared his remarkable laugh.

Joanie, who knew nothing of his past, instantly liked him.

* * *

For Ballard Trout, all the emotional jive was just that. The kind of thing white boys raised on Little League dreams got caught up in. He had seen too much of life right from the start to buy that. His mother died having him, due, he was later told, to some disease of the womb. Not because his head was shaped like a bullet, like his cousin Rathel always said, which gave Mama such a fright she up and died. His father, Big Robert Alonzo Trout, was hit-and-run, catch-as-catch-can, hello-good-bye. Big Robert decided that the passing of his wife was a definite message telling him to git.

So Ballard was raised by his Aunt Lea, who had six of her own and was a good and gentle woman with a hum that could put you to sleep on the worst toothache or the fiercest thunderstorm.

His father did stop in when he got in the area, but never for long. The family called him Neutral, because he never stayed long enough to shut the motor off.

Ballard Trout's childhood was spent in a little shack with no running water on a gravel road outside Idlewild, in the northern lower peninsula of Michigan, once the barbecue and blues capital of the Midwest when rich black folk came up on vacation but long since gone to seed as the poorest county in the state, bunches of little colored kids running barefoot in the fields. It was something long ago and poor. Sweet if you remembered only the coo of the mourning doves and swimming naked in the creek; damn bleak if you thought of the bacon-fat meals and dead dogs and winters when ice formed white on bedroom walls.

So emotion was something Ballard had no time for. Especially when it was attached to a game, a ball and a bat. He played and played well, in the fields as a kid at Cadillac High School, where he hit .674 his senior year. When a representative of the St. Louis Cardinals offered him $10,000 to sign a contract and a $2,000 monthly salary after that, Ballard thought Auntie had died right there and gone to heaven.

194

Then he said, "Don't let the old man get at it, Auntie," and smiled.

The rest was history, recorded by the scribes of the *Baseball Encyclopedia*, updated each year on the back of a full-colored Topps trading card.

Ballard Alonzo Trout. Nickname: "Big Train."
Born 8/11/41, Idlewild, Michigan. 6' 2", 190 pounds.
Bats left. Throws right. Outfield.

He stayed in the Cardinals' system for three years before going to the Chicago Cubs in the Ernie Broglio-Lou Brock trade. Played with a bunch of no-names—except for a kid named Ernie Banks.

How he performed, year in and year out, batting left-handed with a clean, level, effortless stroke and that impassive expression. Not power, though with his wrists he could jerk any ball out of the park if he got his pitch, but machinelike consistency, eight seasons of 200 hits and a .300-plus average.

He was so low-key, so consistent, that it worked against him. People took him for granted. Affixed terms like "dependable" and "underrated" in preseason stories. That would have been a general commentary on his pro tour had not a wonderful thing happened to him, a bit of justice in a career of obscure excellence. It happened when free agency hit baseball, when players were free to negotiate new contracts with the highest bidder. Texas millionaire A. Hebert Armstrong decided that Ballard Trout, at age thirty-six, was a superstar, and he gave him $1.2 million to sign with the Texas Rangers. Over three years, guaranteed, with a $100,000 bonus to sign.

It brought that same rare, sanguine smile to Ballard's face, a strange cap to his head, and nothing but grief to his batting average. He hit moderately well in the Texas heat, his ninth .300 season, but he was not the Ballard Trout of Wrigley Field. He was just an aging ballplayer.

And a millionaire.

The contract made him more money in three years than in the previous sixteen. And with a portion of it his lawyer bought him a seat on the Chicago Board of Trade.

At the time the purchase of the seat had no effect on Ballard. He did not know a commodity from a glass of Gatorade. But in only a few years the seat changed his life. It transformed his entire character and brought out a personality that he never knew existed, one never seen by the millions of fans who watched him play baseball, a character that could have come only from his father, Big Robert, the gambling man with numbers in his head and grand larceny in his soul.

Ballard "Big Train" Trout became BAT, one of the boys, a trader, a solo player in a game where there were no teams, no reliance on someone else to bring you home. It was a game of guts and instincts and drive, and it brought fire to Ballard Trout's dark eyes, made his blood pulse, brought dancing lines to that heretofore impregnable veneer.

BAT loved to trade, and he was damn good at it.

The pits were full of hunks and studs, guys with tans and chest hair. And money, of course. From the moment Joanie's Reeboks touched the trading floor she caught their nods, both innocent and lascivious, but mostly the latter, fielded the flip, inviting small talk on the elevators and the steps of the pits. She snickered at outrageous but bona fide propositions scrawled on trading cards and slipped into her jacket pockets. Bids, offers, positions, and phone numbers.

Yet Joanie remained drawn to the wafer-thin bond trader, a guy who looked like your best friend's older brother. There was no explaining it.

Or maybe there was. As brave a front as Joanie had put on after quitting Korngold, she trembled at the very thought of him. Korngold had been her sponsor, her mentor, her lover, her whole reason for being in the pits. She hated him for what he had done to Brian Boyer, and how he had come to treat her, particularly when he was drinking. Yet he remained a large figure in her life, a presence, no matter if she was working for him or not. He was still a strong, paternal, assuring figure in a business where nothing was assured or certain. She could never forget him, never really extricate herself from him.

Her flight to Steve Stamford came naturally. She fell headlong for him. He was not physical, no slab of beefcake. He was not loaded, no million-dollar kid. His appeal to Joanie was immediate and obvious: he could talk. Not just the howl and the postpit trader swagger, not just grabass, towel-snapping nonsense left over from fraternity days. Steve said things, about himself, about her, putting English on his words. He turned a phrase like a comedian, and usually turned it on himself. Traders did not do that. They were bombast and egomania, rowdies with Rolexes, boys with bankrolls and BMWs eager to convince the latest blonde that they were the smoothest, most self-assured creatures to ever whisper in her ear.

Steve did none of that. He spoke in plain tones and compound sentences.

At dusk, late by a half hour, she showed up in front of his loft. The tardiness was due to a last-minute errand. She had made a few hurried phone calls, then aimed the Honda to the Northwest Side and a secondhand bicycle shop on Roscoe Street. Inside she spied a $22 fat-wheel bicycle with a toy license plate reading "Mary" wired to the seat. She knew it was the one. In her peach-colored velour jogging suit she pedaled the bike east to Steve's place, wobbling over the potholes and the pavement fissures, finally turning the corner and coming into view. He buried his head in his hands.

"Don't you love it? Isn't it great?" she yelled.

Steve walked around the two-wheeler, a Roadmaster, shielding his eyes from the glint of rusting chrome fenders.

He lightly kicked the rear tire.

"I haven't seen tires that big since I was in Little League," he said.

"Like riding on fudge," Joanie said.

"Fudge?" he said.

Steve began loosening up, stretching, running in place. He wore a baggy pair of gray shorts and a Miller High Life T-shirt. Side by side they looked like a fashion model and a furniture mover.

"You can park it behind the gate. Nobody'll touch it. Shoot, they'll die laughing at it."

"Forget it," she said. "I gotta break it in."

He shook his head.

"Ride interference for me. And don't wind yourself," he said, and started off, running on the parkway east toward Lincoln Park and the lakefront.

Joanie's ponytail bobbed about her shoulders as she pedaled. She had not ridden a bike in years, and never one like this. She tried to maneuver her rear end into a comfortable position on the hard seat. The front tire rubbed against the fender in a rhythmical groan. Steve ran smoothly, without talking, occasionally looking sideways at her and the bike, and grinning.

"This is getting boring," she finally said.

"Buy a newspaper," he snapped, now breathing harder.

"Sep beans closed at six-thirteen even, down a cent. Sep corn at two-oh-eight, up a half. Wheat even—" she said.

"Stop! I'll talk. I'll talk. Tell you anything you want to know," he said.

"When did you know you first wanted to trade?" she said.

"I smell something with that question," he said.

"Shut up and answer," she said.

"Is that what Barbara Walters would say?"

"Who cares?"

"When I knew it was bullshit, that's when," he said, punching his words between breaths. "Capitalist greed. A

198

market with no reason to exist except for the speculation."

"So why'd you get in?" she said.

"My life, for one. My marriage, my career, a friend who traded beans. Et cetera."

He began running harder, sweat darkening a circle on the back of his shirt. Joanie stood up to pump the bike and stay with him. She took no notice of the stares the two of them got from pedestrians and other joggers.

"So go on," she said. "Before you're too tired to breathe."

"Jesus," he grunted, stumbling.

"Minor melodrama," he said, now back in stride. "I was raised to be a lawyer, and I became one. Early seventies. Back when people my age still had the faith. McCarthy— Gene, not Joe—the sixty-eight Democratic convention, Vietnam. I passed the bar, went to work for the public defender's office."

They had reached Clark Street, which was alive with traffic. They continued east toward the green expanse of Lincoln Park as it fronted the lake.

"Represented the tired, the poor, the wretched refuse," Steve continued. "Wretched, and guilty as sin. Maybe not what they were charged with, but of something at least as bad. I had guys trying to beat burglary raps who'd committed ax murders. 'Oh, yeah, Mistuh Steve, I forgot 'bout that.'

"Then I joined a storefront legal clinic. They existed back then. You didn't even consider working downtown. That was a cop-out."

"The poor man's Perry Mason," she said.

"Clarence Darrow, if you please. The work was more social than criminal. Office was a former massage parlor in Uptown. Wallpaper had a hundred and one sexual positions on it."

"Ooooh," she said.

"That's what Ricky, the office rat, used to say, and he was only twelve. People had *problems*. Lockouts, rape, immigration hassles, drugs, beatings from cops, politics, gangs. I was as much a community organizer as a lawyer."

"Depressing."

"Yeah. And I loved it. It was the common good. We won some big ones for the little people."

"Big money, too?"

"Oh, yeah. A cool eight thousand bucks a year and unlimited privileges at Park District restrooms," he said.

They crossed Stockton and cut down to the jogging path adjacent to the lagoon. Joanie leaned forward and inhaled the misty lake air, now feeling the muscles in her back and legs.

"Let's take it easy," Steve said. "You're doing real well on that thing."

"Easy rider," she said.

"That's my era," he replied.

She got off and walked alongside him. A constant procession of joggers weaved past them, their shoes lightly throwing the path's gray cinders.

"Eight thou?" she said, eager to have him continue.

"That's all. But so what?" he exhaled, his hands on his hips. "We were fighting big money, not trying to make it. I worked in blue jeans and army fatigues and had my hair in a ponytail like yours."

"SDS," she said.

"Power to the people," he said. "Hell, we thought it would happen. We did. Rallies, boycotts. We got out the vote. Even elected some good people—community types, independents—instead of the machine hacks. We worked our butts off for McGovern and got clobbered. By then it was in our blood and we got involved in the Singer campaign against Daley."

"Tell me about that. I don't know anything about Daley."

"Neither did we, it turned out. We thought if we ran an intelligent, liberal candidate who could articulate the issues and expose the machine for what it was, we'd win."

"And?" she said.

"If any one of us had grown up in the neighborhoods,

200

we'd have known better. But we didn't. So we worked like dogs — eight months of sixteen-hour days, living on coffee and cigarettes, paying the rent with chits. None of us had a dime and we were still donating money to the campaign."

"You got beat, right? Like everybody who ran against Daley."

"Creamed. Humiliated. Election Day was the worst experience of my life."

She laughed. "I didn't mean to laugh — it's just that those days must have been something."

"Duh Mare," he repeated.

"What if you'd won?"

"We were gonna take ours. The top guys would get the big departments — my buddy Michael Holland wanted Streets and San. The rest of us would be mayoral aides at sixty K a year."

"Not bad."

"What we got instead is the hell out. Scattered to the winds like a bunch of wounded animals. Some moved out of the city, like they were punishing it or something. A lot of us started looking for jobs. I went back to the clinic, but it wasn't the same. Didn't last six months. It was the beginning of the end of a lot of things — my politics, my law career, my marriage."

He began to jog again, and she got back on the bike.

"We've never talked about your marriage."

"No, we haven't."

"Soon as I met you I knew you were married. Or had been."

"How?"

"You're just . . . well, you're just very *married*."

"I don't know what that means."

"Never mind. How'd you meet her?"

"You don't want to know all *that*," he said.

"I do. I'm a fiend for details."

"College," he said. "She was an ed major. Got a job

201

teaching high school. Put me through law school in Champaign. We came to Chicago and she taught at Marshall High and I got on with the PD. We'd come home at night and compare stories about the savages."

"What was her name?"

"Barb. Still is."

"And she was involved in the campaign?"

"Had to be. That was our life. But not like I was."

"So what happened?"

"In a nutshell: it got to her. Ten years of teaching school, wearing blue jeans, driving beat-up Volkswagens, having no money. Got to me, too, but I didn't know it at the time. When it did it was too late."

"She sounds interesting."

"She is."

"Live in town?"

"No."

"Still see her?"

"Yeah."

"Sleep with her?"

"Wait a minute—"

"Well?"

Joanie was beginning to tire, her feet pushing against the pedals. Steve seemed to want to run on forever. They had gone north past Diversey Harbor and its bobbing yachts and perch fishermen, past the driving range chocked with crazed, flogging Orientals, past the flood-lit, polite tennis courts.

"I don't sleep with her. Sometimes I wish I did. It makes me a little crazy," Steve said.

"Of course, it's none of my business," she said, then smirked.

"No?" he said, and turned to look at her. She looked back at him. He stepped off the path into a calisthenics area. It was an array of platforms and exercise bars ostensibly meant to give runners a means of testing their flexibility but which were really only fancy devices that served to interrupt the tedium of running. Joanie let the bicycle fall and went over to a balance bar. Steve kept running, lengthening his strides and reaching for speed, finally sprinting a hundred yards before turning around and jogging back.

It was not like him to talk as he ran, much less to divulge the personal details of his past. But he had done just that. He was not sure what this meant, or of what cosmic effect Joanie Yff seemed to have on him. At that moment he pulled up in the exercise area and came upon her rear end, upraised, straining against the fabric of her pastel velour as she bent over and clutched her calves. Her ass was a dream, and all rational thought left him.

Then she stood upright and turned around, her face flushed and sweaty, wisps of blond hair falling about her forehead. She put one arm straight out and rested it on his shoulder.

"My crotch is killing me," she said.

"You say that to all the boys," he said.

She punched him. He yelped.

"What's your normal distance on a fatwheel like that?" he asked.

"Athens to Sparta," she said.

"No, that's my event," he said. "And it was Athens to Marathon, twenty-six miles, three hundred eighty-five yards."

"I suppose you even run in them," she said.

"I have."

"Spare me," she said.

She exhaled and leaned in back of him. Spotting a patch of white, she reached under his shirt and snapped the band of his jockstrap.

"My God!" he yelled and whirled around.

Joanie back-pedaled, smacking into a jogger, a rolypoly woman in shorts and tights and smeared makeup. Joanie grimaced sheepishly.

"I want an ice cream cone," she said.

"It would negate everything we just did," he said.

"Good," she said.

They headed west on Belmont, beneath Lake Shore Drive, and into New Town.

"I'll fix you a tuna and avocado salad back at my place instead," he said.

"What is this, L.A.?" she said.

"Luckily neither of us has any money for ice cream," he said.

Joanie leaned and poked a finger inside her shoe. She pulled out a $5 bill and held it up in front of her nose.

"There's a Thirty-one Flavors around here someplace," she said.

They saw a lot of each other, over beers or a bottle of wine, walking hand in hand down North Side side streets after dark, munching Mexican food at a neighborhood cantina. For Joanie it was relaxed and comfortable, a tonic after the pits. Steve was not aggressive or physical, but he was extremely charming, well mannered, gracious almost to a fault. He held doors, offered his arm, made introductions, and immediately put Joanie at complete ease whenever they were together. Maybe it was his age, his experience, his basic intelligence, she did not know which, but he seemed to be totally in control and unforced.

Or maybe, and she did not dwell on this, it was just that he was a complete contrast to Korngold, another man who had swept her off her feet in a different way. That had soured, things had changed, or she herself had, and Steve was the right person at the right time.

Joanie remembered a snatch of a conversation she had had when she was doing hair. It was one of those endless conversations with women customers in which the topic was usually men—boyfriends, husbands, lovers. This time the customer, a newly divorced woman in her early thirties, was complaining about the new men in her life.

"I just want someone," she said, "who can pick up a menu and *order*."

Joanie never forgot the remark. Especially now. Steve was someone who could order.

He pampered and complimented her, bought her small appropriate gifts—an album she said she liked, a book, a raunchy postcard, a lapel button with a photo of the Little Rascals, even fat, whipped-cream treats from a favorite bakery. He did it all with a smile and a squeeze, and she loved him for it.

If only, she reflected one night alone in bed, if only he told her what he felt for her. He never said a word about that, and she was afraid to ask.

"Why don't you leave some clothes here? Wouldn't that be more convenient?" he said one night after another bicycle-escorted run.

"Why don't I move my whole wardrobe in?" she said.

He smiled, but shook his head no.

As much as she ached to do so, she did not protest.

As the summer days passed, the bicycle's seat molded to hers. She deftly maneuvered it up and around curbs as she accompanied him. Out of respect for his hard work and sweat, she refrained from sucking on popsicles or drinking soft drinks as she rode. Each night Steve pushed himself, lengthening his distances, noting his times. He had given up trying to get her to run with him.

Then one night he did not immediately change into his customary cut-off shorts and one of his crummy T-shirts. He poured himself a beer, offered her one, and leisurely drank it before dressing. The next night he did the same, but took even more time to get dressed. She waited for him and said nothing, but took note of the change. Each night he seemed to take more time, dressing reluctantly, like a little boy getting ready for bed, a resigned, bored look on his face.

205

Finally he came out with it.

"Why don't we just bag the work-out tonight?" he said.

"For shame," she said.

"I decided to jog for two reasons: to stay in shape and pass the time. Well, I'm in shape. In fact, I'm too damn skinny. Weigh less now than I did in high school. And when I'm with you the time passes quite nicely."

"Well, aren't you sweet," she said. "Does that mean I can bag the bike, too?"

"No. I still like to see you sweat."

"There are other ways, you know."

"How well I know," he said.

Instead of jogging that night, they rented roller skates from a lakeside concession. It was a complete disaster. Steve's legs flailed about like those of a new colt. With Joanie's fatwheel back at the apartment, they rented bikes, and soon they were pedaling along the lakeshore south into the Gold Coast and down to Navy Pier.

On the ride back they crossed Lake Shore Drive to the Northwestern University complex of law and medical schools. The law library was newly completed, and Steve was interested in seeing the inside. The building was relatively deserted in the summer, and only a few students and personnel quietly padded about. Not a person was in the lounge area with its overstuffed sofas and polished wooden desks.

In the corner of the lounge was a piano, an old upright apparently moved from the old building, and Joanie brushed a finger along the keys, lightly plinking a few.

"Mozart," Steve said.

Then he slid onto the bench and began to play, not Mozart but Debussy. His hands moved effortlessly, the prelude echoing through the room.

Joanie was amazed, and watched as his fingers reached for chords, his foot lightly vamping the pedal.

"That's wonderful," she said.

"Kind of awful, really. A maestro of missed notes."

He trailed off, playing with a few themes, thundering a refrain until he got it correct, then drifting into a tune with a couple of fingers.

"Is there anything you can't do?" she said.

"My classical Indiana education," he said. "Do a little bit of everything, and nothing really well."

Her eyes widened.

"I can't believe you said that," she said. "You are—I bet not one person in the pits could sit down and play like that."

"They don't have to. They can trade. Make bundles and buy digital recordings of Vladimir Ashkenazy. Now *he* can play."

"Why do you do that?" she said.

"What?"

"Trash yourself."

"Longhours of practice," he said, and raced into the opening salvo of *Rhapsody in Blue*.

He finished and slid off the bench. Joanie walked over to one of the deserted sofas in the center of the huge room.

"Come here and talk to me," she said.

She sat sideways, kicking off her sandals and tucking her legs beneath her, and faced him with her chin in her hands.

"Sometimes I think I'm really getting to know you," she began. "Then you say something like that and all bets are off."

"Like what?"

"Like how you do everything but not well."

"Well?"

"Well, it's just not true," she said.

"Look," he said, "I know all the slogans, all the believe-in-yourself stuff. Zig Ziglar. Art Linkletter. The lingo that makes insurance salesmen froth. I can forgo all that. I know I'm good at things. I have ability. I'm educated. I can read and learn. If all this goes to the shitcan, I can always get a job as a bank teller."

She said nothing, her unwavering attention inviting him to go on.

"I knew I could make it as a lawyer, go with a firm, be a solid associate and then a partner. All I needed was the wardrobe. But I knew I wouldn't be great. I haven't got the brilliance to be great, or the guts, maybe. Anyway, I felt better helping people, so I went the public defender/law clinic route, like I told you about. And that was okay, too. I helped a lot of people. I was no Clarence Darrow and never would be. That takes brilliance and guts, too.

"When my marriage went south I thought of going back home and putting on my father's mantle. Some would see that as a triumph. Others, me included, would see that as, well, somewhere between failure and death.

"So I figured I'd give the law a rest, figure out if I even wanted to practice. And I went this way—trading, the pits, for all the reasons I told you about—my ex-wife, bookshelves out of bricks and boards, a Volkswagen with a heater that never worked in winter.

"And one other reason which I may or may not have mentioned: because trading takes so much energy and effort that it takes my mind off myself, off all those things I think I should be and ain't."

He stopped, thinking she would be tired of listening, but she continued to look intently at him.

"So now I'm trading and I'm pretty good at it, absolutely challenged by the action and the intensity, proving to myself that I can do it. If things go along as they have this year, I'll probably make forty, fifty K, which is nothing down there—you know that—like being a failure, but which is a damn good living, especially for a single guy with no debts to speak of.

"Look at how I live, right? When you compare it to the rest of the world I'm wealthy, thriving, making a whopping sum for a few hours of work a day. Enough to cut the crusts off sandwiches. Order a filet mignon and complain about the fat. Hell, I *eat* filet mignon. And when I do I

208

think of my former clients, and my salary, the ticks I lose in a day, and it's crazy. It makes no sense. All perspective is long gone.

"I think I was happier when money was evil—I didn't say when I didn't *have* any money, because even when we were manning the barricades and wearing jeans with plaid patches we had a certain amount of money—but money was evil so you only used it to subsist.

"You donated ten bucks to Medgar Evers's political campaign in Mississippi even though that left you eight bucks to buy groceries. And the rent—do you even *know* how many times we stiffed the landlord, or ran out on the last month, or bounced a check? God, we were felons, out-and-out felons for the cause."

Joanie found herself listening as if he were telling her tales from the *Arabian Nights*. She watched him as he spoke, noting how the movement of his lips altered the lines of his eyes, the cleft of his chin. She merged his words and the images they evoked with her thoughts about him, how she admired him, even idolized him.

"But it was a hell of a lot better than all this Yuppie crap," he said, jogging her attention back to him. "Which just shows that the idealists of the sixties are the assholes of the eighties."

It was another self-deprecating zinger, and it bothered her. He hung criticism like clothespins on his abilities, picking and nipping at what he did and how he did it.

"What must you think of me," she said, "if you are so hard on yourself."

He shrugged.

"You know what I think of you," he said.

"I do?"

"I think you're fine, Joanie Yff, or I wouldn't be spending so much time with you."

"That's it?" she said.

Steve groaned and rubbed his palms together.

"All, how about this: I'm still knocked over by you.

209

You're the most beautiful woman I've ever been around except for the time Miss America came to Noblesville—"

"Which one?"

"Nancy Anne Fleming."

"Don't remember her."

"—and I'm still kind of astounded when you're here and I wonder where all the other guys like that beefcake in the Porsche are hiding or if there might be something despicable in your medical history that keeps them away. I also *know* you ain't here because of animal magnetism because a stud I'm not.

"And don't think I don't appreciate what we do in the hay and that I don't think about it but a few thousand times. And each time I do I wonder if I ought to talk you into doing it all the time, like overnight, or maybe for a few years or so.

"But then I think no, let's not push it."

He said it all in one breath and then, despite the shape he was in, he gasped.

She grabbed his collar and pulled his face close to her. She gritted her teeth.

"Push it," she said.

Chapter Two

"I have a question," Ballard Trout said.

He was standing with one foot on top of his desk, as if it were a chair seat instead of a desk top, looking like a manager gazing out of the dugout at his team. Except that Trout was looking at the crowded quarters of his small office and Joanie, who was leaning against the partition. Trout's tie was loose, and his button-down, oxford-cloth shirt was open at the collar. It was after the close, and Trout was tired and hoarse.

"When you gonna get in?" he said.

"Excuse me?"

"You're excused. You been workin' for me three weeks now, bustin' your tail, doin' a *job* down there. You know what's happening. You're on to it."

"Don't think the idea hasn't come up before," she said.

"Then believe it. You got a handle on things like it took me a year to get. But you got to use that brain for yourself instead of for me. I'll miss ya, don't get me wrong. But I'll live. In the short run, you got to give it a go," Ballard said.

She smiled brightly.

"For a black dude, you're all right," she said.

Ballard roared.

The steps to becoming a trader were not much different from becoming a cabdriver. For each it was mandatory never to have committed a felony. Each demanded a lead-lined stomach and a good set of legs. Each required the ability to keep one's head amidst total chaos.

The two jobs differed, however, when the meter was running. Being a hack meant long hours, a precarious life span, hemorrhoids, and a predictable, if modest, wage. Trading commodity futures involved short hours, a longer life, perhaps, hemorrhoids, premature varicose veins, not to mention hosts of other maladies, yet no guarantee of any wage at all.

Trading, however, also carried the potential for vast wealth, something a cabdriver might only achieve if a commodities trader were to leave a valise of cash in his backseat. Traders liked to say that the floor was a last frontier of the true capitalist. Mere hacks disappeared in no time.

No set amount was necessary in order to get into the business. What was required was an arrangement with a clearinghouse, the firm that provides backing for all trades. While some traders went into the pit having put up no capital at all, most houses required a margin sum of $20,000 to $25,000. The figure varied widely. In return the house collected a small fee for each trade.

What mattered was the amount of faith a clearinghouse had in the individual. What it was extending was credit in exchange for monetary backing on every trade, win or lose. Its legal responsibility was to supply and transfer funds after every trading session. How it dealt with member traders was its business. Ballard Trout, knowing Joanie and having every confidence in her trading temperament, told Joanie that she herself could decide on how much capital to put up.

Joanie well remembered Korngold's crying chair, that tear-stained piece of furniture that absorbed the reality of loss.

"I'll take your house," Korngold had said.

She would never forget those words. To become a Trout trader she decided she would put up $20,000, half her personal worth. She withdrew cash from her money market account, sold her shares in a mutual fund and all of her silver.

Her hands shook when she held the money. It made

212

trading more than just a neat idea, more than a whim, more than a dream. The statistics were brutal: four out of every five new traders were wiped out within six months. Some died slowly, bleeding from little wounds; others were executed in days. All saw their capital — savings, inheritances, windfalls, funds from second mortgages, loans from banks, relatives, or friends — simply evaporate.

Joanie knew that, had seen faces come and go, had tallied up devastating losses for stricken traders who stood by her desk and trembled. She knew it all, and still she put her money on the line to capitalize herself, her talent, her belief in her ability to compete in the toughest financial market on earth.

For $625 a month, she rented an associate membership on the Chicago Board of Trade and was issued a badge. She ran her fingers over the red plastic and the white initials that identified her to the rest of the pit. JOY: Joanie Olivia Yff.

She was ready to trade, ready to be one of them.

That night she called her mother. Before she could explain what it all meant, Joanie sensed that her mother's voice was cracking. She knew, Joanie thought. Her mother knew all about reaching and grasping. And Joanie felt her own eyes water.

Her decision was not the only major change in her life. In the last week of August she moved out of the Taylor Street apartment. Its owner, the itinerant professor, had returned from Europe and though he immediately welcomed her to stay, Joanie declined. He was very bright, talked rapidly, yet the top of his head came up just about to her shoulder.

She had moved north, and only a few blocks from the Board of Trade into a rented two-bedroom loft-condominium in Printers' Row, a fashionably renovated complex of factories and warehouses in the South Loop area. She had found the condo on the bulletin board outside the trading floor. Initially an in-house repository for messages and decrees, the board had become a register of profit and loss. Traders who had taken hits and had to raise quick cash used the board to sell their worldly possessions—cars, skis, condominiums, yachts, country homes, jewelry—anything but the shirts off their backs. The prices were usually rock bottom, the conditions cash.

Joanie's apartment was a condominium belonging to a highrolling broker in the bond pit who had moved back in with his wife and needed the $800-a-month rent check. Part of the arrangement was that he would leave his furniture there, which was perfect for Joanie since she had little of her own. The rent was considerably higher than she had been paying and more than she could afford, but she might remedy that with a roommate. Somebody on the floor was always looking for shelter.

The apartment was lovely, full of space and light and sleek angles, a layout, she had to admit, not unlike Steve's place. When she first showed it to him, she could not contain herself.

"Isn't it great? Look at all the space! Two bathrooms. A Jacuzzi. A fireplace. Even a garbage disposal," she exclaimed as she went from room to room.

"Well, maybe some of his stuff is a little rich, but I'll work around it," she went on.

Steve stood in the middle of the living room, his hands in his coat pocket. He looked around but did not follow her into the rooms.

Joanie stopped.

"God, Steve. I'm glad you're so excited about this place," she said.

He shrugged his shoulders.

"I can't see the expense," he said, then he paused, and exhaled. "You had other options, you know."

She put her hands on her hips.

"I was never asked," she said.

214

For the rest of the day he helped her move in. He was extremely quiet.

The new apartment also was only a short walk from work, something Joanie immediately appreciated. The South Loop area was burgeoning with new restaurants and shops catering to people like her, so she could shop on foot. Her concern was what to do with her car. To park it in the garage below would cost her $100 a month, more than the wheezing Honda was worth.

That problem was secondary, however, to what she faced as a trader. She spent hours in front of her bathroom mirror practicing hand signals. There were schools that taught potential traders the techniques, simulating actual conditions in the pit. Joanie did not need school, having learned all she needed to know in her months as an assistant to Korngold and Trout. Still, she was nervous, uncertain, even frightened as she faced herself in the mirror, flailing and screaming, pencil and cards in her hands, scribbling fictitious trades with imaginary traders.

Then, after a perfectly warm, dry, and dull Labor Day weekend, Chicago ended summer and began fall. The beaches closed, the public school teachers went on strike, fewer fans showed up at the ball parks, and the weather, that ogre Joanie had heard so much about but which had hidden its hoary head since her arrival, turned hostile. With no warning whatsoever, benign, beautiful days turned gray and windy, laced with a cold, often rainy bite in the air. The wind off the lake, dubbed the Hawk by songwriters and anyone unfortunate enough to walk against it, swooped down upon innocents on the city's streets as if they were prey. Once, coming out of the Board of Trade, turning east on Jackson toward State Street, Joanie was buffeted by a gale that sent her stumbling backward, reddened her cheeks, and brought tears to her eyes.

"Is this what it's like?" she asked her companion.

"This is a piece of cake," came the reply. "Wait 'til it really gets cold."

She did not have to wait long. That Sunday morning she found herself in Grant Park, the narrow expanse of grass and gardens between the Loop and the lakefront that contained everything from a band shell to softball fields.

Joanie, wearing jeans and a bulky wool sweater that stretched to her thighs, blew into her palms and bounced up and down on her toes in an effort to keep her blood circulating. Her exposed ears were stinging with cold.

Steve had brought her here, and he stood next to her dressed only in a thin jogging suit. He did not shake or shiver, in fact, he revealed nary a trace of a chill. They were spectators at a football game, an organized, officiated match between two seven-man teams, the Goons and the Tap Outs, in ripped blue jeans and makeshift headbands, loose jerseys and wool stocking caps. Many had wrists, thighs, and knees wrapped with elastic bandages. They were part of the LaSalle Street Football League, a circuit made up of executives, traders, and clerks on the Board of Trade. The parking lot nearby overflowed with Saabs, BMWs, Mercedes', and Jaguars.

The rules prohibited pads, cleats, one-hand touches, and airborne blocking. But the rules were shit, and regarded as irreverently as trading etiquette in the pits. The games, it was generally felt on the floor, were legalized revenge, a chance to work out frustrations or grudges or out-and-out animosity toward someone who had gored you in the pits last Friday, or last week, or a year ago. Like most sporting events, traders took odds and placed bets on the outcomes, and showed up with wives, girlfriends, and paramedics to watch and howl.

When the whistle blew, the players tried to take each other's heads off. Front lines crashed together with clenched fists, guttural grunts, and unoriginal obscenities. Legs churned, mud and sweat — despite the cold weather —

and occasionally blood and teeth flew like sparks.

Joanie stood and grimaced at the contact, at the shoving and tackling and unbridled fury. She knew several of the players, and had seen many others on the floor. The substitutes and other male spectators who recognized her from the trading floor looked her way, some trying to make eye contact, their interest much greater now than during trading hours.

She stepped back for the Goons' coach, a bond trader named Jack Leimer, who paced the sidelines screaming, "Pound 'em! Pound 'em!" no matter what was happening or if his team was on offense or defense.

Just then the Goons' quarterback went back to pass, searched in vain for a receiver, then sprinted for the sidelines where Steve and Joanie stood.

"Goose it, Spuds!" Steve yelled just as the charging back rushed toward them. He tried to turn upfield before going out of bounds but as he did a defender came over for the touch and sent him sprawling face-first into the muddy grass. Seconds later a Goon lineman jumped on the back of the defender and the two of them fell in a heap of flailing arms and legs. The lineman managed a few good rabbit punches to the defender's left ear before he was jumped. Joanie screamed. The referee's whistle shrieked and players tried to pull the battlers apart.

"This is awful!" Joanie cried to Steve.

"Wojack's a fuckin' maniac!" Coach Leimer screamed, running into yet another flare-up.

A few minutes later the ball was back in play, and the war of knuckles and knees and head butts continued. Joanie and Steve moved along the sidelines with the plays, cheering and exhorting the Goons even though they were being mauled by the Tap Outs, one of the LaSalle League's powerhouses.

"Freddy Barr played for Colorado," Steve said, nodding at the Goons' huge center.

"Pre-beer gut, I hope," Joanie replied.

217

"Shit, Sarsany had a year with the *Bears*," said a guy standing in front of Steve.

Denny Sarsany, who wore three days' growth of beard and a baggy gray sweatsuit that could not contain his hairy stomach, was the Tap Out's hulking, grunting one-man front line. When the ball was snapped he shoved Barr of the Goons into the backfield, then lumbered in the general direction of the ball carrier, knocking over anyone in his way. His play was not unlike his trading style, for as a corn broker he huffed and bellowed and belly-bashed his way around the pit like a crazed steer.

Sarsany was one of several former high school and college athletes in the LaSalle Street League, most of whom were above their school playing weights and out of condition but who made up for it with reckless, uncontained fury. In the second quarter Ray Kotlarik of the Goons ran out to block for his halfback and was suddenly leveled by a flying block from a Tap Out lineman. Kotlarik collapsed in a heap and did not get up. Nobody paid attention to him until it was time to huddle, then the referee called time.

"This guy's cold-cocked!" the ref yelled.

A few of the Goons went over to the prone Kotlarik.

"Play ball!" a Tap Out player yelled.

"Get the stiff off the field," barked another.

Coach Leimer and the team medic, a premed student with a collection of splints and some smelling salts, ran on the field.

"God, he got whacked," said Leimer, watching as they administered to Kotlarik.

"This is one of the dumbest things I've ever seen," Joanie said.

Several guys along the sideline looked at her.

"Just an excuse to beat each other up," she went on.

"It's a game," said a Goon substitute.

"Bullshit," Joanie said.

Steve heard her but did not respond, his attention still on Kotlarik. Finally they helped the stunned trader off the

218

field, and the game went on.

In the second half another fight broke out. Though a few good punches were thrown, the bout lapsed into shoving and spitting. One of the Goons had his shirt ripped off him, and the sight of his white belly convulsed everybody, even Joanie.

"Are there always so many fights?" she said.

"With the Tap Outs, yeah," Steve said. "They figure since you get fined a thousand bucks for fighting in the pits, they might as well do it out here for free."

"And they still fight in the pit," growled a Goon.

At noon the game ended, the Goons on the short end of a 33-16 score, and the players headed off toward the parking lot. The teams did not mix, and there was little postgame sportsmanship. Several players limped noticeably, others had open cuts on their hands and arms that mixed blood with their grime. A Tap Out halfback had broken a finger; Ray Kotlarik had a headache that blurred his vision.

A few of the Goons asked Steve and Joanie to join them at a nearby pub where they would dampen their injuries with beer and catch the Bears on a big screen.

Steve declined, having promised a shivering, thoroughly chilled Joanie Irish coffee and a warm brunch.

They caught a cab to a small restaurant on North Broadway run by a bevy of fey young men in brush cuts and flannel shirts. Called Mom's Apple Pie, the place specialized in stuffed omelets, French toast, champagne, several brews of coffee, and every cheesecake and whipped cream dessert.

Joanie was ravenous and desperate for a cup of coffee.

Into her second cup, with her blood warmed and once again reaching her extremities she said, "So, did you enjoy that as much as I did?"

Steve laughed.

"Just a little insight before you make the plunge," he said.

"What do you mean?" she said.

"Well, having seen how the big boys play, do you still want to be a trader?" he said.

She sighed and sat heavily back in her seat. He was serious.

She leaned forward.

"Now more than ever," she said.

She chose to trade Treasury bonds, a commodity for which she had no particular affection apart from the fact that the bond pit was big and liquid. In it she would be able to start small, feel her way in, and have the company of several new and small traders like herself.

Then, one morning not long after she had walked out of Korngold's office, she emerged from the offices of Trout Trading wearing a new, Cubs-blue trading jacket and JOY, her gleaming trader's badge. She strode onto the floor and toward the U.S. Treasury bond pit: today as a trader.

One of the first to see her was Tommy Haggarty.

"What in the hell are *you* doing here?" he said. He was wearing the yellow coat of his new firm.

"Lookin' for trouble," she said.

"Trout," he whistled, eyeing her jacket. "The man with the big bat."

"Jeez, Tommy. I thought you were history," Joanie said.

"Kenny K. know about this?"

"Do I care?" she said, knowing all too well the answer.

Then she walked on.

Her response had been immediate, yet she was not sure how she would react to Korngold when he saw she was trading. On that first day she made every attempt to stay away from the soybean pit.

The specter of Korngold was but a trifle compared to what she had to face stepping into the bond pit. She was a virgin, as naked, vulnerable, and scared as she ever had been in her life. For months she had run up and down these very steps, in and out of the pit, living and breathing it, knowing it better than the rooms of her flat. Until she pinned on her badge and stepped inside as a trader, as one of the *players*, she knew nothing of the pit at all.

She was careful to pick the right place to trade. It was on the first step of the pit, near the center, on the north side. It was also the domain of no particular trader. That was crucial. Position in the pit, especially one as big and crowded as the bond pit, was important to traders, due to tradition or luck or its proximity to other brokers and traders. Any trader careless enough to take someone's spot risked physical injury. Fights broke out so often that the Board of Trade instituted an automatic $1,000 fine on anyone involved.

So Joanie positioned herself carefully. She stood next to Wilson Hartz, a friendly North Shore kid who had also just started, and near Margie Finamore, who, Joanie thought, might help her out if necessary. Several traders nodded in mild surprise when they saw her. Some gave the thumbs up. Margie Finamore came over and hugged her. But most of the pit paid no attention to her at all. She was just another player in a game where it was every player for himself. They studied the board, their cards, rubbed their ties, complained of bad stomachs, bad backs, bad trades, bad weather, and the general gamut of maladies so common to the moments before the opening gong.

Joanie fingered her trading cards, cards that now had her name printed at the top. She tried to tell herself to be cool, yet her heart was racing, pounding so hard she could feel it in her throat. She had spent the night staring at the ceiling, repeating to herself the admonitions of veteran traders:

"You'll never learn until you jump in and do it."

"You can only be wrong half the time."

"It's like being a chicken sexer: you don't know what you're looking for, but you know something's there."

"Try to feel the market, not fight it. Fight it and it will

221

drill you a new asshole."

And finally: "New traders always buy at the top and sell at the bottom."

Yet she had also carefully reviewed her plan. She had plotted what her research told her the price would do, then set rigid stops on where she would buy and sell. She was reviewing those limits when the gong sounded and the maelstrom began. She was pushed from behind and nearly lost her balance. She dropped her pencil and fumbled for a new one. She looked up to see where the tick was and could not focus on the board. Someone reached over her shoulder and jabbed her ear. She was surrounded by outstretched arms, bids and offers. In the precious seconds that it took her to get her bearings she realized that the market had run right through her stops.

A hand was shoved into her face.

"One at three," the voice screamed.

"Yes," she screamed.

The trade came from Jim McMahon, JMM, a broker for ComCot whom Joanie knew. He smiled at her, nodded confirmation, and scribbled the trade on his card.

She suddenly realized that she had just bought her first contract, her very first, at a price way above the limit she had painstakingly set for herself. But she was in. She scribbled the price on the card, the initials of the trader. In the seconds that she considered what she had done the price went even higher.

"One at five!" a voice shouted at her.

It was Barry Snider, BAS, another broker who stood right next to McMahon.

"Sold!" she boomed, then she laughed out loud.

BAS and JMM laughed with her. She had taken her first ticks, two in all at $31.25 apiece. The two brokers gave her the thumbs-up sign. Joanie blew them a kiss.

After the rush of the first half hour, trading settled down. Joanie made another trade, then another. She was scalping, buying and selling the closest month in order to

222

make money on minute price fluctuations. That meant constant trading, getting in and getting out, grabbing a tick here or there, trying to avoid a loss. At $31.25 a tick it seemed to add up in a hurry. Now that sum was not just a figure she calculated for other traders but one that was added and subtracted from her own ledger.

Her nerves gave way to concentration, the strain of standing and staring at the boards, of trying to feel the market. By noon, having left the pit only to go to the bathroom, her neck was stiff and her feet sore.

That is when she saw him, and the sight nearly took her breath away. Korngold had learned of her new status and come over from the ag side to see for himself. He stood on the bridge between the bond and T-bill pits. It was impossible not to see her, standing among the one- and two-lot traders on the first step, that smart, lush head of blond hair, the tough, determined thrust of her jaw.

He stood there gazing down at her, as if he expected her to peer up at him. Hey Joanie O, pivot those gray-green eyes.

Though she saw him there, though she could feel his stare, she was determined not to turn his way. She continued to trade. In so doing she was for Korngold, amidst all of his staggering successes, a notable loss. Losses were to be cut and cut fast, then forgotten. He knew that. And yet, dammit, she would not even look at him.

At 2:00 P.M. trading finally ended. Joanie was exhausted, aching all over.

Those hurts, however, were nothing next to the pain she got from her totals. She had bought high and sold low. After that first winning trade, she had been a loser, not a big loser, but a loser. She was off seven ticks, just over $200 for the day. That and her overhead. She knew, however, that it could have been much, much worse.

Back in the office she sat and studied her cards, nursing a can of grapefruit juice. Other traders came by with knowing smiles.

223

"You looked great down there, slugger," said Rick Murtaugh. "I heard your first bid clear across the floor."

Ballard Trout put a big paw on her shoulder.

"You clean me out today?" he said.

"Started on it," Joanie said.

"The bingos'll come, don't you worry," he said.

She smiled and shook her head, appreciating the two of them. They knew what it felt like; and she now knew a little better what they were all about. The virgin metaphor struck home: she hurt like hell, but she was glad she had done it. She wanted to do it again and get it right.

In the meantime she was hungry. She had not eaten all day and she realized why traders came back to the office after the close with sacks of burgers and fries. That was exactly what she wanted.

Stepping out of the elevator in the lobby Joanie saw her, that fresh, unmistakable face, the coal black hair. It was Rachel Korngold. Their eyes met.

"Hi," Joanie said.

Rachel smiled, but uneasily, as if she had encountered something forbidden. She immediately noticed Joanie's trading jacket, however, and the JOY badge. Her mouth opened.

"You're trading!" she exclaimed.

"First day," Joanie said.

"Too *much*," Rachel said, smiling excitedly.

"That's what I said," Joanie replied.

The two of them laughed together. Then Rachel stopped, her expression once again turning solemn.

"I'm going up but I'm really in no hurry," she said.

Joanie hesitated, then sensed the invitation.

"Come on. Food fix. Double cheeseburger, fries, you know."

Rachel brightened and followed. She was wearing a pair of soft leather camel-colored slacks and a matching short jacket, a black cashmere, cowl-neck sweater draped with gold chains, and low heels. It was a stunning, God-only-knew-how-costly outfit, Joanie thought, and one that made Rachel look a half-dozen years older than she was. Only the suffocating, musk-scented perfume said otherwise.

The two of them, Joanie, the braided blonde, Rachel, with her olive skin and dark hair, parted the sidewalk, fielding looks from all directions as if they were in a television commercial and the men on the street were hired extras. Rachel, young and self-conscious, returned the looks and blushed; Joanie walked on as if the vultures were not even there.

"So how are you?" Joanie said when they sat down.

"Okay, I guess," Rachel said. She sipped a Coke.

"My dad and I had a big argument about you," she said.

"I figured as much."

"He'd kill me if he knew I was telling you this—"

"Nah—"

"Yes, Joanie. You don't know. You really get to him. You do. Boy, I found that out. Cuz I told him I thought you were right about that kid who killed himself."

"Wait a minute. Your father is way out of my league—"

"No way! He really has it for you. And when he wants something, he takes it."

"Like me, huh?" Joanie said.

"Well?"

"Sorry."

"Really? Then I'm *right*. He wouldn't give a shit about you if you were just like all the rest. You mean you never—"

Joanie stiffened, looked down at her food. Rachel did not complete her sentence.

"I didn't sleep with him," Joanie said evenly. She fiddled with a packet of ketchup, then tossed it on the table. "I was tempted, okay? Your father comes on. Boy, does he come on."

Rachel nodded vigorously. "He usually gets what he wants, too."

"Listen to you. You're really down on him," Joanie said.

"I know. I'm just mad, I guess. He can be so selfish. You should see all the times he doesn't come home. It's always something—that shitty soccer team, or he just goes somewhere else."

"Stays downtown?"

"Yeah, or he goes to his condo in Myrtle Beach and golfs with his jerk buddies down there or to Telluride, which I love cuz we got a really neat chalet there or to Vegas or who knows."

"Check my math—three condos?"

"Four if you count Bubba's—my grandma—in West Palm Beach, which we own."

"Of course, I forgot," Joanie said.

"And, it's just, oh, he's weird lately. Different about things."

"Or maybe you are."

"You're so—" Rachel began, then stopped. "This may sound really bizarre and utterly pushy, but who do you talk to?"

Joanie smiled.

"I have friends. One in particular."

"Don't you, like, get lonely?"

"Yeah," Joanie said. "Most of the time, though, I'm too busy to let it get to me. But, sure, I miss my mother most. I miss our talks. I miss having coffee with her after work, even if it was in our little house trailer in Florida. She'd sit doing her needlework—she always had a project—and you could hear the thread pulling through the fabric. It'd be dark outside, maybe midnight, and things kind of ticked as they cooled off. I really miss that. . . ."

"Yeah," Rachel said.

"Who do you talk to?"

"My friends. Well, sort of. And Daddy. I mean, I did."

She paused again.

"Your mother?" Joanie said.

Rachel's eyes wandered. Finally Joanie crumpled the wrappers, finished the rest of her soft drink, and the two of them got up to leave.

"God, I can't believe you're a trader!" Rachel beamed.

"I told you, this is my first day," Joanie replied.

"That's really great."

"Not when you see how I did."

"Oh, yeah. Real bad?" Rachel said, looking sideways at Joanie.

"I'll live."

"How is it, I mean, how is it being a girl and all?" Rachel asked.

"Well, I wish I was a foot taller and built like Sly Stallone. You wouldn't believe how you get pushed and shoved."

"Yes, I would. I seen Daddy. And some of those guys are the biggest jerks."

"You should hear 'em bitch about chicks and broads and how we don't belong in the pit. Sometimes I just look at them. Just stare at them. They haven't got the balls to say it to your face. But when you put up the bid and offer they trade with you. They have to."

"You must feel great when you beat 'em."

"I don't know. It hasn't happened yet."

"Daddy does. He comes home and I hear him on the phone saying, 'I really fucked that bastard. Tore him a new asshole.' "

"Such talk," Joanie said.

Rachel laughed. "Don't ya love it?" she said.

They left and retraced their steps to the Board of Trade. Waiting at the elevators was a group of noisy traders, their ties loose and coats open. In the center, talking louder than all of them, was Ken Korngold. Suddenly he spotted Joanie and Rachel. He broke off his conversation and pushed his way out of the group until he reached Joanie and his daughter.

"So what the hell is this?" he said.

Rachel cocked her head slightly.

"Hello, Daddy," she said.

A far elevator opened and Joanie walked quickly to it.

As she did she caught a trace of Rachel's smile, and, as the elevator doors closed, she looked no further.

Steve was waiting for her at her office.

"Hey, trader. Buy ya a steak after your first day?"

She groaned, feeling the bulk of $4 worth of fast food in her stomach.

"What say I watch you eat a piece of fish and tomato— you know, your usual pig-out. Then we do would-have, should-have, could-have with my cards. Then I collapse into a black sleep," she said.

"Hot night," he said, wincing.

"You know us traders," she said.

Chapter Three

For days she struggled, trying to feel the market, trying to trade well. The novelty of trading soon wore off. What remained was the brutal task of making money at it. Her goal in the first three months was to break even, which meant she had to meet her overhead, rent on her seat, and the cost of trading each day. After two weeks of trading she was woefully short of that goal. The few days in which she traded well could not keep pace with the days she scratched or traded poorly.

She fell into all the traps. She violated the Cardinal Rule of Trading: Cut your losses, let your profits run. Instead she "ate like a bird and shat like an elephant," trader jargon for taking profits prematurely and holding losing positions too long. She groped for a rhythm, a knack, a sense of what the market was about to do. She quickly realized that so much of trading was feel. "Two percent intellectual, ninety-eight percent emotional," the saying went, yet after her first week in the pit she decided even that 2 percent was an overstatement.

She began to take on the haggard look of a trader, a look of worry, of strain, of a person perpetually late for a plane. Her eyes grew hollow. She scratched and twitched, jiggled the pencil that never left her hand, squinted at the price boards until the skin around her eyes bunched into tight lines. In the pit she was anxious and expectant, often leaping into the air and screaming, then waiting and watching.

She chewed a great hunk of gum at all times, chewing it violently, partly for the saliva that lubricated her throat, partly for the pounding it provided her jaws. Once when the tick jumped and she saw a profit she jumped and screamed with such force that the gum slid back into her throat, nearly choking her. She dropped to her knees and gagged, finally dislodging the wad into her palm. Gasping, she shoved it into her pocket and fought through the melee above her, already having lost a tick, desperate to sell.

Her cushion each night was Steve. His dining room table was open to her charts and her trading patterns. He meticulously reviewed them with her, trying to get her to recognize and avoid weaknesses and fatal tendencies. Her first week was a loss, but not a disaster. On two days she had broken even. She was trading small and conservatively, one contract and one contract at a time.

"If everyone had your control, there wouldn't be any tap-outs," Steve remarked.

"But we'd all be broke," she said.

On Tuesday of the second week she had her first winning total: a gain of seven ticks, $218.75. She took them in a sideways market, a period in which the price traded in a narrow range. That kind of market was the worst of all worlds for traders, especially scalpers like Joanie who lived off price movement. Not caring if it went up or down, they could play it both ways—soaring like a Roman candle or dropping like a stone—as long as it moved. So Joanie's profit was hard-earned, and satisfying.

She soon realized that for her, and for most beginning traders, trading the downside of the market was the hardest. The natural instinct was to buy something at a low price and sell it higher. The notion of selling something at a high price and buying it back lower—selling short—was uncomfortable. To make money, however, you bought and sold in either direction, holding no regard whatsoever for the direction of the price (or, for that matter, its consequences on the rest of the world) as long as you were on the right side of the move.

Then came Thursday, a day that started out flat and gave no indication of changing. She put on a short position at the day's top price when word came in that a major

New York bank was raising its prime lending rate a full percentage point. The short-term effect on bond prices was devastating, sending them immediately downward. The pit erupted in sell orders, with major brokers and traders trying to cover their long positions and go short. The price immediately plunged ten ticks, held, then fell three more.

Traders and brokers screamed hysterically, some of them losing thousands of dollars with each tick. Whole rows of traders stumbled and jostled each other in the panic. Joanie had never seen anything like it, not in her months of running, and certainly not as a trader.

And now she was in the center of it, literally in the eye of the pit, nearly suffocated by the churning mass of flesh, arms flailing, voices cracking, drops of sweat and spittle flying about. Joanie hung on, her heart and ears pounding, eyes riveted to the board. In minutes the price had dropped a full basis point—thirty-two ticks in all—and she was still short, having made in this single move twice as much as she had lost in her first week. Then as more brokers evened out their positions, the price held, the pit calmed with only sporadic pockets of furious trading.

Just then, in the wake of the inferno, she felt very different. It was as if her whole body had become caught up in, but not swept away by, the tide of the market. She felt as if she were riding on top of it, like a foaming, cresting wave. A sensation emanated through her in the tips of her fingers, her arms, the hair on the back of her neck, the muscles in her legs, as if her body had suddenly become a sensory instrument, a gauge, a prompting, prodding indicator of the market's course.

It was a remarkable feeling, a secure, powerful sensation, and she threw up her hands to buy and three traders lunged at her. She made the trade and closed out her position. Then just as quickly she got back in again, buying another contract, reading the ticks, the board, the feel. Then she unloaded it, making a few more ticks. She sold short once again, rode the swing of the market, the pit now exploding, simmering, churning, then settling, and she covered. She was in and out, again and again, as if the market were a whip in her hand, one she could crack or coil at whim.

Finally she was out. She had done it, traded the whirlwind and filled her cards with a blur of transactions. She gasped. She looked unbelievingly at her totals, the figures. She broke out in a smile, a beautiful, unabashed grin that lit up her face.

Her gloating was the reaction of an amateur, and she quickly erased it. Every dollar made by one trader, she well knew, came from the pocket of another. The pit was a zero sum arena—everybody put up an ante—and for every winner there was a loser. All around her were traders who had won and lost, a lot and a little. Some had made enough in that afternoon sizzle to buy a BMW—and would. Others had taken staggering losses that threatened their very existence in the pit.

Most all of them accepted it as part of the business, showing the strain but trying to bridle their emotions. Some, but not all, succeeded. On the steps of the pit Joanie saw a trader, a guy with the build of a linebacker, suddenly break down and weep.

She eyed the clock and saw there was less than an hour left before the close of trading. But she was done. She would not chance getting back in and risk giving back her profit.

She wound her way through the traders and out of the pit, heading over to the agriculture side and the gold pit. She literally danced as she walked, focusing on none of the faces around her, hoping to spot Steve. He was not there. A Cunningham runner said she thought he was up in the office.

She was tempted to go there, to rush through the door and show him her cards. But she held back. Even in her present state of euphoria she could not go there. Instead she headed for her own office, stepping inside the elevator,

232

punching the button, and letting out an ecstatic whoop. The three riders already in the car did not have to be told, and just laughed with her.

When she saw Ballard Trout she hugged him.

"Caught it, huh?" he said.

"Yes!" she screamed.

"Where?"

"Seventy-two ten."

"Pretty high."

"Yes!" she said again.

"Ten, twenty ticks?"

"A hundred and ten!" she squealed.

"Good Lord, Joanie, you choked it to death!" Ballard said.

She laughed wildly and started punching him in the ribs.

"Tell me this—" he said.

"Anything, Mr. Ballard," she said.

"Will you marry me and keep me in grits?"

"You should be so lucky?" she hooted, and pushed him away. She reached for a phone to call Steve, had three numbers dialed, then stopped. *I've just made $3,000, she thought. Me, just little old me.* She replaced the phone. It was still only mid-afternoon, and she deserved a treat.

She took off her trading jacket and grabbed her wallet from the top drawer of her desk. On Jackson Boulevard she hailed a cab and aimed the driver to Marshall Field's on State Street. It was a $1.50 ride, and she gave the driver, a thin-faced Lebanese who had stared at her in his rearview mirror for the entire drive, a $5 bill. She waved her hand as he began to make change.

"Keep it. Buy figs," she said.

In Field's she browsed slowly through the women's clothing and specialty shops until she saw what she wanted: a caramel-brown, waist-length, leather jacket. Cost: $410. It was her size—today everything was—and she put it on and sauntered in front of a fitting mirror. Her fingers caressed

233

the leather, the ridges of the seams. The jacket was her, the former Joanie Olivia Yff of West Palm Beach, Florida, presently JOY, Chicago bond trader and damn good one. The leather would keep her warm in the face of fickle Chicago winds, make her a little tough.

She wrote a check on her money market account as the clerk boxed the merchandise. All she needed now was a new pair of jeans and some boots, and those, the clerk said, were one floor down.

What seemed like short moments later she was back on State Street, her packages bulging under her arms. She loved it, the effortless scribble of her signature on the checks, the feel of the shopping bags, the secret thrill, even power of being able to buy anything she pleased. She looked around her, at what people were wearing, driving, at the scents that trailed behind them. She could have it all.

In her mind she made a list:

> A thirtieth-floor condo with a cherry-wood four-poster bed
> A wardrobe of silk, cashmere, and more leather
> A sleek, solid-gold watch
> A strand of real pearls, diamond earrings
> Two dozen pairs of shoes
> A BMW 520e
> An IBM PC AT
> A Sony CDP 302 compact disc player
> A JVC video cassette recorder

She would have gone on had she not bumped into a newspaper vendor. He was blind, his eyes marbled and aimed somewhere over her shoulder, but he sensed a sale and quickly rolled a paper and tucked it under her arm. Joanie was startled, but she held firm to the warm paper. She quickly dug into her pocketbook and handed the vendor a dollar bill. He nodded and mumbled.

She found Steve in his office. She went up to him and kissed him hard on the lips. Then she whirled around, her hands on her hips, the musky smell of the leather jacket filling the air.

"A hundred and ten ticks," she said, raising her hands in fists.

Steve nodded. His day had been a wash.

"New coat," he said.

She groaned.

"Asshole," she said. "My best day ever and you say, 'New coat.' "

"Sorry," he said.

"Asshole," she said, then she went over and tried to kiss him again.

He leaned away.

"What's your problem?" she said.

"It's your problem. You took away three K?"

"Damn right."

"And you went right out and bought the coat?"

"Damn right."

"Stupid shit. You put profits in your account. Not on your back," he said.

"Go to hell," she said, and she walked out.

Joanie did not have another hundred-tick winning day again, yet she did not lose big either. She now adapted well to the pit, picking up its rhythm, staying within her limits. That was key. She knew herself and her strategies. She continued to scalp, trading the last month and playing the minute changes in price. She assimilated the numbers—the prices for each month's contract, the cash markets, the whole array of flickering digits—to where they were second nature to her. She scanned the price boards like a primer, heard and registered bids and offers throughout the pit. She felt totally comfortable, in control even during days of tepid, unproductive trading. She could make a go of this business.

Steve could see the transformation, an exuding sureness, as if she had suddenly, dramatically matured. She was now a trader, not just a wide-eyed, frizzy-headed clerk.

"You like this whole thing, don't you?" he said in the dining room of his apartment a few nights later and an hour after they had made peace.

"I love it," Joanie said. She was wearing his white terry-cloth bathrobe.

Then she stopped and looked at him.

"Wait a minute. Don't get on me again. I still like the leather jacket. I had a great day and I rewarded myself. Don't make a big material-girl argument out of it."

"You said you love it."

"Yup. I said it."

"Trading, right?"

"Yes!"

"Beating the other guy?"

"Yeah, I guess. No. Strike that. I love to make a good trade," she said.

"Too late—you hesitated. You gotta love to trample your mother. The trade is secondary."

"I don't know about that," she said.

"Of course you do. Look around the pit and what do you see? You see guys who don't give a damn about anything but number one. Cowboys. Spoiled brats. Worse— you got dealers. You know what I mean? You got the bikers and dealers of the sixties. Like in the Brando biker movie: 'Whatta you guys rebellin' against?' And Marlon says, 'Whatta ya got?' "

"*The Wild One.*"

"That's it. The pit draws them like lice. They don't know anything about *what* they trade and they don't care to. They just trade and step over the bodies."

"I think I've heard this before."

"It's true."

"So what?" she said. "You'd rather have traders who

236

cared deeply about soybeans, brought them home at night and tucked them in?"

"Well, maybe a few farmers down there would help."

"Like in the gold pit? Maybe you'd like some South African gold miners to trade with."

He looked away. He looked back.

"The mentality of the pit doesn't bother you, Joanie?"

"I haven't really thought about it," she said. "I'm so knocked out by the energy of the place—God, I still can't believe I'm in it."

"I envy you," Steve said.

"Wait a minute—you think liking what we do is bad?"

"No, as long as you don't become one of the boys."

"I want to be successful. I want to trade well. I want to make money. Does that qualify?"

"Those are nice ways to put it."

"Okay, how about this: I want to get rich so bad I'd eat babies to do it."

"Getting warmer."

"Jesus Christ, Steve," she said.

She clenched her teeth and blew a stream of air through them. She stared at him, remembering that just the other day he said he was considering going in to the office at 4:00 A.M. in order to get a better fix on the European gold markets.

"I read *The Pit,*" she said.

"Great," he said. "What'd you think?"

"The women—what an uptight bunch."

"True to the times. What else?"

"Rotten weather."

"That's eternal. What else?"

"Well, let's say that trading hasn't changed very much," she said.

"Yes! God, I'm glad you caught that. You can take whole passages out of that book and apply them to the floor today," he said, suddenly springing out of his chair.

He went over to his bookshelf, looking only briefly before he plucked a volume from the top shelf.

"Look here," he said, holding a brittle, yellowing copy of the Frank Norris novel.

Little slips of paper stuck out of the book, and he turned to one.

"Let's see . . . no, not this. Okay, listen. They call it buying and selling, down there in LaSalle Street. But it is simply betting. Betting on the condition of the market weeks, even months in advance. You bet wheat goes up. I bet it goes down. Those fellows in the Pit don't own the wheat, never even see it. Wouldn't know what to do with it if they had it. They don't care in the least about the grain. But there are thousand upon thousands of poor devils in Europe who care even more than the farmer. I mean, the fellow who raises the grain, and the other fellow who eats it. It's life or death for either of them. And right between these two comes the Chicago speculator, who raises or lowers the price out of all reason, for the benefit of his pocket.'

"I could go on. Here, listen to this section on retail, the old lambs to the slaughter routine—"

"No, Steve," she interrupted. "I read it. I told you."

"It's a classic," he said.

She got up from the table and went to the kitchen, coming back with a slice of cheese.

"I don't understand you," she said, still standing. "You think everybody on the floor is a jerk. You think the whole system stinks. And yet—"

"I'm part of it," he said.

"Yes."

He clicked his teeth, motioning for a bite of her cheese. She ignored him.

He shrugged. "Maybe I hate to see you digging into this with such glee."

"Steve! You're the one who changed his mind and told me to trade," she said.

"I know. I know. It's just, well, you're infatuated with the

238

damn market."

She put her hands over her face.

"Try this," she finally said. "Maybe you're just contrary. Maybe you just thrive on going against the flow. Maybe you feel good only when you feel bad."

"Psychology one-oh-one, thank you," he said.

"Go to hell."

"I've heard that before."

She looked away.

"I don't want to start another fight," he said. "It's just the way I was raised. You always question what you're doing and why you're doing it."

"And while you're at it, you whip yourself," she said. "Like those crazy Iranians with the chains during that hostage thing."

"I could get into that," he said, a smile creeping over his face.

She sat down, eyeing him, not sure if he was toying with her, not sure of how far she wanted to take it. She looked absently at the charts and cards and data on the table, their nightly homework. She picked up one of his charts. Steve was neat and precise with his data, an absolute demon for detail.

"You want to know what really bothers me about you?" she said.

He waited.

"You're so smart. I don't know if you're sincere or just toying with me. Like some cute exercise in law school."

"No. That's not true," he said, getting up and coming over to her. He bent down, slipped his hand inside the bathrobe, and lightly kissed her.

"Don't ever think that," he said.

"Then don't ever *do* that," she said.

Friday of that week began as a dull, predictable, sleeper of a trading day in the bond pit. Then it suddenly flipped.

239

The action came in a rush, based on pent-up demand and a spate of unsettling news reports. A widely quoted interest-rate guru put out a message of doom regarding broker loan rates, the chairman of the Federal Reserve Board threatened to quit, the bankruptcy of an energy-loan bank in Louisiana spewed rumors of another Penn Square fiasco.

In a sudden wave of trading, the pit came alive. The price gyrated, and previously somnolent traders leaped into the action. Orders poured in. The big brokers were mobbed, with traders pushing to get close to them, climbing onto each other's backs, pushing, elbowing, screaming bids and offers. Joanie was gouged and trampled, then gouged and trampled others to make trades of her own. She madly scribbled the numbers on her cards, hoping to God that they were right, knowing that such frenzied action was a rat's nest of out-trades.

Out-trades were unavoidable, the result of heat-of-the-moment mistakes and misunderstandings, and every trader dreaded them. A trader might signal a five-lot and have it mistaken for fifteen. A trade with one trader may be claimed by another, often one standing nearby, both of whom insist they confirmed the trade and that it is theirs. According to the rules of trading, such misunderstandings must be settled in out-trades—settlements outside the pit—between the traders involved. That usually meant splitting the difference, and often at a substantial loss to one of the parties. And there was usually nothing that could be done about it.

An hour after the close of trading Joanie finally made her way up to the office. Her head was spinning, her right thigh throbbed from having been kneed by another trader, her voice was nearly gone. Coming through the door she nearly missed the secretary's signal. Her name was Susan and she waved her arms, motioning toward Joanie's desk.

"You have a visitor," Susan said, making a face that Joanie could not decipher.

She looked over and saw the head of hair, the clothes. It was Rachel Korngold. She was sitting hunched over on a folding chair next to Joanie's desk, her head in her hands. She did not look up until Joanie was nearly by her side. She had been crying, her makeup was smeared.

"Hi," she said softly.

Joanie crouched down next to her.

"Hey, what's the matter?" she said.

"Him. Mr. Big," she said.

"Your dad?"

"Who else?"

"What happened?"

"He said he didn't want me in his office all the time. Like it's some clubhouse or something," Rachel said.

Joanie made a face.

"He says he can't get his work done if he has to take me home all the time and that's a lie. What he means is that if he takes me home, then he can't go to his *whores*," Rachel said.

"You said that?"

This time Rachel made a face.

"I can't *imagine* somebody would come all the way downtown just to make her father take her back home," Joanie said.

She lowered an eyelid and looked sideways at Rachel.

Rachel would not look her way.

"Whattaya say I total up and you hang with me? When's the last train to Highland Park?"

"Nine-oh-seven."

"You can tell me what you think of my new place."

"Okay!" Rachel said.

Joanie tossed her trading cards on the desk.

"I'll total them for you," Rachel quickly volunteered.

"No, please," Joanie said.

She had always done her own totals, knowing what was on the cards and where the problems were. And today there were problems, in fact, she would need a lot of time

241

to settle up.

Rachel turned away. She was a master at looking hurt, and Joanie got an instant insight into what her father was up against.

"I forgot," Joanie said. "You're the data entry whiz."

Rachel smiled. A few minutes later she was logging Joanie's cards into the firm's computer. As she did, Joanie looked over at her: the daughter of one of the richest men in the building, beneficiary of a God-knows-how-fat trust fund, decked in a wardrobe of the toniest of labels, yet sitting at a computer terminal doing the drone work of a $200-a-week secretary. And loving it, Joanie added.

An hour later they walked out of the building together, again appearing like friends. Rachel beamed and occasionally nudged Joanie as they walked.

It was after six and beginning to get dark. They made their way south and east toward Joanie's apartment, stopping on the way to buy Chinese food, then a bag of home-made coconut-macaroon cookies from one of the overpriced cookie shops that had spread through the Loop. At each cashier Rachel produced a $20 bill before Joanie could even get to her wallet.

"Us suburban kids are loaded," she said.

When Joanie opened the door to the apartment Rachel looked around and headed for the kitchen.

"I crave Mongolian beef," she said.

Joanie followed, realizing that Oriental delicacies and gooey cookies were more important than any new apartment or its view, at least to Rachel Korngold.

They spread the boxes of food about the countertop and ate on a pair of stools, Rachel using her fingers to pull out great gobs of food, which she stuffed into her mouth. She talked in grunts and swallows, mostly about the food, comparing it to places near her house, mentioning other Oriental dishes she craved, among them sushi and sashimi. She lovingly recounted how she and three of her friends once devoured $162 worth of the raw delicacies while watching TV one Friday night.

Joanie mostly listened, noting Rachel's first mention of friends, finishing off what Rachel left in the various boxes.

"So. You and Steve still a thing?" Rachel suddenly asked.

"A thing?" said Joanie.

"I like him. He's not brain-dead like most of the jerks on the floor," Rachel pronounced, then chewed on a pea pod.

"No, brain-dead he's not," Joanie said.

"I can't handle those guys," Rachel said.

"Who do you date?"

"Losers. Nerds. A wimp or two. Sometimes a real dumb jock so I can rub his muscles and laugh at him."

Joanie laughed, pitying the poor kid who might ask this girl out.

"I thought Friday night was a big date night. Football, cheerleaders, go team, go," she said.

"Yeah. Kids do that," Rachel said, looking away.

"But not this kid."

"Not this kid," Rachel said.

Joanie got up and ground some coffee beans, feeling distinctly at that moment like a mother.

"I go out some," Rachel continued. "Or I hang out. You know. There's always a party house. Lotta kids' folks take long weekends to ski or something so we trash it. You ever seen that movie *Risky Business?* They filmed it in a kid's house I know."

"Where would you be now if you weren't here?" said Joanie.

"Ask Daddy."

Joanie made herself a cup of coffee.

"He just wants to run around with his sleazy girlfriends. He's got one now—she's a redhead with this phony accent—and she wears *musk.* Like that's really *in,* darling," Rachel said, her fingers kneading rice into little balls.

Just then the phone rang and Joanie reached over to answer it. All things considered, she was pleased to hear the

243

voice on the other end.

"I know you want to see it and it's your turn and I'll go," she said. "But I'll hate it. I always hate Third World movies."

With a few more nods and chuckles, several phrases in code that made no sense to Rachel, she hung up.

"Your squeeze?" Rachel said.

"Uh-huh. He's making up."

Rachel's expression sank, and she exhaled.

"So much for me," she said.

"You feel like a movie about a coffee farmer in Brazil?"

"Does he trade coffee futures?"

"Twenty-lots," Joanie said, laughing.

"I'll go," Rachel said.

Joanie frowned, then caught herself, but not before Rachel noticed. It was a fatal lapse.

"Wait a minute. I gotta get home, I just forgot," she said. "Can I use your phone?"

Joanie began to protest, then decided not to.

Rachel took the phone and walked a few steps around the corner. She punched several numbers, waited, then punched more. After several tries she spoke.

"If you've been trying to find me, which I know you haven't, I'm at a friend's downtown and I'm going to take the train home unless you might want to pick me up yourself," she said. "Oh, you *would?* Imagine my surprise."

She poked her head around the partition.

"What's the address here?"

"Seven-ten South Dearborn."

Rachel repeated it, then hung up.

"Who'd you call?" Joanie said.

"Daddy. He's picking me up. Feels guilty."

"Oh, come on, Rachel!" Joanie said.

"What?"

"He's picking you up here?"

"Yeah."

"Oh, get a grip! You know what he thinks of me,"

244

Joanie exclaimed.

Rachel smiled.

"I know," she said.

Joanie slammed her palm on the counter.

"I don't like the idea of being in the middle of you and your father. That's not what I had in mind when I invited you over."

"I paid for the food," Rachel said.

Joanie scowled. "Yes, you paid for the food.

"Calling him up from here was a shitty thing to do," Joanie went on. "Why don't you think of somebody else besides yourself once in a while?"

Rachel looked at her, stung, her lips turning down. She began to cry.

Joanie waited, wondering if this was just another routine.

"I'm sorry," Rachel said.

Now Joanie felt lousy.

"C'mon," she said.

When they got to the lobby Korngold's Mercedes was parked outside. His head suddenly appeared above the roof and he glared at his daughter, then at Joanie.

Rachel got into the car. Joanie held her ground as Korngold continued to stare at her.

"I warned you," he said.

Joanie turned and walked down the street, cursing herself and him and Rachel Korngold and all that was unfair in the world.

It was after 2:00 A.M. when she returned to her apartment. The phone was ringing.

Joanie guessed who it was, considered not answering, and finally lifted the receiver. She had guessed wrong.

"He was awful and cruel and I hate him," Rachel sobbed. "He said you were nothing but a *whore* and that you'd turn me into a whore, too. It was so *rank*, what he

245

said about you. He said he screwed you on the floor, on the sofa, in the car, anywhere. I said he was a *liar*, just a fucking *liar*."

She was panting and crying. Joanie waited, feeling her own exhaustion, feeling for Rachel.

"You should go to sleep," Joanie said quietly.

"My own father threatens to kill me and I should sleep!" she said.

"He did that?"

"He said he'd kill me if I turned into a fucking tramp like you. I *hate* him for it."

"Don't hate him. Don't fight him. Don't do anything. Just stop it for tonight."

Joanie listened and heard muffled sounds on the line, the rustling of sheets, Rachel's breathing.

"Are you okay?" Joanie said.

"I hate him," Rachel said.

"Okay."

"And I love you."

"Okay."

She was certain her head had only just taken the chill from the pillow when she was awakened by the buzzing of her intercom. It whined continuously, as if someone were leaning on it. She staggered across the bedroom, seeing 4:12 on her clock radio.

"Who's there?" she rasped into the intercom.

"Me. Rachel," came the reply.

"Shit, shit, shit," Joanie moaned, pressing the door entry button.

She was exhausted, her mouth tasted like cardboard. She yawned and felt her jaws crack.

Moments later she opened it to Rachel. She was wearing Georgetown University sweats, her hair pulled back and wrapped with a terry-cloth band, an oversize canvas tennis bag, makeup, and a look that made a weak attempt

246

to pass for sheepish.

"Do you believe it cost me fifty bucks to get here? The bitch wanted twenty dollars extra," she said.

Joanie closed the door behind her.

"The bitch?"

"Yeah. The cabbie. Some bag lady they imported to Highland Park to drive their one and only taxi. She was gonna bring me to the cops."

"What's going on, Rachel?"

"I couldn't spend another night in the same house with him."

"Him?"

"My father."

Joanie rubbed her palms over her eyes.

"I'm out. Gone. I got two thousand dollars, my clothes and things, and I'm gone. I can live where I want to."

"No, you can't. And I'm not going to argue with you," Joanie said.

"I know. I'm sorry. I'll just stay here for a while until I get set up," Rachel said. She swung the tennis case over her shoulder.

"No, you're—oh, *shit*, Rachel. Shit! That's what I think of this trick. So I'm going to bed and try to salvage what sleep I can and when I wake up you're going to fix this. There's the sofa."

"Hey, look, Joanie. So don't do me a favor. There's hotels."

"Come *on*, Rachel! You're fifteen years old—"

"I look seventeen easy."

"—yeah, sure, and tell me if you just walk into the Ritz and check in."

"I could."

"Look," Joanie said, now irritated. "You can do this with your father. This pissing, this arguing. But not with me. I'm not your parent and I don't want to be. Sorry."

Rachel's bottom lip turned inward.

"You did fuck him, didn't you?"

247

"Don't *talk* to me like that."

"That proves it."

"No, it means you don't come into my door and insult me."

"You sound just like him."

"You're pushing it."

"I thought you were my friend."

"I am."

"Is this the way you treat your friends?"

"Is this—! For pity's sake, Rachel, why don't you think before you say something? Just try to think how it'll sound when it comes out."

"Okay, how about if I go off somewhere and take some pills and—"

"That's it. Good night."

"You didn't say that with that little Brian. You were all *concerned* over him."

"What next, Rachel? What'll you use next? Poor little rich girl. Designer clothes, ski trips. How 'bout that two thousand dollars? Your allowance?"

Rachel rushed for the door, struggled with the locks, and finally pulled it open and stumbled into the hallway. The elevator was waiting for her.

As soon as she closed the door behind her, Joanie knew. There was no way she could go back to bed with Rachel Korngold on the street. Once again she cursed.

It was 4:30 when Steve answered. She knew, too, that he would, that he would grouse and complain and, finally, help her. In the time that it would take her to dress and get her car, he said, he could cab over. It was before 5:00 A.M., still dark, the street prowled only by cabs and the dawn's early workers, when she pulled out of her building's parking garage. She drove. Steve tried to figure where to search.

"Michigan Avenue. If you're from Highland Park, born in a Gucci manger and wrapped in swaddling diapers by Yves Saint Laurent, you run away to Michigan Avenue,"

248

he said.

"I don't need this. I don't need some little bitch adolescent to screw up my life," Joanie said.

"So turn around and go back to bed."

"I came to this city to learn the markets. Make a buck. Toss the dice. Not baby-sit. I could have stayed south and baby-sat."

"Yeah, dammit. What in hell is something like real life doing getting in the way of my career?" he said.

"You know what I mean," she said.

"No, I don't. I don't understand anything you just said. You wouldn't either. You should hear yourself."

"Kids like Rachel Korngold have no goddamn right to . . . to . . . ah, shit," she said. She thumped the horn on the steering wheel at a bus that was taking up two lanes. "Move your ass!"

"Turn here. There's a little park just down from the Water Tower. Let's try it."

They drove on, winding through the partially deserted streets off Michigan Avenue, exclusive, moneyed blocks whose residents arose at this hour by choice, not necessity. They saw no sign of Rachel Korngold.

"Where is the little bitch?"

"Cut it, Joanie. I didn't get out of bed to hear you rant about Korngold's kid and pity yourself."

"Admit it, Steve. She pisses you off just as much."

He turned and faced her.

"No. You piss me off. Lately a lot more than she does. She's fifteen and so fucked up she can't see straight. What's your excuse?"

Joanie swung the car over to the curb.

"Excuse? I'm the one she comes to, right? And now I'm out here looking for her, right? That's my excuse," she said.

He sniffed.

" 'Cept you really don't want to find her," he said.

"Go to hell," she said.

"Been there," he said.

"Belong there," she said.

In silence she drove toward his apartment. When she got there she stopped and he got out. She drove off.

When she returned to the South Loop and drove onto her street, now a full hour since she had gone out, she saw the silver Mercedes in front of the building. In the front seat was Rachel Korngold.

Joanie turned into the drive. She went over to the passenger side. The tennis case on her lap, her expression rigid and tear tracks staining her cheeks, Rachel looked straight ahead. Joanie knocked on the window. She tried the door. Rachel would not look at her.

Ken Korngold emerged from her building's entrance. His hair was mussed and he was unshaven. He was wearing his brown leather jacket. Joanie turned and stared at him.

He started for her, stopped, then walked quickly around the front of the car. Looking over the contoured roof, he pointed at her.

"You blew it," he said.

Chapter Four

They started out in the dead of night, pulling out of their barns and rutted drives onto gravel roads, then onto county roads, and finally onto the two-lane blue highways that lead from town to town. They made agonizingly slow time, just over twelve miles per hour, with the nubby, hard-rubber treads of their tires slapping against the pavement, blue-white smoke shooting from dual exhaust pipes overhead.

By the time yellow spears of dawn shot up over the fields, they had been joined by dozens of others of their kind, a ragtag, grunting, belching procession stretching over a half mile. And still more joined, drivers nodding, raising clenched fists of solidarity to one another. They sat two, sometimes three, in a cab, men wearing worn seed company caps, women with cropped hair and print blouses, kids in T-shirts.

The State Police cruisers picked them up on I-55 about twenty miles outside the city and led them onto the Adlai Stevenson Expressway. The troopers had come from the Joliet Post with orders to escort the procession front and rear. They had performed such duties before, for circuses, over-sized construction convoys, mobile homes, and visiting politicians. They had never escorted something like this.

Most of the vehicles were tractors, from open-seated Massey-Fergusons and Deeres that putt-putted along as if cultivating a bed of squash, to massive, $60,000 International Harvesters with air-conditioned, stereo-equipped cabs and engines that roared like those of a Mack truck. And there were also the bulky combines, threshers, balers, and harvesters, all awkward, tentacled machines that looked like space vehicles as they lurched along the freeway.

Driving them were farmers who knew damn well they

could better use the day in the fields. They were taciturn men with copper faces who had come together on this brilliant day in September to make a point. They were headed for a stone building in the heart of Chicago, the home of a market that dealt in the commodities they produced with these machines. They were going there to create as much ruckus as they could in order to protest that market, whose prices seemed to bear no relationship with reality, with what it took to plant, fertilize, and harvest a crop. It was a market that affected their lives and their livelihoods, over which they had no control, and which, in this deadly summer, sustained prices so dismal as to threaten their very survival.

They wanted to get that message across to whoever would listen, the media, the populace, the politicians. But they especially wanted to confront the traders, those boys in the grain and meat pits who, the farmers believed, set the prices that were killing them.

By mid-morning the half-mile-long parade had chugged into the perimeter of downtown, leaving the expressway and winding along city streets. The State Police cruisers gave way to white and blue city police cars and three-wheel motorcycle cops, officers who would have ordinarily blocked such a brigade but who, on this day, had orders to accompany it. The noise of the farm vehicles' engines, the clapping tires and groaning metal, brought people into the streets of Chicago who gawked as the procession passed, people who thought they had seen everything.

At Jackson Boulevard the parade came tightly together, the wider vehicles taking up more than a full lane and stopping traffic in both directions. In minutes most of the South Loop traffic was bottlenecked. The rural invaders slowly proceeded east, past the Amtrak station, over the Chicago River and past the black-clad Sears Tower, across Wacker, Wells, and finally to LaSalle and the Board of Trade Building itself.

At the sight of the fabled stone building they opened up with their horns, honking, hooting, and bellowing. They shook their fists, yelled, whistled. The thunderous noise, the deafening roar of unmuffled engines and bleating horns shook the canyon of buildings up LaSalle Street, vibrating with a commotion worse than the wildest Independence Day parades. Pedestrians in business suits held their ears. Cabbies got out of their taxis and cursed. And still more tractors, more fuming, gyrating, otherworldly machines came up Jackson Boulevard until their number totally ringed the Board of Trade Building and clogged the streets from Jackson to Van Buren, Wells to Clark.

In front of the building they were joined by picketers hoisting placards and passing out leaflets. A man on a loud-speaker began chanting, "The market's a fraud!! The market's a fraud!!" In no time television crews arrived and began filming, moving from the picketers to the tractors, isolating some of the drivers for interviews.

Although those inside the building knew it was coming, they were not prepared for the fury. The noise penetrated the trading floors, even the modern, acoustically sealed agricultural floor. Traders and clerks abandoned the pits and clustered eight-deep around the windows on the north wall of the financial floor, which looked out onto the intersection of LaSalle and Jackson. They climbed onto the sills and leaned on each other's shoulders in maneuvers not unlike those inside the pits, laughing and jostling and generally enjoying the event. A squat, rugged clerk hoisted a squealing female co-worker with brilliant red hair onto his shoulders and the crowd cheered.

"Who in the hell *are* those guys?" yelled PTT, a bean trader.

The crowd erupted in laughter.

"Farmers, I think," came a reply.

"So *that's* what they look like," PTT returned, the crowd still with him.

The quips and jeers came from all directions, each one followed by howls and guffaws.

"I wanna hat like that, Jack!! A green one with a *pig* on it."

"Is this what happens if I take delivery?"

253

"Hey! One of those things just took a *shit* in the street!"

Then PTT chimed in with the clincher.

"That cat's drivin' a John Deere Four-fifty SL!!"

The crowd came apart.

Someone managed to swing open one of the windows, and the noise trumpeted in. As if on cue the traders and clerks began tossing trading cards outside, hundreds of them raining like cardboard confetti upon the street below. The horns of the tractors bellowed in response, fists were raised, cameras rolled.

Away from the windows the phones rang and generally went unanswered, tapes raced by unnoticed, hundreds of millions of dollars worth of commodities contracts stood idle. Traders who couldn't get close to a window strolled off to the cafeteria. Others went down to the street. Among them was Steve Stamford.

He went off alone, at first curious and interested in the march, then peeved at the nonsense of the mob of traders by the windows. He had known of the farmer protest but, like most other traders, was not prepared for the ferocity of it.

Once on the street it hit him, not the sound or the spectacle of the demonstration, but the blunt fact that today he was on the other side. His jacket signified that, the Cunningham insignia certifying that he was a member of the very Establishment that these little men and their angry machines were protesting. Right here on LaSalle Street, an avenue of finance and commerce that he had at one time despised but was now a part of.

He stood there transfixed, stunned, not at what he saw before him but what he saw in himself.

A blast of horns and a shout from the crowd brought him out of his reverie. He suddenly focused on the commotion before him, the machines that looked so out of place in the city, the crowds and the cluster of picketers. They were looking back at him. Then a pair of eyes from a face atop a tractor, a weathered old face beneath one of those soiled hats, locked onto his. In a moment of direct, unerring rapport amidst the chaos, those eyes in that old face connected with those of Steven Stamford, son of Samuel Stamford, former public defender and community organizer, presently trader in commodities. And the look was one of primary contempt.

Steve wanted to turn away, then caught himself. Instead he waded into the crowd of farmers. If nothing else, he wanted to talk to them to set himself apart from the ridiculing smart-asses in the windows above.

He was met by a group of three men, all farmers, and more came up.

"Your quarrel isn't with us—" he began.

"Show me your Mercedes-Benz, hotshot," one man yelled.

"How many bushels did you dump today?" added another.

"We don't make the market—" Steve said.

"No, you destroy it."

"Let the son of a bitch talk."

"Look," he went on. "I know prices are down, but we don't set them. The market seeks its own level."

"Horseshit!"

"Damn middlemen! You take our profits and none a you ever seen grain in your lives."

By now a crowd had gathered around, including a television crew, all leaning in on Steve in the center. He tried to talk, singling out one face or one response, but was drowned out.

He was rescued by the television crew. A cameraman as big as a house barged in and parted the crowd, and a reporter thrust a microphone in front of him.

"I respect what these people stand for, I really do," Steve said, "but their quarrel isn't with us. We don't make the market for farm products, we simply work in it."

He could barely hear his own words and he did not much like the sound of them. He looked like a professor in front of a renegade classroom.

"The market is really very efficient—" he continued, but was butted on the chin by the microphone, then pushed from behind.

"The *hell* with this," the reporter said, and pulled away.

The TV crew began to push out of the crowd, taking Steve along. An elbow speared him in the back. He lifted his arms in front of his face and pushed ahead. As he did a hand tried to grab his stack of trading cards. He swung his fist up and caught someone on the side of the head. Finally he got free of the crowd, got up on the sidewalk and headed for the side of the building. His jacket was ripped, his badge hanging by threads.

He stood there collecting his breath, feeling for his cards and trading data. In the street police began breaking up the crowd and herding the procession away from the building, west down Jackson Boulevard and back where they came from. Just then another cluster of trading cards came hurtling out of the trading floor window, accompanied by a muted cheer from the traders, showering down on the exiting farmers and their machines. One of the cards sailed and caught Steve in the ear.

"Dammit," he yelled, but his voice was lost in the roar of the passing engines.

He turned into the building's revolving door, into a crowd lingering just inside the entrance. His ear rang and he cursed to himself, cursing his torn jacket, this building, the fraternity of jackasses three floors above him. Pushing his way through this jumble of bodies, he walked swiftly toward the elevators and caught an open car just before the door closed. He stood alone, hearing his own breath, and realizing as he rose to the twenty-first floor that he was trembling, his left heel fluttering up and down against the parquet.

Once inside the Cunningham office he sat down heavily on the sofa, then got up and took a beer out of the refrigerator. He drank deeply and stared, still breathing heavily, feeling his pulse in his neck. He paid no attention to the giggling from the clerks in the adjoining office. Several minutes passed. He absently pulled his cards from his torn pocket and studied his positions. On top of everything he had just gone through, his cards told him that so far today he had not done shit in the market.

He tossed the beer can toward the waste basket. It missed, splattering beer against the wall and rolling across the carpet. Steve got up, retrieved it, and placed it into the trash. Then he changed jackets. The screens told him the price of gold was moving. The fun was over and the boys were back in the pits.

In minutes he too, was, back in his spot, once again trying to get a fix on the tick. The price of gold *was* moving, and the traders were caught up in it.

"Two at two," he screamed and thrust his hands into the air. "Two at two! Two at *two!* you sons of bitches."

His howl turned the heads of those around him. He paid no attention, screaming once again, bidding with new intensity. He was buying for the men on the tractors, dammit, for the faces beneath the visors of those worn feed and grain hats.

"Two at three! Two at three!" he shouted, seeing the grizzled, grimy face that fixed on his on the street only moments earlier. *"Five* at three! *Five* at three!" he bellowed, thrusting his hands into the air and leaping off the step.

He bought and sold, scribbling wildly on his cards, trading with a fury he had never known before. He generated a maelstrom around him, of elbows and arms, of buying and selling. He locked into the market, riding it, shocking it, feeling the tick, the pulse of the price, reading his fellow traders as if they were children. He felt it, finally, deep in his gut, knowing beyond everything that he was doing it for himself. He had discovered, this day, right now, who he was, and what he had become.

It all clicked, all came together, all crystallized before him. He saw every face around him; he saw no one around him. He read badges, initials, digits, the coats of the same cut as his but now belonging not to fellow traders, but to enemies. His enemies. People who would eat him alive if he

257

did not eat them first. So he thrust his hands, his weapons at them, making kills, slicing into carrion and tossing it aside.

He went after every tick he could get, lunging, pushing. He spied an offer he wanted, desperately wanted, would kill for, and he leaped across the backs of a row of traders and grabbed the offering trader's shoulders.

"Sold!!! Sold!!!" he screamed, his spittle showering the trader as he slashed the trade onto his card.

Another trader grabbed his elbow, jerking him around.

"Fuck off, asshole!!!" he shouted, and plowed his way back to his spot.

He stopped only with the closing gong. His pockets were jammed with cards, his shirt pulled out of his trousers. He was flushed and panting, his fingers black with pencil lead, one bleeding from a puncture wound. He was hoarse, gasping, barely able to speak.

His fellow traders looked at him as they peeled away from the pit. Their looks, however, were looks not of horror or pity, but, in this strange cannibalistic world, of admiration. They knew when a trader had finally come into his own, had clicked, had grabbed the muscle and frigged it with all his worth.

Steve Stamford, gold trader, had done just that.

After all his cards were totaled, all the trades recorded, the ticks checked and double checked, he was handed the total: $25,120.

He stared at it. He was speechless.

He had just made more in a single day than he had made in the previous three months. He absently acknowledged the raves from other traders, then from Jack Cunningham himself. The word had raced through the office.

Neatly folding the tally sheet, he placed it inside his briefcase. He felt strangely numb. He peeled off his jacket and hung it in the closet. Instead of lingering around the office like a giddy winner, he picked up his case and drifted out into the hallway and onto the elevator. Soundlessly the car dropped, the doors opened, and he was deposited into the bustling lobby.

Caught in the current of traffic, he found himself walking toward the Van Buren Street exit, the silver facade of the new Helmut Jahn — designed addition and the walkway to the Options Exchange across the street. But this afternoon he hardly noticed the brilliant exterior panels or the warm, fume-clogged afternoon air. His head was buzzing and his feet were light. He had just made a killing in the market.

He began to walk, listlessly, leaning with the slant of the pavement, holding his briefcase limply by his side into the rejuvenated South Loop.

Here was the new darling neighborhood of downtown Chicago. For years the Board of Trade Building looked north upon the power and formidable grace of LaSalle Street money while its back end abutted the elevated tracks along Van Buren, the Post Office to the southwest, and a shabby stretch of half-empty warehouses, small factories, parking lots, a mission, flophouses, railroad tracks, and empty lots. But now that was all changed, transformed by a wave of renovation and development, the Options Exchange, the pink marble of the Midwest Stock Exchange, and a Yuppie heaven of lofts and condominium developments that catered to the very money made on the trading floors.

Yet there were still pockets of the South Loop's former self, of wandering vagrants and addicts, guarded, littered parking lots full of precision-made automobiles whose owners lived in villages thirty and forty miles away. Steve wound his way through it, reminding himself how obvious it all was, wondering if the naked contrasts ever struck other traders. He wondered if the owner of the silver Rolls Phaeton parked illegally — but under the watchful eye of a nearby lot attendant — on Wells Street cared one whit about the broken concrete and the broken bottles strewn all about his $200,000 machine.

He wondered what traders thought as they hurried past

the greasy spoon grills and shot-and-beer saloons, past the inevitable derelicts who picked through trash containers and sucked mustard out of Burger King packets. Or the street hustlers who walked with a shuffle and cupped hot watches and zircons in their palms.

Was it all too sublime? he thought, as he went on. Just a block east, a jagged piece of reinforced concrete overwhelmed him. The Metropolitan Correctional Center. Could any of his fellow freemarket mavens, participants in a business many thought was out-and-out larceny, could they *not* appreciate the fact that the city's newest jail was built right here? It was a rest stop, however brief, for the best as well as the baddest of federal ne'er-do-wells, for the most wanted cross-country kidnappers and bank robbers and whitecollar forgers and mail frauders, for just-bagged mafiosi, kinky politicians and their political hacks, a former governor or two.

The Met held them while their lawyers pressed their appeals, or until they were transferred to a federal country club in another state. In the meantime the building was an architectural wonder, a soaring gray triangle with vertical windows so narrow they did not need bars. On its roof was a recreation area, and from blocks away on a sunny day, you could see basketballs lob lazily toward hoops. Yet the Met was still the Can. Just a few steps down the street from the Board of Trade. Such a neighbor.

It *was* too obvious, and Steve snorted.

When Joanie got to the gold pit Steve had already gone.

"Probably downstairs getting shit-faced," said a fellow trader.

Then he told her of Steve's afternoon.

From the house phone she called Steve's office and was told he had left for the day.

"I don't believe it," she said out loud, thumping the receiver down. She dialed his home number but expected no reply, not this early, and she got none. If he wasn't in the building, and not at his place, she had no idea where to find him. She felt a real urge to kill him.

Had she looked two blocks east down Van Buren she would have seen his back. He continued to stroll, his long legs stretching in just about any direction they wanted to go. He looked into the faces of those around him and most looked away or locked eyes only momentarily. All of a sudden he had the urge to stop a man with a particularly soft, wattled face and tell him, "I just made twenty-five thousand dollars." But the man was past him, the light had changed, a traffic cop was madly gesturing at a cabbie to stay in his lane.

At Wabash he turned right past a $1.98 steak joint, then the flickering window bulbs of a porn store. For no reason he turned in and pulled open the door.

Inside he was confronted by a turnstile, and young man with a blond crew cut and tight beard sitting behind a counter on a raised platform. To his left was a wall of gadgets and devices, most of them made of shiny rubber and looking like exotic varieties of zucchini. The young man on the platform had what looked like a studded dog collar around his neck.

"One dollar to browse," he said in a whisper.

"A dollar?" Steve said, then laughed.

The clerk stared at him. The world was full of deadbeats. Steve gave him a five.

"Tokens?" the clerk said.

"Why not?" Steve replied.

From a cylinder on the counter the clerk released a handful of tokens. They were currency for the video booths, a dark, dank arcade in the rear. Its entrance was bordered by blinking colored lights. On one side was a video poster of a punk-haired blonde in black leather boots, chrome chains, and the title "Trashy" between her legs.

Steve walked in, momentarily blinded, seeing only red lights on the booth doors, holding his tokens like a handful of cookies. The place smelled like bleach. He went inside a booth, closed the door, and deposited a couple of tokens in a

261

slot. Suddenly the wall came alive with a close-up of an undulating vagina stuffed from behind by a penis. Somewhere a woman gasped and a man grunted.

Steve stood and stared. The tokens became warm and moist in his hand so he dropped them all in the coin slot. Minutes passed. The video couple was unrelenting.

Suddenly the door to the booth opened. A man in a business suit, wearing glasses, at least fifty years old, squeezed inside. He looked down at Steve's crotch.

"Let me do it for ya," he said.

Steve froze, then pushed past the man and bolted.

Chapter Five

The trading floor being a small community, there was no way for Joanie to avoid Korngold. When they passed he looked at her, even tried to make eye contact. Joanie always looked away. She could not help it. At times she felt her throat tighten. Korngold, however, made no attempt to encounter her. He did not speak or show any expression. He only looked at her.

Other traders were not so aloof. A few days after she had begun to trade, Bob Penneman, the Rope, one of Korngold's bean-trading buddies, came over while she was huddling with another trader near the old smoking bullpen.

"Hey, Joanie, baby," he said, and put his arm on her shoulder. "They say you give good fill."

He cackled, and was joined by laughter that seemed to come from every direction. She lifted his arm from her shoulder and walked off.

To almost everyone in the area, it appeared like harmless nonsense, the kind of exchange that thrives in the pits. But to Joanie it was intentional, probably orchestrated, liable to happen again at any time.

Then one day she looked up during trading to see a gaggle of laughter among some of Korngold's bond traders. They were playing finger games, ad-libbing on the arcane system of signals traders use to confirm transactions. After a trade, particularly a large one, a trader often flashes the sign of his clearinghouse instead of communicating its cumbersome three-digit number. The signal system was devised half in fun and half in necessity. A finger goring the palm like a bull meant Merrill Lynch. Bear, Stearns was a hug; Cargill, the motion of a steering wheel; Goldberg Brothers, a finger on the nose; E. F. Hutton, fingers shaped like a

hut; and so on. One firm known for its heavy use of mari-
juana used the sign of toking on a reefer.

Joanie realized that she had been added to the repertoire.
It started with a Korngold trader and one from Virginia
Trading. Virginia's hand signal was normally a salute.
When they got Joanie's attention they put two fingers in a V
over the mouth, with a tongue wiggling in between. Their
corner of the pit convulsed in laughter.

Joanie ignored them. Yet it went on for days, usually
during lax periods when traders were telling jokes and betting on the ball scores. In no time the hand signals started,
the variations, the raucous laughter. Joanie had little choice
but to gut it out, to steel herself against the onslaught, hope
it would pass. Other women in the pit, seeing what was going on, weren't as patient.

"I'd file a complaint," railed Margie Finamore, a bond
trader herself, after stopping Joanie in the entrance tunnel.
"Go in front of the Business Conduct Committee and name
names. Nail those baboons."

"You know I can't do that," Joanie protested. "Not if I
want to keep trading."

"No way should you have to put up with them," Margie
said.

"It's good training," Joanie said.

"It's abuse," Margie countered.

Steve disagreed.

"You saw it the first day here," he said. "You don't have to
like it. But if you let them get to you, you're beaten. You'll
have proven to them what they'd love to believe: that
women can't take it. By law you can trade, but you really
aren't traders."

She knew he was right. Especially about being a woman.
She had heard it over and over again: it was a man's game.
Rather, she knew, it was a boys' club. To survive she had to
be one of them.

Privately, however, she vowed revenge against Korngold
and the jerks who did his bidding. Yet on her down days,
after long hours and hectic trading, of taking the usual
physical pounding and an occasional jagged loss, the sight

of yet another wagging tongue between the fingers was too much. She went off by herself and cried.

In the middle of it all she was confronted by Tommy Haggarty.

"I hear you're gettin' the needle," he said.

"Get out of my face, Tommy," she hissed.

"You wanna get even?" he said.

"With who?"

"You know who," he snapped.

"Sure, Tommy. Like that's possible."

"Anything's possible."

She started to move past him.

"There are ways," he said, wiggling his head. "I got ways. I got hooks."

"You'd be the first place anybody'd look."

He laughed, as if that were a compliment.

"There's an old Outfit saying—you know, the Boys, the Mob. Goes 'Not today, not tomorrow, but someday.' Capeesh?" he said.

She sighed, looking at him.

"You ever heard of Faust?" she asked.

"Used to be football coach at Notre Dame?"

She threw up her arms and started to leave.

"Hey, just remember, when you had it up to your eyeballs, Joanie, baby, ol' Tommy's here. I got ways," he said, lifting the words just over her shoulder as she walked away.

The more Joanie tried to steel herself against the obscene signaling, the more it persisted. It was Rick Murtaugh, a Trout bond trader, who finally did something. He told Ballard Trout what was going on, how Joanie was putting up a valiant front, but that the assault was wearing her down.

"She's getting gun-shy, Bat," he said.

Trout cursed, full of sympathy for his new trader but peeved that Joanie had not told him about the situation herself.

"You tell me, Murt," he said. "Did I take on some bad trouble here or is this worth a fight?"

"Just for a minute putting aside what she looks like — and, Jesus Christ, Bat, you went and hired the premier *fox* of the building — she's damn good. Got a chip on her shoulder once in a while, but she can trade bonds," Murtaugh said.

Ballard Trout nodded and thought for a moment, then gave Murtaugh a message for Ken Korngold. Later that day Trout made his way up to the public observation deck. He leaned on the wooden railing, scanning the floor below. All around him visitors gawked with perplexed and astounded looks at the action in the pits. None recognized him as Ballard Trout, the ballplayer, but they took notice of his trader's jacket and badge and knew he was one of them. As for Trout himself, he looked altogether bored.

A few minutes later Korngold appeared and stood next to him at the window. Trout nodded at him but continued to stare out onto the floor. Korngold, who was a solid six inches shorter than the former ballplayer, gazed sideways at Trout, at those wondrous hands, the long, slightly bowed legs now wearing loose-fitting casual slacks instead of Cub pinstripes, legs that once took him from first to second base in seven steps and a slide. Korngold knew Trout's statistics, could still see those frozen ropes he hit up the alleys, Trout going into second base standing up.

Korngold had traded with Trout but did not know him. There were a handful of former pro athletes on the floor, but none were of the stature of Ballard Trout. And here was the man in the flesh, looking, to Korngold, almost alien out of a Cub uniform.

"How's your soccer team goin'?" Trout finally said.

"Crap, that's how. I got a German superstar out with the clap. My Brazilian forward broke three of his toes. And my Haitian forward is in love with my Italian goalie," Korngold said.

"Short pants. Grown men shouldn't play ball in short pants," Trout replied.

"When they play they're okay. It's all the fuckin' around I can't stand," Korngold said.

Korngold liked this, the jock banter, the jargon. He continued to gaze up at Trout as he talked, waiting for the man to look back at him.

"Got a game tomorrow night. Come on out. Sit in my box," Korngold said.

Trout did not reply, his look still locked on the trading floor below.

"You know, my trader lady ain't said zip to me about the shit your boys are givin' her," he finally said, rubbing his big hands together. "She's tryin' to prove how hard she is. Which she don't have to do. She could just write your ass up and be done with it."

Trout's voice was barely audible.

Korngold opened his mouth.

"But I figure you just havin' some fun," Trout went on, "and was just about to call off the game."

He turned finally and looked down at Korngold.

"I figured that cuz you're the pro in this ball park. Best there is, they tell me. And next to you I'm a damn rookie trying to hit for an average," Trout said, standing straight.

"Damn bean oil," Trout said under his breath, his eye once again on the boards. "You in it?"

"Nah, topped out in May. You're spinning your wheels," Korngold said.

Trout nodded, a pained expression on his face.

"You remember the time you got four hits off Harvey Haddix?" Korngold finally said.

"Like yesterday," said Trout. "Whole team only got five."

"Six," said Korngold. "I was sitting behind third base. You guys lost five-two."

"Yeah?"

"My favorite was Marichal."

"Not mine," Ballard said.

Korngold laughed, shaking his head up and down. "I know what you mean, yeah," he chuckled.

"We straight on this mess with Miss Joan?" Trout said.

"No problem, no problem," Korngold said, swinging his arms back in the motion of a pitcher's wind-up and lifting his left leg up so quickly he almost kicked a visitor.

"Ol' Juan had a kick, didn't he?" Korngold said.

Ballard lifted a palm and was gone.

267

* * *

In the days that followed, the market did not open soon enough for Joanie. She was out of her apartment at 6 A.M. and on the floor an hour later. At the opening bell she locked into the rhythm of trading, sensing it, feeling the flow up or down, staying patient when it languished. She pounced on rallies and retreated with setbacks. She shook off losses and recorded gains. Her trading days acquired a pattern, a sequence that she herself controlled. She was a trader, and getting to be a good one.

Her success — she now saw winning days edging the losers and more losing days turning into scratch-even sessions — meant that she had to work even harder. She prepared more, set technical data solidly in her head, and she concentrated on the market's patterns. It was not a matter of predicting or outwitting the market, simply trading with it. Trading wisdom held that you could play the market, goose the market, goad it, cajole it, even flog it, but you could not fight it.

Most of all, Joanie felt akin to the ebb and flow of the bond pit. She was no longer a visitor, the sharp kid from Florida with a good luck wish and a prayer. She was an ingredient, a part of the fraternity of traders and brokers who made up this powerful market.

One immediate effect of her new success was tunnel vision. She moved quickly, intent on where she had to go, looking straight ahead and seldom seeing the faces and the sights around her. She had no time for small talk with the clerks and runners with whom she had once been so close. She seldom varied her route from the Trout office to the pit, the floor desk, and back again to her office. Were it not for a certain gold trader whose pit was on the ag side, she would never even see that side of the floor.

And finally, most significantly, Joanie's fortunes seemed to extinguish her contact with Korngold. She occasionally saw him in the soybean pit, but he was no more than one of many faces there, or so she kept telling herself. So, too, his cronies, "Rope" Penneman, and the others in the bond pit

268

who were now just anonymous badges to her. If a smirk, or the salacious hand signals appeared, she ignored them or, in her utter concentration, did not see them at all.

When Joanie got back to the office that afternoon she had a phone message.

"Who's this?" she said, studying the memo.

"I think he's a reporter," said Renee, a small, chunky black girl Ballard Trout had recently hired.

Joanie returned the call and found that Renee was right. Louis Lange was a writer on the *Wall Street Journal.* He was interested in doing an article on women in the pits, and he said he had heard that she was among the best new female traders. As he spoke Joanie smiled, felt downright flattered.

A few hours later she sat across from Steve in a Szechwan restaurant in Chinatown.

"Can you believe it?" she said, leaning halfway across the table and grasping his hands.

Steve smiled back at her.

"You'll be a star," he said.

"God, the *Journal.*"

He let her go on, her enthusiasm surpassing even that of her first days in the bond pit. He nibbled on shrimp wrapped in seaweed.

"Brian Boyer," he said.

"Huh?" she said, her voice dropping.

"There's the story," said Steve.

They paused as more food was spread before them: spicy hacked chicken, willow beef, hot-and-sour soup, crispy Peking duck. Joanie ate like a starved woman.

Steve went on. "The whole Boyer thing's been swept under the rug. Unauthorized trading. Korngold taking none of the rap."

"He skated," Joanie replied.

Just before the fried bananas, Steve said, "I think you should put off the *Journal* guy."

"What?" she said.

"Don't bust a gasket, but I don't think you ought to do it."

"Why not?"

"You don't need publicity. It might make you feel good,

but it won't help you as a trader."

"No, of course not—"

"In fact, it might even hurt you. You know how the guys are."

She looked at him, her expression deflating.

"You said it yourself the other day, Joanie, they don't bother you anymore. You're one of them. No more hassle. Something like this sticks it right back in their faces. Especially the big guy," he said.

Joanie's fork dropped weakly to the plate.

He reached out for her hand.

"Hey, it's just my opinion. Do it if you want to," he said.

She groaned. "The *Wall Street Journal*."

"Then do it. Forget I said anything."

"No. As usual, Mr. Wise Father, you're right. Those ass-holes would never let me forget it."

"The timing's wrong, that's all," he said.

He smiled, then got out of the booth and slid in next to her. He put his arm around her shoulder. She was limp.

"Just keep trading. The news dogs'll be back," he said.

The next day Joanie called to cancel her interview. She told the reporter she had decided it would be bad luck. Luck was something quite precious to traders, she said.

No sooner had she hung up the phone than she got another call from another reporter, this one from the *Chicago Tribune*. She held the receiver away from her ear when he identified himself, wondering what this sudden media blitz was all about. But the *Tribune* reporter did not inquire about her.

"Did you know a kid named Brian Boyer?" he said.

"Of course," she said.

The following Monday morning, while he listened to an all-news radio station and plodded along in the outer lane of the Edens Expressway with the crush of morning traffic headed into Chicago, Korngold's car phone buzzed. The caller was the Rope.

"You better get a *Tribune* before you come in," Penneman said. "Your ass is reamed all over the business page."

"For what?"

"That kid runner who hosed himself."

"What about him?"

"Seems now it was your fault," Penneman said.

Korngold swung his car onto the shoulder, his tires squealing and throwing stones, and passed the stalled traffic until he reached an exit ramp. He found a *Tribune* at a convenience store. He read it in the parking lot.

At that same moment, just about every employee on the floor of the Board of Trade was reading the same page. The piece had been written by one of the *Tribune*'s most popular business columnists.

JOHN LARKIN

The tales that usually come from the commodity trading floors of Chicago are of dizzying profits and staggering debits. It is life in the fast lane.

The pits. Those gyrating arenas of lions and lambs, predator and victim.

But once you get past the glitter, the noise of the pit and the immense, even outrageous capacity for gain or loss, some of the stories aren't so pretty. They are tragic. They involve more than the loss of a few bucks, but the waste of young lives.

This story involves two people, one big and one little.

The big person is Kenneth I. Korngold, owner of the Chicago Clout and one of this town's fiery sportsmen, and also one of the richest, shrewdest traders on the Board of Trade. He is said to have personally amassed soybean profits of more than $20 million alone in the drought summer of 1988.

The little person was a boy named Brian Boyer, 18, a runner for Korngold's firm, and one of the many faceless workers who make Chicago's burgeoning futures markets work each day.

Being a runner is one of the many unglamorous, low-paying jobs on the floor. Most runners are young men and women, many of them students, who take on the job's rigorous demands—they literally *run* to bring orders into the pits—in order to learn the business.

So it was with Brian Boyer, a June graduate from St. Rita High School on the Southwest Side.

"Brian was a good kid. He was well liked and he seemed to have a knack for the business," said a Korngold employee who wished anonymity.

But, as it turned out, Brian was doing more than just earning his spurs as a runner, he was succumbing to the lure of speculating. Only weeks after he'd been on the job, he bought a Treasury bond contract. He did not do this on his own. Like most 18-year-olds, he had limited funds, certainly not enough to qualify him for a brokerage account with the Korngold firm.

Instead, Boyer was able to speculate in bond futures with the help of registered traders who winked at the rules and traded a contract for him.

His first trade was a rousing success, and deadly bait. Putting up a sum believed to be $200, Boyer saw it become $1,100. Not bad for a few hours' work, or, more accurately, a few hours of risk.

Unlike the public, floor traders do not have to put up collateral—often as much as $2,000 to 4,000 per contract, depending on the contract and the brokerage firm involved—in order to trade. Being on the inside, they simply have to take care of the modest overhead fees. Such an arrangement permitted a neophyte like Boyer to trade, though he had no business doing so.

Heady with success, Boyer continued to speculate, pressing traders to get him into the various markets.

"He wanted in. Brian had the taste of fresh blood in his mouth and he wanted more," said a trader.

Then young Boyer lost, not once, but again and again. His losses slowly but surely ate away the profits from his initial bond trade.

The fatal blow came in trading the German mark on the International Monetary Market of the Mercantile Exchange. Boyer somehow persuaded a D-mark trader to buy him several contracts. When the D-mark market collapsed several weeks ago, Boyer was wiped out. His losses were estimated to have totaled in excess of $5,000.

Now that is not a great sum in the halls of the commodity exchanges. Traders win and lose $5,000 in a single trade. But to Brian Boyer, it was a disaster, a debt he thought would not only take him months to repay but would probably lose him his job.

Faced with such a prospect, Brian did something altogether irrational, emotional, and sad. He left a love note and what cash he still had to his fianceé. Then he went into the garage of his parents' modest home on the Southwest Side, closed the door behind him, and turned on the ignition of the family car. The next morning his father found him dead of asphyxiation.

Brian Boyer isn't the first youth to take his own life. But Boyer's life perhaps could have been saved had someone said no. The finger must be pointed first to Kenneth Korngold. Korngold is considered one of the most knowledgeable veterans of the exchange. If not Korngold himself, then other traders, men and women with more savvy than Brian Boyer, should have stepped in. Instead, an everyman-for-himself ethic prevailed, and, sadly, prevails.

"Runners are bodies. Nobody gives a damn about them," said an anonymous trader.

As far as this columnist can see, no crime was committed, though several exchange rules against unauthorized trading were violated. But a life was needlessly lost, and that's a crime.

As for Korngold himself, a Korngold spokesman stated he was upset by what happened and fired the employees involved. But that was too little too late.

Finally, it's up to the exchanges to clean their own house, to supervise trading and exact severe penalties to unauthorized activity. Given the nature of the markets and the traditional, honor-bound method of trading, that may be a difficult task.

For the sake of other Brian Boyers, the little people down there, however, it is much overdue.

Instead of going to the office Korngold went to his apartment in Lake Point Towers. Once there he checked in with Mary Beth and Ira, forbidding them to tell anyone where he was but to log all calls. Then he had the Rope paged. A half hour later Penneman returned the call.

"Keep your ears open about this thing," he said.

"It's all anyone is talking about," said Penneman.

"I wanna know who gave it to that Larkin asshole."

"How 'bout Haggarty?"

"He's too obvious."

"That's my point."

"If it was him, he's done. Dog meat. He'll never get his face on the floor again."

"And the Pope had an abortion last week," said Penneman.

"Fuck off, Rope."

With that Korngold turned on the computer and the wall of price screens he had had installed in the apartment and tuned into the markets. In a matter of minutes he was on the phone to his floor desk with a trade.

About an hour later his phone rang.

"Talked to a friend of mine at the *Journal*," Penneman said. "He said he was pitched the Boyer story but he turned it down. The pitcher was some chick."

Chapter Six

For the rest of the day Korngold traded badly. He had stone hands, devoid of any kind of feeling. The market went south and he was in Canada. When it came back home he was in the Caribbean. He looked around him and blamed the apartment, the four walls, the dull, blipping machines. For some time he had considered trading off the floor completely, leaving the drubbing of the pits. But he hated this—this isolation, these soundless monitors. You couldn't feel a thing.

At mid-day a sportswriter, the soccer beat man, called.

"The paper asked me to find you," he said.

"Well, you did. You wanna talk soccer, let's talk."

"They don't want me to talk soccer."

"Then fuck 'em," he said, and hung up.

Vodka helped, but not his trading. That remained bleak and costly. The liquor removed the cobwebs and the funk. Good spirits could do that, just move right in, kill the offending brain cells, and make things obvious: he could not trade because of that woman. Who was he trying to kid? Joanie Yff had come onto the scene, and, like some *agent provocateur*, had scalded him. Cut his legs off at the knees. Dangling that cute ass and those rock-solid tits in front of him, fucking his brains out on his office carpet, for Christ's sake, then taking it all back, shutting him out.

Then Rachel. Rachel. Rachel.

And now this newspaper shit.

She had gotten him and gotten him good, just snugged up close and laid a shiv between his ribs.

Finally the markets closed and he turned the machines off. He replaced them with the cassette disc of Gladys Knight, the VCR with *Little Caesar*.

A half hour later Ira Roth called with the day's results.

"I'm a pissant receptionist," Roth started in. "That's what I am all day. Phone ain't stopped ringing. You're the talk of the place, Kenny."

"We lose any business?" Korngold said.

"Hell, no," Roth said. "Three little pricks applied for Boyer's job."

Roth listed the callers and rang off. Korngold returned none of the calls, business or otherwise.

Soon the phone buzzed again.

"I knew you'd be there, Daddy," Rachel said. "There's a Channel Seven mini-cam truck parked outside. They been here since *noon*."

"Call the police."

"Come on! I wanna get on the tube. This beautiful man reporter has been to the door four times and I think we got something going." She started to laugh, then cut it short.

"This ain't a goddamn comedy, Rachel," he said.

"Daddy—!"

"I'm in no mood. Not for you and not for your fucking friend."

"Who? Joanie?"

"Who else?"

"What does she have to do with it?"

"She's behind the whole damn thing, that's all."

"She is not."

"Dammit, Rachel!" he shouted.

The phone receiver shook in her hand. She was silent, shaken.

"I'm sorry," she said.

"Yeah, you're sorry," he said.

"Come home and I'll fix you an artichoke omelet. Park in front of Levinson's and come in the back," she said. "I'm going nuts all alone here, Daddy."

He exhaled. "Where's your mother?"

"Give me a break. She's at the Hyatt. She said she'd stay there until the TV guys are gone," Rachel said.

Korngold said nothing.

"Please?" Rachel said.

"If I can," he said.

He hung up and threw the telephone on the sofa. He had to get out of there, go someplace, get out of touch. He took the elevator down to the restaurant adjacent to the building's lobby. Called Jovan, it catered semirecognizable *nouvelle cuisine* mostly to the building's dowagers. But it did have a small alcove bar, and a bartender named Lally who loved to hear dirty jokes.

He sat down heavily.

"See, there was this ventriloquist in Indian country," Lally began, and she started to giggle.

Three drinks and a basket of goldfish crackers later he left the bar and headed for his car. He was in no condition to drive to Highland Park and he knew it. Instead he aimed the Mercedes, like a bird dog on the scent of a quail, toward the Board of Trade. Passing a Kentucky Fried Chicken store just off Van Buren he turned in, filled with a sudden craving for the original recipe.

When the girl at the drive-in window handed him the box he tossed her a $20 bill and drove out. Immediately the inside of the car became so overwhelmed by the smell of herbs and spices that Korngold pulled to the curb and started to dig in. With a thigh in one hand and a biscuit in the other, he looked around and realized he was in Printers' Row, parked across from the same building where he had picked up Rachel that night, home of Joanie, the one and only.

He absently checked the entrance as he ate piece after piece of the warm, greasy chicken, wiping his hands on his pants and the car seat, spilling bits of skin and coleslaw everywhere. In no time he consumed nearly all nine pieces. Grease coated his chin. The inside of the car smelled like a deep-fat fryer. He was stuffed, still a little drunk, and he laid his head back on the soft leather seat and fell asleep.

The knock of something against the window jolted him awake. Korngold looked into the scowl of a traffic cop on a rumbling, three-wheel motorcycle. The cop motioned at him to move. Korngold nodded blankly and started the car, and the cop drove on. Korngold rubbed his hands over his face, not sure of what time it was or how long he had napped. His neck was stiff, and the inside of his mouth tasted like a wet towel.

He was about to start the car and go home when he saw her. Coming out of the building, wearing a terrific leather jacket, a pair of jeans and espadrilles, her hair pulled back and kept in place by a comb-sized barrette, was Joanie. He watched as she paused and waited at the entrance.

Just behind her appeared a tall, skinny guy. Korngold recognized him — what's-his-name — the gold trader. The guy came up beside Joanie and she snaked her arm around his back. The two of them said something to the doorman, laughed, and walked down the sidewalk toward his car. They faced each other as they walked, coming within a few feet of his Mercedes and walking past without seeing it, lost in some private exchange, some sweet nothing.

Ain't love fucking grand, he said, and felt the chicken coming up.

Several nights later Korngold remained in his office long after the others had left. A few minutes after eight three traders filed in and lounged in separate corners. Each seemed surprised to see the others. They knew, however, what they had in common.

They were all bond traders, and they had all at one time cleared with Korngold. All had traded badly — or had taken one-time losses far in excess of average daily gains — had moved on to different firms, and continued to trade badly. All were struggling to stay afloat, to meet monthly overhead and put bread on the table or to repay long overdue loans or both. One still owed Korngold several thousand dollars. Unless they made dramatic turnabouts, their remaining time on the trading floor consisted of days, a week or two at best. If they went belly-up, they would go back to the real world and do what they could: sell cars, work construction, rejoin the old man's accounting firm, work for years to pay off their debt.

So when Korngold beckoned they quickly appeared. The three were nervous, strained, irascible young men, and they

278

were anxious to know what Korngold wanted of them. They stood and fidgeted, feeling the cold drafts of their own breath against their teeth.

What he said astonished and scared them, churning the walls of their stomachs like a thirty-tick loss. It was ruthless, dangerous, and, they all well knew, illegal. But in their precarious financial positions, they could do little but blink their eyes and listen. Korngold's was an offer that afforded them a ray of hope, a salvation from the specter of bankruptcy. They had little choice but to do what he asked and to do so in complete secrecy. Korngold had chosen his troops well.

The next time they called, a meet was set up at a lunchroom on Milwaukee and Chicago avenues on the near northwest side. Tommy objected, saying he'd never even been in the neighborhood before and didn't know how to get there, but the agent hung up on him.

The place was called F & T, and was a holdover from the time this stretch of Milwaukee Avenue had been dominated by Polish. That had been years ago, and apart from the F & T, a few undertakers, newsstands, the offices of the *Daily Zgoda,* and a bar or two with the code words *Ziwne piwo* on the sign, the neighborhood had gone mostly Spanish.

To Tommy it was no-man's-land, a pain-in-the-ass cab ride from the Loop, and he walked into the harsh light of the restaurant with a scowl on his face. The agents were already sitting in one of the wooden booths. One, the sport coat, was devouring a plate of *gulumpke,* the fist-sized stuffed cabbage in thin tomato sauce.

"Class joint," Tommy said, sliding in across from them.

"Great food," said the sport coat, ripping apart a piece of rye bread.

"Things look like floaters," Tommy said.

"Jesus," said the sport coat.

"We don't want any of your sushi bar friends to stumble on us," said the other agent.

"No threat here," Tommy said, looking around.

Then he looked at the two of them.

"So what's the beef?" he said.

"You," said the sport coat.

Tommy stared at them.

"Time you made a few things happen, Haggarty. We're just about done with your social reports."

"What's that mean?"

"Take your best shot. Give us somebody who counts."

"Come on, man. Park your ass at the entrance and grab anybody who comes out," Tommy said.

"Look, asshole. We're at a point where we justify this thing or we dry it up. We take somebody out of there with some weight — not some half-ass clerk or a few gofers from some street gang. We take some million dollar sweethearts."

"That's cool."

"Is it? Or maybe we get out of there and go after different fish. Like put a wire on you and use you as bait for sharks. You know? Juice guys love to make loans to traders."

"No way," said Tommy.

The sport coat laughed and looked at his partner.

"You hear that?" he said. "The kid said, 'No way.' "

His partner spoke.

"We need a big local. One of the North Shore guys with a stable and a Rolls and a big nose full. That way we take him down and we bargain. Get everybody eating everybody's asshole out. Turn the place over," he said.

"You got that, Haggarty? Enough fuckin' around."

That trading day, a Wednesday, started off like all the others. Joanie lingered on the floor, chattering with other traders, waiting for the open. She was now an old face. In the months since she had begun trading several new traders had come in, some of them women, all with the same taut, expectant expressions. Many looked to her, no doubt, just as she had looked to other experienced traders when she first began. Their expressions oozed admiration — you're doing it, you're good — and supplication — give us guidance, give us hope. Each fleeting glance was pleading, flattering.

As for the others, the traders who had been there far

longer than she had, they paid her no attention other than an occasional, salacious daydream. To them she was another badge. That she was also part of the good-natured, locker-room butt pats and well-directed—often a little *too* well-directed—elbows in the boobs was a fringe benefit of the action. The pit was a physical place, and while scores of bond traders would have traded body parts to get physical with JOY, their first mission was to push and claw for the trade.

As for Joanie herself, she keyed on the major brokers, many of whom were Korngold's cronies, and the big locals on the upper steps of the pit. Brokers were her lifeblood—ready buyers and sellers, sometimes the only people who could get you out of a position—and the pacesetters of the pit's ebb and flow.

In the minutes before the gong that day she and the others assumed their usual, quiet look of panic, replete with restless calisthenics, fidgeting, itching, tugging, and complaints about the business of risk. Lately the market had been flat; ticks were hard to make.

When trading began the market drifted. It listlessly gave and took a few ticks at a time. Like the others, Joanie groped for a sense of rhythm. She scraped for every tick she could get, then struggled to keep it. At the end of the first hour her cards were frustrations, memos of a trader doing nothing but treading water.

Then things began to change. With movement by some of the big brokers, prices gyrated somewhat due to pressure from clients anticipating glitches in interest rates. Then as quick as it started, it leveled off. There was little volatility or volume. The pit grew quiet, with few bids or offers. Traders' eyes flashed impatiently, jaws churned gum.

"One at four," Joanie shouted, her hands in the air. It was a plaintive bid to buy a contract, but a tick below the current bid. She bid it to the pit in general, her voice a stone thrown into the pond, and like other bids at the current asking price, none elicited a response.

Except this time.

"Sold," shouted MMP, a pudgy Hayes-Brookins trader standing just over her shoulder.

281

She scribbled the trade on her card, then confirmed it.

"One at four," shouted another trader, then another, but neither received a taker.

"One at three!" screamed a trader, this time somewhere among the bigger locals and brokers. A flurry of trading broke out, and suddenly the tick dropped to three, then two.

"Sell at two!" Joanie cried, desperately trying to rid herself of the contract.

It was this time snapped up from her by GLA, a Lipitz trader.

"One at two! One at two!" came the shouts.

More traders came in. Joanie felt a surge of anticipation, a rush of courage. The tick was plummeting, she could feel it.

"Sold!" she screamed, suddenly going short, selling a contract she did not own with the intention of buying it back at a cheaper price. Then she sold another, then a three-lot. She was short five contracts, more than her limit.

Then suddenly the far end of the pit erupted, with traders leaping over one another, their shouting frantic, arms and hands furiously clawing for trades. In seconds the tick rose to four, then five, then hopped up to nine. The rest of the pit was swept into the surge.

Joanie was stunned. With each added tick she was losing, and she frantically tried to buy five contracts and cover her short position.

"Five at nine! Five-nine! Five at nine!" she screamed in anguish, desperately searching for a taker. The tick rose to ten, eleven, and her voice cracked as she howled her offer.

"Yes! Yes!" came the offer, and she spun around to see the hands in her face. Once again it was MMP of Hayes, and Joanie made the trade, then slumped in agony. The tick rose another tick but she was out, damaged and damaged badly.

Then, almost as quickly at it had mounted, the flurry subsided, the tick held, the pit became quiet once again.

Joanie recovered and calculated her loss. She had lost forty-seven ticks. At $31.25 a piece that came to nearly $1,500. She was staggered. It had all happened so fast, a wave that had washed over her, swept her away, then spit her back on shore.

The rest of the day she feverishly worked to make back the deficit. She never came close.

That night she studied her cards and cursed herself for the lapse. She had jumped in, abandoned her strategy, taken on a five-lot — she had vowed never to trade more than one or two at a time — and gotten scalded. It was incredible! Stupid! Incredibly stupid!

She lay awake for almost an hour scolding herself.

The next day she began well, if overly cautious, getting in and out of the market with scratch trades, managing to be ahead a few ticks going into the last hour of trading. The final hour usually saw the pace pick up somewhat, with traders trying to get out from under losing positions or simply giving the session one last shot.

The tick began to bounce, up one, down one, up one, then two, and Joanie got in, buying a contract from Lipitz's GLA once again. Then she bought another from HHH, Harry Henegan of ComCot. The tick held and she tried to get out even, scratch both trades.

"Two at seven!" she yelled, fanning her arms out in front of her, scanning faces.

Then it happened again. Trading exploded across the pit. A knot of heavy hitters on the top steps descended upon each other, their palms out with twenty- and fifty-lot offers. The tick responded, down one, two, then four, with small traders soon leaping into the action until the pit was again in chaos. When it ended Joanie was out at one, a twelve-tick loss. She stared at her cards, not believing the debacle of those few moments.

The following day she traded even. The day after, however, was a disaster. Three separate times she was whipsawed, caught in long positions when the tick took a violent jump backward. Each loss was acute, a total loss of thirty-five ticks in all. When the closing bell sounded she could not help herself. She stood in her spot as other traders fell away, standing alone like a forlorn choir girl. Her hands started to tremble. Her fingernails dug into her palms. Then she started to cry. She stood there amidst the lights and the litter of the emptying U.S. Treasury bond pit and cried in muffled, fitful sobs.

That night she and Steve spent long hours studying her trades, trying to spot a fatal pattern, a newly acquired hitch. They felt like ballplayers appraising film of batting stances, swings, pitching motions, all the physical ingredients that made for bad outings. They could not identify a thing in Joanie's trading that might help her avoid future problems.

"It happens," Steve finally said. "Traders get into slumps like anyone else. They get out of them by staying the course, fighting the fight.

"And blah, blah, blah," he added, knowing he sounded like a commodity trader's version of Knute Rockne. Joanie smiled and put her arm around his neck. She hurt all over.

The next day a spurt just minutes after the opening cost her eleven ticks. After it happened she did not lose her composure. She did not cry or show any emotion whatsoever. She had resolved the night before not to do anything of the kind. She simply left the pit and went into the washroom. There she stared at the trade, this time with Henegan of Com Cot, the numbers scrawled on the card by her own hand. Then she went into a stall and vomited.

She ended the day down seventeen. For the week she had lost 107 ticks, more than three full basis points, more than $3,200 in all. Part of her loss came from two out-trades, those miscommunications among traders that result in trade discrepancies. Floor rules dictate that out-trade losses be shouldered equally. In Joanie's case that meant an additional loss of twenty ticks. When the Trout accountant handed her the printout of her week's totals, she nodded listlessly. She was pale, drained of tears, too sore to curse. She sat down and closed her eyes and heard the whine of dozens of hair dryers, saw rows and rows of chairs in a beauty salon, a station with her name on it.

She was taken from her reverie by Steve.

"Come on," he said. "I'm parked in a tow-away zone."

He pulled the trading coat from her shoulders.

"You don't even own a car," she said.

"I do now," he said.

He had rented a Mustang, complete with sky roof, a full tank of gas, and handwritten maps of Wisconsin on the front

284

seat.

"We got a weekend ahead of us," he said.

She looked at him in amazement. Steve Stamford was a person who planned *every*thing in advance, who did nothing spur-of-the moment. Until now.

"Uncle Manny is waiting," he said.

She followed him to the street and the cherry-red Mustang. She obeyed meekly when he dropped her off in front of her apartment and told her to pack a bag for two days in the wilderness.

His therapy, one he had devised that afternoon after learning of yet another of her losing days, consisted of his uncle's cottage on a blue lake in Wisconsin. No trading cards or related paraphernalia were allowed. An hour later they were on the Kennedy Expressway heading north into Wisconsin. Joanie sat against the door in the front seat and smiled a forlorn, altogether appreciative smile at the person behind the wheel.

Three hours later, minus a quick pit stop, they were at Stark Lake, twenty miles north of the Wisconsin Dells, and Uncle Manor's hand-hewn, two-story log cabin. Manny, along with his brothers Steve and Obie, had moved up here upon retirement six years earlier and built similar log homes within a few acres of each other. Included was a two-room guest cabin around the bend of the small, spring-fed lake. It was available to Steve, whose mother was the younger sister of the three men, any time he wanted. Manny and the others, with spouses, Rose, Betty, and Verna, three dogs, and plenty of Point beer, were waiting when they drove up.

They spent the weekend drinking the Point, playing long hands of gin rummy and euchre, wandering in the woods, fishing for bass and bluegills, and on Sunday, with much fanfare and bickering among the uncles, they roasted a twenty-four-pound suckling pig. On a clattering, makeshift rotisserie welded together by the brothers at a local sheetmetal shop, the skewered pig slowly turned over an orange bed of charcoals. For hours the heat browned and cracked its hide, and fatty drippings oozed out and sizzled in the coals.

Joanie had never seen anything like it. With the others,

285

however, she devoured the pork when it was served, chewing the delicate meat, savoring the fresh ham, washing it down with ice-cold Wisconsin beer. As the guest, she was offered the most prized delicacy — the ears. She declined. Uncle Manny beamed, then ate them in two bites, crunching the little flappers like potato chips.

When she and Steve got back into the city Sunday night Joanie felt wonderful. She had not spoken a word about bonds or trading or anything whatsoever concerning her dismal week past.

Monday morning she bounded into the pit. The weekend had put great distance between her and the previous week, and she began trading well. She was cautious, perhaps overly so, reluctant to take what she should have, skittish at the possibility of holding a profit too long. The market was not exciting or particularly active, but she did okay. By the end of the day she had avoided disaster of any kind, and made a little money.

The next day was much the same, and she finished the day by buying Steve dinner at a neighborhood Thai restaurant. They talked about Manny and Rose and the others, of pig roasts past.

Then Wednesday, again during a lull, while she was watching her cards, she got hit again. This time it was during a double bear trap, a sudden but small drop during which she was long and lost six ticks, a momentary pause where she got out, in, out, then in again, followed by a lightning-fast free fall in which the price began to plummet.

At the start of the slide traders erupted. Joanie was kicked, then shoved from behind and nearly pushed off her step. She struggled to get her balance, and she was pushed again. She floundered headlong against bodies that twisted all around her. It was as if she were caught in the crush of a street mob, carried along, her arms twisted and pinned. She struggled to get free, to see the boards, to trade. Who was pushing her?!! Suddenly an elbow cracked her across the ear and she screamed, then nearly blacked out. Still the crush continued, the tick's mad downward spiral putting new frenzy into traders, and they slammed against her in their frenzy to make trades.

Finally she pushed away and out of the knot of traders. Her head was spinning, one of the pockets of her trading coat had been ripped. She was breathing hard, still clutching her trading cards and her pencil. The tick! She looked up at the boards at the damn tick. In the melee, it had fallen sixteen, half of a basis point, before firming. She was holding a deuce, two contracts, and she had not even had a chance to see the price, much less cover it. Again, she had been pounded.

The next day she was pecked to death. She made several trades, dozens more than usual—there always seemed to be a bid or offer to meet hers—and lost a tick or two here or there. At midafternoon she stepped out of the pit to count up, to see exactly how she was doing and she was startled by the figures. Though she had not lost more than two ticks in any one trade she was down forty for the day. She was getting reamed.

Again she spent hours reviewing, trying to figure why she was just a beat behind the market, why she was no longer in control. She considered changing her strategy, taking a position and weathering short-term setbacks. But position-playing scared her to death. If you were right, you could make a fortune—the legendary ones were made that way. But if you were wrong, you were wiped out. And quick. She had no choice but to scalp, to do what she knew best, even though it was agony.

The next day, the last of the week, she made several good trades, taking profits of four, six, even eight ticks at a time. The market was moving on good interest rate volatility, money supply figures, overseas monetary ripples. Yet for every winning trade she gave one back. Then another. At the end of the day she was dead even. She had scratched. She had not made a cent.

A few minutes later she had lost even that. A ComCot trader came over to confirm a trade and showed her numbers she could not believe.

"Bullshit!" she screamed.

She riffled through her deck and found the trade, then thrust the card in his face.

"This is the trade, dammit!" she said.

It was her scrawls against his.

"Not by my numbers, JOY," the trader said.

"I don't *believe* this!" she shouted.

Other traders, knowing what was going on, walked past the two of them and hardly took notice of the feud. The ComCot trader held firm. Joanie knew she had no way of winning her point. Out-trades, those damnable, festering mistakes, were a fact of the pit. Joanie had to take half of the hit. Another twelve ticks.

This time no weekend retreat could help. She stayed in the office, wandering around with little direction. Steve stayed away. He said he would call a little later. By five all but a handful of employees had left, and Ballard Trout came out of his office.

"You got a bad case of hangdog, Miss Yff," Ballard said.

She nodded.

"Takin' your lumps, I see."

"I don't know what to do, Bal. At this rate I'll be gone in a month. I can't make any money, and I can't keep from losing it."

"Fun, isn't it?" He laughed. "This damn business. People think we're just having a hell of a good time. Makin' millions. Driving Mer-ce-dees-Benz automobiles. Oh, if they could see the look on your face right now."

He laughed deeply, then saw his attempt to humor her had scant effect.

"You got to stay in there, Joanie O. It's like a batting slump. I can't tell you why it's happening or when it's gonna end."

"Do you change strategy when you lose?" she said.

"Hell, what strategy? Half the time I get in there and leave my strategy in my pants somewhere."

"You, too?"

"You got the jumps, that's all. You're nervous 'cuz if you keep on losin', your cushion'll dry up. And if you worry about your cushion, you're gonna keep right on losing," Ballard said.

She bit a fingernail.

288

"Now if you were like some of those boys down there, I'd tell you to jet on out to Vegas and shoot craps all night. That'll clean out the head as good as anything.

"But you, Joanie O., I don't know. Look at your cards. See what the hell is goin' on. Maybe get off lead month for a while. Do some spreads. Break up your rhythm.

"Otherwise, all this tired old bean trader can tell you is to get back in the box every day and go at it. Find your juice. Get so you can hump a little bit. Feel that tick. Kiss it and send it back to its momma."

Again he laughed loudly, slapping the desk and scratching his belly with both hands. "How's that for financial counseling?"

Joanie couldn't help but smile. Ballard Trout's personality was too kind to be believed. It made her wonder what he was doing in this business.

But his words stuck with her as she left the office. Maybe she should get off the lead month. Maybe she could try spreading—buying and selling contracts for different months and waiting for the difference to go her way. It was a slightly different game, involving different thinking and a different pace.

Her mind swam with the possibilities, but one of them, she determined, was not to involve Steve. He had tried to help her, to bolster her spirits—that weekend in Wisconsin was wonderful—but so far it had not helped and she felt guilty about that. She had to get through this herself, not drag him and his trading down to her present depths.

When she met him that night she would not talk trading, not hers or his. She would leave the miserable pits on Jackson Boulevard while she and Steve skittered about different avenues.

She left the office alone, meandering down the hall, nodding to the cleaning ladies who had already begun their nightly raid on the building. The elevator was empty, as was the lobby when she stepped out of the car.

Just then someone tapped on her shoulder. She turned to see Tommy Haggarty.

"I wanna talk to you," he said.

289

"C'mon, Tommy—" she groaned.

His mouth tightened.

"Right *now*," he said.

"I'm in a hurry," Joanie said.

"To go belly-up?" he said.

"Haggarty, kiss off," she said.

He turned and leaned close to her, his nose centimeters from hers.

"With what you been droppin' lately you can't *afford* not to hear what I have to say," he said.

"What are you talking about?" she snapped.

"You're getting nailed in the pit and I know why," he said.

She looked at him, angry, and yet dumbfounded.

"Follow me," he said.

Chapter Seven

She walked a step behind him out of the building, turning west toward Wells Street. A half block up, Tommy went into Wing Yee's, a Chinese joint that was all but deserted at this time in the evening. Tommy slid into a booth.

An old Chinese man in house slippers offered menus but Tommy waved them away.

"Two Cokes and an order of fried rice," he said.

"Huh?" Joanie said.

"Never mind the hospitality. Just listen," Tommy said.

He bent over the table.

"You're being picked off," he said.

She scratched her scalp with both hands and exhaled loudly.

"What are you talking about?"

"What you drop this week—two, three K?" Tommy said.

"How do you know?"

"C'mon, Joanie. Everybody's bare ass in the pits. You suck gas and the whole world knows."

"You're canned—"

"I'm with Hargrove now. No sweat. And that's beside the point. The point, Joanie baby—" he said, leaning across the table and causing her to lean backward, "is that they're picking you off."

She stared at him.

"Correct me if I'm wrong, which I ain't. You been hit for two, three weeks now. You been trapped long and short. A few ticks here, a few out-trades, then wham, they cut your legs off. I know the program."

Joanie was stunned. How could he know? *What* did he know? *What* was he up to?

"You check your cards. Check your out-trades. You get in

deep shit when you trade with Palmer. Marty Palmer, that fat buttfuck with Hayes. And Arneson with Lipitz. That's two guys. There's another one, too, but I'm not sure who."

"Henegan," she said quietly.

"Could be. It don't matter. The point is that those guys are feeding off you. Setting you up, then taking you down. And they're being put up to it."

"How do you know?"

"You forget who I used to work for."

"Yeah, sure . . . sure, but how?" she stammered.

"C'mon, Joanie. Use your head. You're getting nailed when the market jerks, okay? Always when things are real slow. One big tug is all it takes. Who do you think's got the muscle to jerk it?"

Her chin dropped into her hands; she stared stupidly at the table.

"I seen Kenny do it all the time. Like clockwork. He don't even get hurt too bad."

"I don't believe it," she said.

"Well, when you start siccing the newspapers on guys like King Korngold you can believe in anything."

"But you—"

"Hey, hold on, sweetcakes. Sure, I talked to the guy and told him what he wanted to hear. But he found me thanks to *you.*"

"You put that out on the floor?"

"I have no fuckin' secrets."

"Shit! Tommy, you're a lowlife."

"Hey, watch the adjectives. I have feelings. I mean, let's get it straight: some press guy comes to you. Why? I don't know. You send him to me. So okay. But I cover my ass. Dig?"

"You bastard—"

"Hey, it happens. It's you he really wants anyway, Joanie O."

The waiter brought the order of fried rice.

"Tea?" he said.

"Is it that green shit?" Tommy said.

The waiter smiled and Tommy shook his head. He pushed the plate of fried rice aside.

"Stuff looks like a maggot convention," he said.

Joanie didn't hear him. She was seething, her mind running, in re-creating the events of the last few days.

"How do you know" — she blurted — "about me getting picked?"

"Put three and one together. Somebody said you were gettin' hit. Shit, said you started bawlin' on the steps the other day, which ain't real good form. Then I heard that fat ass Palmer in the john talkin' about nicking you for a mess of ticks. So I do a little research."

She shook her head wearily and drank from her glass.

"I — I just can't believe it. . . ."

"I'm right, though, about you getting gored."

Joanie nodded.

Haggarty whistled.

"Boy, you must a squeezed his nuts good for him to go after you like that. We're talkin' high crimes and misdemeanors here."

"I didn't squeeze anything of his."

"A figure of speech."

"I'm still not sure I believe you," she said, sitting up.

"Hey, are you losing money or are you losing money? Another week or two and you'll be into your savings — if you ain't already. Then you borrow from friends. Then the house. Hey — I know the scene.

"And he won't let up. We're talking about Mr. Big here who got his ass reamed in the Chicago *Tribune*. He's pit mentality — don't get mad, get even."

"So what do you want from me?" Joanie said.

Tommy grinned, displaying both rows of teeth. He did a two-finger rim shot on the table.

"Thought you'd never ask," he said.

She waited.

Once again he leaned across the table.

"For obvious reasons I wouldn't mind seeing ol' Kenny take it up the giggy. I mean a good one, and I don't mean in the pit. He's too big there. He's got reserves, man, maybe three, four million just for trading losses alone, so forget it.

"But he could be got. You already got under his skin for

him to go after you like he did. That's risky. Palmer or one of those other jagoffs could make some noises upstairs, okay? and K's in big trouble. Even you could scream and yell, if that's what you're thinking. He'd beat it, though."

He slid a piece of ice from his Coke into his mouth, crunching it loudly.

"If he's gonna be got, it's gotta be done different. Something even he can't cover, okay?" he said.

She stared at him, at his wiggly, expectant mug, not sure if she should thank him or spit in his eye.

Then she straightened up in her seat and thought for a moment.

"Tommy, I don't know what the hell you're up to. Or who's behind you. Or why," she said.

He smiled tightly.

"And I trust you like Richard Nixon," she said.

"You got no choice, Joanie," he said. "Without me you're out on the street in a month. With what I told you, you can go back in the pit and survive. Then it might be hard to admit but you'll come back and say that Tommy Haggarty saved your gorgeous ass, okay?"

She lifted her eyes and rubbed her forehead. It was getting late.

"Then what?" she said.

"You owe me one," he said.

He swirled the remaining soda in his glass and gulped it down. Then he slid to the edge of the booth.

"A *real* big one," he said.

He winked, and walked out.

She stared at the empty seat across from her. Her face burned. Then the waiter arrived with a fortune cookie and the check.

Joanie hurried quickly back to the Board of Trade, signed in with the front security guard, and went up to her office. She located her cards and printouts of her trades for the previous two weeks and spread them out on the floor.

Now that she knew what she was looking for it took her

only a few minutes. She went right to her disastrous trades, and each one involved the traders Haggarty had mentioned. There they were, as brazen as bad checks, and just as fraudulent. The only thing missing was the smug, guttural smile that Korngold must have worn with each one. The bastard!

She pounded her fists against the carpet.

"Tommy's full of shit."

"Look at my cards, Steve. It's there. The three guys he said. They *nailed* me time after time."

"They're the only ones?"

"No, of course not, but when you're going bad—"

"That's a far cry from being picked off."

"Why don't you believe it? Why is it a 'far cry' at all?"

She had not been even close to ready when Steve arrived at her place later that night. Trading cards and printouts, the same ones she had strewn about the floor in her office, were now scattered on her bed. Steve picked through them, studying them while Joanie made vague motions at getting showered and dressed.

"Because Tommy's duplicitous as hell."

"Sure, and what better person to know."

"What better person to get a load of your problems and exploit them."

"It started with that newspaper story on Brian Boyer."

"Maybe Haggarty started it. Ever wonder how that reporter found you?"

"He called the firm—"

"Yeah, but somebody had to tip him off in the first place."

She did not reply. She stared at the cards.

"He couldn't be—I mean, I just don't think even Haggarty could be that much of a manipulator," she resumed.

"Why the hell not? The floor's full of them."

He looked up at her and frowned. "Maybe you want to shake a leg? I haven't eaten since last Tuesday."

Joanie had managed to take off only her skirt. She circled the bed, her mind miles away from what the two of them had planned to do that night.

295

"But he's *right*, Steve. That son of a bitch is going after me."

"Bullshit. If Korngold wanted to get you, he'd do it with a monster out-trade, not the pissant ones here. Have somebody make you eat a fifty-lot."

"No, Steve, you're wrong. *This* kind of thing is just his style."

Steve looked at her, then in the direction of the bathroom. She went in and turned on the shower.

"Even if you're right—or Haggarty's right—what can you do? You bark and he'll deny it. He's covered," he said.

"I'll get those three traders," she shouted.

"No way. Korngold's probably got markers on them longer than their arms."

She didn't respond. Droplets of water came flying over the shower curtain as she scrubbed herself. Then she finished and turned off the shower.

"Stay away from them," he went on. "Don't even get near a trade with them. Same for Haggarty. Even if he is right, don't confirm him."

She walked in the bedroom with the bath towel around her waist, her bare arms and breasts still slick. She faced him with her hands on her hips, her marvelous nipples erect.

"So what do I do?"

"God, Joanie," he said, staring at her. "The graduating class of Notre Dame would kill to lick that one drop of water right there."

"C'mon, Steve, I'm serious."

She turned her back and began putting on her underwear.

"If it's true, which I doubt, forget about it. Walk away from it."

She turned around. "Are you kidding?"

"No. Trading doesn't give you the luxury of revenge."

She slipped a light, peach-colored sweater over her head, then pulled on a pair of pleated jeans. She went to her bureau and picked out jewelry, some yellow art deco earrings and matching bracelet. She returned to the bathroom and put on fresh makeup, then tousled and played with her hair. She didn't like it, and decided to pull it back into a ponytail. All the while she said nothing.

296

When she was finished she reappeared in the doorway of the bathroom. She was fresh, bittersweet with cologne, gorgeous as ever.

"There's a principle involved here," she said. "Real moral, ethical stuff. And there you sit, Mister Nineteen-Sixties Radical Protester, Mister Defender of the Public Good, and tell me to forget about it. That stinks, Steve, and you know it."

"Oh, grow up, Joanie," he snarled.

Then he tasted blood in his mouth. He had bitten the inside of his cheek.

The following Monday morning the bond pit was crowded—more than four hundred traders packed into the eighty-foot-wide octagon—and Joanie had all she could do to wedge herself into her spot. Second step, middle, on the window side, in the heart of the highest concentration of small traders like herself. But she only cared about three—Palmer, Henegan, and Arneson. They were all in place.

She stood with her elbows jammed into her ribs, her cards in her left hand, pencil in the right, one eye riveted to the quote board above her right shoulder, the other casting about the faces around her.

Yet this morning was different. She could feel it. The anxious tension of the opening was there, but it was as if she was in control of it instead of vice versa. Interest rates were moving, which meant bond prices would move. And when they moved, up or down, traders could make money. No, *JOY* could.

Then the gong sounded, the price at 72-6, and the pit erupted, hundreds of traders leaping and screaming in a frenzy of opening trades.

"One at six!!" she screamed, her voice cutting through the baritone roars all around her, lunging and thrusting her blood-red, razor-sharp nails into the air.

Only now she was not trading the pit, with any trader who would accept her bid, but with only a few faces. She did not look at Palmer, Henegan, or Arneson, but she knew exactly where they were and what they were dealing. Then she shut them out of her mind, preferring to slap the market, stay a half second ahead of it, step aside when it charged, take a slice when it reared.

She got in and out of several trades, making a tick here and there. She felt comfortable and confident once again, like a gambler sure of his odds. She knew, however, that the real ante would come when things slowed.

An hour or so later, as if on schedule, trading did slow. She noticed Marty Palmer give her the eye. It was on. She glanced at Arneson, then Henegan, and back again to Palmer. She made sure not to stare at any one of them, though it was difficult not to linger on the sight of Palmer.

Martin M. Palmer, MMP. It was not the hair, which was thick and combed straight back from his forehead, or the fact that he was heavy and out of shape. Marty Palmer's real problem was that the moment he set foot in the pit he began to sweat. His face became an oily, glistening, dripping mask. The perspiration drenched his collar, soaked his shirt, and formed a wide, dark stain on the back of his trading jacket. When he shouted bids and offers sweat sprayed from his upper lip as though it were a lawn sprinkler.

At first she saw him as an unctuous villain. She caught herself, thought a moment, then smiled at the fat, leaky tub. For as Joanie looked at him, she suddenly appreciated him. She appreciated every sweaty, rotund part of him. Because she was going to get him.

Her card was clean. The tick at 72-12. Palmer offered twelve and she made a move to take it. But she held off. He kept at it, staring at her, thrusting his fingers in her direction. Then Henegan came in, offering two contracts at twelve. Suddenly another trader bought from Palmer, the tick moved to thirteen and several more traders came in. Palmer offered once again. Joanie fidgeted, looking uncertain, bluffing as well as she could. The volume increased, the pit now swelling with noise and flailing arms — Palmer, Henegan, then Arneson — all three of them selling.

Suddenly Joanie joined them, not buying, but selling. She was going short, offering to sell contracts she did not own. She offered a tick lower than Palmer and the others, screaming her price, and she made the trade, one contract, then two, scribbling furiously on her card.

It was as if the gates had been opened, because the action increased even more, and all on the sell side. The price dropped, two, three, then four ticks. The pit was now alive, with traders on every level coming in on the move.

Then she covered, happily buying two contracts from Marty Palmer himself who had taken a bath on them. The price had dropped eight ticks, sixteen in all on a two-lot.

It all happened in minutes. Joanie clutched her deck. She was elated, her system racing, the pit a frenzy all around her. Yet she was out and would stay out for the time being, having taken a nice profit. She kept her hands folded tightly against her chest, her body being buffeted by the sway and the churning of the manic traders all about her. It was as if she was hugging herself.

Then it hit her, in the glow of the sweetest trade she had made in weeks, that Tommy Haggarty was right. She looked up at Marty Palmer, sweating like a pig and trading wildly, at Henegan and Arneson, and wanted to choke them.

As for Korngold, choking was not good enough.

The rest of the trading day passed in a blur. The veil had been lifted from her eyes. She was renewed as a trader, efficient, savvy, back in the game.

At the closing bell she raced over to the gold pit. It still had a half hour of trading left but Joanie could not wait. She stood on the steps and got Steve's attention. She motioned to him and he came out to her.

She thrust a trading card on which she'd scrawled her day's totals in front of him.

"He was right!" she exclaimed. "I kept away from those pricks. They came at me—you wouldn't believe it, Steve—and I wouldn't budge. And it worked!"

She literally bounced as she spoke.

"That little creep was right," she said.

Steve nodded, his eyes on her cards, and said nothing.

Joanie took a step back and looked at him.

"Don't be so happy for me," she said.

He shrugged.

"I grew up," she said.

"I gotta close out," he said, and stepped quickly back into the pit.

The following sessions repeated the pattern. Joanie either avoided the three traders completely, or watched them try to mount a pick-off and jumped in with an opposite position. She guarded against any chance of out-trades. By Thursday they were not even trying anymore. On Friday Marty Palmer was absent from the pit. Somebody said he was bankrupt.

"In debt ten K to his laundry lady, no doubt," cracked a trader.

"She's still underpaid," said another, and those around him snickered. It was a fitting, and not uncommon eulogy for another slain trader. Joanie broke not a trace of a smile.

Later that morning she stopped Tommy Haggarty. Before she could speak he raised his hands in front of him.

"Not here," he said, looking behind him, then back at her, as if he was being followed. "This afternoon. Four o'clock. The lobby of the Marquette Building, Adams and Dearborn."

Then he walked quickly away. Joanie shook her head.

Yet that afternoon after trading had ended she discarded her jacket and walked the three blocks to the Marquette Building to meet him. It was a landmark building with a magnificent lobby made of marble and decorated with murals depicting "The Deerslayer." Tommy motioned her to a stone bench in a corner near the stairwell.

"Too many fuckin' ears on the floor," he said, looking furtively around him.

Then he turned to Joanie and clapped his hands together.

"So-o-o-o-o, back in the money, huh, babe?" he said. "Did the kid know his beans, or did the kid know his beans?"

"I didn't come here because of your looks," she obliged.

"That's a shame. We're a natural couple, Joanie. I don't

know about you, but I can go all night."

"To the bathroom, probably," she said.

"You're quick, you're quick," he said.

"Cut the shit, Tommy. I got things to do."

"Okay, okay. Now you know I was right. Korngold went for your throat. I mean he wanted you out, right? Big league hardball. And he damn near did until look! in the sky! it's a bird! it's a plane! it's *Super Tommy* to the rescue!

"So I *know* you'd love to get a little payback. And I got just the idea for you."

"And just what would that be?"

"We bust him."

"Right, Tommy. That and maybe turn him into a Baptist."

"I mean it. We get him in handcuffs. FBI agents, the whole she-bang."

"How?"

"Blow."

She laughed.

"Like that auto guy a few years ago," she said.

"Yeah, what *was* his name? Made that tin can car. They nailed him in some damn hotel room on a VCR—I remember now. But he got off. Our boy won't, and the cameras, we can get him right out in the open."

"Oh, really," she said.

"Like right on the trading floor," he said.

She exhaled, then stretched her arms over her head. Her blouse went taut against her torso.

"God, I'd sell my mother to the ayatollah if you'd do that again," Tommy said.

Joanie quickly lowered her arms and scowled.

"Tommy, I came here because you saved me. I hate to admit that but it's true," she said. "I also detest that man more than anybody on earth. I don't mind admitting that. But I am really not interested in hearing some drug fantasy of yours."

"No fantasy. This is serious shit, Joanie, you better believe it. I happen to know the G is just achin' to raid the floor. There's a blizzard of blow down there as we all know and they'd love the PR. And when they do come in, we just happen to see that they take him, too. Got it?"

"How?" she said.

"Leave that up to me, if you're in," he said.

"How much coke does Korngold do?"

"Who cares? It'll take him a year to fight it. He'll be suspended from trading. His name will be shit and his firm will go down the tubes. You catch the sketch?"

She looked off across the lobby.

"Couldn't happen to a nicer guy," she mused.

"Now you're talking," he said.

She caught herself when she said it. She was not sure what put her off more, Tommy Haggarty's scheme or the fact that she was sitting here and listening to it.

"And someone like you can pull it off, Joanie. Nail him good. Get real close, like rub up against him 'til he's hard as a cucumber. Then put the blade in his gut."

"Oh, brother," she said quietly.

"I knew you'd like that," Tommy said, tilting his head slightly.

She exhaled loudly. He expected her to respond, and tapped nervously on the bench between his legs. She got up to leave. He grabbed her wrist.

"This ain't fun and games, Joanie. This is a big hit for me. Someday I'll tell you why," Tommy said.

Chapter Eight

Korngold did not make the rules, but he knew them. He traded by them, took advantage of them, even abided by most of them. One of the rules had to do with good news and bad news. Good news in the world of business — gains, higher sales and profits, new products, sound acquisitions and mergers, top personnel — was expected, even occasionally rewarded. Bad news, however — losses, lower-than-expected earnings, suits, disasters, scandals — was intolerable, and always punished.

Neck-deep in bad news, in the publicity surrounding Brian Boyer's suicide, Korngold knew he had to face the onslaught. He expected a few ripples from customers, and snide, self-righteous asides from competitors. He did not look forward to it; he would not enjoy it. But he would face it. And in the final tally, he did not expect any real losses.

The bulk of the crap, he knew, would come from the outside, the press and the public, particularly in light of his ownership of the Clout. But the unwashed understood nothing of the futures business, and they overreacted to what they thought they did know. As long as the press and the public were dogging him, he had no choice but to answer the phones, tell the employees to go about their work no matter what, and persevere. He would hang tough, wait until the smoke cleared.

It did not. No matter what Korngold personally said or did, rumors swept the trading floor concerning the health of his firm, pending lawsuits from customers, and traders and employees who were supposed to have jumped ship. Irv Kupcinet, the city's ageless gossip columnist, wrote that Brian Boyer's family was conferring with attorneys about filing a multi-million-dollar suit against him. Kup's competition at the *Tribune* wrote that the Board of Trade was considering suspending Korngold's seat. A TV sports commentator ended his broadcast by repeating a rumor that the Clout were for sale.

Korngold cursed every word, every new report. He vowed to stand firm, but that was getting more and more difficult. He wondered if it might not be time to retaliate.

Nowadays it took Joanie three seconds of contact with Steve to know his mood. Usually his was a quiet, even, engaging temperament, sometimes detached and preoccupied, occasionally cynical and short, but always obvious. At least to Joanie.

Just after trading that afternoon, she met him for a late lunch in a cafeteria in the Insurance Exchange Building across from the Board of Trade. As soon as they were seated she knew he was depressed. Still depressed. He had been that way with her since the icy night of the weekend before. She knew it because when Steve was down or angry or sulking, he became stone quiet. He responded but did not contribute, did not jabber or quip or radiate his usual energy. Right now, no matter what or whom she brought up, he offered little.

"Look, Steve, this is just stupid. I'm sorry if I offended you. I don't know exactly what I did but I'm sorry anyway," she said.

He looked up.

"Don't be sorry. You said what you felt the other night," he said.

"I'm still sorry."

He nodded, his mouth full of corned beef.

"If you're going to sulk about it, why'd you even want to have lunch together?" she said.

"Habit," he said.

She scowled.

"Okay, I'm going to think out loud and if you'd like to comment on anything you hear, just feel free," she said.

He looked at her, then laughed approvingly.

"That's a start," she said. "Anyway, having confirmed in my *own* mind that three traders — with or without, but probably *with,* the support of KIK — were definitely out to pick me off, I went over to Tommy Haggarty, the slimy but useful little creep who alerted me to what was going on, in order to thank him.

"Haggarty acts like he's some kind of secret agent or some-

304

thing and tells me to meet him in the lobby of the Marquette Building so nobody will see us talking together. Okay? So I meet him there and he pats himself on the back so hard he probably separated a shoulder. Then he says he's gonna get Korngold back. Revenge of the Clerk, or something like that.

"How is he going to do this? He claims that drug agents are about to raid the cokeheads on the floor. He knows all about it. And he says it's the perfect chance to nail Korngold. With my help, he says, though he didn't say exactly how. He did suggest that I should renew contact with Korngold. 'Rub up against him' was the way he described it, while someone else, probably him, gets him from behind.'"

Steve lessened his attack on his sandwich and paid attention.

She went on. "Well, the idea carries some appeal to a person in my shoes, having gone through what I just went through. Not the rubbing-up part, the revenge part. I mean, I'm only human."

"Tell that to the judge before he passes sentence," he said.

"Hello there, glad to have you back."

"You're not serious? Tommy didn't throw that at you."

"That and more."

"Goddamn snake. You'd rather link up with G. Gordon Liddy than him."

"Easy for you to say, Steve. You're not the one who was almost bankrupted. He was going to wipe me out. He went after the fillings in my teeth."

"Look, you're convinced of that, so I'm not going to argue with you. Everybody loves a conspiracy—"

" 'Cuz it's *true,* dammit."

"All right, so maybe it is. It looks that way when things go to shit. But you're out of it now. You survived—with or without Haggarty's help, I don't care—and the only thing for you to do now is to go on as if it never happened. You don't have the luxury of getting even, especially with a guy the size of Korngold. Not in this business."

She scowled, and bit into her chicken salad sandwich.

"If I don't get back at him, he'll just come back at me. You know what they say, 'Maybe not tomorrow, maybe not next week or next year, but someday he'll be back.' So I've got to stand up to him," she said.

"That's just plain stupid. Almost as stupid as Tommy Haggarty's schemes," he said, and stood up to leave.

"You're always the voice of *reason*," she said, as they walked out of the nearly empty cafeteria.

"You say that word with such disdain," he replied.

"Just one time I'd like to see you do something totally reckless," she said.

"What is this coat I wear, a Century Twenty-one salesman?" he replied.

"Might just as well be," she said.

He turned his back and kept walking.

"Indiscreet," she said, trailing behind him. "Maybe just once Steve Stamford could do something indiscreet."

He kept walking.

"Reckless," she said.

"Dangerous," she said.

"Knock-your-socks-off incredible," she said.

He kept walking.

The Board of Trade was very much like a big club, and likewise had its committees. They dealt with everything from dress codes to trading rules. Like every other full member, Korngold had from time to time served on some of them. He had made friends, and knew just about everybody necessary to know. When the rules committee notified him of its inquiry, he reached out to one of its members.

"You know I can't tell you anything, Ken," his contact said, cupping his hand over the phone receiver.

"I know. But I'm sure you'll find a way to get something to me," Korngold replied.

Korngold was confident because of what had happened to this trader, a soybean scalper, one cold, windswept day about ten years earlier. On that day soybeans fell out of bed. The market whipsawed so badly that dozens of traders were wiped out. One of them, a young man with a lisp and glasses so thick they distorted the shape of his eyes, was hit so badly that he broke down in an aisle and started wailing hysterically.

Korngold knew the trader as a friend of his uncle's, and he went over to scrape him off the floor. As he did, the kid began pleading with him.

"Twenty K, Ken!" he sobbed. "I gotta have it or I'm wiped out, Kenny! Please, ya gotta help me."

He rose to his knees and clawed at Korngold's pant legs. Other traders looked over at the scene without a smattering of pity. They would have been touched had they not observed similar scenes before. Most simply stepped around him.

"Gimme twenty large, Kenny," the kid pleaded as Korngold ushered him off the floor and into the lobby.

When Korngold got the trader cleaned up and collected, he told him he was an asshole and that he never wanted to see him be an asshole again. Then he gave the kid $20,000.

Within a few months the trader repaid him. Today, nearly a decade later, the same trader, now devoid of hair, still wearing thick glasses, but possessing a comfortable fortune, paid Korngold interest on the debt.

He told him that the Board of Trade was not interested in the Boyer episode or in any of the firm's more dubious accounts. Instead, it was investigating a brief partnership he had formed several years before with another trader. It was just after Korngold left his uncle's firm and before Korngold Commodities had come of age.

He and his former partner had set up a separate trading account in the Cayman Islands, a favorite offshore financial and tax haven for creative American businessmen. Korngold understood the account to be a form of tax avoidance, not as a method of pursuing secret — and potentially illegal — futures trading.

The government and the futures commissions thought otherwise, and considered almost anything having to do with offshore accounts as illicit. Korngold's exposure was brief, the partnership dissolved after only a few months. But the Cayman Island account had been utilized, and it remained in Korngold's financial past even though Korngold had literally forgotten about it.

Until today.

* * *

Every pit has its day, its week, sometimes its year. When that day comes, interest in the commodity dominates the floor. If it persists, due to an act of nature or politics or both, news of the frenetic trading makes the pages of the business sections in daily newspapers, occasionally even splashing onto front pages and nightly television newscasts. Nothing lent color to a story about a shortage or an unstable market—in sugar or silver or soybeans—like the flailing, howling antics of an infused trading pit.

In the late 1970s just such an explosion occurred in metals, mostly gold and silver, but also in others such as platinum. The surge was fueled by double-digit inflation. Dubbed "runaway inflation," and there was no other kind, it was the ogre, pronounced legions of gloomy economists and financial gurus, that would ultimately annihilate the worth of paper money.

The dollar, as well as all other currencies, was doomed. Times would be no different than when the deutsche mark collapsed in pre-World War II Germany and thousands of marks were needed—always transported in wheelbarrows—just to buy a loaf of bread. Even worse, things could go the way of the Netherlands in the seventeenth century, when the tulip bulb became the only accepted currency and frenzied Hollanders hoarded the precious root.

No inflation/currency collapse scenario was too farfetched. And gold, said the experts, was the best refuge. The price of the metal soared, from $50 an ounce at the beginning of the decade to over $800 an ounce in 1981. As if inflationary fears were not enough, gold prices gyrated with news of every international fracas, an oil boycott, a shortness of breath by the president of the United States. Network television crews taped action in the gold pits. Investors big and small, savvy veterans and rank amateurs, followed gold quotes like they did the ball scores, and inquired about cashing in savings bonds for bullion.

In the 1980s, however, inflation began to ease and the price of gold fell. The dollar, which had taken the brunt of attacks from the financial community in the wake of gold's rise, displayed remarkable strength on foreign markets. By the mid-1980s the price of an ounce of gold stabilized to the $350 to 400 range.

The dollar broke new trading highs day after day. Gold bugs faded into the background.

Yet gold never lost its gleam. The financial world remained populated with worry warts, with gnomes ever willing to contemplate the worst: breakneck world inflation and monetary collapse. If that happened, gold would trade for $1,000, even $2,000, an ounce. Currency-rich individuals again would need their wheelbarrows.

Such was the reality of Steve Stamford's trading world. Though he personally considered gold to be no different from any other commodity, with a supply and a demand and a proper niche in the workings of the industrial world, he knew the price of gold was a political and social barometer of sorts. He knew that the orderly market for the metal was vulnerable to world events, to cataclysms and coups, to wars and rumors of wars, to assassins and tyrants and every kind of maniac that might give people cause to worry about peace on earth.

When he first began to trade he stepped aside whenever the market heaved. He did not want to be an incidental victim of an ayatollah or a torpedo in the Strait of Hormuz. He traded best when the market was stable, taking his morsels where he could, scalping and spreading with reason and design, following carefully researched technical strategies. By traders' standards he did modestly well — he survived and made a little money.

Since the day of the tractor brigade, however, the day Steve Stamford truly realized what trading commodity futures was all about, he made much more than that. He traded shrewdly and ruthlessly, his profit and loss ledger showed much greater swings than he had ever before imagined. It was as if his entire personality had undergone a metamorphosis, from a cautious, bean-counting, former barrister to a bareback rodeo cowboy. He whooped and hollered and wrestled with the market, and took away $10,000 to $15,000 a month. A six-figure year was virtually in the bag.

The better he did, the fatter his account got, the more chances he took. A scalper no more, Steve found himself looking ahead and around, taking a broader view of the market and where it was going. In so doing he took on positions, buying contracts and holding them, no matter which way the price went. The risk was enormous. The market could run against his position and mount up staggering losses, even wipe him out. Steve knew that, yet he began to put on positions anyway. It was not that the potential gain was so great, though there was no denying it, but rather that he possessed a smug sense of being right, or, even more significantly, of being able to handle things if he were wrong. He savored the feeling.

Position players, conventional wisdom held, made most of their money in just 5 percent of their trades. Which meant that 95 percent of the time they twisted in the wind. They sucked gas, absorbed losses big enough to send lesser traders to the stalls, and did so without flinching. They had balls, conventional trading wisdom also held, the size of cantaloupes.

Steve's research and his instincts told him the gold market of the 1980s had nearly bottomed out, that the dollar had run its course on foreign markets, that the Federal deficit was finally going to rear its ugly head in the form of higher interest rates and higher inflation. It was a dismal but conventional forecast, a return to the dog days of the late 1970s, and a bonanza for gold. The key ingredient, and the very crux of the existence of men who traded wasting assets, was timing.

He went long with a ten-lot, ten contracts for delivery of 100 troy ounces of gold each in June of the following year, a full seven months away. At $345 and change an ounce, the gross worth of his position was just over $345,000. Going long on a ten-lot was nothing—Steve traded in excess of 200 contracts a day—but staying long, holding the position from one session to the next was something new and something bold. Then, as if to buttress his new strategy, he took on another ten contracts.

As the days passed, he held firm, ever eyeing the board and his indicators. He occasionally scalped contracts for small gains here and there when the price jerked but he did not waver from his long June position. In fact, on a weakness in gold prices two weeks later he doubled it, then doubled it again. He amazed even himself when he did it, and physically shivered when he confirmed. He stood in the pit stunned by what he had done, but the sensation was only temporary. Everything inside him told him he was right, that gold was due to break out. He was long 80 contracts, over $2.5 million worth of gold bullion. He

310

had rolled the dice.

Yet he did it in solitude, without the knowledge or the counsel of Joanie.

"Your cards are empty," she said during one of their nightly review sessions.

"The market's flat," he said.

"That never stopped you before," she said.

"These days it's quality over quantity," he said, coming closer to the truth than he cared to.

" 'Cept you're not making any ticks," she said.

He shrugged.

"When the market gets off its ass, I will too," he said. "In the meantime, I'm not going to worry about it."

Except, she noticed, he *was* worried, or at least concerned. Steve was as intense and occupied with the market as he had ever been, even though his daily trading was listless. That was not like him. In the days that followed she wondered about it, even worried, and found herself slipping over to the gold pit at different times to watch him. Invariably he stood motionless, intent on the action but seldom trading with the ferocity she had come to know in him. Something was wrong, or different, or both. She pondered if indeed she did not understand him, as a trader, as a lover, as a friend.

"It's a loser's market," he said when she probed, but would say no more.

He did not have to say anything to his firm's accountant, as he knew the position of every trader. The firm's managing partner also took notice.

"You're digging in," he said to Steve, in more of a question than a statement.

Steve nodded, knowing full well the stakes, the gravity of his position in pure dollars and sense, and also knowing that he did not owe an explanation. If he was wrong, he simply had to pay for it.

As time passed, the price did little, and Steve's position stayed relatively static. He was not making any money, which meant he was losing it, but slowly, a drop of blood a day. It was a lull, he told himself. His charts repeated the reassurance. His timing was a bit premature, but, then, nobody could nail market breaks right on the nut. He would wait, grit his teeth, find out what he was made of.

But the waiting started to work on him. His daily trading ground nearly to a halt. He stood in the pit like a stone, but one that by the end of the day became clammy from an anxious sweat. He began to bite his nails. He ate bag after bag of Cheetos, the orange, cheeselike snack puff that left his fingers greasy and his stomach empty, yet he had no appetite for dinner. He sat across from Joanie night after night and nibbled on rolls and bread sticks while she attacked fresh fish and choice red meats.

"You must have an ulcer," she said, trying to get a response. "Or a virus or maybe a dose of prostate cancer."

"Real funny, Miss Yff," he said.

"Somebody around here should be," she said. "You're a lotta laughs lately, Steve."

"Sorry."

"Don't be sorry, snap out of it."

He grimaced.

"The trouble with you, Joanie, is that you make no allowances for mood swings. You know what I mean? Everything's up or down, and there's no room for, say, melancholy," he said.

"You make your own fun, my mother used to say. God, this tile fish is good."

"Everything with you is physical. Tactile."

"Hey, lighten up, Steve. If something's really bothering you, tell me. I've tried to be sympathetic and you say nothing. So I figure maybe it *is* physical."

"Just an occasional attack of proctalgia fugax."

"What's *that?*"

"Sharp, unexplained rectal pains common to young men."

"That's *wonderful.*" She laughed.

"Easy for you to say. I read about it in a magazine."

"I *must* remember that," she said, her face beaming. "Proc—What?"

"Proctalgia fugax."

"Got it. I mean, you got it. I don't want it."

He smiled slightly, then looked away, his expression once again falling blank.

She sighed and blotted her mouth with a napkin.

"Boy, I'd love to have you back," she said, her voice now direct. "I'm serious. You're preoccupied or obsessed or depressed, I don't know. Is it me? Is it another girl? Is it work? You put on some big position or something that's driving you up a wall? I lie in bed at night, Steve, trying to figure it out."

He turned quickly to her.

"Just take it easy," he said.

The slide that followed in the price of gold was at first almost imperceptible. A few cents here and there. Though Steve agonized with each penny, he did not panic. The market was fishing for a bottom. Support levels, those crucial indicators to traders who heeded the technical indicators, generally remained firm. For Steve's positions, the crucial support level of gold was at $340. So far whenever the price approached $340, it held steady or even rose a shade. His next support level was at $300, and he was prepared, though he dreaded the notion, of holding on to his position even at that level.

Then the price slid below $340. Just a few cents, and it held there for days, but Steve worried. His position was beginning to hemorrhage.

By this time Joanie knew what was going on. She had studied his trading and asked a few questions around the pit. The discovery stunned her, yet she tried to keep it to herself. She followed the price of gold as if the position were hers.

Finally she could no longer keep quiet.

"Why are you doing this?" she asked.

"What am I doing?" he said. "I took a position. So what?"

"So it's destroying your life, that's what," she said. "And not doing great things for mine."

"I'm sorry about that," he said.

"*Dammit,*" she shouted.

She could not help but get angry. At night there was nothing for them to review, nothing to talk about, so Joanie saw no choice but to see less of him. He went home alone, staring at his charts, wondering how long he could hang on. At her place, Joanie cursed the walls, wondering why in hell he was doing this.

It was Ballard Trout who offered a different angle.

"Maybe it don't have anything at all to do with trading," he said to her one night in his office.

The insight, forthright as it was, followed by Ballard's cool, analytical gaze, made her shudder.

Finally the market broke. The jog came not from any domestic developments, not from economic indicators or government reports, but from the Russians. Faced with their annual economic failures, most of which were precipitated by their moribund harvests, and their staggering defense budget, the Russians needed cash. To get it they sold two commodities they owned in spades: oil and gold.

Their oil glutted an already glutted world market for crude, sending prices downward from the OPEC $19.50-a-barrel benchmark. Their gold sent prices in the London and Hong Kong markets sprawling. Traders scrambled to sell; the price fell by the minute. When Steve came to work at 6:30 that morning the foreign exchanges were in chaos.

Steve sat in the office and held his head in his hands.

At the bell trading in the pit erupted. Traders crammed themselves into every available inch of space and convulsed like a massive, berserk animal. And everyone, including Steve, was frantic to sell. The price dropped like a rock. Within minutes the price had dropped down limit—selling below $300 an ounce—the full $50 change allowed in any one session unless circumstances dictated otherwise. Traders howled "Limit bid! Limit bid!" like coyotes in the night. There were simply no buyers, for until the price stabilized, not even those traders who were short, thus profiting from the decline, felt compelled to cover their positions and buy back into the market. They would gleefully let the decline run, and that might be for days, until the rest of the world, including the Russians, decided just how precious gold really was.

The day ended as one of the biggest massacres in the history of commodities trading. Those traders who were long were locked in, and their losses were staggering. At the close the floor looked more like a colosseum than a trading pit, with bodies barely able to walk off on their own power.

Steve was one of them. He had managed to shed only a few of his contracts, and those at a substantial loss. His position was still largely intact. He stumbled back to the office like a dead man.

Joanie was a few steps behind him. She did not know whether to go to him and hold him or to leave him alone. He walked steadily, seemingly unaware that she was there, his eyes fixed straight ahead. She stayed in his shadow, seeing only him amidst the rush of bodies all around, trailing after like a scolded child behind an angry parent. For while she felt awful for him, she also felt afraid. For him and of him.

That night she went to his place. She let herself in and immediately heard an unfamiliar sound. It was a television. Steve never watched television. She stepped quietly into the living room and saw him lying on the sofa, facing the small black-and-white set. It was tuned to "Wheel of Fortune."

Steve looked up at her.

"The rain in Spain," he said blankly, winning the game.

"I brought you a present," she said.

She had stopped at an Italian delicatessen and picked up an order of pasta primavera — which he craved — Italian vegetable bread, a green salad, and a bottle of wine. She went to the kitchen and began to prepare it. He did not move from the front room. The aroma was persuasive enough to get him to the table, however, and for long moments they ate in silence.

"I'll get through this, but I think I have to do it alone," he finally said.

"Be serious, Steve."

"I am."

"What is this, some kind of macho rite?"

"I don't know what you're talking about."

"Look, I thought we meant something to each other. We buck these things. Not just when they go bad for me, but for you, too."

"I don't need a team effort. I fucked up and I'm paying for it. Alone," he said.

"That was the plan all along, wasn't it? To go it alone."

315

"Of course not."

"How else can you explain it?"

"I don't want to. I don't have to."

"What? Come on, Steve. After all this time you just blow us off like that?"

"I'm not blowing anything off. I'm losing my goddamn shirt — hell, I'm getting murdered — in the goddamn gold market! That's all I know right now. No kissy face, no sweet nothings. I'm trying to survive. And you, Joanie, just have to get out of the way."

She glared at him. He looked down at his food. Then her face collapsed and she fought back tears.

He reached out for the plate of pasta. With a swipe of her hand she grabbed the plate away from him. She went over to the countertop, retrieved the plastic carry-out containers, and scraped the pasta back into them. She went to the table and did the same with what was on her plate. She picked up the salad, wrapped up the bread, pushed the cork in the wine, and stashed it all back in the shopping bag.

At the door she turned to him as he sat there.

"There. I'm out of your way," she said.

Steve felt the door slam, then heard the outer door close behind her. The fork dropped out of his trembling hand.

Outside the building Joanie stopped, put her face in her hands, and began to cry. The tears washed over her fingers. As she stood there sobbing a taxi pulled up alongside, the driver having driven on the wrong side of the street to get to her.

"Ride?" he said, leaning his head out his window.

"Go to hell," she scowled, and hurried down the street.

A half block away she saw a wino probing the insides of a private dumpster. She walked up to him and thrust the shopping bag into his midsection.

"Bon appétit," she said, and walked off.

The bum looked after her, then into the bag, and, spotting the jug of Chianti, had kittens.

Chapter Nine

For Joanie the days and nights that followed were a blur. She knew she could not stand to be alone. She dreaded the four walls of her apartment, a place that lent itself to self-pity, to sulking or pining away suddenly available hours. So she went from the pits to the spots, eating little and drinking too much, moving from Rush Street to Division Street to Lincoln Avenue to a kick-ass punk rock club across the street from Wrigley Field.

She went alone, or with Margie Finamore, or she called up some of the stylists at Paul B., who gained entry to the private clubs because of their green hair. One night she tagged along with a trio of T-bill traders who took her to a sports bar, got four dark beers into her before a single bite of food, then challenged her to a tournament of drunken table hockey. Later she found herself staggering into a strange automobile, exchanging wet, groping kisses with beery lips, raking her fingers over sweaty chests as thick fingers raked over her own.

It did not matter where she went each night, from Yvette on North State Parkway, to Harry's Cafe, Thunderbird, Butch McGuire's. Somehow she ended up back at her own apartment, negotiating the door locks out of instinct in the bleak hours of the morning, reeking of smoke and spilled booze, some of her best outfits stained or ripped.

In the light of day she could not remember the night before. She had no idea what she spent or what was spent on her. One morning her wallet was picked clean of at least $500 cash. She did not know if she had lost it or given it away or had had it stolen. She was just as uncertain about the bruises that appeared on her legs and arms, if they were friendly or hostile. She felt sore all over, in every recess and orifice, and could only guess about the offending instruments.

The binge went on for a week, until she flopped onto her bed after work on Friday and did not get up until Sunday morning. When she paused to take a light-of-day look at herself in the bathroom mirror, a look that revealed coal-colored hollows beneath her eyes, puffy skin, and a gauntness that looked as if she were a veteran of silent movies, she knew this had to stop.

She took a scalding shower, inhaling the steam deep into her lungs, and washed her hair. She shaved her legs and manicured her nails. She kneaded moisturizing cream into every square inch of skin. She felt renewed, and famished. In the refrigerator she found a container of raspberry yogurt free of mold and a box of stone ground wheat crackers. She would have killed for a platter of lox and fresh bialys but that would mean going out and she did not want to go out. Instead she reclined in her white velour bathrobe and spent the rest of the morning absorbed in the Sunday papers.

She felt somewhat healthy once again, until the thought struck her that she was alone. She was unused to being alone in the calm of a Sunday morning. She did not like it. She missed him awfully.

When the phone rang she lunged for it, then caught herself before she answered too quickly. She waited three rings.

"Aren't you the party animal," a voice said.

She did not recognize it.

"Who is this?"

"Mr. Haggarty."

"Tommy to you," she said.

"Word is you were torrid on the street last week," he said.

"How would you know?" she said.

"Tommy sees all, hears all, knows all."

"Tommy knows nothing."

"Okay, how 'bout three bill traders putting enough blizzard in your beak in the back of Gamekeepers to cover Squaw Valley? For starters," he said.

Joanie's forehead began to burn.

"You know what they say," Tommy went on. " 'Wild women don't get the blues.' "

318

"Is that what they say?"

"Yeah, so why didn't you tell the kid you were hot to—"

"Tommy, do I hang up now? And how'd you get my number anyway?"

"No number is safe from these fingers," he said. "Not to mention many other things."

She sighed.

"Listen, sweetcakes, that little operation we talked about is about to happen. It's due bill time."

"What are you talking about?"

"I'll tell you at Burger King on Washington in exactly three hours."

"Forget it, Tommy—"

"After what I did for you, Joanie, you have no choice on this."

She cursed the phone after hanging up. He was like a leech, an insidious tick that would not let go. And a spy yet. What did he know about the other night? What did anyone know? She bit her knuckle and cursed again, this time at herself.

She moved angrily about her apartment, picking up the papers, seeing Tommy Haggarty's smug face, repeating what he had said. Steve had been right: Korngold's evil was nothing compared to what this little creep had up his sleeve. Suddenly what she had to do became clear. She had to forget her preoccupations with Steve and Korngold and get rid of Tommy and whatever he was up to. The kid was trouble.

Steve, Tommy Haggarty. Korngold. Three wonderful men in her life, she thought. She wished they were tin cans on a backyard fence in Tampa, and she was fondling a rifle.

She argued with herself about what to do. She was tempted to call Steve. Now more than ever. But she could not, and she resented him for it. She put on a pair of jeans and a loose jersey top, pinned her hair back, then let it fall, then pinned it up again. She was not going to put on a look for Tommy. He would interpret anything as license. He was like the masturbating chimp in the zoo: if you so much as winked at him, he took it as a cue.

She put on a pair of running shoes and a trench coat, then shucked that in favor of a windbreaker. Then she pulled that off and threw it against a chair. What was going on? What was she doing? She'd meet the jerk and get it over with. No big deal. Or was it?

Then it hit her. If Steve were here he would tell her to cover her ass. He would figure all the angles, including Tommy's, then decide how to outstrip him. She was compensating, subconsciously settling on a pose—she'd learned a lot. More than anything else, she knew, she had to protect herself against Tommy. She had to palm a card.

She decided on the cassette recorder. Steve had persuaded her to get one, a pocket-sized mini-recorder to have around for notes, good ideas, and random dictation. It was typical Steve: never letting a moment's inspiration or thought pass. You talked into the recorder every so often, he said, just to articulate passing thoughts, to take advantage of daydreams, to plan. If that didn't work, he said, you could use it to write twentieth-century letters. Prop it up next to the bathtub and dictate a letter to Mom. Then send her the cassette (along with a recorder of her own) and tell her to do the same. Nobody wrote letters anymore.

No, a recorder was ridiculous, she thought. Something out of TV. Then, again, this whole thing was a bad script, a series that should have been canceled long ago. Hell, she would take the recorder. Life imitates video. And if they can do it on "The Young and the Restless," she could do it in Burger King. She checked the recorder's batteries, then slipped it into her purse.

"Thing is, you don't have to set the asshole up. He'll do it all by himself if you just goose him a little.

"I scored shit for KIK all the time so I know he likes the candy. But here's the genius of the thing—you ready? What the G needs is for Kenny to make a buy himself. A big one. And that's where you come in.

"See, Joanie baby, the guy still has it for you. Horns as high as the Sears Tower. The more shit you gave him—like when you just cut him off—the more he had to have you. Or get you. It's a thing with the big hitters, I think—now this is just my theory—that they are so used to gettin' what they want that it drives them up a fuckin' wall when they can't get it.

"So what happens — *God,* I love this part — is that you come on to him. You tell him you want a truce. You know what he done to you and he knows how you got him back. But both a you gotta survive in this racket and you can't be duckin' his spears all the time. Some shit like that.

"He'll buy it. Hell, he'd buy Lower Wacker from you if you offered it. And that's when you tell him you want him to show some good fuckin' faith and liberate a kilo for you. Some Bogotá Blow.

"He won't flinch because he knows — as many of us know — that Joanie baby likes to get wired nowadays. And then what happens — and I like this part, too — is that he comes to me like he always has. Bygones be fuckin' bygones when it comes to shit.

" 'Cept this time I say, 'Hey, Kenny baby, that's out of my league.' And I send him to this guy. And this guy — bam!! — is wired better than the phone company and the next thing you know KIK is facing ten years of buttfuckin' in Marion. He being not the fuck-er, but the fuck-ee.' "

At that Tommy's laughter buffeted the microphone, and she snapped off the recorder. He had gone on, and the machine had swallowed every word, sitting across from her at a two-man table in the far corner of the nearly deserted hamburger joint. Tommy talked, talked like a wired disc jockey on a runaway mike, jabbered and giggled and just enjoyed the hell out of his caper.

"But you gotta move 'cuz from what I hear the G is ready to move. And if I know about it then the whole goddamn floor'll know and it'll all be off. You'll see the cleanest noses this side of a Vicks factory. So you gotta get to him and quick."

She stopped the tape again, then started it again, anticipating something at this point that stuck with her, bothered her.

"See the G know who's doin' it so it's a matter of who they wanna take. You and me are just pointin' them in the right direction. And we're *sticking* it to that asshole. We're gettin' him back, Joanie. He's the big one they want. Trust me on that. Especially if you got second thoughts, Joanie. They have these meetings downtown and decide whose ass is gonna cook. I mean, nobody's immune. Not the boys *or* the girls, sweetheart."

She played that last part over and over, vividly seeing Tommy's queer, cocky grin when he said it.

"Whattaya mean, how do I know all this? I *know*. Believe me, I know. . . ."

Hours later, in the dawn's light before trading began, Joanie stopped Tommy in middle of the low, smoky corridor leading onto the financial floor. She spun him around and faced off with him in front of a dozen traders and clerks who hurried by and others who were huddled over the red phones. Tommy tried to pull away, livid at being seen talking to her right out in the open. She held him fast.

"*Now* I know, Tommy," she said, her voice rising above the din of the nearby pits. "I know why Korngold went after me like he did and when he did. Just after the article about Brian Boyer, wasn't it, Tommy? Remember that?"

By now every head in the corridor had turned their way. Tommy glared at her. His fists were clenched, his lips tightened into a grimace.

"Like he thought I had something to do with the press getting on to that," she went on, ignoring those around them, fixed on his fixed eyes. "Just a prejudiced guess on his part, I thought. But no. He was told that, wasn't he, Tommy. He was tipped that *I* was the one. Joanie Yff did it. And he bought it. Just like he bought all the tips you threw at him, right?"

She released his arm and he snapped it away.

"Which means count me out, Tommy. Stay far away from me with your little slimy deals," she said.

He lifted his palms outward and started to tap dance.

"Hey, you got the wrong guy, okay? *I* ain't the one tried to nail you. I'm the one saved your *ass*."

"No more favors, Tommy. I'm off your list."

She began to retreat when he reached out and grabbed the front of her trading jacket. He turned his head from side to side as if to check his flanks.

"Hey, Joanie baby," he said, tightening his grip when she

322

drew back, his face flushed and coated with a mist of perspiration.

"Now the fist goes up your ass," he hissed.

She pulled free.

Although running a business involved more paperwork than he ever thought possible, Ballard Trout hated sitting behind a desk. Any conversation that went much further than a yes or a no drew him onto the sofa where he sat with his lanky legs crossed and his hands cradling the back of his head. Which is what he did when Joanie came in late that afternoon. The look on her face said she wanted more than a yes or a no.

"Well, I'm flattered you asked, young lady," he began. "Most people want to talk ball. I can appreciate that and I oblige as it's kind of my debt to the pastime. 'Cept most of the time I believe people think all I know about is baseball. Oh, the many times I've had people replay my career for me . . ." he said, and sighed.

He went on.

"So for you to ask me how I fell in love is just damn refreshing."

"Twenty-some years?" she said.

"Twenty-two next July twenty-fifth."

"God, I was two years old—"

"Hold that right there, Joanie."

"Sorry."

"I met Linda playing ball. St. Louis. She hung by the bus outside Busch Stadium. She asked for an autograph and I asked for a date. She got the autograph and I got a maybe. When we finally did go out it was to her parents' house for supper. No kiddin'. She said later she wanted to find out if I could carry on a conversation. She wasn't interested in any stiff who didn't know how to talk. Didn't matter what he was hittin'.

"Well, I *can* talk and we got married about a year later, after some convincing on my part because she said she wasn't crazy about being a full-time cheerleader and a part-time wife to some night-ridin', two-timin' ballplayer. Yeah, she wised up in a hurry to how many chicks the players have in each port. You might say she had no awe for my profession."

"Whew," Joanie said. "She laid all that on you?"

"Just for starters," Ballard laughed, leaning into the subject. "The woman was tough. *Is* tough. And I liked that. Gettin' a fill on soft little girls was no problem. A woman with some spine took some bidding.

"Course that came along with the animal instincts. I *did*, and still *do*, find her mightily attractive. Sexy damn woman. Just gets the mojo runnin'. That's important — you got to have the lust.

"But what surprised me over the years was that she'd grow so much. I mean, more than just mature, but put on some character. You catch what I mean? Linda's got character, *style*, whatever you want to call it, in spades — a term I usually avoid with white folks. Everything she does — how she dresses, spends her money, makes her house. Hell, the way she eats, the way she walks down the street. Ain't no doubt about it and never was.

"And the *big* thing for me, I mean we're talkin' a rehab job, is that she carried me along with her. I mean it, Joanie. You're looking at a guy who came from nothing and didn't know nothing 'cept how to use a baseball bat. I wore what the salesman sold me. I ate greens and ribs and wiped the grease on my sleeve. I was interested in what the crowd — that meant my baseball friends — was interested in. I watched television and laughed at the dumb damn jokes.

"But Linda shaped up my program. Put some savvy into me. I started eating things I couldn't even pronounce. Like foreign food, Chinese, Japanese. Can you believe a kid from Idlewild, Michigan, been raised on pork 'n' beans and fried chicken would get himself a tempura jones?

"I could go on. We got three Class A kids that just make me proud. She stays interested and gets excited and makes plans and I could go on. Instead of watchin' the TV and gettin' fat she reads. Reads everything.

"I just *like* the girl, Joanie, and she likes me. I still make her laugh. Can you imagine that? And we're goin' on twenty-two years of this business."

He sat back and laughed, filling the room.

Joanie smiled at him, her face alive with utter admiration. For her, for him.

"What does she do?" she said.

"Computers. On the set-up and sell side. She did my system here."

Joanie sighed.

"But misery is 'sposed to love company so my thing doesn't help you much, does it?"

"Oh, yes and no. I'm jealous and I'm inspired."

"And screwed up?"

She shrugged. She went on to describe what had happened with her and Steve, from the early, easy times, to the breakup. She described his moods and hers, how much he had influenced her, changed her, and how much she thought she had changed him. It flowed out of her, and Ballard Trout listened intently, locking onto her batting, beautiful green eyes.

"It was everything I thought was impossible to find," she said. "We talked about everything. He listened. He was just — I don't know — he just seemed a part of me. On the tip of every thought in my head.

"And then it all stopped. He put on that position — and that is just *so* out of character for him — and he closed me out. He wouldn't talk about it. He got real moody and down. He just wasn't the Steve Stamford I knew. It was as if we never had anything going between us."

"Then gold blew," he said.

"He really got hurt," she said.

"Which doesn't make it any easier to patch things up."

He paused, waiting for her to reply.

When she did not, he said, "His taking a position in gold was the first thing. I seen it and I seen a lot. You don't know why you do it. As if the tradin' you been doing for the last month or the last year just ain't *interesting* anymore. Or it ain't a challenge, or some damn thing. So you look around the ring and you see guys and what they're doing and the next thing you know you got a position. Some guys buy new shoes. Some guys buy cars. Some guys — like your man — put on a position."

"Because of me?" she said.

"He probably doesn't even know."

"You tell me, Ballard. If it were you."

"Hey, I don't do things like that — well, maybe a little bit. So none of this is gospel. I don't even know your boy. But what I see in a lot of guys is ants. They just get 'em when things start going good, when things start falling in place. They don't know what to make of it. They get suspicious. They worry. Sometimes they just up and take off.

"I knew a guy who said he wanted to get married in the worst way. But it had to be Miss Right. No, Miss Perfect. So he offered a bounty. Set him up with Miss Perfect and he'll pay you a grand cash. She had to have certain qualifications, and all that. And what happened is that he got women from all directions. Easiest way to get action since the invention of the birth control pill.

"And you know what happened? He got Miss Perfect. To every detail. She was a cookie. Just made for this guy and he knew it. Knew he'd fallen for her, too. So you know what he did when he realized what happened? He took off. Up and left town."

She shook her head.

"Now that's just a story, Joanie. Your man is still around. But what I'm saying is that sometimes for some reason people have a way of fighting what is damn right and good for them. Like kids, 'cept kids usually come around.

"I cant talk for your friend. If it were me I'd be pinching myself every time I thought of a girl of your class being interested in me. I'd be jealous and suspicious and worried and happy as hell."

Then Ballard Trout leaned forward in the sofa, placing his hands on his bony knees and looking intently at Joanie's increasingly crestfallen face.

"And if I was as smart as you say your man is, I'd be back," he said.

Joanie smiled through the curtain, not worrying about whether he said it sincerely or out of sympathy, only feeling that he was one of the nicest people ever born.

"You're sweet," she said.

She lifted her eyebrows.

"You got a twin?" she asked softly.

Once again he roared.

When Joanie went to the gold pit the next day she did not find Steve in it. Another trader told her he had walked away a few sessions before and not returned. The price of gold had stabilized — though in a range nearly $120 an ounce lower than only a week before — and the action in the pit had gone back to normal. There had been scores of casualties, losers shaken out so severely that some would never return.

Was Steve among them?

Chapter Ten

The thousands of traders and floor personnel on Chicago's commodity exchanges live by the brightly lit quotation boards and the telephones. The quote is life. Every moment of their trading days depends on a continuous supply of precise, split-second market data.

That is why the information networks servicing Chicago's commodity trading floors — the Board of Trade, the Mercantile Exchange, the Chicago Board Options Exchange — are massive and intricate. The phone systems serving these buildings are bigger than those serving many good-sized towns, and are instantly capable of accommodating usage surges of astounding magnitudes.

Apart from holidays and weekends, nothing — not a crisis or a catastrophe, indeed, trading thrives on misery and doom — is able to shut down the trading floors except a power or a telephone failure. Should either occur, the entire system of commodity trading, contracts worth billions of dollars, stops cold.

That is why the event of that afternoon, in the midst of active, normal, chaotic trading on the Board of Trade, was so startling. It had the effect of momentarily halting trading, of bringing traders to a pose of stupefied, slack-jawed paralysis.

There were twenty visitors in all. They were men, many of them trim and athletic-looking, clean-shaven with short hair and tight neckties. Each wore the baby blue jacket of CBT employees, though it was obvious to all that they were not in the employ of the Board of Trade. They walked quickly past the guards in the lobby, then split up and headed for the separate trading floors. As if on signal, they broke up into pairs and strode directly to the trading desks of specified commodity firms. There they spoke briefly with a clerk, then waited or were directed to a person nearby.

At first the twenty men were mostly ignored, but once they spoke to the clerks, and were overheard by other clerks, the word spread like a silent alarm—they were heat, federal agents, the law. The floor was being raided.

The agents displayed arrest warrants for several floor personnel and they were serving them en masse, here and now. Suddenly heads began to turn and hands holding fortunes in contracts stopped in midair. The action in the pits floundered, then stopped altogether. The din of shouting leveled off, as if a curtain of silence had been dropped over the huge halls. The quote boards froze.

The agents, all of them from the Chicago Bureau of the FBI, quickly displayed gleaming badges on their breast pockets and moved about the floor, weaving through the mass of traders and assistants in search of the persons named in warrants. They ignored the dumb stares and the mutterings from traders who, after their initial surprise, became agitated at what was happening. Above them, peering through the windows of the visitors' observatory, were the FBI officials who had planned the whole thing. Behind them, clamoring for a better view, were news reporters.

Joanie was in the pit when the raid came down and she stopped trading like all the others.

"Who in the hell are they?" traders around her exclaimed as they strained to see what was happening. They pushed and crowded up to the top steps of the pits, trying to get a glimpse of the movements of the stern-faced men with the badges.

Some uttered sharp expletives, and anxiously felt the contraband they had stored on their person. Others literally sprinted for the elevators and their offices.

Joanie, suddenly realizing what was happening, craned her neck to scan the floor. She was looking for one person. She did not see Tommy Haggarty anywhere.

That left one other person. She pushed her way out of the bond pit and hurried quickly through the milling bodies on the financial floor, through the tunnel, and over to the ag side. There the scene was identical, with traders clustering around FBI agents at several desks and at nearby pits.

One by one the agents collected their prey, identifying themselves and stating the charges, then handcuffing the individual and leading him off. Most were clerks and runners, the drones of business and pleasure. Some of the arrests precipitated pushing and scuffling by traders furious at what was happening, at the invasion of their castle by the feds.

The biggest flurry of attention centered on two agents, one the size of a professional wrestler, ascending the steps of the soybean pit. As usual it was crowded, and scores of traders were jostled and pushed as the agents came through. Traders began to shout and curse, as if caught in a surge of trading, except their gestures were directed not at each other but at the hulking trespassers.

The stone-faced agents moved among the top steps to a cluster of some of the bean pit's major brokers and locals. As they did the pit became still, almost eerily so, entranced by what was happening, breathless at the prospect. Then the agents stopped and spoke, and the pit erupted. They were arresting Ken Korngold.

Like they had with the others, the agents made their declaration, then produced a pair of handcuffs.

"What!" Korngold yelled indignantly, snatching the arrest warrant from them. He saw his name, and the signature of a federal prosecutor. He whirled around, jostling traders who were pressed against him, as if he were searching for help or some kind of escape.

"This is *shit!*" he screamed, and shook the warrant over his head.

"Fuck 'em!" shouted a trader just behind him.

The others cheered.

The agents curtly told Korngold to come along quietly or the situation would only get worse for him. One snapped a cuff around his wrist. Korngold's face turned ashen with disbelief. Then his arms were pulled together in front of him as the agent cuffed the other wrist. He stumbled alongside them as he was led through the crowd and down the steps of the pit. His mouth curled in a clenched scowl, and he began to breathe rapidly through his nose. Yet he had no choice but to follow meekly. Instead of the cocksure, sauntering, millionaire floor trader, he looked every bit like a hostage, as if he had been singled out not for arrest and arraignment, but punishment.

His fellow traders were stunned, and they clamored incredulously. Ken Korngold. KIK. One of the major figures in the exchange. One of the city's wealthy entrepreneurs. Owner of a professional sports franchise. A seemingly untouchable force now shackled and taken off like a stray dog.

Joanie, frozen where she stood on the floor, watched it all. Her thoughts spun, racing back to the boasts of Tommy Haggarty, seeing his cocky smile. She strained to get a glimpse of Korngold as he was led toward the exit. She followed the silhouette of his head, his thinning but styled hair.

Then, just before he reached the tunnel, he turned momentarily to look back at his firm's trading desk. Joanie saw his familiar puffy face and the baggy pouches beneath his eyes. Yet she was stunned by something quite novel: an expression not of smugness or defiance, but of confusion. For the first time in her life she saw Korngold appear addled. He was furious, of course, yet frustrated, awkward, and, most obviously, in complete submission.

Then he was gone. For long moments floor personnel stood paralyzed. All trading had long since stopped. Then the din returned, traders began to mill about, many went for the phones.

Joanie could not move. Her stomach ached. Her eyes burned. She felt no elation, no joy, no sense of justice or revenge. She tasted the acid in her throat and she tried to swallow.

The confusion of the trading floor brought about by the arrests spilled over into the lobbies. Reporters and television camera crews were everywhere. They climbed over each other, mimicking traders in a bidding frenzy, to get to Korngold as he was ushered out of the building and into the unmarked FBI sedans. He was front-page stuff. When he was gone the reporters turned back inside the building and ambushed anyone wearing a trading jacket.

In the mad lunge to get close to Korngold, however, the newsmen missed an incredible event going on right behind their backs. It involved not arrests, agents, or handcuffed traders, but the near destruction of the infrastructure of the massive Board of Trade Building. As word swept through the building of the raid on the trading floors, hundreds of employees in offices on each of the twenty-four floors rushed to rid the premises of contraband.

They grabbed leaves, buds, pills, and powders of every quality and hue, with a total street value of hundreds of thousands of dollars, and chucked them into the toilets. The nearly simultaneous flushing of so many water closets in an interconnected plumbing system caused a charge of water and a succeeding vacuum that nearly destroyed the building's pipes. Had they burst, the resulting destruction and chaos, not to mention the deluge, would have dwarfed the raid that brought it all about in the first place.

Joanie pushed her way through the pit and went looking for Tommy. She half walked and ran, dodging and weaving through the milling mass of floor personnel, her face taut with an urgency so common to the floor. Yet now she was not seeking an order or a trader or some other mundane piece of the market, she was looking for the fuse, the source, the button which, she knew, had been pressed.

She saw him nowhere on the floor, not at his company's desk or in the pits he worked. She was about to ask, then stopped herself, thinking quickly, realizing that she should not even ask, not give anyone a chance to link her to Haggarty. That would come, she feared, soon enough. She hurried across the street to the Insurance Exchange Building, where Haggarty's offices were, and from a pay phone she called and asked for him. A secretary said he had not come in or called or given any word at all of his whereabouts.

She retreated to the street and headed for her office. Trading was all but a dead issue for the rest of the day. In addition to the Board of Trade, the Mercantile Exchange and the Options Exchange had each experienced raids. A total of twenty-three arrests had been made, though none as spectacular as that of Ken Korngold. The entire commodities industry in Chicago reeled from the crackdown, and news of it spread throughout the world. Only prices remained unaffected: holding unchanged and unattended on blipping terminals like abandoned waifs. For long, rare, extraordinary moments, traders ignored the tapes and huddled around screens tuned to news stations in order to get a glimpse of the breaking coverage.

When special afternoon editions of the daily papers arrived, the delivery boys could barely get them to the newsstands. A *Sun-Times* truck appeared first at the Board of Trade, and a kid began tossing bundles of the tabloid onto the sidewalk. Its front page consisted of a three-inch headline reading "GOAL! Feds Bust Clout Owner" and a photo of an anguished Ken Korngold. Traders scrambled to get a copy. The *Tribune* featured a similar photo from a different angle over the headline "Drug Net Hits 23 on Trading Floors."

A clerk who had managed to buy both papers no sooner passed through the door of the Trout offices when he was surrounded by traders eager for details. The articles said the raid was the result of a fifteen-month investigation involving agents who worked undercover on the exchange floors as well as floor personnel who served as informants. Most of those arrested were charged with selling cocaine on the premises: the bathrooms, offices, even the trading floor itself. Korngold, the articles said, was charged with the purchase of a kilo of cocaine from a federal agent.

Joanie furiously scanned the copy, almost holding her breath in anticipation. She could feel furtive glances cast her way from those around her, but her concern was elsewhere. Tommy Haggarty. The name coursed through her brain as she read. She had to know what he had done. Neither paper mentioned his name, and she felt palpable relief. Yet she left the office that afternoon with her head spinning. She was sure Tommy was involved, had to be, and yet where was he? And had he dragged her in?

Emerging from the Board of Trade, slammed by a wind that made her eyes water, she clenched her teeth and bowed her head and walked east down Jackson Boulevard toward her apartment. She moved by rote, feeling other bodies but not seeing anyone, hearing traffic and horns but oblivious to streetlights and vehicles. She could see and hear and think

only of that conversation in the restaurant, of her confronta-
tion with Tommy on the floor. She could see his face and only
his face, the pods of spit at the sides of his mouth. She could
hear his cracks, his trash talk, his threats. And then she
thought of the micro-cassette tape back in her apartment.

She finally reached her building, swept past the lobby mail-
boxes, and heaved forward to her door. In her bedroom she
saw it, the damn tape, rushed to it, clutched it like a treasure, a
grail, a curse.

She slept fitfully that night, awaking to scenes and conversations that pitted her against Korngold and Tommy Haggarty.
She endlessly replayed her words with Tommy. At times she
opened her eyes and stared into the semidarkness of her bedroom, then she scolded herself and tried to sleep, hearing the
ticking of her quartz clock and every creak in her apartment.
When she finally did drop off she slept for a few hours, then
was awakened suddenly by a dream that had her on a witness
stand being cross-examined by an angry, shouting prosecuting
attorney. That prosecutor was Steve Stamford.

She sought out the papers' morning editions and read them
on the curb. The stories ran front page and were updated.
Joanie's eyes raced over the copy. The *Sun-Times* said that in-
vestigators built much of their case on the undercover work of
a Board of Trade runner. She breathed heavily. The runner
was not named. But there it was. Joanie visibly grimaced
when she read it, knowing in her guts what was sure to follow.

It came the next day. Again it was the *Sun-Times*, an exclusive that named Tommy Haggarty as the Board of Trade mole.
Haggarty, the story said, had not been seen since the day before the raid and was believed to be in the protective custody of
federal agents.

With each succeeding edition, the bead on Haggarty narrowed. He was painted as a white knight, as a kid who had gotten mixed up in drugs — the story detailed his trip to Colombia
and the overdose death of his cohort — and had vowed to do
something to clean up the rampant drug trade on the futures
floors.

Radio and television reporters sought out his family and
friends, anyone who knew him. Camera crews camped in the

lobbies and roamed the corridors. When Joanie saw them she fled into the women's room, staying clear, knowing, dreading the day they would be looking for her. One television reporter stopped anyone wearing a trading smock and asked if he knew Haggarty. That same newsman said on the ten o'clock news, in a report taped in front of the Board of Trade building, that Tommy was a kind of "new American hero."

The very mention of his name among traders, however, brought unbridled scorn.

Korngold retained Patrick Lollar Tulet, one of the city's top criminal attorneys. At Korngold's arraignment, Tulet entered the perfunctory not guilty plea. Before the scrum of reporters and cameras in the hall outside, he proclaimed his client's innocence. Korngold, free on bond, stood mute at Tulet's shoulder. Though he was free to come and go on the street, his trading privileges had been suspended pending the outcome of the case. That meant he was barred from the trading floor. To the public that seemed routine. Fellow traders and habitués of the pits reeled at what the suspension would cost Korngold in missed revenue. It would be several months, maybe as long as a year, before the case went to trial.

Joanie watched and read it all, and in so doing cut in on her own trading routine. When she could contain her feelings no longer, she called Steve.

"We have to talk," she said.

"Why?" Steve said.

"Because this whole thing is killing me. Us, the drug raid, everything."

"You bagged him. You should be on top of the world," Steve said.

"Steve —"

"Hey, come on, Joanie. You know how I felt about Tommy Haggarty. Now Korngold's facing a federal pinch and Haggarty's a star."

"It's a farce. It's ridiculous."

"Glad you feel that way. You're a little late, that's all," he said.

335

She exhaled loudly, steeling herself.

"You think I had something to do with this, don't you?" she said.

"I'm a technician — or was. I look at the data and let it speak for itself."

"No," she said.

"No what?"

"I've got to see you. Not on the phone."

He paused and thought for several moments. The silence was painful for both of them.

"Maybe when I get back," he said. "I'm going to Indiana for a few days. My mother's sick."

She wished him well.

The tape was still in the recorder. The recorder was on top of her dresser. The dresser loomed large in her bedroom like an ogre.

She saw the tape every morning when she got out of bed, as she put on her makeup and her jewelry, then again at night when she returned to remove her makeup and jewelry and get into bed. Her routine was motion; the tape was motionless. It lay there, a lifeless device — no, a presence as vivid as anything alive. She tried not thinking about it, she pretended it did not exist.

Fat chance. Every minute of every hour, she knew, the tape consumed her. In all but her busiest moments in the bond pit she thought about it. Saw it lying there. In her more rational moments she told herself that the tape was what she wished to make of it: a weapon, a test, a tool of deliverance. The rest of the time she knew too well that the tape dominated her, controlled her, dictated her thoughts, her fate. She found it impossible to touch it, to move it, to remove it from her sight. She could depress the right buttons on the recorder and erase it from the earth. Not a soul on earth would know.

She would know.

By then it was December and Joanie was so preoccupied

that she nearly overlooked the postcard. The photo of Santa Claus on water skis caught her attention.

"Joanie," the card began. "Coming on the 12th as planned — 5:12 P.M. Cheapo flight — no booze. Make up for that later — oh yeah! Can't wait. Line up scads of men. Studs and hunks with no brains — I like 'em big and real dumb! Love ya — Duda."

Joanie groaned. Duda was her cousin, Susan, and she had called months ago to plan a visit. She was a sophomore at Florida State and she and a couple of girlfriends were doing a reverse jaunt during winter vacation — going from warm weather to cold. Five days in Chicago. Joanie had volunteered to put them up and show them around. That was months, seemingly ages, ago. The twelfth was this Sunday.

In many ways the visit was a blessing. It gave Joanie a deadline of three days to clean the apartment, stock the cupboards and refrigerator, and plot suitable entertainment for Susan and friends. She looked around her place. She had all but neglected it for weeks. Dust bunnies mated in the corners. Piles of mail and assorted junk had collected on counters and tables. The refrigerator was clogged with moldy leftovers and carryouts. Joanie would need every bit of the time she had before Susan's plane to shape up the place, to give it a fresh face for her adoring cousin.

By that Sunday, and because of a favor she had delivered in the bond pit earlier that week, Joanie was able to borrow Margie Finamore's car. It was a mint BMW, shiny black, complete with cellular phone, and, incidentally, much bigger than Joanie's aging Honda. Margie smiled when Joanie said that was her only reason for asking.

Before she spotted them coming off the plane in the terminal, she heard them. Susan and her two friends, Gina and Gina T., were all giggles and hoots, shiny hair, makeup, fingers clogged with rings, copies of *Cosmo*, perfume, tight designer jeans, and clacking heels. They turned heads and pretended not to notice. They primped and gushed and fairly fell all over Joanie. Joanie laughed and hugged Susan, then ushered them to the baggage pickup, wondering to herself what she must have looked like to the civilized world upon her arrival only a few short months ago.

They had enough baggage for a rock band entourage and three skycaps. Joanie shook her head at the prospect of loading it all into the BMW. When they saw the shimmering black auto they cheered.

"I *knew* you'd have something like this," said Susan.

Joanie shrugged and, with the help of a skycap who should have retired before their plane arrived, hoisted and secured the bags into the trunk and on the rooftop luggage rack. One scratch, she said, and you die. They crammed themselves inside, pushing the car's suspension system to the limit, and scooted off back downtown and Joanie's place.

The girls' rapture over the BMW was second only to their awe at Joanie's apartment. The prints, the hand-knotted rugs, quilted fabrics, lush draperies, the stereo and video equipment, the bedroom of print sheets, plush carpeting, and crystal curios. It was everything their dormitory rooms were not. Joanie was only a few years older, yet light-years beyond.

"This is even better than I *dreamed*," said Susan as she unconsciously caressed the pastel print wallpaper that matched the footdeep down comforter on Joanie's bed.

From there Joanie took them to a newly opened fifties cafe', complete with carhops and six-ounce Coke bottles, hamburgers and onion rings. Before they could add and divide, Joanie snatched the check and sent it away with a $50 bill. Six eyes widened.

Then they swung around North Michigan Avenue, ablaze with white lights of Christmas, the marble and glass of I. Magnin, Neiman's, Bonwit's, Water Tower Place, then down to the Loop and City Hall, LaSalle Street to the Board of Trade. Sunday night traffic was sparse, the buildings dark and forbidding, the city seemingly asleep, or, perhaps, just catching a weekend breath.

They finished the night in a Near North singles joint featuring a lip-sync contest, and howled at the would-be rock stars, the mimics, and the impersonators. Though only Joanie was legal, none of the girls was carded at the door, and men exuding cologne and testosterone soon pressed around them. Susan and the Ginas were besieged and loved it; Joanie sipped white wine and flicked away the hounds.

Much to Joanie's relief, Susan and her friends had their week scheduled, and as quickly as they could arise from the dead of sleep begun in the early-morning hours of the night before, they rushed out of the apartment each morning to hit stores and sights.

"Y'all can have the temperature, but I'll take this city any day," cooed Gina.

"Me, too," said Gina T. "I could fairly *thrive* here."

On Tuesday they had a group hair appointment with Joanie's former roommates at Paul B. They returned that evening changed women: plucked, gelled, cut and shaped in styles North Florida had never seen. If that wasn't enough, when they approached the cashier they were told it was a gift of the management, of Paul B. himself. They were staggered — "D'ya know what it all had to *cost!*" — and that night they promenaded before an approving Joanie, who tried not to reveal how pleased she was with her investment.

The next day Joanie invited them to the Board of Trade. She met them in the lobby and escorted them to the credentials office where they were given visitor's floor passes. Like almost every other visitor lucky enough to get on the trading floor itself, they were overwhelmed, and they huddled closely around Joanie.

She tried to explain the pits, the boards, and the trading, but mostly she just let the chaos of the place pelt them from all sides. When she thought them completely overwhelmed, she led them from the floor and to the fifth floor observatory, where they could look down at what they had just been in.

From there it was easier for Joanie to explain the principles of futures contracts and trading. The girls listened, responded with intelligent questions, and Joanie elaborated on the intricacies of her job. Her lecture, and the authority of her trading badge and coat, drew the attention of other visitors, and for a time it looked as if she were leading a tour.

Susan, the Ginas, and other visitors glanced alternately at Joanie and the pits, trying to hear her over the incessant din and clamor of trading piped in through the overhead speakers. On their faces was a look of confusion and amazement, and, most unmistakably, of admiration. Here was a person, an articulate, attractive woman, who was one of them, a trader, a warrior in those incredible arenas.

Even Joanie, as she spoke about what was now second nature to her, sensed it.

As she talked, her eyes bouncing from person to person, she suddenly saw a figure across the room. Joanie stopped in midsentence, lost her thought, then stuttered. For standing there, gazing through the wide window onto the trading floor, dressed in a black cashmere sweater dress, was Rachel Korngold.

Joanie was startled, more so than she might have ever expected. She wanted to avert her face, duck out, somehow avoid any chance that Rachel might see her. Then she froze, and stared, staring at Rachel where she stood, alone, motionless, quiet, overdressed as usual, young, beautiful.

"Hang here a minute, Susan," Joanie finally said.

She left the group and walked over, pausing a few feet away. Rachel turned, then visibly winced.

"Oh!" she said, her eyes widening. They narrowed as quickly.

She turned back to the window.

"How are you?" Joanie said. It was more than a greeting.

"Okay, I guess," Rachel said. "Considering. . ."

Her stare remained fixed on the floor below.

The two of them said nothing for long moments.

"This whole thing has been a zoo—" Joanie began.

"*Tell* me about it," Rachel exclaimed. "All the TV stations camping around the house. My ma went nuts. Then when they couldn't find you-know-who cuz he never came home they actually hired this scuz ball guy to just sit there on the street and wait for him. Day and night. It was unreal."

The words clattered out, high-pitched, emotional.

"How is it at school, I mean, shouldn't you be there now?" Joanie said.

"Oh, that's another *joke*. Half the kids look at me like I'm a criminal, right? Like none of their parents ever got in trouble. Like none of their hotshot dads who are lawyers and judges don't get indicted about every other day. Right? Shit! And

340

then there were these guys who came up and asked me if I could score some coke for them off my old man."

"You're not serious."

"I'm *serious,*" Rachel said.

At that her lower lip began to quiver. Her eyes watered. She fought to keep control.

Then she turned and faced Joanie.

"And Daddy's gone. He never even came home. He doesn't call and he's changed his phone numbers. It's like he just cut me out of his deck. Like I don't exist."

At that she sobbed. Tears skidded down her cheeks. She choked. She raised her fists to her mouth and bit into her knuckles, trying to stifle the keening sound that peeled from her throat. She cried and cried.

The sight of her ripped Joanie apart. She put her arms around her and held her, unable to say anything or give comfort or do anything at all to make the wrenching pain subside. Her own tears hung on her chin, then dropped and disappeared into the rich, black pile of Rachel's dress.

For the remainder of the visit she saw little of the girls. With each passing day they became more dedicated Windy City natives. By the Friday of their departure they were telling Joanie where to go and what to do there, of deli countermen with great lines and stunning men in clubs with even better lines.

The return trip to the airport was accompanied by a taxi jammed full of their luggage and loot. For starving coeds they had managed to amass enough cash, or plastic, to go retail.

Joanie kissed them all, savored their glowing thanks, and told them they looked big city. In a last moment before she boarded, Susan hugged her.

"God, Cuz," Susan said. "You have it all. You're really *doing* it." Joanie smiled. There was no way to evade her cousin's fresh, adoring face. Yet in that brief but indelible moment, Joanie saw much more. She saw herself, the person she was in Florida, the person who drove off in the packed Honda on a northern adventure. She saw her mother. She saw the face of the Old Trader in Pensacola and the girls who danced for the

341

Navy flyboys. She saw the Baby Hueys and their bare behinds.

For long moments after Susan and her friends boarded their flight, Joanie stayed and watched as the ramp was pulled away and the plane maneuvered out toward the tarmac. Though her eyes were fixed on the plane's taxi, she saw none of it. She was miles away, lost in events recent and past, her life and what it had become. In very cold and grainy terms, still in the echo of her cousin's sweet words of awe, Joanie realized what she had become.

She shook herself back to the present. The lounge was empty, the plane gone. She turned and walked quickly to a pay telephone and called Steve. She was coming over, ready or not.

He spoke first.

"I saw what was happening to me and I didn't like it. I compounded matters by blaming you, as if you were some kind of Old Testament temptation or something. I didn't like my life or what I was becoming, and you were part of it. You were too, oh, too easy — no, too flip, too up, too blithe — dammit, all the things I love you for. I mean that. I really loved being with you. I looked forward to it to the point that nothing else mattered. You gave me the feeling that I somehow *deserved* it. Life was good, and so was I, or something like that. And I couldn't take it. The pit just made it worse. Here I was in the middle of the most irresponsible, self-centered, selfish, rat-fucking business in the world and doing well at it. And you were, too, and the two of us were licking up the spoils like frosting off the beaters, just rolling along oblivious to the rest of the world. It's like Babylon. But I knew better, or thought I did. And . . . and . . . and I cracked. I'm sorry. I apologize because I hurt you. You didn't deserve that. All you'd done was make my life happy and fun. You're so damn . . . so damn *healthy,* Joanie Yff, and that makes it tough on a pisser and moaner like me. So I dropped out, scuttled the whole routine. I did nothing but sit and watch my positions, which I had put on in violation of all my own rules. The old death wish. Watch Stevie self-destruct. The market puked. I got killed. But, if you really want to know, the worst thing that could have happened, I think, is if I'd been right. If I'd been on the right side and taken out a few mil, just *raped* the damn market. Oh my, oh my, oh my . . . So now I'm out. On the side. I could trade. There's a balance, a few coins, but Jesus A, I was a lot healthier three months ago. I've still got my coat and my badge. But I'm out, and I have to decide if I want to get back in. Ever. And on top of it all you hit me with the Korngold thing. And that bastard Haggarty. You were crazed, smoked, blood in your eye. Vengeance with a capital *V.* You'd become a pit animal. 'They took from me,' you said, 'so I take from them. They hit me. I hit back.' And no matter what had happened to me, or what I'd become, I wasn't about to help you with that. In fact, maybe that was what woke me up. I couldn't live with it, or with you if that's the way you were going to deal with things. And that was that. Except it wasn't very simple. I didn't sleep very well. Haven't really since. So, having said all that, I now, right now, want to make a very selfish, mundane, simple statement: I miss you, Joanie Yff. I miss your face, and your laugh and your slinky body and the way you breathe when you're asleep. I miss being around you. You're good fill. Great fill. And I'm miserable without you."

Then he stopped. His right knee was shaking. His mouth was dry.

"Of *course* you are, you dumb shit!" Joanie said. "We're *good* together."

She clutched the sides of his skull and kissed him all over his face, slobbering and smothering him until he began to laugh.

Then she spoke.

"Sure, I was smoked. I've never felt so much hatred, just right in my gut. What Korngold *did* to me. He and those sweathog traders of his. But it wasn't as if I was going to hire some knee crackers or a hit guy to take 'em out. I just wanted—oh, I don't know what I wanted. Yes, I do. I wanted to sauté their private parts. Maybe I still do. But I couldn't. Things changed, and maybe I grew up real fast. And that's why I'm here. No sleep. You're looking at a zombie. I need you, Steve. I have to tell you everything like we used to and

343

you have to look into my head and sort it out. But get this straight: you can't cut me off. If we can't talk about things, we're doomed. You can pout and sulk and I can pout and sulk and, well, look, our whole thing started because we jabbered to each other. I just crawled inside you a lot, Steve, and I liked that. I loved it. Loved you. Right from the first, you big, bony goose. If I want strong and silent, I'll date a hockey puck. Look at me, yeah, like that. What I know all too well about most men is that they can't face you and say what's on their mind. Most of 'em talk best on the telephone because they don't have to make eye contact. And we women put up with it and try to communicate through signals and code and all that. Well, bullshit. Big bales of bullshit. I don't want that. Not with you. Especially not with you."

Then she stopped, having said enough. In violation of what she had just vowed, she was not going to tell him everything. She would not tell him anything about the cassette tape recording, not ask him his advice or direction of counsel. For in that golden, glowing moment she knew in and of herself exactly what she would do.

What followed was mostly unspoken communication. All night long.

The next morning, before going down to the trading floor, Joanie telephoned Patrick Lollar Tulet and left a concise message for him. When she returned to the office at noon she found that Tulet had returned her call. He would see her at her convenience, and as soon as possible.

Tulet's LaSalle Street offices were a fascinating mix of legal art — *Spy* caricatures of The Jury, The Judge, etc. — political knickknacks from Tulet's close ties to Chicago's Irish politicians, several of whom he had represented, and Chicago White Sox memorabilia. Joanie would have lingered over it had she not been swept into Tulet's inner chambers as soon as she announced herself.

The attorney was a stocky, square-jawed man, a graduate of the city's neighborhoods who had become a top attorney through a combination of street-smarts, work, exhaustive attention to detail, and a far-reaching network of political friends. No courtroom defense was better researched and better prepared than one put together by Pat Tulet. His reputation was fearsome, his track record nearly flawless.

Yet he was a friendly, unpretentious man, and Joanie, as nervous and unsure as she was about being in his office at all, was subtly disarmed by him. He greeted Joanie with a handshake and asked if she wanted something to drink. When she nodded, he fetched the soft drink himself.

She sat down in a soft, quilted, leather sofa that looked as if it had been lifted off the set of "Masterpiece Theater." Tulet sat on the other end, crossing his legs and turning to her.

"Before you say anything," he said, "I want to tell you that there is no legal reason for you to be here. We're in the very early stages of this case, really just beginning research and discovery."

"Okay," she ventured.

"But I'm not going to kid you. My client has told me something of his past relationship with you —"

"Have you ever defended killers, Mr. Tulet?" Joanie said.

"Accused, yes," he said.

"Rapists, drug dealers?" she said.

He looked directly at her, his prominent eyebrows arched, his dark eyes fixed.

"The Mafia?" she went on.

"Your point?" he said.

"They've got nothing on your client," she said.

Patrick Tulet did not react. He did not smile or frown. He only waited.

Joanie reached inside her purse and withdrew a mini-cassette tape and handed it to Tulet.

"It's all there. The guy on the tape is Tommy Haggarty. I'm the other voice. He pretty much explains it all himself."

Tulet looked at the cassette and back at Joanie.

"Will you personally corroborate this?"

"Pardon me?"

"Will you testify, if need be?"

Joanie nodded.

"What do you expect for this?" he asked.

345

"Nothing."

"I don't understand," he said.

It was her turn to smile.

"You wouldn't. Your client wouldn't. But for the first time in a long while, Mr. Tulet, I do," Joanie said.

She got up and put out her hand.

"That's the original tape. The one and only, no copies," she said.

Patrick Tulet shook her hand. Once again he smiled, all the while looking keenly into her eyes, as if he was not sure what he was seeing, or that he was seeing everything. Then he slipped the cassette into his pocket and got up to show her out.

Back at his desk he put the cassette into one of several minirecorders he possessed. Before the tape had run ten minutes he was on the phone to Ken Korngold.

Thut! Thut! Thut!

The sound was absorbed by the padded wall in the massive interior room. To make it, Korngold had bought the condominium next to his and knocked out the common wall. The resulting open space was the size of a banquet hall, or, in Korngold's scheme, a small gymnasium. He lined the walls with three-inch-thick, Naugahyde-covered foam, screened the windows, installed a juke box, stereo speakers, TV and market monitors, soda machines, and Astroturf. When he was finished, Korngold had his own indoor soccer arena.

Since his indictment and arrest, he had rarely left it. Just he and he alone, usually crouched at the goal mouth at the room's far end. In the middle of the floor was a remarkable, costly, automatic soccer ball shooting machine. It held a dozen soccer balls, and could be programmed for direction and velocity.

For hours, his body rinsed with sweat, dressed only in the black-and-gold shorts, knee socks, and shoes of the Chicago Clout, Korngold played goalie. Over and over, one ball after another, the machine's piston punched shots at all points of the net.

Thut! thut! thut!

And Korngold leaped and dove after them. The machine

346

was incessant and unmerciful, spoke no German or any other soccer language—only its unremitting *thut!*—and, given the circumstances, was Korngold's perfect companion.

He stopped only to eat or drink, take an occasional look at the market, or to answer the phone. Only a select few people had the number. One of them was Patrick Tulet, and it was he on the line. Korngold lifted the receiver and listened. He breathed heavily, a towel around his neck, a light steam emanating from his milky-white flesh.

Then his head began to spin. Patrick Tulet spoke slowly and concisely, laying it all out for him, and the effect was numbing.

Korngold sank to one knee. The telephone trembled in his hand. In his entire life, in the pits, in professional sports, in any stratum that he had coursed, he had only been stunned like this once before, and that was with his arrest in the pits only weeks earlier.

Though he heard Tulet's words, the various legal details, even bits and pieces of the tape as the attorney quoted them, Korngold saw only the countenance of Joanie Yff. It washed over his mind's eye like the sun in the sky.

"You got a hell of a pass," Patrick Tulet said.

Korngold laid the receiver on artificial turf.

Behind him, the piston of the kicking machine, now empty of soccer balls, methodically punched thin air.

Thut! Thut! Thut!

What followed was silence. For days Joanie heard from no one, not Tulet, not Korngold, certainly not Tommy Haggarty, who, since the day of the raid, had not been seen by anyone on the floor. The newspapers intimated that Haggarty would probably be given a new identity and moved to another state after the cases had been disposed of. That could take months, maybe a year or more, and until then he was in the care and feeding of the federal government.

Then it broke. Joanie first heard while she was trading. A rumor shot through the pit that Korngold's case had been dropped. She rushed to the foyer, then down to the first floor lobby to catch any news reports. She ran into the Sign of the

347

Trader, where dozens of traders and floor personnel were huddled around a television monitor.

A local newscaster repeated the information: federal prosecutors had been given information that impugned the credibility of Tommy Haggarty. The new material severely jeopardized their case against Korngold, if not all the defendants. No charges had been dropped as yet, but unnamed sources speculated that that was a matter of time.

Joanie stood motionless as she listened. Then the station returned to its regular programming and the restaurant erupted in shouts. Moments later bulldog editions of the newspapers arrived with headlines bannering the break in the case. Accompanying photos showed Patrick Tulet and Korngold. Joanie seized a paper and anxiously scanned the article for any mention of her name. It did not appear, only the repeated yet unspecified mentions of the startling new evidence. Patrick Tulet had handled things adroitly. Korngold was a free man; the government's entire case was in jeopardy.

"We're not encouraged," a federal prosecutor had said at a hectic press conference, "but we have no plans as yet of suspending prosecution of the other defendants."

The prosecutor did not say much more. He said he would not comment on Tommy Haggarty, not about his character or his whereabouts. He did not divulge any of the choice words he had for Tommy upon hearing the taped conversation between him and a certain young woman.

For his part, Tommy, who was being housed in an apartment inside the Great Lakes Naval Facility thirty miles north of Chicago, took the lashing without a word, his face the color of paste. An assistant federal prosecutor, a former amateur boxing champion from Notre Dame, had personally driven up to confront him. His outburst shook the walls.

"You cost us the friggin' farm!" he roared.

Steve spotted the headline on a newspaper box outside the Board of Trade and quickly bought a paper. He folded it under his arm and took it with him not to his trading office or the floor, but to the CBT's library. Nowadays it was the only room in the building in which he truly felt good.

He went there not to pore over the blinding array of financial newsletters and technical reports, but to read books on the law, economics, and history. The silent hum and subdued rustle of the library was a dramatic contrast, a true oasis amidst the chaos of the Board of Trade. Those around him who had found it, a few traders and research assistants doggedly searching through materials, were as quiet as he was. Yet they were there for only a few moments and gone. Back to the floor, that churning, enticing, magnetic, impossible place.

Steve stayed, through the morning, the rest of the day, able to resist the pull outside. He would never go back.

Now, with the newspaper hot under his arm, he strode quickly to a corner table and began reading. He devoured the words, the data, the layered sequence of events and information. The details made perfect sense, almost too perfect. It was as if he had somehow known it all along, like a familiar print, a contour. And he saw Joanie's hand in every paragraph.

The page quivered slightly in his hands.

God, how good he felt for her, for himself.

Third row, north side, the black-shaded windows of LaSalle Street behind her, the wrought-iron bridge up overhead. Back in the bond pit. Squeezed shoulder-to-shoulder within the swaying, gyrating crush of five hundred bodies. Buyers, sellers, and both. Millions upon millions of dollars worth of promises. The core of the world banking system, more money here than on all of Wall Street.

That's what they told her. She knew better. Pummeled by hands and fists, knocked, jabbed, deafened by the occasional shout, a shriek, the terrible roar. She was back now, one of them — they all knew, all noticed, whispered and nodded — yet alone among them, solitary, even serene in the pack. She saw all the faces, the bid-offer hands. She heard all the voices, the rasps, barks, and howls. She even inhaled familiar smells. The pit was hundreds of parts fused into a single animal, a beast you saw and heard and smelled.

She sensed it all — as if it were glazed in aspic, plated, crystallized—and she sensed none of it. She was JOY again, the badge, her trading coat loose on her shoulders, open at the waist, bulging with cards. She held her deck in her left hand, a pencil like a stiletto between the stiletto-thin fingers of her right hand. She lifted them to her chin, then held them there.

At that moment she felt so very much at home, as if she had been born if not in, at least to this place, this octagonal pit, this howling arena on the north end of this venerable room in this famous building. She felt at one with the spiraling din, hearing all the yelps, deciphering the code. What was insane, frantic gibberish to the world, to the crowds that leaned against the visitors' windows, was her own language. She had only to speak, raise her hands and thrust her fingers, and her open outcry would be heard throughout the room. Her throat was coated with honey, like a diva, a sweet, glowing, searing peal among the bull-voices. She was one of them.

How far she had come. Not just north into this hard city, past the marble and granite of this building, past the turnstiles and into the pit, third row. Check the blonde.

No, above it all. Skated. Hit the top, scraped the bottom, felt the high, then the ache. She had burned on the carpet, felt sweat on her tongue, his, her own. You feel like that, and nothing can touch you, nothing hurts. Everything hurts. Go.

She held her hands at her chin. Not parting her lips, she smiled. It was easy now. A poem she read and loved. The boards and the cries and the motions and the fury were sublime to her now, mere numbers, clicking ticks in a world made of no ticks at all. She could take them or cast them aside. She could add them or shave them. She could spread, straddle, scalp, position. Risk adverse-no! risk-fucking-free. She was an old trader in a Navy flier's town with pictures of naked backsides on the wall. Her wall. Her backside. Here in this pit, oh yes, JOY, trader, five at nine, five at none. She smiled. The market was hers.

William Brashler is the author of three previous novels and several books of nonfiction, including *The Bingo Long Traveling All-Stars and Motor Kings* and *The Don: The Life and Death of Sam Giancana*. A former police reporter, columnist, and contributor to a wide range of national magazines, he began work on *Traders* after spending months of research for an article on the Chicago Board of Trade's U.S. Treasury bond pit. Mr. Brashler lives in Chicago with his wife and two children.

PINNACLE'S FINEST IN SUSPENSE AND ESPIONAGE

OPIUM   (17-077, $4.50)
by Tony Cohan
Opium! The most alluring and dangerous substance known to man. The ultimate addiction, ensnaring all in its lethal web. A nerve-shattering odyssey into the perilous heart of the international narcotics trade, racing from the beaches of Miami to the treacherous twisting alleyways of the Casbah, from the slums of Paris to the teeming Hong Kong streets to the war-torn jungles of Vietnam.

LAST JUDGMENT   (17-114, $4.50)
by Richard Hugo
Seeking vengeance for the senseless murders of his brother, sister-in-law, and their three children, former S.A.S. agent James Ross plunges into the perilous world of fanatical terrorism to prevent a centuries-old vision of the Apocalypse from becoming reality, as the approaching New Year threatens to usher in mankind's dreaded Last Judgment.

THE JASMINE SLOOP   (17-113, $3.95)
by Frank J. Kenmore
A man of rare and lethal talents, Colin Smallpiece has crammed ten lifetimes into his twenty-seven years. Now, drawn from his peaceful academic life into a perilous web of intrigue and assassination, the ex-intelligence operative has set off to locate a U.S. senator who has vanished mysteriously from the face of the Earth.

Available wherever paperbacks are sold, or order direct from the Publisher. Send cover price plus 50¢ per copy for mailing and handling to Pinnacle Books, Dept. 17-460, 475 Park Avenue South, New York, N.Y. 10016. Residents of New York, New Jersey and Pennsylvania must include sales tax. DO NOT SEND CASH.